A Spark of Romance

OF

ROMANCE

ANTHOLOGY

PAULLETT GOLDEN

Cover Design by Fiona Jayde Media
Interior Design by The Deliberate Page
Illustrations by Doan Trang

Also by Paullett Golden

The Enchantresses Series
The Earl and The Enchantress
The Duke and The Enchantress
The Baron and The Enchantress
The Colonel and The Enchantress
The Heir and The Enchantress

Romantic Encounters
A Dash of Romance
A Touch of Romance
A Spark of Romance

The Sirens Series
A Counterfeit Wife

Romantic Flights of Fancy
Hourglass Romance
Romantic Choices

This book is dedicated to two souls who transcended during my writing of this story: Mercury and Carolina. They remain in my heart, forever loved.

A Letter to the Reader

Dear Reader,

This is the third book of the Romantic Encounters series. Within each anthology, you'll find a novel followed by a special bonus: a collection of flash and short fiction.

The flash fiction pieces are those featured in the periodic newsletter. All stories from the previous year's newsletters are featured here, but you can also find the fan favorites included in the Romantic Flights of Fancy series, which is reserved for flash and short fiction only.

There are many types of flash fiction, ranging from micro fiction of only a few words to short fiction of a couple thousand. Within this anthology series, you'll find pieces ranging from approximately five hundred words to two thousand. I hope you'll enjoy them. Each is a stand-alone story, regardless of brevity.

The addition of bonus fiction to accompany the novel is unique to the Romantic Encounters series. You can look forward to a similar combination of shorts plus novel in every publication within this series.

Enjoy!
Paullett Golden

Table of Contents

A Spark of Romance

Chapter 1

1796, March
Devonshire

For any hero worth his salt, scaling a stone wall to steal a maiden's kiss ought to be surmountable. A fingerhold here. A shimmy there. No self-respecting hero would be daunted or deterred. Certainly not the Comte de Corentin. With the grace of an Ossenfelder vampire, the French nobleman *could* mount the stone.

But would he?

Miss Isobel Lambeth drummed her fingers against her desk.

The ink-stained paper with its cross writing stared back at her, expectant but offering no insightful reply. For the better part of the day, she had crafted with ease and wit the Comte's rescue scheme of the fair damsel. This bit, however, stymied her. *She* would not scale a wall, so why would her fictional hero, even if for dramatic effect?

Quill into inkpot, she refueled.

Corentin scoured the wall along the ground floor
for a servant's entrance, some inconspicuous oak
panel wherein he might sneak. Around the corner,

*he spied his quarry. A look from right to left, hand
on pommel, he entered.*

Quill to inkpot. Isobel tugged her bottom lip
between her teeth, breath poised.

*Up a winding stair. A glance down, then up. His
hand wrapped about the hilt. Corentin's heart
pounded.*

Quill to inkpot.

*Belowstairs, a door slammed, shaking his resolve.
Should he retreat? No, he had come too far. With
renewed vigor, he launched himself up the stone —*

Downstairs, a door slammed.

Isobel shrieked, dropping her quill, ink dribbling.
She snatched a handkerchief from the top drawer and
dabbed the ink as best she could from the desk — at
least nothing had spilled on her writing. Her shoulders shook with laughter at being so easily startled
by a door. Unlike her character and his current plight,
Isobel did not need to worry about guards or villains who desired to imprison maidens for nefarious
intentions. She thought it best not to tell Mrs. Thomas
her reaction. The housekeeper would take offense to
being thought a villain for slamming a door.

Rewetting the quill, Isobel resumed.

*Round and round the tower, he circled, searching
for the elusive door barring him from his beloved.
A scuffling sound, as if boots against stone steps*

*alerted him. He was not alone on the stairs. He
stilled, ears strained. Too narrow of a stairwell to
draw his sword, he hinged to reach for his knife.
A guard? Or was he about to face his nemesis?*

Outside Isobel's small parlor, she heard a scuffling sound, as if of slippers on wood stairs. No doubt
about it. Thieves out to steal her moth-eaten curtains.
She grinned at the unmistakable overture to Mrs.
Thomas' interruption—off-key humming. Returning her quill to its stand, she waited as both humming
and steps drew closer.

Following a light scratch on the door, Mrs. Thomas'
capped head appeared. "I'll be off, then, Miss Lambeth. You'll find enough ready meals in the kitchen
to survive the remains of the day. Won't have you
starve on my watch. Any word for Benji? You know
he hates not being here."

Isobel shooed her with a wave of her hand. "Go
before he disobeys you and shows up at the doorstep.
Send him my love alongside your best soup. May he
take as long as he needs to mend."

With a bob, Mrs. Thomas left. Every morning, she
and her son Benji arrived, then left before sunset, their
home not far, the pair being the only staff in the Lambeth home, each serving a multitude of roles, from
butler to groundskeeper and from housekeeper to
cook. Isobel was ever thankful for their kindness. A
shame Benji was under the weather this week, sneez-
ing more than talking, according to Mrs. Thomas,
and for Benji, that must be quite a feat, as he rarely
stopped talking once he started. Born too early, they
had said, and never fully matured, despite being in

his thirties now. No one in the village of Sidvale loved him any less for his curious and almost childlike ways.

Now, where had Isobel paused in her story? Ah, yes, the Comte was ascending the stairs. As Isobel reached for her quill, her eyes fell on the vase of flowers on the mantel. She blushed. A single vase was poised to be admired in the small parlor, but in the large parlor were two dozen more. *Two dozen!* That they were not accompanied by as many gifts was only due to Isobel's scolding of her suitor that a gentleman ought not to gift a woman who was not *yet* his betrothed. Flowers, she could accept. Grinning up at the bouquet, her eyes caught the hands of the timepiece.

Nearly sending her chair flying behind her, Isobel leapt from the desk. She was late! Inexcusably late. Her flower bestower would be at the inn by now, awaiting their completely-coincidental-and-not-in-the-least-clandestine meeting. Isobel grabbed her bonnet and raced out of the small parlor through the large parlor and into the great hall, her destination the front door. As she tied the ribbons beneath her chin, she thought, *but what if he is late? He is always late. What if I arrive first with nothing to occupy my time? Can't be seen* waiting *for someone, now can I?* She raced back through the great hall into the large parlor and darted into her small parlor to shove, unceremoniously, her story into her slope desk — praying the ink had dried, or she would find a smeared mess later — and tucked the box under her arm.

Racing back through the large parlor and into the great hall, she realized she had forgotten shoes. Shoes!

Who forgets shoes? Another dart back into the small parlor. Shoes… shoes… She searched around the clutter of books and chairs, set her box down, and then crawled under the desk for the long reach to slippers that had been kicked off hours before. There. Shoes over her stockings, she dusted her skirts and headed back towards the great hall. *Ah!* She almost forgot the writing box. Turning back, she grabbed it.

Only after she closed the front door did it strike her that her hands were covered in ink stains and, more mortifying still, she had forgotten to dress for the day, still adorned in her morning gown.

Mr. Alistair Trowbridge looked his last at the newly renovated abbey before turning to the solicitor. "If I've not mistaken my lady's taste, I believe this a contender."

The solicitor nodded in approval. "An excellent choice. A word of warning before you decide — better forewarned, I say. Some neighbors won't be favorable to someone of your kind taking residence, but it's nothing you can't remedy in time, assuming your betrothed has the necessary familial connections." He arched his thin brows.

Alistair ignored the probing use of *betrothed* and resisted asking what the man meant by *his kind*. Instead, he countered with, "The cottage with the farm may be my choice yet. I'll be in touch."

A glance at his pocket watch sent him reeling into panic, but he affected the leisure ease of a gentleman while in sight of the solicitor. He was late. Inexcusably late. Isobel would be waiting for him at the inn.

The morning had not been unproductive, yet it had not brought a smile. Five properties he had viewed, ranging from a wee cottage fit for two to a sizable estate with a handful of tenant farms. He kept in mind what he believed Isobel would favor while also considering what he could afford, neither being points of confidence. After all, he had only known Isobel for one month and courted her for two weeks, no betrothal yet set. For that matter, she still thought he would return to India in July—with or without her. As to his purse, everything depended on his father. He had enough set aside for a cottage, but if he could secure his father's approval and support.... No, he should not look back at the abbey. Best to keep his eyes forwards on the foreseeable future.

As he rode back to the village of Sidvale, he ignored his voice of reason, dreaming about a life with Isobel, the two of them masters of their own domain, he a respected English gentleman of means, and she a published gothic novelist, both welcomed by neighbors with as much fervor as he had been on his estate in West Bengal. At times, dreams were all one possessed.

He arrived at The Tangled Fleece precisely half an hour late.

His first sight when he stepped into the public room of the inn, after his eyes adjusted to the cozy darkness inside, was of his ladylove laughing at something the innkeeper had said. She sat at one of the tables, her writing box next to a teapot before her, while the innkeeper stood next to her chair, looking down at her guileless smile.

Rather than jealousy, Alistair felt pride, pride in *her*. Artless, she shared her enthusiasm, her laughter contagious. Her appearance deceived all but the most sincere, for she bore an air of dishevelment at all times, ill-fitting gowns that aged and plumped her, hair lobbed in a lopsided knot, a drabness always shadowing her. Yet it took mere moments to discover the inner glow, so warm one must bask in adoration. Her frazzle was nothing more than excitement to live, the gowns an indication of circumstance, not person, all a wrapping to hide the gift within, a gift Alistair had been *un*wrapping steadily since his first introduction to her.

Not until Isobel and Mr. Bradley turned towards him with questioning gazes did he realize he was still standing in the entry, practically drooling on himself.

Louder than necessary, given the sparse crowd, Mr. Everitt Bradley, innkeeper, welcomed, "Mr. Trowbridge, come in! The Tangled Fleece aims to serve. Might I beg you to keep our Miss Lambeth company while I fetch a fresh brew for you?"

"My pleasure," was all Alistair said as he made his way to the back table, removing his traveling coat and cocked hat as he did so.

Isobel waved a hand to the chair across from her. "Do please join me. I thought I might write at the inn today. No one wants to write alone in an empty house." Like the innkeeper, she spoke a touch too loudly, her audience anyone in the public room with roaming ears.

Alistair grinned his amusement and said with hushed words, "No one is fooled, *pastilam*, my sweet. All in Sidvale know I aim to woo you."

Her cheeks pinkened. "Yes, well, we must still play the game, at least until my mother returns to give respectability to the courtship."

Draping his coat and hat on the empty chair next to him, he crossed one leg over the other and folded his hands on his thighs. "Good news? She has written with her anticipated arrival?"

Isobel fiddled with her writing box, avoiding his gaze. "Her letter arrived, yes. At last. However pleased she was to receive Mrs. Owen's letter introducing you and your intentions, and however much she delighted in my subsequent letter, she regrets to inform me she cannot return on every little whim, not when her sister needs her company." She rocked the unevenly constructed writing box with a solitary finger. With a tug to the edge of the slope, the box teetered one way then the other with a rhythmic knock against the table.

Every little whim? Mrs. Lambeth, a woman he had yet to meet, thought a gentleman wishing to court her daughter *a whim*? From what Isobel had shared over their acquaintance thus far, he was the first and only gentleman to pay her court, and he was not just *any* gentleman if it was not arrogant of him to say. Regardless of how his circumstances may change once he consulted with his father, Mrs. Owen would have painted his current status in a favorable enough light to send any mother with sense racing home to begin her own courtship of the suitor, not foolish enough to let this one get away. Alistair was, after all, an exceedingly wealthy and powerful settlement governor in West Bengal, courtesy of the East India Company. His estate and house would put to shame any manor in and near Sidvale. And yet, she would not return *on a whim*?

He believed this was more a reflection of what Mrs. Lambeth thought of her daughter than what she thought of his accounting. With a sweep of his gaze, he took in Isobel. Her mother did not believe Isobel could hold a gentleman's interest. *Zan-e ahmak*, he cursed to himself in Persian. *Foolish woman.*

"There is but one resolution," he said, then waited for her to look up at him. "We must elope. Who will say 'whim' then?"

Isobel covered her face with her hands and tried not to laugh so hard that she drew attention to their table. His esteem would be wounded if he did not know her better. Instead, his grin deepened.

Leaning closer to the table, he said, "Or we could cause a scandal, yes? That will bring her home. We are each alone, you in your home, and me a guest at the Owens' Nasrin Manor. No one to stop us, not while the Owens are away, meeting their daughter's future in-laws in Hampshire. Not while your mother is away. I will come to you, or you to me, and we will make a scandal."

Isobel squealed behind her hands, still hiding her face. She mumbled against her palms, "*Stop*. My sides hurt from laughing."

Alistair leaned back just in time to greet Mr. Bradley with the fresh tea. Isobel waved her hands to cool her cheeks.

As the innkeeper set the tea things on the table, Alistair said, "Mr. Bradley, I request assistance. A quandary it is I face. Without Mrs. Lambeth, I cannot court my lady in the proper English ways, and Miss

Lambeth refuses my offer to elope or cause a scandal. What options have I?"

Mr. Bradley, accustomed to the Persian's bluntness, did not blink, cough, or sputter, rather said to Isobel in response to Alistair's request, "Mrs. Bradley's been wanting to call on you, Miss Lambeth. Our little Everitt Jr. has kept her busy, but what with her sister staying with us now, she'll be able to make her calls. If she had someone to escort her from the inn to your house, she could call as early as tomorrow. Would you have the time, Miss Lambeth?"

Try as she might, Isobel could not hide her smile. She opted instead for nonchalance by pouring the tea as she said, "If it's not presumptuous of me, I believe Mr. Trowbridge here would be the perfect escort. I'll ensure my *entire* morning is free of distraction." Her voice edged with laughter.

"She'll be delighted," Mr. Bradley said, winking at Alistair before he bowed off to see to his other patrons.

Chapter 2

Isobel's morning, since she did not know what time to expect Mrs. Bradley, consisted of dashing between the small parlor — to make a note of something for the Comte de Corentin's story before she forgot it — and a mirror — to confirm her hair had not escaped its confines — and finally to the nearest window — to glimpse for callers — then back to repeat the process again. Alistair was coming to see her! Granted, it was Mrs. Bradley doing the calling, Alistair merely escorting her, but.... Alistair was coming to see her! This would be his first time seeing her residence. Her house was what it was. She would not be embarrassed by it, even knowing how grand his estate and house must be in comparison.

Would they have an opportunity to talk privately? She did not know Mrs. Bradley well. It was Mr. Bradley everyone knew well, his inn being the heart of Sidvale and one of Isobel's and her friends' haunts. Mrs. Bradley made the best pies Isobel had ever tasted, but the innkeeper's wife spent most of her time tending to her six children, the youngest being about four months. Would Mrs. Bradley be a strict chaperone? Isobel hopped from foot to foot, eager to discover the answer.

With no sight of anyone along the driveway, she slipped into the small parlor again to jot down Corentin's clever lines as he faced his nemesis. Corentin did not know that Isobel wrote the scene to not end well for him, despite the witty repartee. Oh, nothing so gruesome as death or torture. The nobleman was merely in for an unpleasant surprise, a moment when it would seem his nemesis held the winning hand.

A knock on the door trembled her quill. With a squeal and bounce, she tossed the quill into its stand and darted through the large parlor into the great hall where, shortly after screeching *they're here* in hopes Mrs. Thomas would hear her, she touched a hand to her hair, swept a palm over one of her nicest gowns, and tried not to skip to the front door. She turned the front door key just as a second knock resounded.

"Welcome!" she said with far more enthusiasm than she ought.

Standing before her was the strikingly attractive Mrs. Bradley. If anyone expected the stout Mr. Bradley to be married to a dowdy woman, they would be surprised to meet his wife. Isobel ought to wish she were this comely. A beautiful woman such as this would be a better match for the handsome and mysterious Alistair, would she not? And yet, one look over Mrs. Bradley's shoulder at Alistair's smoldering gaze had her forgetting to feel or think anything other than being the luckiest woman in England.

Mrs. Bradley squeezed Isobel's hands as she entered. As they exchanged greetings, Isobel showed them into the large parlor just as Mrs. Thomas arrived with the tea tray.

Since it was a surprisingly warm March, no one would look twice at the empty fireplace. Then, with two dozen bouquets adorning every visible surface, no one would be tempted to look anywhere except at the blooms. The curtains had been thrown open earlier to brighten the room with sunlight, and earlier still, the windows had been opened to air out the musty scent of "old house." Now that Alistair's ample dose of cologne filled the room, Isobel and the guests could inhale the enticing aromas of fresh air, spices, rose water, and *man*. Isobel's pulse quickened.

Mrs. Bradley, with her quaint West Country lilt, said, "I hope I've not missed my chance for a chinwag with Mrs. Thomas. I heard Benji's not feeling his best. Thought I'd bring him a pie. If he wouldn't mind the company, my girls were hoping to read to him one afternoon."

"Oh, Mrs. Bradley!" Isobel held her hand over her heart. "He would love nothing more."

Alistair looked from Isobel to Mrs. Bradley and back, his eyebrows asking his unvoiced question.

"Benji is Mrs. Thomas' son," Isobel explained. "They both help around the house, for which I'm eternally grateful. Benji hasn't felt his best this past week. The worst part? He'll be more concerned about the repairs he promised to make than with mending himself." Both Isobel and Mrs. Bradley shared a laugh, each knowing all too well Benji's devotion to keeping his word.

"Repairs?" Alistair questioned, his gaze strolling around the room.

Biting her bottom lip, Isobel turned to the tray to prepare the tea in hopes he would not see the grimace.

Of all the opening conversations she had practiced and planned, discussing the condition of her family home was not one of them.

Muttering, she said, "A few odds and ends." With a bit more gusto, she added, "Benji is our butler, gardener, groom, and manservant-of-all-trades, you see. Little does he know I will impose strict rules when he returns that he's not to take on any task too arduous until at least two weeks after he's revived full health." She followed this last with a smile and the passing of teacups and saucers, only in hindsight chagrined that she had not asked Mrs. Bradley how she liked her tea. Thankfully, she knew how Alistair preferred his.

However uninviting the house, at least the tea tray was bountiful. Thanks to her dearest friend's father, Mr. Owen, she stayed well-stocked with the best tea from China, imported through India. Add the most decadent and unadulterated tea, with its floral aroma and earthy flavor — a forest after a spring rain — to Mrs. Thomas' biscuits and cake, and Isobel was surprised she did not have half of Sidvale paying her calls. Then, perhaps she should not boast of her tea collection — thieves and smugglers would line up at the kitchen, all wanting their share. After locking Isobel in her room to keep her out of their way. Would she be able to climb out of her bedroom window to reach help? Not likely. But if she could, she would find Alistair, and he would save her tea things by dueling the thieves. Then, was tea important enough to risk Alistair in a duel?

Isobel blinked to notice both Mrs. Bradley and Alistair looking expectantly at her. Oh dear. Away with the fairies again, was she? Well, who could blame her once they tasted the tea? She smiled at her guests.

Alistair chuckled under his breath as if he knew she had drifted into storyland. "Shall I take your silence to mean you decline my offer, or are you so surprised you will have me repeat myself?"

"I must be that surprised," she said with an innocent bat of eyelashes.

"If I knew of the repairs," he repeated without hesitation, "I could offer my services."

Isobel blinked again, this time in confusion.

"I possess an abundance of skills," he teased.

Stuttering her way through a response, she said, "I don't believe a gentleman's *skills* are quite what's needed." She ignored the tumble in her stomach at what else his seductive tone implied. "It's labor the house requires. Two doors in the long gallery are sticking; at least one set of shutters needs to be rehinged; three windows are leaking when it rains; there's a mysterious odor in one of the guest rooms neither Mrs. Thomas nor I can uncover; there's a draft from two of the fireplaces, and… well, you see, not the sort of repairs a gentleman can see to. The trouble is, Mama wanted them all done before she returned, but then, I suppose if she's staying longer with my aunt than planned, there's no rush."

Alistair, the provoking man that he was, arched his black brows and said, "You doubt my abundant skills. Allow me to be your hero, Miss Lambeth. I shall return tomorrow with tools."

While Isobel tried to overcome her shock, Mrs. Bradley said, "My boys will help you, Mr. Trowbridge.

Not my little Everitt Jr., of course, but my other boys
will be glad to busy their hands."

"It is done," Alistair said. "I have apprentices now,
Miss Lambeth."

Isobel looked between the two of her guests,
hoping she was not as slack-jawed as she felt. On
second thought, her eyes narrowed as she wondered
if they had planned this all along, a conspiratorial
scheme devised during their walk here. How... bril-
liant! And flattering. And... she almost squealed at
the thought of Alistair here two days in a row.

Mrs. Bradley turned her attention to Alistair.
Between bites of her cake, she said, "Your story must
be interesting. A gentleman who also labors? A gentleman who, noticeably, is not from England."

He angled his head in a nod. "My father is British, deputy chairman for the East India Company.
During his earlier years with the Company, he lived
in Calcutta, where he met my mother. Although
Persian, my mother lived in West Bengal for many
years. They married, and I brought them joy soon
after. I stayed with my mother while my father
traveled to and from England, as the Company
required."

"Is your mother here with you, then?" Mrs. Bradley asked.

He looked down at his folded hands. "She died
a few years past, but not before seeing my success in
the Company. I am a settlement governor in India. I
came to England with Mr. Owen, who works in West
Bengal for the Company, as you may know, to help
him win the election in April for a director position,
which will allow him to remain in England with his

family, as he wishes." Moving his gaze to Isobel, he said, "I have also come to make a wife of my ladylove."

Isobel spluttered her tea as she took a sip.

Mrs. Bradley laughed. "Does your intended know of your plans?"

Before Alistair could answer, Isobel set down her cup in its saucer and, with a face as warm as a June sunrise, said, "Mr. Trowbridge is not yet engaged for his intended to know anything of the sort. He *was* supposed to marry Leila Owen, all part of their fathers' plans, but that arrangement did not suit him. Leila is, as you already know, currently in Hampshire with her family and her betrothed to meet her future in-laws. And so, here sits Mr. Trowbridge, *unattached.*"

With a sly grin, he said, "Only because your English etiquette will not permit me to wed my rose petal until I have courted her. What I do not understand is for how long I must pay this court."

Mrs. Bradley offered, "I have it on good authority, Mr. Trowbridge; you cannot rush a woman to the altar, no matter how ardent feelings may be on both sides. The best way to a woman's heart is through patience. Show her you're prepared to wait forever."

Alistair uncrossed his legs and sat up straighter. "English rules confound me, Mrs. Bradley. I may not gift my love until we are betrothed. I may not betroth my love until we have courted. I may not court my love until I have acquainted myself with her family and friends."

She winked. "You're proceeding quite nicely, young man, just as you are. Don't you agree, Miss Lambeth?"

Isobel hid behind her teacup, not wanting them to see how feverish she must be blushing.

Her embarrassment did not last long, as the conversation turned first to Mrs. Bradley asking after Leila Owen and her betrothal to Mr. Jules Knowlton, which then prompted a brief explanation of how Isobel met Alistair while staying at Leila's home this past month to avoid being left home alone while Mrs. Lambeth stayed with her sister, as she did at increasingly lengthier intervals since the wedding of Isobel's cousin. Following that, the conversation shifted to Mrs. Bradley's new baby before the mantel clock rudely informed them it was well past time for departure.

As they reached the front door, Mrs. Bradley said, "Oh! Mrs. Thomas! I had almost forgotten. I want to ask her about calling on Benji. Would you think me terribly impolite to invite myself into your kitchen, Miss Lambeth, or would you prefer to ring for her?" With a laugh and a hand to Isobel's arm, she added, "Your shutters may be coming unhinged, but this is the first house I've been inside with bellropes."

Isobel pulled a face before directing the innkeeper's wife to the kitchen. When she offered to escort, Mrs. Bradley waved her away with a wink and nod towards Alistair and a whispered promise she would be more than a minute.

Taking the cue without hesitation, Alistair reached for Isobel's hands and placed them against the warmth of his waistcoat, just over his heart. "Until tomorrow, *nazanin*."

After a quick glance behind her to ensure they were alone, Isobel stepped closer to Alistair. He was enchanting, casting a love spell with his heady beauty. Long, black hair was bound by a riband at the nape of his neck. Eyes the color of obsidian invited her to express her affection, eyes framed by long, dark eyelashes and olive complexion. She inched onto tiptoes only for nerves to leave her flatfooted rather than acting on her desire.

As though aware of her intentions, as well as her nerves, he gifted her a knowing smile before pressing a kiss to her temple. "*Nazaninam*," he whispered.

Chapter 3

A listair eyed his pocket watch, reassured by the fact he had not set a definitive arrival time. If he had, he would now be a quarter of an hour late. There was still the walk to the house to consider. He hoped Isobel was busying herself writing rather than waiting for him to arrive with tools in hand.

"Lemme carry it," pleaded nine-year-old Daniel.

"It takes a strong grip," said Cedric. "I should carry it. Here, you carry this." The eldest at eleven, he moved the toolbox behind his back, out of reach of his brother, and handed Mrs. Bradley's wrapped pie to Daniel.

Kicking the dirt, Daniel said, "I'm not a baby. Let Brayden carry the pie."

Alistair spared a glance at seven-year-old Brayden, who paid no heed to his brothers, far more interested in kicking his toy up and down the road.

Rather than feeling impatient with their antics, Alistair followed a memory that tugged the corners of his lips into a smirk. When he first met Isobel at Nasrin Manor, they had the pleasure of entertaining two young boys, twins not much younger than ten, the cousins of his arranged betrothed at the time, Leila Owen. The twins had traveled with him and Mr. Owen on their journey from India to England, their new, permanent home to be with the Owens. It was not the twins that had him smirking so much as the memory of Isobel with the twins. He suspected she would enjoy the Bradley children's company today. Assuming they ever arrived.

Alistair tried for the fourth time to herd them farther from the inn. "I wish to carry the pie. This way, I may sample as we walk."

Daniel gaped. "Not fair! Marm made it for us." Holding his hands out to Cedric, he said, "Gimme before Mr. Trowbridge eats it."

Again, Alistair urged them to begin the journey.

The distance to Isobel's house was not far. In truth, it was closer to Nasrin Manor than it was to the inn, so Alistair undertook a brief backtrack, but the extra leg was worth having the Bradley boys darting about him. It would not be a dull day with their company. However eager the boys were to ply a trade, they had managed every excuse possible to postpone departure. At least his delay had not been entirely his fault. Not entirely. Only partially.

He had needed further fortification that morning from Mrs. Owen's exquisite tea supply, which he thankfully had the leisure of sampling despite the lady of the manor's absence — and oh, what leisure sampling he had enjoyed these past days, each sip bringing the flavor of home to his lips, wild yet delicate. Add an extra teapot — admittedly, two extras by the time he left Nasrin Manor — to his search for tools and then the collection of his three helpers from The Tangled Fleece, and the morning had quite passed him by.

Ah, but the delay would have offered more time for his flower petal to write. She would be thankful for that.

The winding drive to the house was longer than the road from the inn but, all in all, no farther than two miles. A good thing, too, since the leaden sky added an atmospheric drizzle to their journey along the overgrown woodland encroaching on either side of the driveway. A steady dribble of misty rain wet his hair and the coat about his shoulders. He tried tucking the bouquet and box he carried beneath his coat, hoping the blooms would not flatten.

As they drew closer, the house came into sight beyond the veil of tree branches. Expressing their excitement, the boys alternated between running forwards and backwards — the latter literally — while singing sea shanties with nonsense lyrics.

He gazed up at the house to take it in more fully, this time with the eye of a carpenter come to repair rather than a guest seeing his love's family home for the first time. It was a sizable Medieval farmhouse built of timber frame and white wattle-and-daub walls. At one time, he suspected it had been impressive. It was not the sort of impressive of Nasrin Manor, but it had been undoubtedly built for a wealthy landowner. Time and lack of care had done it a disservice.

One side of the first floor had shifted unevenly due to wood sag and warp, now ever so slightly crooked, but that could not be helped and, from Alistair's perspective, added to its charm. What could be helped was the upkeep of the woodwork along the jetties where the first and second floors overhung the ground floor. He could spy rot even from this distance. Not something he could address today, but it would not be a challenge to repair.

The shutters Isobel had mentioned must be on the back, for he saw no shutters on the front. A relief since not only was the rain steadier now, which would make rehanging shutters difficult unless he wanted to stand and climb in the rain, but visually, shutters would detract from the beauty of the Tudor design. He could not recall if she mentioned which windows leaked, but he suspected at least one of them was on the first floor where the house slanted.

To its credit, the upper stories boasted ornamental paneling with decorative motifs, the eaves carved with animal faces. The windows were mullioned and transomed with three to five lights, and two windows on the first floor were fitted with stained-glass panels.

While one should not make assumptions, especially since a limited amount about a person could be assumed based on their residence alone, Alistair could not help but discern a few things about Isobel, things he could neither confirm nor deny from their month's acquaintance. Despite the poor condition of the house, only someone of means would have been able to afford it. He did not know the acreage attached or if there were farmlands included or tenancies, which would all add to the value. For all he knew, it was only the house, drive, and immediate land on which it sat. The poor condition was due to the recent upkeep, or lack thereof, meaning if she had lived here for any length of time — and his understanding was this was her childhood home — it would have been in good condition at the time of purchase. At one point in their conversations of old, they had spoken of losses, he of his mother and she of her father. Mr. Lambeth had been a gentleman in every English sense. Although now the poorest of her friends, she was, technically, the daughter of a gentleman, as all her friends, including Miss Leila Owen, were daughters of employed men earning a salary.

He could not ask Isobel, and she may not know, and for that matter, it served no purpose, but Alistair did wonder at the loss of the wealth. Had it been Mr. Lambeth who poorly spent or Mrs. Lambeth after her husband's death, or yet still a poor inheritance from Mr. Lambeth's father? Alistair would likely never know, and, again, it did not matter. But he wondered since this was the home and familial situation of his ladylove, and he wished to know everything about her, good and ill.

By the time the boys reached the front door and took hold of the door knocker, the rain had doubled its efforts. Alistair bemoaned the sodden state of the bouquet.

The front door opened to a bemusedly smiling Isobel. Alistair's heart skipped a beat. She had, indeed, been writing. He spied an ink stain on her chin.

She spared him a cursory glance before turning her attention to the boys, exclaiming her delight at their arrival, her pleasure over their preparedness to bring the toolbox and ever-important pie, and her wish for them to come inside where Mrs. Thomas awaited.

When his eyes met hers at last, the bottom of his stomach dipped.

Voice low, never mind that he competed with the cacophonic voices of the children, he said, "*Salaam, khoshgele.*"

Isobel tilted her head. "I know *salaam* from Leila, so *salaam* to you, too, but what else did you say? Wo-ho-sh-kel?"

His pulse quickened, hearing her trying to pronounce his language. "*Khoshgele*," he repeated slowly. "It means beautiful." When she blushed, he was prompted to flirt further. "*Khoshgelam, Khoshgele khânum*. My beautiful Miss Beautiful."

Ignoring the waving arms of Brayden to get their attention and the two older boys racing around the great hall behind Isobel, Alistair beheld the wilted bouquet and small, wrapped box.

"Oh!" Isobel's eyes widened. She reached for the gifts, then hesitated, looking from them back up to him, then down again, then behind her at the boys running amok around the dining table in the center of the room. "You're standing in the rain," she finally said, almost hopping from foot to foot in her indecision as to what to do first.

He laughed. So taken with her, he had forgotten to notice the rain. Blinking away the droplets streaming from his forehead, he stepped past her inside, then decisively put the box in her hands. He swiped a hand through wet hair as he searched for a place to stow the soggy but once-perky bouquet. Ah, he would add them to one of the vases on the mantel of the inglenook fireplace overlooking the dining table. With luck, they would right themselves when dry.

The boys, thankfully, were now occupied with the housekeeper. Isobel, he saw when he turned back towards the door, was unwrapping the box. He grinned in response to her scolding expression — how many times now had she told him she could not receive gifts until they were betrothed? Bah! To Alistair's mind, they were already betrothed upon his first declaration of love. He went to her, lacing his fingers at his waist, expectant and hopeful of her reaction.

As she tugged at twine and paper, slow and anticipatory, she asked, "What do I say to you?"

He frowned. "That you are vexed I brought a gift?"

"No, I mean, when you call me whoosh-kill, what do I say to you in response?"

"*Khoshgele*," he corrected her pronunciation again, enunciating slowly for her benefit. Then, after some thought, he answered, "*Koshtip* would be your response. Or *kheili koshtip*." He waggled his eyebrows. "No, no, more better, I wish you to say *shirinam* to me, and often."

Isobel blinked, her hands paused in the unwrapping.

"I am teasing you," he said. "*Koshtip* means handsome." He struck a pose. "Yes? *Kheili koshtip* means very handsome."

"And the other? Shee-re-nam?"

Alistair cleared his throat and had the courtesy to appear abashed. "An endearment. It means, let's see, in English, it is 'my sweet.' But not one for you to use yet."

"Oh? Why not? I like it. Sherry-nam. Cherine-am. Shear—"

He placed two fingers on her lips as she tried various pronunciations. "It is used between lovers."

Her eyes widened again, and she turned her attention back to the box, although he could see the darkening blush on her cheeks. Tucking the wrapping under her arm, she lifted the lid and laughed in delight.

Inexplicably nervous over what he thought was a rather silly gift, he said, "You instructed no more jewelry until the banns are called. But will this do?"

"Oh, Alistair. A collection of new quills. Thank you! They're lovely. How did you know I'm down to nubs? No, don't answer. You always know these things about me. These will last me at least a month."

"Good. You must write more so I may read."

With a mock scoff, she said, "A self-serving gift." She followed this with a bat of eyelashes. "If Mrs. Thomas and the boys were not here, I would hug you!"

Alistair turned back into the room and commanded for all to hear. "You must all retreat to the parlor and await my attendance. *Khoshgele khânum* wishes to embrace me with gratitude but will not do so in your presence."

Isobel closed the lid of the box with a squeak. "No, no, no, he doesn't mean that! He's... he's... oh, he's *Persian*." Her voice cracked with laughter, incredulity, and desperation, or so Alistair imagined.

He joined her laughter, winking at Mrs. Thomas and the boys, although he had been serious with his command for them to leave the room. Would he ever understand English reserve?

To fuel their hard work to come, the boys nibbled on their mother's pie in the kitchen under Mrs. Thomas'

supervision. Isobel took the opportunity to show Alistair some of the most pressing repairs, which turned into a home tour after his endless stream of questions.

"The great hall's best feature," she explained with a sweep of her hand, "is the high ceiling. There's not much else to boast about it. It's the dining room, obviously, as well as the main thoroughfare for the ground floor." However grand the name, the great hall was moderate in size, with all doors and stairs leading from this central room. White walls, a fireplace, a table. A plain room, unadorned, undecorated.

Guiding him through the large parlor that he had already seen the day before, she opened the door to the adjacent small parlor. "This is where I write. I don't know what purpose the room would serve otherwise since it's too small for guests, but it's perfect for me. The best part is that door." She nodded to the back corner. "It opens into the garden. I've no idea why the door is here rather than in the large parlor, but there it is. Technically, there is no garden, but I don't let that stop me from enjoying a patch of wilderness, especially on a warm day when I can leave the door open."

She cringed at the great mess on the desk, papers scattered, ink spilled, quills past their prime lying in disarray. The room was so small it only held the one desk, her chair, and a brick fireplace. At least the bird and leaf paper hangings made it cheery. Before he could comment on the mess or size, she closed the door and directed him back through the great room to the opposite hall. They stopped on the threshold, one foot still in the great room.

"This," she said, leaning into the hallway, "leads to the kitchen and all that is Mrs. Thomas' domain when she's here." Isobel glanced up at the coffin drop in the ceiling, blanching rather than pointing it out to Alistair. Not every feature needed to be part of the tour, especially those steeped in memory. Her last look at her father had been his coffin's descent through that drop. Her eyes burned, but she blinked away the sight and recollection. "Come. Upstairs is next."

Alistair looked about him as they returned through the great hall and entered the enclosed stairwell leading to the first floor. Isobel wondered what he was thinking. He left no surface untouched by his gaze as if cataloging every sprig of muslin-papered wall, molding, or brick. Was he impressed by the bones or horrified by the condition? Unlike Leila's manor, Isobel's house lacked personal affectations, at least in the public rooms. No paintings hung on the walls, no embellishments, no pianoforte, or fanciful furniture. Both her domains were cheerfully papered, and her mother's room had tapestries, but that was all. She could not explain why. This was as it always had been.

She did not think he cared if she were a pauper or otherwise, but it was unnerving for him to see so much as though she had been caught undressed and unawares. To say she felt exposed was an understatement. But then, the house was not *her*, and yet this was her childhood home, a reflection of all that comprised her youth. Every inch of this house had inspired her writing in some way, from the squeaky floors and coffin drop to the painted wall she had discovered in her bedroom, an indecipherable design that had been hidden behind paper hangings for decades, perhaps centuries. She had wanted to keep that one wall displayed, a testament to her discovery and the history of the house, but her mother had papered it, not wanting to waste the muslin paper hangings she had already purchased for the room.

Curiously, Isobel hated to be alone in the house, although she could not say why when it was not haunted and truly did inspire her writing. But with her mother spending so much time away, Isobel found herself staying with her friends rather than at home.

Up the narrow, creaky stairs they went. She touched her fingers to the scorched timber behind the empty candleholders as they progressed to the landing, then around to the first floor.

"This floor has all the main bedchambers, including the guest rooms," she explained. "We'll look at the long gallery and four of the bedrooms. Those are where most repairs are needed. There's no need to tour the second floor because it's unused attic space. I think, at one time, the household staff might have stayed there since the downstairs is used for storage. Given we only have Mrs. Thomas and Benji, and they never stay overnight, we ignore the second floor."

"I understand," Alistair said, his gaze traveling down the long gallery stretching before them. "Once I retrieve my apprentices, we will look in the attic, with your permission, in case there is a leaky window or wood rot you've not seen."

She strolled down the long gallery, not sure how much to say about the house itself versus the needed repairs. The gallery was another plain hall, wide enough for a promenade on a rainy day but not for country dancing. Once more, no paintings or tables or chairs, simply white walls interrupted by timber framework. However, the long gallery, as with the high ceilings in the great hall, spoke volumes to anyone who knew Medieval architecture. No Tudor farmhouse would have had a long gallery except one built by an exceedingly wealthy person, someone with local prominence. Long galleries were for manors and castles and the like, not farmhouses. To say that to Alistair, though, would call attention to her *lack* of wealth and familial prominence.

Deciding it best not to mention anything of the sort, she instead opted for, "All rooms are accessible from this gallery. Don't mind the slight slope of the floor as we move to the far end. It's always been like this."

"As charming as your ink." Alistair slid his arm in front of her and palmed the wall to block her path.

"My *what*?" So taken aback by his odd words, she forgot to be startled by the impediment in her path.

Then she caught his expression. Dark eyes caressed the curve of her face, resting on her lips. His own lips curled into seduction. This close, his cologne intoxicated and dizzied her senses. His mane had escaped its riband, strands falling and tickling her cheeks as he leaned forwards.

As her eyelashes fluttered, he said, "Your ink, *nazanin*. Just here." He reached up and pinched her chin between his thumb and forefinger.

"My *ink*?" Dawning distracted her from his proximity. Isobel pirouetted away from him with a peal of laughter. "You should have told me I had sneaky ink smeared across my face! For shame!"

She darted into the first room on the left to peer into the mirror there. Sure enough. Ink. Right there, across her chin. And she thought he had been eyeing her lips! Isobel could not hold back her laughter as she dipped a bit of linen into the washbasin to clean off the stain. In the mirror's reflection, she saw Alistair leaning against the doorframe.

"*That* is shameful," he said. "I wish you had not washed it. I thought it charming."

"As charming as my sloped floor. Yes, you said." She shook her head, still humored. With a last look into the mirror, she tossed the linen next to the basin and turned to face Alistair. "This, as you might have gathered, is my bedchamber."

She looked about her little sanctuary with its oriel window and coal-burning fireplace. It was not impersonal, but as she spent most of her time in the small parlor, there was little to show in her room. A four-poster bed, washstand, and wardrobe were the only pieces of furniture. The best feature was the window overlooking the back wilderness. It brightened the room no matter the weather.

The room's location was another matter. She both loved and hated that it was the first room after the stairs. It allowed her a swift retreat to her writing parlor without having to pass any of the other rooms — a luxury she was thankful for when she wanted to stay up late to write after her mother had retired for the evening. By that token, however, she heard every footstep to and fro since anyone wishing to enter rooms or use the stairs must pass her bedchamber door.

That Alistair stood in her chamber, a room no gentleman ought to see, did not faze her. It was merely a

room, after all, and she did not consider herself genteel enough to be embarrassed. There was no lady's
maid to think her scandalous, no parent to fuss about
propriety. Besides, how could he repair anything if
he was forbidden?

"The window leaks." She walked to the window
and tapped the latch on the casement. "I don't know
if the leak is with the latch or the hinge or the mul-
lion or one of the panes or…." She waved a hand.
"But it leaks like a sieve in a rainstorm. Oh goodie,
a puddle." With a swipe of her finger along the
narrow seat board, she flicked water. "Lucky us, it's
raining."

"I will fix it," he said unequivocally.

She studied him, appreciating more than his
kindness. All her thoughts of being unperturbed to
have him in her chamber, yet he stole her breath. His
raven hair fanned about his shoulders, loose and wet,
primal in comparison to his usually pristine appearance, nary a strand out of place. His coat, too, had
been removed downstairs so Mrs. Thomas could hang
it to dry. Although he wore a drab suit in preparation for labor, he somehow made egalitarian English
dress look positively regal. *And he was standing in her
bedchamber*. Her only hope was she was not wearing
her adoration in her expression.

"How did you learn all this?" she asked. "The car-
pentry and like. I had imagined you, and don't take
offense, as being so important in West Bengal as to
have servants carrying you about on jeweled pillows
while questionably clad beauties fanned you from
the heat. But here you are, wanting to fix my broken
bits and bobs."

Without hesitation, he answered, "I saw to my mother's happiness. As she wished, I granted. A bench in the garden? I built it. A folly for shade? I built it. A book to enjoy? I read it aloud. A play to see? I acted it. Someone else could build or repair, yes, but each sanding stroke, each cutting chop, each falling hammer would not possess the loyalty or love one can infuse in his own work. Flawless splendor. She knew with every gift she was loved."

Unshed tears stung Isobel's eyes. To love and be loved so ardently. She did not know it could be that way.

At a loss for words, she said, "You're magnificent."

"And *koshtip*, yes?" He grinned, his eyes half-lidded. "I will fix your window, my sweet Isobel." He stepped into the room, closer to the window, closer to Isobel. Rather than approach her, though, he studied the window. "I think young Cedric will be best to help with this. He'll know to be careful around glass. Now, guide me to the next ghost haunting you."

Dipping her head so he could not see her rub the wetness from her eyes, she showed him the other rooms along the gallery, including the guest rooms, her mother's room at the far end — which was the largest and most well-decorated room in the house — and finally her father's study. She did not linger in her father's study. It was smaller than her writing parlor, little more than a closet, but he had loved the view overlooking the front door and the snugness. At one time, she thought she would find solace in this room, but it always felt empty. Why could she never feel anything of her father here? It left her melancholy, this cold and forgotten space.

As they surveyed the rooms, she showed him the two doors that kept sticking when closed, a few more leaky windows, the drafty fireplaces, and the mysterious odor in one of the guest rooms. The shutters, which had been added to the back of the house not long ago to reduce the wind that whipped around that side during winter nights and storms, would have to wait for another day. Outside, the rain continued its steady fall.

Tour completed, they headed for the kitchen. Eyeing his strong profile, Isobel ventured, "Should I learn Persian?"

He turned to her, slowing his steps. "To compliment me daily? Tell me how *khosh ghiaafe* I am?"

With a chortle, she said, "That too. But no, I meant for moving to West Bengal with you. If we wed, that is. I would move to India with you, wouldn't I? I wouldn't want to be like Mrs. Owen, living here while Mr. Owen resides there, or like your parents when your father moved to England and left you and your mother in India. I would want to be with you. Am I being too forward? Too presumptuous?"

He stopped, one foot on the last stair step, the other on the herringbone flooring of the great hall. "We *will* wed, Isobel. I will court you as long as it takes to please your English rules. One week more? One year more? Two? We *will* wed unless you decide you do not want me." He hesitated but then said with confidence, "That will not happen. I am too— how did you say?—'magnificent' for rejection. Once wed, we will not live apart, although we will leave for another day our decision as to where we wish to reside. You may not have considered my desire to become a privateer on the open seas rather than return to India. You will be my first mate, yes?"

She swatted at his arm and then blushed when her fingertips met his shirt sleeves rather than his discarded coat. "You are impossible! How do you follow the most romantic words with silliness about privateering? You positively ruin a poetic moment. And I *know* you're not serious. I would sooner be a privateer than you." Tugging at his hand, she said, "Come, the boys will have driven Mrs. Thomas to Bedlam by now."

Had he answered her question about learning Persian? She thought not. Best to ask again later.

If Persian was the language of the wealthy society in West Bengal, to which Alistair would undoubt-edly belong, it would be imperative she learn. But then, perhaps they spoke other languages of which she was already fluent. Definitely a conversation to explore with him further.

The whole of it both excited her and knotted her stomach. Did she *want* to move to India?

She did not doubt his sincerity, but it was all so soon, so rushed, so confusing. She had spent the first two weeks of their acquaintance convincing herself to dislike him because he was the forced betrothed of her dearest friend Leila, and Leila had wanted to marry Mr. Knowlton, not Alistair. What little Isobel had thought of him at all outside his villainy was to think of him as Leila's future husband. Then suddenly, without any warning, without any hints, without any-thing save a few conversations wherein Isobel had aimed to distract him so Leila could spend private moments with Mr. Knowlton, Alistair had declared his love for *her* — for *Isobel*. It took nearly a week to believe it had happened and then another week to accept his addresses.

He had time to assess his feelings about her, time to make his decision to recuse himself from the betrothal to Leila in favor of Isobel, but Isobel had not had that luxury. And soon she must move to India. From her understanding, she had until July. Alistair would attend two meetings with the Company, one in April and one in June; following that, if wed, she would leave her homeland for his. A little over three months to choose her fate.

Chapter 4

The Comte de Corentin pulled her against his chest.
'Je suis ici. Tu es sain et sauf. C'est sans danger.'

Isobel rewet the tip of her new quill, still hearing Corentin's words said in Alistair's voice.

As the words left his lips, the tower door behind him
slammed to the sound of maniacal laughter — his
nemesis! Corentin listened as the man's footsteps
receded down the spiral steps. Tap, tap, tap.

Her candle flame flickered. She eyed it, brows raised. Outside, heavy rain beat against the windows. After a warning squint to the candle, she returned to her story.

The beast was off to report Corentin to the
authorities, no doubt, to have him transported back
to France to face the guillotine so the dastardly
villain could have the maiden for himself. Sobs
wrenched anew from his beloved as he released
her to try the door.

Isobel's hand jerked as the wind rattled the garden door. Pursing her lips, she ignored it. The storm was determined to interrupt her, and she would not have it. This was an important scene!

> *He tugged. He pushed. He kicked. Solid oak and solidly locked. The villain had made a prisoner of him. The window! Corentin moved across the room, a hand touching his beloved's arm, and peered out the narrow window. Enough room for him to escape, but then he would need to climb down — what of his beloved? He could not leave her in the tower.*

The flame guttered violently.

Isobel sat back with a huff, surrendering her quill to its stand. Earlier, Alistair and his helpers had seen to the many necessary repairs, although they had not been able to finish everything, not by any stretch of the imagination. It would appear she had another repair to add to the list, a mysterious draft in her writing parlor. She suspected the garden door had shifted. Either that or the fireplace chimney was the culprit.

She glanced out the window, but only darkness stared back. The panes trembled against the wind and rain. Judging by the dance of her candle flame, it was time to retire. If this candle went out, she would be in the dark for the walk to bed, not that she was a stranger to lightless strolls through the house, but there was something about promises of stubbed toes that marked her reluctance to allow the candle to snuff.

The disappointment of the evening was leaving Corentin trapped in the tower. Granted, he had his beloved with him, but she was in no state to assist or entertain. Now, if it were Isobel trapped in the tower and Alistair came to the rescue, a simple matter of a locked door would be of no concern. Isobel tugged her bottom lip between her teeth. Alistair would not find a distraught damsel in distress. Oh no. He would find a most grateful heroine eager to shower him with affection for his efforts in rescuing her, and then, she would find a way for them to scale that wall together.

The flame ducked and danced. Well, pooh.

She tugged at the too-tight and too-short sleeves of her nightgown, wishing she had worn a dressing gown instead — only the dressing gown. No one was around to spy what she wore, so why had she not opted for comfort? At least the dressing gown was loose-fitting. The nightgown, like the rest of her wardrobe, was one of her cousin's discards. She owned nothing of her own. Had never owned a gown of any kind of her own. All clothing had been handed down to her from her cousin, and each article was fit for a woman half a head shorter and at least a stone lighter. If Isobel had been better with a needle, perhaps she could have made everything fit better. Alas, she hated sewing, stitching, darning, embroidering, and all other things involving a needle, so she made do with minor adjustments. Then, if *she* were at least a stone lighter, everything would fit better.

When she stood from the desk, she shivered. The nightgown, after all, stopped below her knees, leaving her ankles and feet bare. Her own fault not to have donned stockings. In her defense, it had been too warm this evening to layer, and with the house to herself, why should she not feel the wood floor beneath her bare soles? With a titter, she squeezed and wiggled her toes, then shivered again.

"Oh, fiddle," she said to the candle. "To Bedfordshire, we're off. Must you be so bossy?"

It dipped low in response, casting long shadows around the room.

Snatching the candlestick holder, she made for her room.

The luminescent orb teased her, lighting her immediate path but nothing else. It cast more shadows than it did light, the strips of elongated darkness haunting her periphery, vanquished by flashes of lightning. Even from the ground floor, the rain pounded overhead, and to each side, thunder rumbled and vibrated the windows and doors.

As she reached the foot of the stairs, she halted, breath held.

A whisper had tickled her ear. A faint whisper of a voice beneath the boom of the storm. With her hand on the banister, she strained to hear, listening past the howl of the wind.

There! An unmistakable wisp of sound. Accompanying was a light tap tap. Footsteps. Was someone in the kitchen? She could not recall if the kitchen door had been locked.

Tap, tap, tap.

She clasped a hand to her throat, clenching a fistful of her nightgown, breathless, heart pounding. *Someone was in the house.*

Bare feet raced up three steps before her world was plunged into blackness.

Had someone hit her over the head? Had she fainted? Was she dead? An acrid smell encircled her nostrils. She clawed at the air, confused and frightened. A flash of lightning revealed the great hall before her. Exhaling in relief, she realized she still stood on the stairs, the candle snuffed.

Tap, tap, tap, tap.

Footsteps tapped louder, closer, the whisper raising in volume but indecipherable.

Releasing her grip on her nightgown, she turned and fled up the stairs to the landing and around, her free hand tracing the wall so she would not trip. At the top of the stairs, she ducked into her bedchamber. Leaning her weight against the door, she pressed it shut, panting. *Someone was in the house.*

Her eyes widened as another streak across the sky illuminated her otherwise dark room. The open window rocked in the wind, sheets of rain streaming inside onto the seat board and down to the floor where a sizable puddle spread. Isobel shrieked. Grabbing her dressing gown from the bed, she tossed it at the puddle and tried to soak the water, then reached up to latch the window. As though angered, the wind howled. The house creaked and groaned around her.

Isobel draped the drenched gown over her washbasin mirror and searched the room with the next flash of lightning. Her tinderbox sat atop the empty fireplace's mantel. Searching the floor, she found where she had dropped the candle and holder in her rush to close the window. With tentative steps, hoping her bare toes would not kick a wall, chair, or bedframe, she retrieved the candle and took it to the mantel. Feeling inside the tinderbox, she grabbed the flint, steel, and cloth. Hands trembling, ever aware of the someone or several someones downstairs, she struck the steel against the flint. A spark. She struck again. Nothing. And again. Nothing. She struck and struck, her hands shaking uncontrollably.

"Arg!" she cried out in exasperation. This was hopeless.

Then, would it not be better to leave the candle unlit? Whoever was inside would see the light beneath the door if they came upstairs. 'Twould be better if they thought the house empty.

Who was inside? Why would they break into a house during a storm? Then, the storm would disguise their sounds. In a way, it was genius. But what if they discovered she was here? Alone?

Panic tightened her throat.

Eyes searching the void, she waited for the next lightning strike. When it lit the sky, she spotted her bed warmer beneath the washbasin. Perfect!

Once in hand, she wielded it as a weapon, thankful it was empty of coal. Step by step, she inched to the bedchamber door. Her aim was to crack it ajar, just enough to peer towards the stairwell and listen for intruder sounds to determine if they were still in the kitchen or had moved further into the house. They would be disappointed to find nothing of worth to steal. Except for the tea. And Isobel.

A hand on the door handle, she eased into a gentle tug, praying the door would not creak or groan to draw attention.

She need not have worried. The door did not budge. She tugged harder. No movement. Setting down the bed warmer, she wrapped both hands around the handle and pulled with a grunt. Nothing. The door was locked from the outside! She was locked inside her bedchamber, imprisoned.

Snatching the bed warmer, she scrambled to her bed. Isobel climbed on top of the bedlinen and pressed her back against the headboard, bed warmer held to her breast as she eyed the dark corner housing the door. Did that mean the intruders knew she was there? Were they holding her captive? Or had they locked all the doors as a precaution?

She strained to hear what was happening beyond the door, but all she could hear was the thunder rumbling, the rain pounding, and her heart thumping in her ears. She clutched the handle of the warmer until her fingers ached. Her breath came in short spurts. Her eyes darted around the room.

Wait. What was that?

A distant whistle.

Releasing her held breath, she realized it was the wind against the chimney of her fireless fireplace.

She resumed her huddling, her listening, her waiting, her watching. Thieves? Smugglers? Occultists?

Tap, tap, tap.

Her grip tightened, and her toes curled.

Straining again to hear, she discerned the distinct sound of footsteps. Increasing with the howl of the wind, as though moving closer, but then as though disguising their movements beneath the storm, the steps slowed and stopped as the wind died down. Did they move from room to room? Were they searching?

A bang and crack in the distance had her shrieking and diving beneath her sheets.

Isobel sharpened her resolve. She would not be frightened. She could not be frightened. It was not as though ghosts haunted the gallery, coming to steal her soul. She was defenseless against ghosts, her only recourse to run and hide and pray, but against flesh and blood people, no matter how nefarious, she could fight. And fight, she would. She refused to be a damsel in distress, some sniveling, cowardly maiden.

Tossing aside the sheets, she sat up, eyes trained on the darkened doorway. *Let them come.* Isobel The Fierce awaited!

Chapter 5

Rather than avoid the puddles along the road, as a sensible person would, the three Bradley boys aimed for every single one, more often than not with a howl, a gallop, and a leap. Alistair slowed his pace to provide them ample room for splashing.

The evening storm had kept him awake. Not the storm itself, although it had been furious enough to do just that. Worry over Isobel had him fretting rather than sleeping. On several occasions, he had to stop himself at the manor door from braving the storm to see to her welfare. He worried about her being home alone and worried about the shutters he had not yet repaired. This morning, he and his helpers headed to the farmhouse prepared with a toolbox and ladder to see to the shutters and whatever else might await their attention.

When they arrived, he surveyed the immediate area for any signs of disaster. Aside from a few felled tree branches, he saw nothing amiss, no visible roof damage, no broken windowpanes, no downed trees, at least nothing to see from the front of the house. The boys reached the front door first and made free use of the knocker.

By the time Alistair reached them, they had grown anxious for Isobel or Mrs. Thomas to open the door.

The knocker rose and fell beneath each of their hands, one after the other. Alistair grimaced, hoping they were not disturbing Isobel's writing.

"Where is Miss Isobel?" Daniel turned to look up at Alistair. "Did she forget us?"

"A morning walk is likely," Alistair said. "She'll return. Until then, we should not waste time. I'll begin on the shutters and —"

Cedric interrupted with, "We can see if Mrs. Thomas is in the kitchen." Before Alistair could respond, Cedric tugged at Daniel's arm, and the two ran around to the back of the house.

Brayden, the youngest of the three, watched them but did not follow. "Can I hold the ladder to help you?"

Rather than laugh or question how a seven-year-old expected to help should the ladder become unsteady or should Alistair slip, he rested a hand on the boy's shoulder and said, "When I need a new tool from the toolbox, I shall depend on you to hand it to me as I descend the ladder, yes?"

Brayden puffed his chest and nodded.

From around the back of the house, Daniel and Cedric came running towards them, both shouting at once, voices overlapping so Alistair could not understand the fuss. He held up a staying hand as they approached, then focused his attention on Cedric, his eyebrows raised.

Cedric said, "There's a flood in the kitchen! Up to my ankles, Mr. Trowbridge!"

"Mrs. Thomas?" Alistair asked.

He shook his head. "I don't think anyone is home. The kitchen door was unlocked, but Mrs. Thomas wasn't inside. Water up to my ankles! Come see."

The boys raced off again, Brayden on their heels this time.

Hoisting the ladder, Alistair followed suit.

As he rounded the corner to the back of the house, he heard his name. A feminine voice shouted, but he could not discern from where. The boys had already disappeared down the steps leading to the servant's entrance. He looked over his shoulder and into the woods. While he saw no one, he heard his name again. Isobel's voice, most assuredly.

When he turned back, he witnessed an arm waving from an open window on the first floor. The oriel window. Isobel's bedchamber. In quick strides, he stood below, looking up.

"*Nazaninam*?" With a hand over his brow, he shielded his eyes against the bright sky.

Isobel leaned over the window ledge. "Thank heavens you're here! My bedchamber door is locked. Can you find a key? There should be one in the kitchen, in the buttery."

Ignoring the bit about the kitchen, Alistair did what seemed the most sensible. He leaned the ladder against the timber and began his climb to her bedchamber window.

She peered down at him, watching his ascent with mouth agape. "What are you doing?"

"Rescuing you," he said, stating the obvious.

"But this is silly. The window's too narrow. And you could fall. And the door is locked from the *outside*, so you'd be trapped in here with me. Wait. On second thought. Quick! Come inside. Hurry before someone unlocks the door and frees us!"

Alistair chuckled as he climbed one foot at a time.

When he reached the top rung, he draped an arm over the window ledge. "Your hero has arrived, fair damsel. Where is the villain I must slay?"

He eyed the door from this distance, wondering how she had managed to lock herself inside. Ah, he understood. This was a game, possibly a test. She wanted him to play the hero. His choice to use the ladder would win him favor, then. He smirked, pleased with himself.

Isobel shook her head. "As I thought. The window is too narrow. You'll have to come around. A pity because I can think of at least five ways to thank you for saving me while being trapped in a locked chamber with you."

He arched a single brow as she blushed. As much as he wanted her to enumerate those five ways, he began his descent. Best to leave the ladder, he decided. Repairs would need his attention once he solved the mystery of the locked door. A shame he could not have lifted her out of the window or climbed into her bedchamber for a gallant rescue. Both scenarios had appeared in more than one of Isobel's stories, he knew. Had he failed the test, then? Was the window itself his heroic quest? Surely not.

Without bothering to see if the front door was unlocked, he went straight for the kitchen. Down the steps into the servant's entrance, he saw the pooling water immediately, the depth deepening as he followed the short hall into the kitchen where the boys were splashing each other as though a flood in the kitchen were the most normal and exciting of circumstances. He did not scold. Let them play. They would be helping to bucket, drain, and mop soon. The water was not as deep as Cedric had claimed, thankfully, but it would need to be mopped, nonetheless.

Ah, he saw the problem before he had crossed the room. A tree branch had shattered the pane of the kitchen window. With the window being ground level, no wonder the kitchen had flooded in the storm. He would wager that when he removed the branch, he would find one of the shutters he had intended to repair. A pity since he could have repaired that one without a ladder yesterday morning had he not been so intent on repairing the inside problems instead. He was to blame, then. Rather than a hero, he was a villain.

Disappointed in himself, he sloshed his way to the buttery. As predicted, a set of keys on a chatelaine hung by a hook. He grabbed the lot, not knowing which would fit her bedchamber door.

His eyes roamed the house as he headed through the great hall and up the stairs. He searched for any other signs of standing water or broken or leaking windows. Everything appeared dry and normal. After resolving the locked door problem, he would do a sweep of the house, attic included, to assess if his repairs had held and nothing else had gone awry, then he would patch the kitchen window and see to the shutters.

Crouching before her bedchamber door, he peeked through the keyhole. Isobel was pacing at the window, looking frazzled but beautiful, a damsel locked in a tower awaiting her hero's rescue. Her stockinged feet were free of shoes, and she wore one of his least favorite walking gowns, one he knew she liked more than the others since she did not tug at the sleeves as often.

His only dislike of it was the color. She looked best in green, he had thought on more than one occasion; not as well in puce, the color shadowing her complexion.

She turned towards the door and gasped. "You're spying on me through the keyhole! You're supposed to be rescuing me!"

"My apologies, fair flower. I was admiring your ankles."

"Alistair!" she said with a squeak. "Gentlemen do *not* speak of a woman's ankles! Now, are you going to unlock me or keep staring?"

"I've yet to decide," he admitted.

Isobel harrumphed and walked out of view of the keyhole.

"I am of a certainty that if I saw more ankle, I would be induced to find the key."

"You're a rogue, Alistair Trowbridge! I demand a new hero, one who will take my plight seriously. You're not even concerned about my well-being. Have you asked how I came to be locked in my room? Have you searched the house for thieves?"

He knew her to be teasing, but at the last word, her voice cracked just enough to cause concern. Was this not a game?

Standing, he tried the first three keys without luck, but the fourth fit. With a turn and push, he tried to open the door. No luck. He tried the other keys on the ring. None fit. He returned to the fourth key. Yes, it fit, but the door was not locked. It had not been locked when he arrived.

He stood back and studied the door. Ah. He understood. As with the two doors he repaired the previous morning, this had shifted. The top corner was wedged into the door frame. No doubt it had been shifting for some time, sticking a little more with each closure. Isobel might not have noticed if she had not closed the door recently. It was an easy repair he would see to today.

With a hearty push, he freed the door from the frame. It swung open to reveal a flurry of puce as Isobel leapt over her threshold and into his arms.

Alistair stepped back, startled, but just long enough to realize he must have won the game after all; the hero come to rescue his lady. With her arms wrapped about his neck and her head buried against his waistcoat, he returned the sentiment by snaking his hands around her waist and drawing her against him.

"My hero," she said with a sigh.

He grinned over the top of her head.

"I'm so embarrassed," she admitted after a time, sliding her arms down his chest and then letting them fall to her sides as she stepped away. "I thought the door had been locked by thieves. I vow I heard footsteps walking through the house, and then there was the whispering, and, and, I was certain someone was in the house. Was it only the storm?"

His chest tightened at the thought of her being afraid or in danger. "I will walk the house and leave no door unopened. Could a broken window have been the sound you heard?"

"The shutters!" she exclaimed, her face brightening with understanding and a laugh. "*That* must have been the tapping I heard. I thought it was footsteps. Oh, Alistair, I'm a silly goose, and I'm so thankful you're here. But, then, where are the boys, and where is Mrs. Thomas? Did you say a broken window?"

After retrieving her shoes, they headed downstairs to find the boys and better assess the situation.
Mrs. Thomas arrived shortly after, singing her apologies with tales of the wicked storm that had busied
her morning with cleaning debris that Benji would
have done if she had not, and with him still in recovery from his recent chill, she dared not take the chance
of leaving the mess. Once she saw the condition of
the kitchen, Alistair had to coax her to a chair in the
great hall with promises he and the boys would set
everything to rights before she could wish for a fresh
cup of tea.

Isobel peered out the window for the tenth time in as
many minutes. The sun had already dipped below the
horizon, the residual glow of the evening rays illuminating the surrounding forest. She searched the trees
for movement. Branches swayed in the wind, leaves
bobbing. No signs of a person, though.

Lifting the skirts of her dinner gown, she loped
upstairs to her room to check her mirror. Nothing had
changed since her last peek — five minutes ago. Back
downstairs, she headed straight for the window again.

What did he think of her for being so forward?
After all the gifts she had denied so as not to be
improper, and after continuing to delay an official
courtship until her mother returned, she had asked
the unthinkable. Which was worse — him thinking her
a coward or him thinking her wanton? Neither was
desirable. She had not hesitated to ask him, knowing

at the time he would understand, for he was not like the English gentlemen she knew, and she was confident he would not judge her question or see more than she had asked, and yet now that she awaited his arrival, she worried about these very things.

No one else would know. No one else would judge. The farmhouse was close enough to Nasrin Manor that he could take the forest walk to remain unseen. He would leave well before Mrs. Thomas' arrival in the morning. No one would know. But *his* opinion mattered to her more than anyone's in Sidvale, and she did not want him to think less of her.

Her fretting was compounded by the memories of him wielding a hammer, climbing up and down ladders, and bucketing water from the kitchen. With his coat removed and his sleeves rolled above his elbows, he had unwittingly favored her with unimpeded views of his tanned, muscular forearms, flexing with subtle movements. Sweat had beaded down his temple as though begging her to swipe his forehead with her fingertips. *Mesmerizing*. Had someone told her when she first met him that she would see him laboring, she would have called them a fibber. He had been so polished at Nasrin Maner, so perfect. Oh, she had not known the meaning of the word perfect! *This* was perfection.

What had she been thinking to ask him the unthinkable?

She watched for movement between the trees, chewing on her bottom lip and fanning her cheeks with her hand.

She could have asked Mrs. Thomas to stay, but there was Benji to consider. Leila was in Hampshire, so not an option. Abbie was visiting her in-laws, so not an option either. That left Hetty, and Hetty was home. Hetty would have allowed Isobel to stay at the manor, although she would not likely have accepted an invitation to stay at the farmhouse. Conversely, Isobel could not imagine staying at the manor. It would always be Lord Dunley's manor to her, not Hetty's new home. Staying with Humble Hetty at her grandmother's home had been fun, but now that Hetty was a viscountess living on the estate in the Dunley Manor with her mother-in-law and husband… well, that was not an option as far as Isobel was concerned. Besides, she would have to devise an excuse for why she needed company because she would never admit to being too frightened to stay alone.

Then, that was exactly what she had told Alistair.

She had not thought to mask her true intention, and at the time of asking, she had not worried he would misinterpret. Only now, with the fading daylight and onset of dusk, did she question if he would judge her poorly and see more into her pleading request than had been intended. Had she really *begged*? Yes, she had. Burying her face in her hands, she groaned.

From between her fingers, she caught sight of movement, a shade of red slipping between the trees, the scarlet of a fine coat, closing in on the farmhouse from the woodland at biped speed. Forgetting her worries, she rocked heel to toe with excitement. Try as she might to wait for him to knock, Isobel opened the door before he entered the clearing. She stood in the doorframe, smiling, unable to disguise her enthusiasm.

When Alistair caught sight of her, his eyes appraised her from a distance, his steps quickening to reach her. "You've not been waiting long?" he asked as he approached.

"Only since the moment you said yes," she admitted, although her tone was teasing.

Isobel stepped aside so he could enter the house without breaking stride. Once in the great hall, with the door closed behind them, he handed her two wrapped boxes. His expression said he would not take no for an answer. Blushing, she accepted, her fingers making quick work with the twine of the first package.

The package open, she mouthed an *Oh*. Beeswax candles!

Looking around the room, she grimaced to realize she had not lit any candles in preparation for nightfall. They would soon be in the dark. How prophetic for him to bring them light.

"Not for tonight," he said, clearly reading her gaze as she looked about the darkening room. "For your writing. So you may write longer into the evening. For tonight, I have another plan."

He did not divulge, merely winked. So enraptured by the beeswax candles, she had forgotten the second gift. The candles were far too good quality to use for writing, but that would be exactly how she used them. They would allow her to write longer and without the unpleasantness of guttering, odor, or smoke, as was the case with her current collection of candles. She might save one or two for the next stormy night, however. Just in case.

Alistair nodded to her other gift, nudging her into action with an expectant smirk.

A tug at the twine, followed by a gasp.

Dizziness undermined Isobel's stability, rocking her unsteadily. She refused to faint, but… *oooh*! Inside the second package lay a turquoise necklace. But not any turquoise necklace. Isobel blinked away tears. Never had she seen anything so breathtaking. The necklace boasted six small turquoise gemstones with a sizable, solitaire of Persian turquoise hanging in the middle, each gemstone set in a bed of diamonds, reminding Isobel of flower petals. For *her*? It was too much, and yet….

Alistair retrieved the necklace and signaled he wished to clasp it around her neck. "Turquoise for protection. Now, you will be safe against all evil."

She reached a hand to the hollow of her neck to touch the cold stone. He had chosen this specifically for her, she understood, in response to her taking fright during the storm. Although she knew he brought it with him to England, and his intention was likely to give it to Leila, he had chosen this from his collection for Isobel. She blinked rapidly.

When she turned around to face him, hoping her eyes were not red-rimmed, he stepped back to admire her fully. She almost crossed her arms about her waist, self-conscious of his appraisal, worried he would see all her flaws compared to the beauty of the necklace. Her dinner gown, after all, was as poorly fitting as the rest of her wardrobe.

"You can no longer reject my gifts," he said. "My staying here wins me the prize of offering gifts as often as I choose."

His sultry smile gave her pause. Her pulse quickened. Her thoughts from earlier returned to taunt her. *Had* he misconstrued her meaning, and rather than be disgusted, he found her forwardness inviting? She swallowed the lump in her throat. All her near swooning over his gallantry fled, replaced with apprehension.

"I have an appetite needing satiation," he said. "Are you, too, prepared to be satisfied?"

In response, Isobel gave a strangled cry and took a step back.

"No? You prefer to eat later? But the food is warm."

It took a moment for Isobel to realize he held up a basket. Oh! How had she not noticed it before? So distracted by the gifts, then his possible double meanings, she had not noticed he brought a food basket with him. If he witnessed her blushing, which there was little chance he could miss it, he would think her flattered by not only gifts but now dinner, and while both were true, she blushed with fervor at having misconstrued his words. *Abominable, Isobel!*

She leaned in to smell the deliciousness wafting from the basket. "I had thought we would split the meal Mrs. Thomas left for me. Now we'll have a veritable feast! Give me a moment to set the table."

"No, wait." Alistair held up his free hand. "I have another plan. A picnic."

Isobel glanced out the window.

"I'll prepare everything, *nazanin*. Your task is to retreat to your writing parlor. You must not peek until I call for you. A surprise, you see? Entrance will be granted with a novel. I wish to read your current story." Holding a finger to her lips to silence any protests and questions, he added, "No argument. Now, go."

Isobel lounged on a blanket before the hearth. Alistair was next to her, his eyes combing her story. A fire burned. A *wood* fire. When she had first entered the large parlor to see the blaze, she had panicked, for the firewood he had found to use and thought to surprise her with was from her mother's personal woodpile. Alistair had assured her in that calm and confident way of his that all he used would be replenished. And so, she could rest as the hungry flames licked the logs. The fire offered more light than heat, the parlor as bright as a sunny afternoon, which Isobel supposed was not a difficult task since the large parlor was considered large in comparison to the small parlor. Her "large" parlor could fit five times in Leila's parlor at Nasrin Manor. The fire, thus, did not have far to reach to brighten all corners of the room.

Alistair angled his current page to read the lines she had finished only this afternoon. "Why a French nobleman?"

"Is it not more romantic? More dramatic? A French count flees for his life, afraid of the guillotine. Now, to live in disguise in Austria, searching for his beloved. Is she dead? Alive? Imprisoned by his nemesis? Forced to wed another? The suspense! It's titillating!" She hugged her arms and sighed at the romance of it all, the hero searching for his long-lost love, ready to battle any villains in his path. "Besides, the French are more entertaining to write. They're daring, uninhibited, and *passionate*! Is that not tantalizing? Who wants to write about aristocrats who never show or express emotion? Rather than fight his way out of the tower to rescue the maiden, the English hero would hand the villain his calling card to arrange a day for his second to conduct a dignified and gentlemanly apology."

Alistair chuckled. "And what would your Persian hero do?"

"I would say he would scale the wall of the tower, fling the maiden over his shoulder, then retreat, all unseen by the villain, but experience has taught me he would prefer the maiden remain locked in the tower so that he might admire her ankles through the keyhole."

Rather than laugh as she expected, his gaze found her stockinged feet and lingered on her ankles, the corners of his lips curling into a smirk.

"Case in point," Isobel scolded, tugging at the edge of her gown.

Rifling through the pages, Alistair arched a solitary brow. "Is a French hero wise? You show sympathy for a Frenchman in exile. In the way of the English, this makes *you* a French sympathizer."

Waving a dismissive hand, she said, "I have no plans to submit this story for publication. I have dozens ready to be read by the world. And then, there are the ones I write for myself. Sometimes, characters speak to me. I can't silence them until I've written their story. This is one of those. No one except us will know it exists." She looked down at her fidgeting hands before asking, "Did you see some of your personality in Corentin?"

He flipped a page or two of her scribblings, as though searching for himself. "I am heroic, my proclivity for eyeing your ankles aside?" His expression was so smug that the question did not need an answer.

Instead, Isobel dove into the backstory. "The setting is 1794. The exodus of French aristocrats is underway. Our hero is an émigré in Austria. To avoid detection, he's disguised himself as an Austrian, for while he's welcome in the country now, his nemesis is sure to report him once he discovers Corentin. You see…" She shifted position, tucking her legs beneath her. "He and another gentleman were competing for the same lady's hand in marriage. During the exodus, the lady was captured by the other gentleman's father. She's then imprisoned until the father can determine his son's whereabouts, as the son — our hero's competition — disappeared somewhere between France and Austria. Once Corentin discovers she's imprisoned, he must find a way to free her. But it's complicated because — "

Alistair finished her sentence with, "Because he will be beheaded in France?" When she nodded, he asked, "Would that not expose the father and son to meet the same fate?"

"Oh." Isobel thought for a moment, then said, "Unless the father and son are Austrian nobles, not French."

"Perhaps," he said with a nod. "And the lady's family? What of them?"

"Hmm. Well… they could have become separated on the journey to Austria, and during that separation is when the villain found her."

Alistair collected the pages and stacked them neatly to the side of their makeshift picnic blanket. "You have ends to tie, sweet Isobel. I like your French count and wish to know how he concludes."

Isobel's lips inched into a smile.

Alistair offered a smile of his own, one that somersaulted Isobel's heart. "Your count's story is not unlike my mother's when she fled Persia."

Her smile slipped into question. In her time of knowing him, he had never spoken of his mother's origins or how she had come to live in India. He had spoken of her with love, but most of their conversations when Isobel stayed at the manor had been about either his childhood or his father. She knew so little of his mother. Clasping her hands in her lap, she angled forwards with interest, nodding for him to continue.

"My mother, along with her family, fled Persia, afraid for their lives. It was no longer the safe place her family had known for generations, now war-torn. India was not immune to this, but her family settled in West Bengal. They hoped to gain British protection, as with your count, hoping the House of Austria would protect him. My father met my mother in Calcutta, and he married her for protection as much as affection. He gave her his name and, by proxy, the protection of the East India Company. You must understand, the Company and England were seen by many in Calcutta, and still are, as an enemy, but to my mother, they were her protector."

"So much like my storybook hero!" Isobel exclaimed. "But then, why did she not move to England when your father moved? That would have sealed her safety."

Alistair stared into the hearth, his brows furrowed. "She refused. My father promised eternal happiness if she would move. She dreamed of returning to her homeland, Isobel, always clutching to her Persian

ways. For years, she opened her ears to news of the
civil war back home, waiting for the resolution so she
could at last return."

"You've never been to Persia. You told me before."

"Correct. I've never been. I was born and brought
up in West Bengal. It may surprise you to know I've no
wish to go. My mother's longing to return wrenched
her soul, and for that, I am embittered, although I see
it is not the fault of the country or people, and I know I
should *want* to go if it was so important to my mother.
But she never saw me in the return to Persia. I confess. She wanted me to be like my father, follow his
steps, and work in the Company. And so, here I am."

With a slow, panther-like motion, he leaned closer
to her. A log shifted in the fireplace, crackling. Isobel
swallowed. He reached a hand towards her, tentative, as though gauging if she would move away. She
remained still, her pulse erratic. His fingertips touched
the back of her hand, light and hesitant, then softly
circling her knuckles until he traced his fingers around
to her palm. A gentle stroking from palm to the tips
of each of her fingers sent a tremor down her spine.
Just when she thought he might add more intimacy
to the moment by holding her hand or lacing their
fingers, he instead reached up to touch the turquoise
of her necklace. His eyes bore into hers as he released
the jewel, his hand settling against the floor to rest.

She did not know what made her say it or even
what she meant by it. But the words slipped, nevertheless. All that was missing was the word *Leila*, for it
was on the tip of her tongue. "You brought this necklace for your intended. All the jewelry you brought
from India. It was all for your betrothed."

He shook his head, his gaze never leaving hers. "No, Isobel. I did not bring jewelry for Leila Owen. I see her name in your eyes."

Perplexed, Isobel remained silent.

"I brought jewelry for the woman who would become my wife." He let the words hang in the air. "The early gifts," he explained, "such as the bobbles I gave to Miss Owen, were ones I purchased before leaving India. As I did not know my intended, I chose what I thought she might like, what I thought would favor a woman. The jewels I give you now are not of those. This necklace is from my mother's collection, an heirloom passed to the brides for generations. I have many more to bestow in good time. These I give only to the one who has my heart. Fortunate am I, this suits you. I thought green your color, but I see now it is blue. Blue is your color, *nazanin*."

She touched the turquoise at her throat. "Your mother's?"

"Yes. They could bring little with them when they escaped, but the jewelry was a necessity. I know many pieces are lost, sold for survival, but all that remains is now mine and will soon be yours, and one day our son's and then for his bride. But I speak of the future and wish not to frighten you."

His smile was so disarming, Isobel could only laugh, even while his words weighed heavily — *their son*.

He continued, "You will not be burdened by jewels, *fandogham*, my hazelnut. That is not the English way. But you will know my affection with each gift I bestow."

"I will accept. I do accept." With a glance at the flames, then at her trembling hands, nervous as to if she should say the next, she took a deep breath and looked back at Alistair. "No more waiting. Who cares if our courtship is unusual and not as proper as it ought to be in the eyes of society? It will be *our* way rather than the English way. I wish for you to court me openly. We've waited long enough for my mother to return."

The disarming smile of his broadened until his shockingly white teeth flashed in the firelight. "Music to my ears, Isobel of the blue jewel. We will make our own way."

Fueled by anticipation, Isobel probed, "What *is* our way? Do we have one? Is there a courtship tradition from your own culture we could regard?"

Alistair leaned back against his elbows, turning his body to face the fire again. He did not look at her for some time, deep in thought. Isobel had considered her question the exciting start of a new adventure in their life, the crossing of an unseen threshold, but his response was hesitant and unsure.

At length, he said, "I am a man in search of myself." Angling back towards her by propping himself on his forearm, he rubbed his chin. "I was born and brought up in India, yes, but I was reared by a proud Persian woman while groomed to become more English to gain a position in the Company with my father, which I did. I am a man torn."

Confused, since he always appeared so confident, Isobel nodded for him to continue, trying to show her encouragement in her expression.

"I am who I was brought up to be, but I wish to create myself as I *want* to be. I wish to create the man I want to become."

The words, so impassioned, inspired Isobel to say, "I've always known you're heroic, just like my story-book heroes. To create oneself is the ultimate heroism. Don't you think?"

His eyes shone, and he reached over to palm her cheek. "I want nothing more than to be your hero."

With her skin tingling from the heat of his palm, she stuttered, "But... what is your plan? Who... who are you creating yourself to be?" She thought she knew who he was and his plans for the future. Were they not moving to India to live in his stately home?

"I am unprepared to answer. I will not leave you in question, and I will not ask you to wed me until I have shared my vision, but I believe in my heart and my head you will favor the man I am to become. Should I proceed as settlement governor in India, or choose to run for Member of Parliament in England, or become the privateer at sea you tease me about, or..." His words trailed off before he continued with, "I believe you will be pleased and supportive. Will you wait for me to form the words? I do not wish to disappoint you with poor poetry when it comes to the language of love."

Reaching for her cheek, she cupped his hand in hers. "You know I'll afford you the time you need. I only wish to help. Your future is my future, after all."

With Alistair's hand still cradling the curve of her face, he leaned closer to her. His cologne, sweet with its spices and heady with its musk, seduced her senses. She swayed towards him in response, antic-ipating what she thought would be their first kiss.

As the space between them shadowed, mere inches from each other, a log shifted in the fireplace, showering them with sparks. Isobel shrieked, and Alistair laughed. With flailing limbs, they patted at the errant embers before any could burn a hole in the linen of their picnic sheet.

Alistair retrieved the screen and settled it before the fireplace. "It is time we retire, *nazanin*. You first while I see to the fire. Gracious hostess that you are, you need not escort me to the guest room. I know where to find it." He held out a hand to assist her in rising. Once she stood before him, he bowed to kiss the air above her hand. "I will be gone before you wake, but should you require my assistance in the night, you need only shout. I am one gallery away to protect you from ghosts, thieves, smugglers, and occultists. *Shab-et khosh, khoshgele khânum.* Goodnight, Miss Beautiful."

Chapter 6

Alistair reread the letter from his father. His teacup lingered before his lips, steam curling around his nostrils with the promise of flavor. Another sip, and he set down both cup and letter. How would his father respond if Alistair requested to bring Isobel? The situation remained delicate.

In one hour, he was to meet the solicitor to look at two more houses, these farther from Sidvale than the others he had toured but still near enough for Isobel to call on her friends and mother. He refused to question his decision to browse availabilities. This helped him plan, helped him think, helped him envision possibilities. Least of all, it showed him the options, all dependent on his conversation with his father, all dependent on his courtship with Isobel.

However much hung in the balance of other people's decisions, he wanted a solid plan for all eventualities. Should one plan fail, another stood at the ready. Nothing would catch him unawares. There were barriers to his courtship with Isobel, ones she was not yet aware of, but he had no intention of hiding them.

The solicitor likely thought him confused, but Alistair's rationale was none of the man's concern. One of the houses they would view today was another modest cottage, one he could afford should he need to pay out of pocket, one he thought Isobel might find an inspiration for her writing given its location near abbey ruins. The other was an estate with a country manor and several farms which could be let to tenants. The two contrasted as dramatically as those he viewed before with the solicitor. The home he provided was important. Home would be important to Isobel, too, but as her provider and protector, he wanted it to be perfect, not only to fulfill his dream but also hers and the generations they would sire.

Of all the points he planned, the one he could least control was Isobel. He did not wish to devise a plan that did not include her, but he knew he ought, in case. With her heart set on India and a gentleman of means, he worried she would not like his confession.

Another cup of tea, he decided, and then he would reply to his father before setting off to meet the solicitor.

"What language do they speak in West Bengal?" Isobel asked.

Alistair served himself from the dishes arrayed on the table. As their first step towards an open courtship, he had invited her to dine that evening at The Tangled Fleece, the private dining room their domain, although they were not alone, as a maid from Nasrin Manor he had convinced to serve as chaperone was seated in a discreet corner, enjoying a meal of her own. He and the maid — along with someone sensible from the inn, if he could persuade them — would escort Isobel home but then leave her at the front door. Although he had offered to return later in the evening by way of the forest walk, Isobel said she felt more confident to stay alone again. His offer would stand. It would not do for her to lose sleep or be afraid.

In answer to her question, he said, "Many languages. One's place in society determines what is spoken. Portuguese is the most common language. English is important because of British settlement. Those with power and status, however, speak Persian. There are many other languages, but none I speak with frequency. The servants have their own language, for instance. The poor theirs. Diplomats must know those of surrounding regions."

Isobel nodded as though her head were on a hinge. He chuckled.

After she finished another bite, followed by a sip of her drink, she asked, "What about clothing? When you first arrived, you were wearing..." She circled a hand, searching for the words. "I don't know what to call it, but you were wearing, you know, Indian garments. Now you wear English attire. Is what you wore before typical, or do they dress as we do here?"

"So full of questions about India."

He wondered if she asked because of what he had shared about his mother the previous evening or if she was thinking about the move. He did not ask. Asking would open the conversation to the latter, and he was not prepared to discuss or disappoint.

Addressing her question, he said, "What I wore when you met me is traditional Indian garb, yes. The dhoti topped with either achkan or sherwani. With

British settlement, more natives dress in the English fashion. Terrible choice. English fashion suits English weather, not the heat of Bengal."

"Oh. So, you'd prefer to dress traditionally?"

"Not at all. I prefer to dress appropriately. In England, it's English fashion for English weather. In India, it's Indian fashion for Bengali weather. You see? I've often worn English dress in India when on Company business. It's expected. When I arrived here, I wore my dhoti and achkan because Mr. Owen let me believe my intended would prefer traditional attire. I wanted to please her." He paused to drink. "You'll laugh when I tell you that she was told the same of me. Once we learned the truth, we were free to dress as we wished. I chose English dress, as she did. Do you have a preference?"

Canting her head, Isobel eyed him with a *hmm* before saying, "You're dashing no matter what you wear. As long as you're comfortable, I'm happy."

He set down his cutlery and leaned back. "And if I prefer to wear a banyan?"

Isobel shrugged. "Most men do. I'm certain you would look dashing in that too."

"*Only* the banyan?"

Her fork paused midair. In his periphery, he saw the maid's cutlery do the same. Isobel set down her fork and swallowed, a blush rising from her fichu and working up her neck.

"Many apologies," he said. "I am impolite. I thought to jest but forgot it is not the way."

Softly, Isobel muttered, "Quite the tease."

The benefit of his jest, aside from the enjoyment of seeing her blush so becomingly, was her distraction from asking the next logical question — would she need to wear a sari when they moved? However beautiful he knew she would look in a sari, he had not the gumption to tell her there would be no need.

Would she be disappointed enough to reject his suit? She had not accepted his advances because she wanted to move to India, but since agreeing to his courtship, she had steadily increased her excitement about the move. It could affect how she saw him. No, it *would* affect how she saw him, if not for the move to India, then for the decision he had made that would keep them from moving. It was *that* point that worried him.

"We spoke much of travel in our conversations at Nasrin Manor," Alistair said as he replenished his plate with other dishes to try. The inn's food could compete with that which he was served at the manor, although he would never dare tell the Owens' cook. "You expressed an interest in seeing the world."

All thoughts of him adorned in a banyan appeared to flee. Isobel's expression brightened. "It has been a long-standing dream of mine, yes. Think of the writing inspiration, the immersion I could create by having seen the places with my own eyes! My stories are always set in other countries, yet I've never left Devonshire. I could write on location!"

"I, too, have wished to travel. While you have never left Devonshire, I had never left West Bengal prior to this year. I am fortunate to have finally made it to this great country. The journey, however…" He shuddered in memory. "…was unpleasant."

"But we could make it an adventure! No trip would be the same. We could playact. I could be an archeologist in search of treasures who meets by chance an exiled and disguised prince–that's you. Or I'm on the run from my wicked cousin who wishes to marry me, and you agree to help me by marrying me instead and stealing me away to some exotic location. Or–"

Alistair's laughter drowned out words. "I see no unpleasant travels with you."

"What made it so unpleasant?"

"Aside from you not being with me?" He winked. "Ah, Isobel, you will not like the journey, but I hope we will both like the destinations. The trip was long, tedious, dirty, and dizzying. The ship rocked many to illness. The cleanliness was… not clean. It took many months. There are two routes, one overland and one by sea. Neither is safe, and both are long. We required safety by traveling in *kafila*, that is, with a caravan of merchants."

He paused to wet his throat. However delicious the food, the inn's tea was not. Weak and scented of horses though it was, his cup was not unpalatable. He now understood why Mr. Bradley had recommended the wine instead.

"You say playacting," he continued, "which is part of safe travel. At various points, we had to disguise ourselves with new names and a different profession. Few suspect merchants, you see, especially merchants with local names. People are suspicious and unwelcoming, more so in times of unrest. Do not be discouraged, Isobel. The lands and sea I saw were worth the journey–such sights! But I think travel to the continent would be superior. Safer and less time on a ship."

"I want to hear about every day of the journey and all the gritty details. Not only do I want to imagine you on the high seas, but I can also have one of my heroes set sail–think of how authentic the details will be based on your experiences!"

Smiling at her enthusiasm but not about to share the grittiest of details, he said, "I'll share during our next fireside evening. For now, I'll say I wish to travel, *nazanin*, and with you by my side."

Isobel fluttered her eyelashes as she flushed pink, an affectation Alistair found endearing, although his reason would have surprised most ladies. She had no knowledge of fluttering them that he could see. She did not flutter them in flirtation but rather when she was most flattered, embarrassed, or nervous. He found it incredibly charming, enough to bring a smile to his lips every time. That she had the longest eyelashes he had ever witnessed drew that much more attention — dark and sooty, although she wore no charcoal or enhancements, and all the more alluring against her alabaster complexion.

Her eyes met his, and then she renewed her blush, casting her gaze to her plate in shyness. He admired her even as she tugged at the sleeves of her gown. Curious, he thought. Not that she tugged at her sleeves, which she often did, but that all her gowns were long-sleeved. An observation he had not considered until now. The maid in the corner wore a short-sleeved gown beneath her open robe. Did none of Isobel's gowns have short sleeves? Was she not warm in the summer months? She needed a new wardrobe, one tailored for her. It was not his place yet to offer new clothing, but it would be a gift he would enjoy bestowing. How different would she look in modiste fashions?

Shaking his head of the thoughts, he returned his attention to her eyelashes. "You have no flirtatious wiles," he said.

Isobel turned her widening eyes to him, her smile slipping into a frown. "I beg your pardon."

He grimaced. "I've chosen the wrong words? Yes, your pink cheeks have paled, and your mouth curves down. I am offering a compliment. Being with you is easy: natural. You have no artifice. Other women... they... how to say... playact. I've not the words. You understand?"

The frown began a slow curve back into a smile. Isobel nodded. "Yes, I understand, Alistair. I understand perfectly. It's the same for me. I'm uncomfortable around most men, most people, honestly. I never say the right things. Nothing I have to say interests anyone, so while you won't believe me for a minute, I'm truthful when I say I never say anything at all. With my friends, yes. With you, yes, obviously. But with other people? Unless I know them well, I stay silent."

The longer she rambled through her reciprocation, the broader his grin. He could listen to her talk all day and all evening without interruption. She was not like the women he knew back home, women who pushed and demanded, always wanting the first word, last word, and every word in between. Neither was she like the English women he had met, who were too reserved to carry on a conversation, flirtatious wiles or otherwise. He had begun to take his interactions personally. Was it he who lacked finesse? Did he inspire the worst in women? But then there was Isobel. His confidence soared listening to her carry on now about how much she enjoyed his company. Almost enough to forget she might not feel favorable towards him after he confessed his decision and the long talk he would soon be having with his father. He brushed this last aside, intent on enjoying every moment while it lasted.

Chapter 7

The vicar's voice rose above the flutter of fans, heartening the congregation for the week ahead. Isobel's pew was near the pulpit since she was a gentleman's daughter, one row behind Hetty, Hetty's mother-in-law, the Dowager Viscountess Dunley, and Hetty's husband, Viscount Dunley. Next to Isobel sat Alistair, his body still, his attention riveted on the Reverend Walsley. Was this his first Anglican service? She would have to remember to ask.

Oh, now that she thought of it, what *was* he? Hindu? She was ashamed not to know and not to have worried over it before — would that not affect their union? Would she be expected to convert? If he was Hindu, they would not be able to marry in the parish church. She knew nothing of Hinduism other than Leila telling her about Mrs. Owen's conversion to Anglicanism. Isobel fidgeted.

Glancing over her shoulder, she searched the faces for Mrs. Bradley, hoping to invite the innkeeper's wife to take tea with her again, with or without Alistair. Now that Isobel had made her acquaintance, she wished to further the friendship. After all these years, she was ashamed it had taken so long to know Mrs. Bradley. The latter had been little more than "Mr. Bradley's wife" and the "inn's best pie maker" for as long as Isobel could remember, which was ridiculous given the woman was a person in her own right, the mother of six wonderful babes, three of which Isobel had offered an open invitation to call on her as often as they would like.

At the back of the church, she spied the tops of the children's heads and next to them, Mr. Bradley. Oh, yes, of course. Mrs. Bradley would be at the inn, preparing for the after-church feast. She and Mr. Bradley traded weeks. Isobel knew this. All the parishioners knew this and were grateful, but Isobel could not recall when she last *thought* about it aside from passing awareness. She turned her attention back to the Reverend Walsley.

Her good friend Abbie was the vicar's daughter. Isobel had spent countless evenings staying at the vicarage throughout the years. Mr. Walsley was, in a way, her second father. He danced attention on her when she visited Abbie, and he was what she imagined her own father had been, what little of him she could recall. She focused her attention on his words, his sermon of the day on a theme of neighborliness. Ironic, given how unneighborly she was feeling, not to know Mrs. Bradley better. She would do well to listen, then.

When the service concluded, the inhabitants of the first pew walked the nave first, followed by Isobel and Alistair. As Mr. Walsley caught Alistair in conversation outside the church, Isobel first exchanged words with Mrs. Thomas and arranged a time for Isobel to call on Benji now that he was feeling better, and then she approached Hetty.

Hetty, in all her viscountess hauteur, greeted Isobel with, "It looks like rain."

Isobel glanced skyward. Leaden clouds hovered. The light had dimmed, and there was a warm breeze, but all was well. She supposed they were skipping spring altogether and headed straight for summer this year. It had been cold and threatening snow only a couple of weeks ago.

"Are you for the inn?" Isobel asked. "Mrs. Bradley's sure to have at least three pies to sample."

Hetty sniffed. "You know my mother-in-law would never approve of *tavern* food." She sighed, her shoulders slumping almost imperceptibly. "I miss Mrs. Bradley's pies. Will our Ladies Literary Society ever meet again?"

"Of course! Once Abbie returns from visiting her in-laws and once Leila returns from Hampshire, we'll find a way to rescue you from the Dunley prison, even if it's just for one afternoon to share stories over endless slices of pie."

With a wan smile, Hetty said, "I would like that. You can always be relied upon, Isobel." Stepping closer, her eyes darting around her, she asked without moving her mouth, "Who is that delectable wildcat talking with Mr. Walsley?"

"Alistair?" Isobel turned to see the two in deep conversation, interrupted by parishioners thanking the vicar before they milled about to talk to each other. "That's Mr. Alistair Trowbridge. He *was* the suitor Mr. Owen brought from India for Leila. Now he's *my* suitor." She stood a little taller when she said the last.

Hetty's jaw slackened. "Isobel!" she hissed. "Where is your sense of propriety? Your mother is away!"

Wounded that Hetty would think of propriety rather than be impressed that frumpy, plumpy Isobel had snared the catch of the century, she snapped back with, "If you would join us at the inn, it wouldn't be so improper, would it?"

Hetty flinched. Guilt stabbed Isobel with the pointy end of its dagger. It was not Hetty's fault her mother-in-law kept her on short leading strings. So much for Mr. Walsley's sermon on neighborliness. As Hetty made to reply, Alistair approached. Hetty instead shared her thoughts with raised eyebrows.

"Would you allow me to introduce Mr. Alistair Trowbridge of West Bengal?" After Hetty nodded regally, her chin raised, Isobel continued with, "This is Lady Dunley. *Viscountess* Dunley. To us commoners, she'll always be Henrietta." She cast an *I-dare-you-to-scold-me* look at her friend. Hetty merely narrowed her eyes.

As Alistair bowed and exchanged a few pleasantries, Isobel spied Lord Dunley and his mother approaching, her heart dropping into her stomach the closer they moved. She had never liked the viscount, but then she had never known him well, either. He spent nearly all his time in London. Of the few interspersed months he spent in Sidvale, he avoided the village aside from Sunday service, treating all he saw with condescension if he bothered to take notice of them. For all his pompousness, everyone knew who ruled the Dunley household: his mother. Her frailty and absentmindedness were deceptive. Her word governed all Sidvale.

The Dowager Viscountess Dunley became distracted halfway to Isobel and company, drifting over to speak with one of her gentleman tenants. And so, only Lord Dunley approached.

Lord Dunley's bejeweled and beribboned cane —
ostentatious for church, Isobel mused — clicked
against the cobblestones, muted once he stepped
onto the gravel. His high heels echoed the sound. In
his opposite hand, he held a perfumed handkerchief,
occasionally wafting it before his nose.

Hetty greeted him with little more than a nod
of acknowledgment. Lord Dunley ignored her, and
Isobel as well, for that matter, his attention on Alistair.
Without a word, his lordship raised a quizzing glass
to his eye. Through it, he gave a head-to-toe perusal
of the stranger in their midst. A single eyebrow arched
in the direction of Hetty, although he never turned
his gaze.

"Mr. Alistair Trowbridge, my lord," Hetty said in
the way of introduction. With an almost apologetic
tone, she offered to Alistair, "My husband."

Not so low to be either insulting or obsequious,
Alistair bowed, sweeping a magnificent leg. The move
was a little too theatrical for Isobel's taste, but the corners of Lord Dunley's mouth twitched in approval.
Not a single word was exchanged, but all in the
party appeared satisfied with the interchange when
Dunley signaled with a cock of his head for Hetty to
follow, and then they were off to gather the wandering viscountess.

Isobel stepped closer to Alistair with a reassuring
smile. Her fingers itched to take his arm, but it would
do neither of them any service to be seen touching.
Only over rough terrain or after an official betrothal
was announced could she take his arm without raising eyebrows or being seen as a scarlet woman. It
was scandalous enough to be conducting a courtship

without her mother in town. A scarlet woman? *Isobel?* Sidvale was a small village with good people, none prone to gossip and none desirous of scandals, but a young lady could never be too careful. *A scarlet woman!* Isobel laughed aloud.

Alistair glanced at her askance.

A single fat raindrop tapped Isobel on the shoulder. Then, a friend followed. All parishioners about the churchyard looked around, then up, then around again, a murmur of alarm working its way through the crowd. Without further warning, a not-so-gentle drizzle bathed their Sunday best. The crowd dispersed, some rushing home, but most heading for The Tangled Fleece, an array of parasols, fans, and gloved hands held aloft to stave off the rain.

With a strangled sound that resembled part gasp, part shriek, and part laugh, Isobel tugged at Alistair's coat and raced towards the inn.

The inn was so crowded as to be standing room remaining. Alistair and Isobel had secured a table solely because two gentlemen offered it to them, a showing of their neighborly spirit following the vicar's sermon. The barmaids moving to and fro about the room served drinks and newspapers. The food was offered on a sideboard; all patrons were invited to take their fill of the sumptuous feast, pies especially, while it lasted.

After securing platefuls for both himself and Isobel, Alistair took his seat and peeked at the newspaper. *The Bard* was printed in bold letters at the top.

Isobel, positively giddy, reached across the table to point at a column in tiny print. "That's mine," she said.

Squinting at the fine print, he read the first line. While he would read the remainder later, he knew from the first line what this was. Why it was in the newspaper was beyond his comprehension.

"One of your stories," he said, then read aloud. "'The tip of Count Alexis' blade invited the band of mercenaries to respond.'"

In answer to his unasked question, Isobel explained, "I write a column for the paper, always a short adventure. It's anonymous, of course, but I never tire of learning my faithful readers enjoy the stories."

"I'm impressed. How did I not know this? We've met here on occasion this past week, and yet nothing was said about published stories."

Isobel waved a dismissive hand. "It's nothing, really. Mr. Bradley knows who writes the columns, though they're supposed to be anonymous. I think he publishes the stories to be kind."

"No. The stories are published because you are skilled. Soon, you will see your name in gold tooling on bound leather spines. I shall be your most ardent reader and order innumerable copies of each novel."

Rather than laugh, as he expected, she ducked her head to hide florid cheeks.

He took advantage of the pause in the conversation to enjoy savory bites of the hearty fare. The two recent houses he had toured had not been far, but he had not liked the route or the distance. Close enough to call on friends but too far to dine at The Tangled

Fleece, participate in Sunday service, or bask in any of the other myriad entertainments Sidvale had to offer, which were not many but were aplenty for Alistair. He had seen nothing of England apart from what he and Mr. Owen had traveled to reach Sidvale, so it seemed hasty to think of Sidvale as the place he wanted to be, but he did like it here.

His thoughts were on Isobel, though. If she rejected him after his confession, he would not wish to stay in Sidvale, no matter how idyllic the village. If she accepted his change in circumstances, he wished to be ready. She called this village home. If it were her home, it would be his too. Unless she did not wish to stay near friends and her mother? He had not considered that, but it would be an important enquiry to make.

Isobel interrupted his thoughts, her cheeks having returned to a normal shade of pale. "Did you enjoy the service?"

Nodding while he swallowed, he said at length, "The vicar is wise. If we took to heart his message, we would be less at war."

In the back of his mind were his mother's experiences. He had never endured or witnessed war, neither local skirmishes nor battles, but they were all around him in India, always on the tips of tongues, whispered in ears, a murmured unrest of how close it would come to West Bengal. The area in which he lived had seen its fair share before he was born, dark days for Calcutta. He had been fortunate to live in a time of peace. Isobel, he knew, would never have heard so much as a murmur, not on English soil.

Isobel asked, "Are Mr. Walsley's sermons the first you've heard? I'm embarrassed to admit I don't know what you believe." Glancing to either side of her, she lowered her voice. "Are you Hindu?"

A corner of his lips inched into a half-smile. She had accepted his courtship, then, believing he could be of a different faith. He was flattered.

"I'm Anglican, just as you are." Was that a sigh of relief he heard? "My mother was Zoroastrian when she fled Persia. Upon marrying my father, she converted. She wished me to be like my father in all ways, and so I was brought up Anglican with little to no exposure to her family's beliefs. I would ask, curious boy that I was, but she wished not to speak of anything that might sway me from being my father's son. She wanted an English son, a true Briton. I am proud of my Persian heritage, Isobel, but I am becoming each day more of what she wished."

Isobel took slow bites of her meal, enraptured.

When she did not respond, merely waited for more, he added, "St. John's Church is in Calcutta, the one I attended. The Reverend Johnson officiated until his return to England. John Owen, no relation to our Owens, resumed in his place. I had the pleasure of attending under both so great men. Of interest, the Company was to fund and build the church. Many a meeting I attended for this, but the Company dragged its feet, as they're wont to do, and so Johnson took responsibility. It is a grand church, Isobel. One that pleases the eyes. Although, if I'm honest, I prefer your Mr. Walsley's modest stone church."

"Leila is Anglican, as well," Isobel said. When he furrowed his brows in confusion, she rushed to add, "I only mention that because she's why I thought you were Hindu. Well, not her, exactly, but Mrs. Owen.

Aaditri, Mrs. Owen, that is, is also Anglican, but she
had converted from Hinduism, not when she married
Mr. Owen, but rather before. Based on that, I thought
anyone living in or near Calcutta must be Hindu."

He followed her circuitous logic with a grin.
"No need to explain, *Khoshgele khânum*. I understand.
Aaditri has been Anglican most of her life. She and my
mother were close friends. I have distant memories
of her before she moved to England, but my mother
spoke of her often. You will be surprised, yes, to learn
most who live in and near Calcutta are Anglican."

"Oh. I wouldn't have guessed." She nodded with
interest, but her attention seemed elsewhere. With
idle absentmindedness, she pushed her fork around
her plate.

"Yes, Isobel? Do not have me guess."

Startled, she looked at him. "How did you know
I—never mind." Giving her food another shove, she
mumbled, "I… I was wondering what happened
between you and Leila."

He set down his cutlery. "You know what happened, *nazanin*. I wanted you, not her."

She tugged her bottom lip between her teeth.

"Ah, I understand. You wish to know *why*. Yes?"
He did not wait for the nod he knew she would offer.
"Miss Leila Owen is… pleasant. After many trials with
conversation, I saw we would not suit. Agreement
between our families or not, I did not wish to subject
either of us to a marriage of kindness, not when there
should be the opportunity for more. I saw no chance
for more with her. She was, how should I say, too
amenable. When I ask a question, I want an answer
of the heart, not acquiescence to please me. I will not

have a meek, servile wife. Conversation with her was stilted, not of the heart. My final decision was — no, I shall not mention her recklessness, for it angers me."

Even as he said it, he recollected vividly Miss Owen's determination to frolic dangerously in an icy lake, heeding no one's warning of the risks, an incident that had sealed his decision she was not the wife for him. Interestingly, it was the moment he realized Isobel was the one for him, although his affection for her had been steadily deepening. So busy saving Miss Owen, he had not been able to aid Isobel in her row back to shore, which had mounted his frustration, and yet once Miss Owen was safe, and he turned to help Isobel, she had already navigated the waters, only needing help to secure the boat. He knew, then, that she was the woman for him. Up to that point, he had been attracted but resisting, wanting to prove himself a man of honor. Their conversations, her interactions with the twins, her talents with writing, and their shared interests, so much weighed his heart with affection. The incident at the lake anchored his decision to break his oath to the Owens and pursue Isobel.

"It is good," he continued, "that Mr. Knowlton was tutoring her cousins so I could matchmake. With their union, I was relieved of Mr. Owen's wrath for breaking the betrothal."

"*You* matchmade?" Isobel questioned with a laugh. "I rather think *I'm* owed credit, for I succeeded in stealing you away on every occasion possible to allow them time alone."

Alistair rested his elbow on the table and his chin on his hand. "You did not wish for my company, then? It was a ruse to distract me from my betrothed?"

Isobel's laugh suspended as her fork clattered to the plate.

"I tease, Isobel. I know you cannot resist my company. Take credit for Miss Owen and Mr. Knowlton if you wish. I will give you the credit. Allow it to be known that you are so skilled at matchmaking, you have captured me, too." He offered a smile until her edges softened.

"*Ethelinde: Or the Recluse of the Lake*," Isobel said.

He looked about him at the crowded room before it dawned she referenced the novel. "Charlotte Smith," he said, searching his memory for a connection to their conversation. "The French nobleman? He's a villain in Smith's book, though, unlike in yours."

"No, not the nobleman. Do you recall when the damsel was drowning in the lake? Every time I think of Leila on that dreadful day, I think of that novel."

"Ah, yes, I see now." He rubbed his chin in thought. "But she is not a reader of the gothic as we are."

"I don't think she's read it, but I can't help to imagine her as the damsel in the story every time I think of her plunging into the blue. If you must know, I'm positive that was the day I fell for you. You rose from the water with her limp body in your arms, your shirt clinging to your torso, and—"

She stopped, eyes widening.

"Go on," he prodded with a smirk.

Isobel shook her head vehemently.

He laced his fingers, ready to tease her further about this clinging shirt of his when a young man in bright livery stepped up to the table and thrust a note at Alistair. He eyed the messenger with curiosity and received a curt bow in response. Rather than leave, the servant stepped back, awaiting Alistair's answer to whatever was in the missive.

With a glance at Isobel, who shrugged, he unfolded the paper.

"Dunley," he read aloud the signature. "The parrot?"

Isobel chortled. "You mean popinjay. He's the viscount you met, married to my friend Hetty."

He read the note three times, although it was quite short, before he turned to the messenger and said, "Yes, and I'll bring a guest." The messenger bowed and left. Turning back to Isobel, he said, "We'll be dining at Dunley Manor late afternoon."

Her mouth fell open, closed, then repeated before she stuttered, "But, but, but *no*! *Why*? No! *We* will be dining there? *Today*? With *Lord Dunley-the-Dandy*?"

Alistair arched a brow but said, "He's invited me to dine. I'll only go with you on my arm. You would not leave me alone to contend with this viscount, would you?" His smirk returning, he added, "If you resist, I shall use my ladder, sling you over my shoulder, and take you prisoner."

"But, but, but… what will I wear?"

"White jade and rubies."

She tilted her head in thought. He knew when she realized what he meant, as her eyes widened again, but this time accompanied by his favorite fluttering eyelashes. If he had his way, she would be wearing more this evening than a white jade and ruby necklace. She would be wearing his kiss.

Chapter 8

The gig swayed, but the drive was smooth. Isobel admired Alistair's handling of the ribbons as they traveled from the farmhouse through the main street of Sidvale and towards Dunley Manor. They had waffled about inviting the maid or Mrs. Thomas to accompany them. When Isobel called on Benji before returning home after church service, Mrs. Thomas had offered, but Isobel did not dare deprive Benji of his mother on a Sunday. It had been bad enough that he missed service, his favorite part of the week since he could see all his friends and hear the good word from Mr. Walsley.

In the end, Isobel decided it was unnecessary to bring a chaperone since the drive was short, the gig open, and the route public. Granted, Alistair would be escorting her home around dusk, which would have them alone off the main road once he pulled into her drive, but could she not live a little? Everyone knew they were stepping out. Everyone knew he intended to propose, and she intended to accept. It was just a short drive, for heaven's sake. Isobel eyed his profile in her periphery.

"You may admire me openly, Isobel. I will not take offense. Of the contrary."

Isobel scoffed. "You are a vain man to think I am admiring you. Should your attention not be on the horse and the road?"

"You will find my attention divided when so beautiful a woman sits close to me. More so when she watches me thinking I'm not also watching her."

"Eyes on the road, Alistair Trowbridge!"

"Same to you." He flashed a smile.

Isobel muttered about the audacity of arrogant men before sneaking another sideways glance at his profile. Her perusal was met with a smirk. Dastardly man!

The journey was far too short for her liking. Before she knew it, they were turning into the Dunley estate driveway, sweeping lawns sloping to each side. The house was not yet in view. However short the journey, she was thankful Alistair had borrowed the Owens' gig. While not far to walk, the weather was warm and muggy after the afternoon's rain shower, and the road would not have been kind to her dinner shoes. The dinner shoes were already unkind to her feet, a hair's breadth too small, as with the dinner gown.

"This parrot—"

"Popinjay," Isobel corrected.

"Yes, this lacy man who minces. Tell me about him."

"I don't know much. His family has been here since time immemorial. He never fraternizes with villagers and only comes for Sunday service, and even that is rare since he all but lives in London. His mother is ancient and needy but kind, from what I've heard. I've had no interactions with her to say, but my friend Abbie—the vicar's daughter—used to be her unofficial companion, and now there's Hetty as her daughter-in-law."

"They appear mismatched, this viscount and his wife."

"They are. Nothing against Hetty when I say this, but he married her because his mother wanted a live-in companion of her choosing and told him to marry her."

Isobel would never understand why Hetty chose that fate. Hetty had no dowry and little family connection, but Isobel knew firsthand about both and still would not sell her soul for financial security. It was shocking enough a family so high in the instep would choose someone like Hetty, but it went to show the will of the dowager viscountess more than anything. What the woman wanted, the woman got.

Alistair questioned, "He could not hire a companion for his mother?"

"It was the only way his mother could convince him to marry." Isobel could just make out the spires of the house coming into view as they began to crest a hill. "I'm not the best person to consult about this. I know so little, and what there is to know is secondhand and thirdhand."

"I understand." Alistair let out a low whistle as the manor rose before them in all its glory. "And what of your friend?"

"Hetty? She's reserved on the best of occasions, but don't think she's a cold fish or rude. She's simply terribly shy, although she'll never admit it. She's a writer, too, you should know. Novels of manners. Her mother-in-law has made her first publication possible, although Hetty did not need the viscountess' help. Her writing is remarkably good. She would have found a publisher on her own, I'm certain."

"Manners? Your friend writes etiquette instructions?"

"Ick. No. Well, yes, for *The Bard* newspaper, she does write a column on etiquette, although her mother-in-law most emphatically does *not* know about that, so don't mention it. The dowager viscountess would swoon from vapors to know her daughter-in-law was writing a newspaper column for the local inn." Isobel snorted a laugh at the thought. "Her novels are… well… novels. Think Fanny Burney. *Those* kinds of novels."

When she glanced at Alistair, he wrinkled his nose and asked rhetorically, "Who would wish to read of the neighboring village over French noblemen in exile?"

"Precisely my point. I would much rather duel a highwayman from the pages of a good book than read about characters enduring a droll dinner." Realizing that was exactly what she was about to experience, she laughed aloud.

Alistair joined her, either because her laugh was infectious or because he caught the joke. On second thought, maybe he simply did not want to seem as if he had missed a joke. She laughed harder still until tears pricked the corners of her eyes.

Before long, they had arrived, entered the mammoth monstrosity that was Dunley Manor, and were being duly entertained in the drawing room before dinner.

Over the years, Isobel had accustomed herself to being the odd one out. Today proved no different. It afforded her the opportunity to admire the ornamentation. Or should that be judge? More like cower, as she found Dunley Manor intimidating. Was she not supposed to be dazzled by the gilding, awed by the portraits, impressed by the imported furnishings? She missed her humble farmhouse. The farmhouse had always been grand to her with its long gallery, great hall, coffered ceilings, and various parlors... despite its neediness for repairs. Anything as old as the farmhouse would need repairs, logically. But to be here in Dunley Manor put her little family home to shame. She felt small.

Nasrin Manor was grand, but there was something cozy about it, something welcoming that reached beyond its owners. Even Abbie's new home at Leigh Hall was comfortable. Both of their homes were larger than the farmhouse, both grander and yet they each felt like *home*. Dunley Manor was a museum. Or should that be a mausoleum? She eyed the elder Lady Dunley.

Crossing her hands about her middle, Isobel rubbed warmth into her arms. A hot and humid day, never mind it was supposed to be a cool spring at this point in the year, yet Isobel felt chilled. Across from her, Hetty tended to her mother-in-law. So demanding of attention was Lady Dunley, Isobel wondered if Hetty would be filling the woman's plate during dinner, or feeding her. No, better yet, would Hetty chew for her? Isobel caught her giggle mid-smile, feeling that stab of guilt again after today's sermon on neighborly thoughts and behaviors. At least she had apologized to Hetty shortly after their arrival for her sharp words after church service. It had not been Hetty's fault, after all, for not accompanying Isobel and Alistair to the inn. Isobel pitied Hetty in that for all her airs, she would have wanted nothing more than to enjoy nuncheon at the inn, a joy now deprived her for marrying Lord Dunley.

Isobel wished she had not eaten so much at the inn. If this had been supper, she might have been hungry again by now, but it was only dinner, and thus, it had been a mere couple of hours since the feast after church. Her stomach grumbled with unhappiness after three slices of pie.

Isobel fidgeted with the ribbon beneath her bosom.

At least Hetty had a mother-in-law, Isobel supposed. Should all go as Alistair and she planned, Isobel would not have a mother-in-law, overbearing or otherwise. In a way, she should be relieved since no one would meddle in their relationship or demand attention like Lady Dunley, not to mention her own relationship with her mother was strained. But how disappointing to have missed the chance to know Mrs. Trowbridge. Isobel warmed to the woman each time Alistair mentioned her. Their relationship had been a close one, and Isobel knew she would have loved the woman like a mother. Had she been anything like Mrs. Aaditri Owen? Isobel adored Mrs. Owen. Aaditri treated Isobel as though she were her own daughter, always attentive and loving, something Isobel did not experience from her mother.

If she was not to have a mother-in-law, then what of a father-in-law? She knew from previous conversations they had shared at Nasrin Manor that Alistair's relationship with his father was as strained as hers with her mother, albeit for different reasons. He did not know his father aside from an annual letter and a handful of meetings over the years. After all his father had done to ensure his family's security, he had moved to England rather than stay in India, only exerting his interest in the family with pleas for them to join him. Alistair had divulged he felt a certain level of resentment that his father had not stayed in India, even if it meant losing his position in the East India Company when his mother expressed her determination to stay.

But what was he truly like? He was as British as she, yet he was Alistair's father. Alistair was Persian in her eyes, so imagining him with a British father was difficult. Was there any resemblance at all?

So lost in her musings, she had not paid attention to the conversation around her. Not that she needed to. No one paid her any mind. Hetty continued to see to her mother-in-law's needs while Lord Dunley monopolized Alistair's attention, ignoring Isobel as though she were the parlor maid. She tugged her ribbon one way, then another. Even imagining Alistair fighting suits of armor come to life or vanquishing living portraits who walked boldly out of their paintings held little appeal. The house was to blame, she decided, rubbing her arms again.

Although her stomach protested, she was relieved when the butler stepped in to announce dinner was served. At least it would be a change of scenery, and

she would have something to do with her hands
while everyone talked to each other.

Once seated about the table, Isobel added a few
items to her plate from the various dishes available,
just a bite here and there for politeness. She sat across
from Alistair, who sat at Lord Dunley's side. She supposed she should have sat across from Hetty, next to
Lady Dunley, but she could not remove the awkward
visual of Hetty serving and chewing her mother-in-
law's food.

"Tell me, Mr. Trowbridge," Lord Dunley was
saying, angled in his chair to better see Alistair and
eliminate Isobel from the conversation, or so it seemed
to her, "of your estate. What does a settlement governor's estate entail?"

Alistair looked at both the viscount and Isobel
when he answered, never mind Lord Dunley did
not acknowledge her presence. "The estate the Company has awarded me will soon increase in holdings.
They wish to turn the settlements into provinces.
With this responsibility will be the inclusion of new
land, expanding the estate size, as well as the raising,
training, and housing of a province army of Indian
sepoys."

"Oh, I say," Lord Dunley said. "And what of the
house? Is it large?"

After another glance at Isobel, Alistair leaned back
in his chair, frowned in thought, looked about him,
then said nonchalantly, "Larger than yours."

Dunley spluttered his wine. Clearing his throat,
he emphasized, "*Larger than mine?*"

Alistair looked about him again, then grinned at
Isobel when he said, "Much larger."

The viscount ignored his dinner plate. "Tell me more. Start with your role as settlement governor turned province governor, then end with explicit detail about this extraordinary possession of yours."

With an apologetic look towards Isobel, Alistair did as he was bid, entertaining the viscount with masterful precision.

Gone was Isobel's boredom. Judging from the look he had cast her way, she had little doubt he thought she would be bored to tears, but this was far from the case. As with the viscount, Isobel forgot her plate entirely. How could she not when, in a matter of a few words, Alistair transformed before her eyes? Aside from her fixation on him, her other awareness was of the white jade and ruby necklace she wore, his gift to her that evening. Her fingers toyed with the cold gems as she listened to him, riveted.

Alistair the friend, Alistair the playful flirt, Alistair the lover set on wooing her smoldered into ash. From his ashes rose a powerful man. He spoke as a politician, a leader, a Company governor, and a Persian. His very essence exuded power, a man who wielded unlimited control and influence, a man not to be crossed. He was magnificent. He was glorious. He was frightening.

Oddly, Isobel did not feel fright but rather fright *for* those who would anger him. She had never felt safer in her life than thinking of this man as her partner and protector. And to think, he had stayed at the farmhouse because she had taken fright during a storm. *He* had been her warrior, a shout away at the opposite end of the long gallery, this man who could and would wield the force of an army.

He wanted to marry *her*?

Was she starry-eyed or feeling ever so insignificant? A little of both.

She looked down at her mostly uneaten dinner. Lost in thought, she missed when the conversation turned to include Hetty and Lady Dunley.

Her head snapped towards Hetty when she heard, "You've read her writing, then?"

Alistair said, "She is my favorite author. I could read her day in and day out without tiring."

Isobel looked from one to the other. Radcliffe? Were they discussing Radcliffe?

Alistair winked at Isobel, and the playful flirt returned. "I had the pleasure of playacting one of her tales at Nasrin Manor. Masterful mind has *nazaninam.*"

Were they discussing *her* writing? Isobel paled, feeling faint.

Lord Dunley raised his quizzing glass. "Playacting, you say?"

"Yes, it is something I enjoy and something Miss Lambeth and I share, amongst other interests. I grew to enjoy it when my mother fell ill. I held home theatricals for her amusement. She had a great love for the gothic, and so, I read aloud and reenacted to please her, developing an appreciation of my own in the process." Alistair locked Isobel's gaze. "I hold hope of my wife and I hosting reenactments. No musical soirees for us. I wish for literary soirees, theatricals, reenacting entire novels from start to finish. What do you say to this, Miss Lambeth? Shall we fill our home with heroes, damsels, duels, and knights?"

She swallowed.

So much to digest, and she did not mean the food. He had implied their marriage in front of Viscount Dunley and his family. He wanted to host reenactments of *her* novels. He...

With a shallow nod, too stunned to offer more, she squeaked, "Like *Vathek*."

Alistair met her shallow nod with a deep one of his own. "Yes. Like the author of *Vathek*."

Lord Dunley, likely confused and bored, said with a flip of his quizzing glass, "I'll be leaving for London soon. One can rust from too much rustication." He chortled at his own cleverness. "You said you're for London soon, as well, Mr. Trowbridge. Should you wish to travel with me, I would not object." The viscount affected a friendly and inviting smile that reminded Isobel of a hungry, feral cat.

Alistair, in turn, cast a smile of his own, one Ares himself would bear while watching minions march to battle, the smile of power and god-like amusement, eternally victorious.

"What were you saying about being promoted to province governor and raising armies?"

The ride from Dunley Manor had been a silent one until they passed beneath the arch of the estate gatehouse. He had felt Isobel's eyes on him as they left, sensed she wanted to ask questions, talk about the dinner, but she had remained silent, and so he practiced patience to allow her to form her words.

To their right, the sky was painted in oranges and yellows, the sun setting. He admired it from his periphery as he formed his own words. This was an opening for his confession, for the talk that could be their undoing, but he did not want to have this discussion on a gig while driving through the village, nor after dinner with Viscount Dunley, a man who had no respect for women, evidenced by his treatment of all three ladies at the table, and thus a man who did not deserve Alistair's respect. Now was not time for his talk with Isobel, but he could not delay it much longer.

He tugged the reins lightly as the hill sloped past the vicarage and down into the vale. "Currently, I am a settlement governor, residing in one of the Company's government buildings, which happens also to be my home. With the April meeting, I'm to be offered both landownership of the estate, not simply residence in the house, as well as the promotion to province governor to expand the holdings and power."

"It's all so impressive, although I must admit I don't understand the specifics. I assume this is good news. Landownership, more property, all that."

"There are two sides," he said, choosing his words with care. "Ownership is a kind of entailment for whoever holds the position of province governor. Even as I hold the position, my land is not my own. In a respect, I wield great power. I can turn oppressed fieldhands who have only known famine into respected farmers, for example. But the land belongs to the Company, and so I must do what they say for its use. If they want to turn farmland into opium fields, that is what I must do. Pastures for sacred cattle into army training grounds? I must comply."

She did not reply hastily. When she did, he could not know what she thought of his explanation. The

situation was not unlike an aristocrat in England, but
he thought it best to avoid the comparison.

"What's the house like?" she asked instead.

He chuckled. "You were not listening over dinner?
As I told the popinjay, it is — "

"Yes, I heard. But that's not what I mean."

From his periphery, he saw her fidgeting, a tense-
ness about her carriage.

She tried again with, "Is it like Dunley Manor, or
is it like Nasrin Manor? No, that won't make sense."
After a sigh, she said, "I was miserably uncomfortable
at Dunley, and it had nothing to do with the viscount.
Everything about the house was cold, from its opu-
lence to its host. Simply everything. I was as small as
an ant and chilled to the bone. Nasrin isn't like that,
though. It's grand, but there's a warmth in the house.
Does that make sense?"

Her words stirred curiosity and hope. Did she *not*
wish to live at his estate in India?

He said, "The house is larger, grander than
Dunley. It is not solely a residence but rather also a
government building. Raj Bhavan is what they call
this type of house, not only my specific residence
but those for anyone in strategic political positions,
be they a settlement governor in the Company or of
the Nawab. A Raj Bhavan, or in English, Government
House, functions first and foremost as a government
building. I am not the only Company man living at
my Raj Bhavan. I have the head of table, as I am the
estate holder, but I must offer a room, a wing, whatever is needed to whomever the Company wishes to
be housed there, temporarily or permanently. I am
not making it sound warm, am I? I believe it is the

people who add the warmth. *My* domain is as a home, warm and welcoming."

Isobel nodded at his side but said little else.

The day was not turning out as he had planned. His vision had been of his beloved on his arm, him bolstering her confidence and singing her praises throughout dinner, followed by a goodnight kiss at her door. Dunley had demanded too much of his attention and made Isobel uncomfortable. Alistair knew how to handle men like Dunley. He did so often in India. He had not, however, balanced well his handling of the viscount *and* attention to Isobel, focusing more on dealing with his host, leaving Isobel feeling alone. Now, she was melancholy. She projected a quiet sadness. Was it Dunley's treatment? The intimidation of the manor? His words now of the estate? He would let it be but would plan for their first kiss another time.

As they approached the farmhouse, he said, "You are much beautiful this evening, Isobel. I am fortunate to have you as my dinner companion."

"Will you come inside?"

Her question startled him. He had thought her upset, wanting him away. "If you wish."

"You could… help me light a candle or two before the sun sets. Maybe take a turn about the house? To make certain it's safe?"

He smiled. "Of course. But on the condition that you tell me about the home of your dreams as I do so. Forget for the moment the estate in India. Do you like cottages? A farmhouse as you have here? A manor with Nasrin's warmth?"

Alistair helped Isobel descend, and then he secured both horse and gig, thankful for the secluded setting that allowed him the luxury of entering her farmhouse unnoticed. He would do well not to linger in case anyone along the main road had made note of the gig entering the drive, for the longer he remained, the longer nosy onlookers would have to wait to see the gig leave, and that would raise eyebrows.

Once inside, he set about the task of candle lighting, a futile task, for he saw not a single candle in the great hall. Isobel held up a hand for him to wait.

Just before she disappeared into the large parlor, presumably to find a candle and tinderbox, he said, "I shall begin my sweep of the rooms. There is light enough for me. Await me here in the great hall."

Her squeak as she continued into the parlor was his assurance she had heard him. The sweep of the house was done in a trice. While in part, he suspected she had used the request as an excuse to extend their time together, and in other part thought she only wanted the comfort of his saying the house was safe rather than being truly afraid someone or something might haunt the house, lying in wait for darkness. Whatever her reasons, he took his task seriously. He left no door unopened, even if he did work swiftly so as not to delay his departure or keep him from her side too long.

When he returned to the great hall, she had two candles and a tinderbox at the ready.

She greeted him with, "Anything with a stable block full of horses. Well, at least one riding horse."

He raised his brows while he emptied the little box of its flint, steel, and charcloth.

"I've always wanted a horse of my own," she continued. "Leila has allowed me free use of her stables, and believe me when I admit I've made ample use, but I want one of my own. I wouldn't mind a coach house for a curricle. Silly as that sounds for a woman to want a curricle, much less to own a curricle out here in the middle of nowhere with our pokey roads. It's a town vehicle, I know. But I want one, nonetheless. I want to ride like the wind!"

Alistair chuckled as his spark ignited the charcloth. He touched the first candlewick to it, then smothered the flame. The second candlewick was held to the first.

Isobel, now animated, with no signs of her earlier melancholy, continued, "As long as the house is filled with love and laughter, I do not care its size or grandeur or furnishings or anything else. A roof over my head with a stable for at least one riding horse, two for the curricle, and then at least one farm horse, and I'm happy."

Placing the candles on the mantel, he leaned against the wall, crossing his ankles. "All your pin money has gone into the stables, I see." To himself, he calculated the costs and necessary acreage should he need to opt for the small cottage.

With a shrug, she said, "I've never thought about where I'd like to live. I assumed I'd stay here forever, tending to my mother as a spinster. Then, she will likely move in with her sister at some point. It's been a long time in coming, and I think her only hesitation has been not knowing what to do with me." She perched against the dining table, her hands on either side of her, idly rubbing the edge. "If she were to move, I had expected to live in the farmhouse. Some form of employment would be necessary so that I might hire a live-in housekeeper. It is one thing for me to be alone here temporarily for a week or two, but quite another to *live* alone. That would not be permitted."

He listened, attentive, fascinated. Why had she never planned for marriage? Try as he might, he could not envision her living in the farmhouse for longer than necessary. It may have been her home all these years, but she was not comfortable here. He could see that.

He offered, "You will bring warmth wherever you live. Had you been mistress of Dunley Manor, it would now feel the welcoming warmth of your flame."

Isobel pulled a face, then laughed.

"This is better," he said. "I prefer your laughter to your sadness. Will you tell me what weighed your shoulders?"

Her smile remained, but it dimmed as she turned to look at the floor rather than him.

"I owe you an apology?" he asked when she did not respond. "I was not attentive enough. I left you to—"

"No, no, no!" She stood, waving her hands. "You were *wonderful*! I only hope I didn't disappoint you. You were... you were *masterful*! I was—"

"You were unfamiliar with the role," he offered. "It is a role I play, not unlike the playacting we spoke of earlier. You could never disappoint me. I hope I was not too theatrical for you. The dinner was my stage, the popinjay my audience, and I was the leading player. Shakespeare was a wise man, and I take his words to heart. All the world is a stage, Isobel. It is my profession to deal with those like the viscount.

It is what I do for the Company, in part. If you did not find me a poor actor, next time, you will play the part with me."

She listened, her smile broadening the more he talked. "*Masterful*," she emphasized under her breath. "However deeply I appreciate the encouragement, it wasn't that. Well, I suppose in a small way. Everything compounded, from the coldness of the manor to the rudeness of Lord Dunley, and being in awe of you, but what's had me disheartened is Hetty. I know it was her choice, and I know her reasons behind the choice. That does not soften the blow to see her unhappy."

Bowing her head, she reached up absently to clasp her necklace and admire the center ruby. The necklace was more elaborate and delicate than the turquoise, the shape that of a central ruby flower surrounded by white jade petals and swirling gold vines with white jade leaves and flower buds. A symmetrical design with the vines curling around the ruby, yet there was a wildness to it, an echo of nature's free will. Curiously, an apt description of Isobel herself.

He did not reply, not yet. She seemed on the verge of saying more, and he did not wish to interrupt again with his feigned witticism. Instead, he studied her profile, admiring the turn of her nose, the rose of her cheeks, the pertness of her chin, but mostly admiring her concern over a friend. He recalled their time together at Nasrin Manor. She had been so devoted to everyone's needs, from her aid during the lake incident to her playfulness with the children. This was the woman he wished for a wife.

"Or perhaps she is happy," Isobel continued, oblivious to his appraisal. "Maybe feeling needed and taking care of her mother-in-law makes her happy. I don't know. I could not stop feeling sad to think of lovely Hetty, always quick with her sarcastic wit, living in a loveless house, and her time devoted to someone who could never appreciate the sacrifices. When Abbie and her husband hosted the literary retreat last month, Hetty had to sneak out of the manor while her mother-in-law napped just to attend. Can you imagine? She had to sneak out of her own home! How is that happiness? Maybe in time, she'll have children to love. That could bring warmth into the house."

Alistair pushed himself off the wall. In short strides, he clasped her hands in his and held her fingers to his lips. "This is one of the countless reasons I…" He stopped short, hesitated, then, with eyes closed, whispered, "*Asheghetam*." When he opened his eyes to look into her questioning ones, he said, "One reason I have affection." He did not wish to translate what had slipped between his lips. Not yet. He did not wish to frighten her away, not this early in their courtship.

Her smile was soft, feminine, accepting of what he said without knowing the depth. "I have affection for you too, Alistair. And I'm relieved you don't think me silly."

"Never. This whole time, I thought you distressed to have been ignored. But no. You had eyes only for your friend, a friend who, I remind you, is now a viscountess in a gilded palace."

"A gilded cage from my point of view, but I take your meaning."

The darkness was settling. He needed to depart. Long shadows swept across the room, the light dim, the candles brighter. The surrounding forest would darken the house before the road, thankfully, but he had already stayed too long. If he stayed longer, his presence would be noticed by anyone watching the road for his return. If he stayed longer, he would have difficulty seeing his way to Nasrin Manor, as he had not brought a lantern for the gig. If he stayed longer... His eyes dipped to her lips.

"I must take my leave of you, my sweet," he said, releasing her hands and heading for the door. "Until tomorrow? I should like to see this library Mr. Bradley boasts of, not something I would expect as part of an inn."

Her voice was close, just behind him, as he retrieved the hat he had doffed when first arriving that afternoon. "Perfect! We can see if the new Radcliffe has arrived. He ordered it for me ages ago."

Turning to face her, his heart in his throat, he ensured a respectable distance between them. All his plans to initiate a first kiss could wait. Her mind was on her friend. He wanted the moment to be right. Her being alone in the house gave him pause, as well. A kiss beneath the forested canopy on the walk from the inn? Yes, that would be better. A kiss to curl her toes.

Alistair took one of her hands in his and, in a reverent bow, kissed the air above her knuckles. "Until tomorrow. With books and tea, I anticipate much toe-curling in our future."

She furrowed her brows.

"Ignore me," he said with a shy laugh. "I said what I thought, not what I meant."

He turned to leave, his hand on the door handle, but before he could tug the door, she hastened, "Wait!"

As he angled to glance her way, she clasped the open edges of his coat. Before he could recognize her intent, she stood tiptoed and pulled him towards her. Her lips met his.

So stunned, so taken unawares, it took slow moments for him to respond. Her kiss was chaste but as full of ardor as if it had been passionate. His pulse raced, and his toes curled. Fighting a smile of delight, he dropped the hat, leaned down, and wrapped his arms about her waist to pull her fully against him.

With a tilt of his head and a sigh on his lips, he deepened the kiss. Only when he knew her toes were as curled as his did he soften their embrace, share a smile with brightened eyes, and take his leave before darkness fell.

Chapter 9

Alistair's first reaction to Sidvale's circulating library was confusion. First impressions were not always accurate, but.... He stood in the same private parlor where he and Isobel had dined a few days earlier. The tables that had been pushed to the perimeter previously were now staggered around the room, with several seated patrons reading over tea or coffee. A few plush chairs could be spotted, ones more likely to be found in a drawing room than an inn, except they showed signs of wear from frequent use.

But where were the books?

Next to him, Isobel chattered about the latest Radcliffe novel and all she had heard about it so far, eager to learn if it had arrived yet. Her excitement had him in a tizzy.

His mother would have loved it, he suspected. As good as his mother's English had been, she struggled to read the language. It had been their tradition since he first discovered the glorious world of books that he would read to her, then act for her, increasingly so after she fell ill. The novels were her window, not so much to the world as to the adventures she would never know, good conquering evil, heroes saving maidens, all the things she had wished to experience in her lifetime.

His mother would have adored Isobel and vice versa.

Interrupting his delicate flower mid-sentence, Alistair said, "I mean not to disturb your speech, but… there are no books in this library of yours."

With a bashful glance, Isobel said, "It's not like a circulating library in a market town or city. We can't browse. For starters, this is a multipurpose room, changing throughout the day, such as being the gentleman's coffeehouse in the evening. My literary society meets here. Well, it did when we held it. We've not had a meeting in over a month, but I'm positive we'll resume soon."

"Yes, but the books?"

"Oh. Oh! That's right. Mr. Bradley keeps them tucked in the storeroom. You'll find we do not have an enormous collection. Rather than the eight thousand or so you might find in a larger library, we have closer to one hundred. Maybe two hundred. No more than five hundred, I'm certain. I'm still proud of our little library." She raised her chin. "You must ask if he has certain titles. *Or*, and how clever is this, you need only describe your mood, and he'll recommend a book or few for you to try. Don't let his being an innkeeper fool you; he's an avid reader. He can order almost any book you would like. To request something be ordered, he charges a minimal fee — yes, I know that is not customary, but we are a small library. Granted, the fee is an *optional* donation, but I couldn't imagine not paying. For general annual membership, it costs ten shillings. Economical if you simply wish to browse what's here."

Illuminating, Alistair thought. Just how often did she request books? Her financial situation was none of his business, but he was still bothered by her poor wardrobe and thus wondered if she spent from household funds for books, used pin money received from her mother, had a credit arranged with the innkeeper, or borrowed from friends. He would never dare ask. He was a gentleman, after all.

She tugged his arm to follow her.

Seated behind a bar in the back of the room, Mr. Bradley read a book of his own, the top of his head visible as he pored over a worn volume. The rustle of Isobel's gown caught his attention.

"Miss Lambeth!" He exclaimed with a welcoming smile, rising from his stool and setting aside the book. "And our esteemed Mr. Trowbridge." With a wink, he added, "Heard you had dinner at the manor."

Isobel dramatized a shudder. "I wouldn't trade places for the world, not for all the gold or thoroughbred horses."

Chest proud, the innkeeper said, "Mrs. Bradley's cooking is superior, I take it."

"No comparison." Isobel eyed the door to the storeroom. "Now, to business. Has *The Mysteries of Udolpho* arrived yet?"

His chest deflated. "Not yet, I'm sorry to say. Can I tempt you to something else? I think you'll enjoy *Things as They Are; or, The Adventures of Caleb Williams.*"

"Last time you offered a recommendation, I read that dreadful *Wolfenbach* novel." She narrowed her gaze. "I'm not keen on trusting you again. I feel you're leading me astray of good writing."

"Or it's my strategy to increase your enjoyment of *Udolpho* when it finally arrives."

"Hmm. Very well. Let's have this Caleb fellow, then. And for Mr. Trowbridge, *A Sicilian Romance*."

Brows raised, Bradley looked at Alistair. "One of Miss Lambeth's favorites? You aim to please, I see."

Alistair merely smiled, allowing Miss Lambeth to conduct their bookish affairs. The *Sicilian* was one of his favorites, as well, so he was curious why she had requested it, namely because they had discussed it on several occasions already.

Once both books were in hand, Isobel guided him to a table in the far corner. Tea soon arrived for their enjoyment. He grimaced at the teapot, remembering it well from their dinner. Would the innkeeper be offended if Alistair brought his own leaves next time?

Thumbing through the first of the two-volume set and seeing the wear of the marble-patterned paper, he said, "You have read this many times. Again?"

"Yes, again! We must refresh our memories of her writing in preparation for *Udolpho*. Did you know I only recently discovered Radcliffe's the author? She revealed her name in the '92 edition of *Romance of the Forest*, but we only had the first edition here, as well as her earlier two novels, including *Sicilian*, all published anonymously. I didn't discover her name until this summer. It was as though a whole new world opened for me! A successful authoress of the gothic. Mr. Bradley found out when he ordered *Udolpho*. Did you know?"

"Did I know you did not know, or did I know the authoress' name? No, and then, yes, respectively." He took a deep breath, not wanting to dampen her enthusiasm to talk about books—they were at Sidvale's peculiar library, after all—but knowing he needed to speak now before he lost the chance and courage. Given finding occasions together was precarious, he wished not to procrastinate further. "Let us set aside books for now. I must speak, and I think you will not like what I have to say."

She looked up from one of the books in her three-volume set, wide-eyed and frowning. With exaggerated slowness, she set the book on the table. Leaning back in her chair, she folded her hands in her lap. If he could best describe her expression, he would name it pensive.

Softly, in little more than a whisper, she said with downcast eyes, "You've said so little since I arrived today. I should have known something was amiss."

No sense in delaying or offering a preamble. Another deep breath. "I must leave for London soon. The East India Company's April meeting fast approaches. I have three weeks to travel and speak with my father. I can delay as long as one week but no more. It would make my heart happy if you would join me."

Jerking her gaze to meet his, her mouth fell open in a silent gasp. "I... I thought you said I would be displeased. You're inviting me to come to London with you?" Her tone wafted between astonished and wistful.

"Yes. This is not the part for you to be displeased. That part is to come. I think, when I have spoken, you will not wish to join me. There are... complications. I'm afraid you will walk away. I should say now, then, you are wonderful in all ways and will find happiness even if it is not to be with me."

She paled.

"You accepted my courtship based on how you see me now, on the person I offer, the life I offer. You see me as a settlement governor, soon to be a province governor, as one who wields influence and political prowess in West Bengal. The man you know me to be is wealthy beyond measure and can offer you stables full of horses, however many you would like, of a quality, a curricle, and any other conveyance. Travel is at our fingertips. All this, you see and accept." He bowed his head. "What if circumstances changed? What if I possessed only my name and a small purse? What if I needed to take up a trade?"

His questions were partially rhetorical, but he waited in case she wished to answer.

Isobel merely stared at him with a pucker between her brows.

He sipped from his teacup, swallowing his grimace of distaste. When she opted to say nothing, he set his teacup to rest in its saucer to continue.

"All will be in my father's hands. It is imperative I speak with him before the meeting. Ample time will help, I think, allow him time to consider my request." He swept a hand down his face, then stroked his chin, unwilling to part with his words any sooner than he must. "There is a new governor-general of Bengal, one whose leadership has not impressed me. He has, in his short time, already unraveled the great diplomacy of former Governor-General Marquess Cornwallis. For my part, I am to do things and make changes against my values. If he continues as he has, a great unrest will rumble, one that could lead to violence, of which I wish no part. I have thought long about this and deeply. I am not without alternatives.

In part, my fate rests in my father's hands, a man I do not know aside from infrequent correspondence and his rare trip to Bengal."

"You want to leave India," she said, her voice low.

"Yes. I wish to relinquish my position." He took another sip. Coffee was not kind to his palate, but perhaps next time, he would try it over the inn's tea. Bitter coffee would be superior to the taste of ditch-water. "There are options. You should know them, as they will determine my circumstances. I could beg for another position, director, for example. It is an option. I no longer desire employment with the Company. A foolish decision when I am wanting to take a wife. But my dream is to be an English gentleman. In part, it is what my mother wanted, except my mother wished me to follow in my father's footsteps as a Company man. I want to be a gentleman with my *own* land, an estate with farming and tenant profits, all my own and for my family to pass to my children. Achieving this is… complicated. It depends on my father investing in me."

He paused to study her expression, hesitant to continue when this was not a polite discussion for a lady.

Isobel surprised him, though, by saying, "It's about money, isn't it."

Rubbing his hands against his thighs, he nodded.

She said, "If he will help you secure the right home, the property and your management of it would then earn its own profits. But what if he won't invest in you?"

With a half-smile, he said, "You speak with knowledge and wisdom. But 'what if,' yes? If he were to toss his ungrateful son on his ear, I would have only what is mine now, enough to purchase a small cottage but no stable. To support my family, I would need work. I am skilled in trade. I could be a village carpenter. Would you be ashamed?" He looked away from her. "I am deceitful to ask to court you without first disclosing my plans."

His mind had been decided for over a year. He had already said his farewells to those loyal to him at his estate, and he had brought to England everything that belonged to him with no intentions to return. Yet now, he panicked. Was it worth losing Isobel? Which fate was worse? He had entered this conversation expecting her to walk away, and he had prepared for that, having decided the right woman would share his vision for the future. But he had not prepared for this emotionally. Words now spoken, he rushed to clasp her hand, reaching across the table to take it between his.

"If it comes to it, Isobel, I will stay with the Company. We can return to India if it will please you. Or I can accept a director position if it is offered. I can —"

"No, Alistair." She did not withdraw her hand. "You have a dream to fulfill, and you will not find it in India or at the April meeting. Did you really think I would walk away? It's you who should have walked away by now. I'm away with the fairies most of the time. My house is falling down around my ears. I have no dowry. I don't have a proper wardrobe. I have no family connections, though I am respectable. It's just me. And yet you think I would walk away because you have a dream? Oh, Alistair. If it comes to it, we can take to the King's Road as highwaymen.

Think how dashing we would look with pistols at our side, capes flapping in the wind, masks for disguise!"

He closed his eyes, warring with his feelings. Relief washed over him, but also fear. Did she fully understand all that his decision meant? It was more than a financial loss, more than a loss of property. These were foremost in his mind, yes, for until his father reacted to his decision, he had no home to offer her and a small purse. What troubled him most was his loss of self. That affected her, as well. Did she not see that? As he was now, he had respect, influence, power, and the backing of a Company title to his name. Without that, he had… nothing. He was but a humble man. He need only point to their dinner at Dunley Manor. Viscount Dunley had been seduced by the power Alistair wielded. How different their interactions would have been had he said he was a village carpenter, a man without consequence.

As a gentleman, though, a landowning gentleman, he retained consequence, more so than with his governor role. But that was little more than a dream.

When he opened his eyes, he was warmed by her understanding smile. "These alternatives cannot please you."

She smirked. "Let me be the judge of what will please me. Now, I seem to recall mention of a London trip."

Isobel watched him fondle his teacup, his mood morose despite her encouragement.

She would need more time to swallow all he had confessed, but the bold truth was she had not fallen for him or considered him because he was a wealthy politician. His position had only crossed her mind in as much that it meant she would need to move away from England. That had been frightening. She had not wanted that but had convinced herself it would be a grand adventure. To stay home out of fear of the unknown was foolish. Leila's betrothal to him had hinged on his being with the Company. The whole arrangement depended on his position. As for Isobel? What did she care?

Gentleman's daughter or not, she had lived a life of near poverty. Yes, there was a difference in respectability, but she did not move in circles where that mattered. She would prefer to dine with the innkeeper's wife than with the viscount, which ought to tell Alistair a great deal about her and how she saw herself. A quaint cottage sounded lovely. Oh — would she need to learn to cook? Oh dear. She had never cooked a day in her life. Mrs. Thomas had always cooked for her. Would his purse allow for a servant or two? She did not dare ask.

Her tea was cold, she discovered. Tipping it to her lips for the first time, she cringed, almost choking. The heat disguised its flavor. Now that it was cold? *Blech*. Rather than order a fresh pot, she sat back and fiddled with a loose thread on her gown's embroidery.

Alistair set his teacup down with a *clink* and cleared his throat. He pulled his shoulders back and tried for a smile, however strained. "London. Yes. Let us discuss London. If you are still of mind to accept my invitation, we must plan. There are things to know to prepare and more to arrange."

Sitting up in her chair, she readied for the excitement that would outshine the dark mood of the table — why should it be dark, though? *He* was more worried than she. She felt a weight lifted. She would not have to move to India! He was so concerned about her response that he had backtracked to reconsider his position — *he cared that much*. Had they not been sitting in The Tangled Fleece with other patrons lounging over books and teacups of codswallop, she might have cried, but then, he would likely misinterpret her tears. She would save them for later.

"You should know about my family," he began. "My mother's name was Shahrazad. My father's is Alexander Trowbridge. In Persia, names are not as they are in England. We have no forename, middle, surname. With each new dynasty, a new preference is given. My mother kept to the old ways and had but one name, Shahrazad, nothing more. She wanted me to have both my father's English name and one of more modern Persian to remember my origin. To the world, I am Mr. Alistair Trowbridge, a name in keeping of my father. To my mother, I was Alistair Aršama Alexanderzadeh Shirazi Calcuttayi. Alistair is of Alexander, meaning 'defender of the people.' Aršama is what she called me, 'strong hero' of Ancient Persia. Alexanderzadeh, meaning 'of my father.' Shirazi for my mother's home Shiraz. Calcuttayi for my birth city, of Calcutta."

Isobel's eyes glazed over. It was all... interesting. But... what did this have to do with London? She could not pronounce his Persian name. Was that terrible of her? Was that insensitive? She was interested, truly, fascinated, really, but....

She said, "I am honored you would share all this. Will it aid me with the London trip? With meeting your father?"

He canted his head. "No. Yes. You should know who I am. I now have only myself to offer. Following my talk with Father, I will not be able to add my governor honorific to my name. I have only myself to offer to you."

"Oh. Yes, I see now." Not really, but she would remain honored, nonetheless. "So…" She hesitated, squeamish to say what she had in mind. It was not *what* she wanted to say, but rather her disbelief in the words. Accepting everything as being real was more outlandish than her fantasy world of writing. "This is real, then? Us? A future together? Your interest in me?"

Confusion clouded his dark eyes. "Have we not been courting? I do not disillusion your affection, *nazanin*. I am sincere. I want my father to meet you and you to meet him before I offer my hand, but it is yours to take." He rested his open palm on the table.

Biting her bottom lip, she blinked to clear her vision, then accepted his hand. With a squeeze, she released it, tucking her hand back beneath the table to loop the embroidery thread around her finger. After several deep breaths, she asked, "Do you think he'll like me?"

"I do not know," he answered honestly. "I do not know him well. He will first be upset about my severing the betrothal with Miss Owen. It was an arrangement made between our families, one much valued. This may cloud his view. It is important you both meet, but I do not deny my worries."

"I *want* to go with you. I don't know if the timing is right, though. You'll be requesting to leave the

Company and all that entails, all while disappointing him about the broken betrothal. And then, there I
will be. I would hate for him to think I've influenced
you somehow. What if you go alone, and then after
everything has been discussed, I can join?" She had
no idea how she would get to London on her own,
but the plan sounded rational.

"Without you, I do not wish to go. You are my
anchor. I must go, but I do not wish to."

Ooh! An idea! A terrible idea. An idea, all the
same. Sitting up with a grin, she offered, "What
about the Owens? Mr. Owen will be staying with
your father, right? He has his election at the April
meeting." Once Alistair nodded in confirmation, she
continued, "What if I go with the Owens? I would be
a family friend. In this way, I'm there with you, and
your father and I can meet, but nothing is said about
courting or marriage or anything of the sort. The two
of you will have time to work things out while he and
I get to know each other without the fog of romance."

Alistair did not answer right away, rather stroked
his chin in thought. "It would solve the traveling
dilemma, as well. We cannot travel together alone that
distance. I will write to Mr. Owen if you will write
to Miss Leila Owen. From each side, we can arrange
travel and your invitation as a guest. It would not be
deception in the eyes of Mr. and Mrs. Owen. They do
not know the depth of our affection, although they
know my intention for courtship, and they would
never deny your accompanying your friend, more
so to ease the discomfort of your friend facing the
father of her former betrothed. I do not know their
travel plans, but I am of a certainty Mrs. Owen and

Miss Leila Owen will be returning with the twins to Nasrin Manor while Mr. Owen continues forwards to my father's house."

At those words, Isobel doubted her plan. Would they really want to return to London after making the trip from Hampshire to Devonshire? It was not likely. They were far closer to London already. She could but ask. No harm came from asking.

"I will write to Leila today," Isobel said, fueled by determination. "I've never been to London. And this is when everyone will be there, is it not? This is when all the snots go on display to find a husband."

Blanching, Alistair said, "I misspoke. The meeting is in London, yes, but my father's house is not. He lives in Reading, west of London. It is a short ride to the city, however, if you should wish to tour. I only saw it in passing. I am curious, as well."

She shrugged. "I'm not going with you to see London, you know. I'm going to see *you*. Yes, London sounds exciting, but I think we have enough to consider, don't you? If it should happen, I accept with enthusiasm. If not, I will be happy to see something other than Devonshire. Do you know that Sidmouth is as far as I've ever traveled? We often walk to Sidbury, so that doesn't count. The exotic Sidmouth." She laughed. "That's the extent of my world travels. I would *love* to see Reading with you, Alistair."

Why was it that when one awaited important news, time moved at a snail's speed, yet when one needed more time, it sped by at curricle quickness? The delay of Leila's letter was interminable. Isobel had written to her within an hour of Alistair's invitation. She had not bothered to go home to write it, rather had written it at the inn so Mr. Bradley would have it in hand to post.

Days felt like decades. Were those age wrinkles Isobel had spied in the mirror that morning? Wrinkles from waiting *so* long? So long, in fact, her hair had greyed, her eyesight worsened, her shoulders slumped, her bones creaked, and to top it all off, she was the only remaining living person in Sidvale, as everyone else had died of old age or withered in the wait for Leila's reply.

At last, Isobel held it between her fingers. The news had *not* been worth the wait. Well, there was some good in it, but also complications.

Most of the letter consisted of descriptions of Jules's family — Leila's future in-laws — and the latest antics of her twin cousins. The part that concerned Isobel had her partly cheering and partly booing. The good news was Mrs. Aaditri Owen would be delighted to have Isobel as her companion since she had decided to accompany her husband to the Trowbridge residence in Reading. Aaditri thought Isobel possessed a touch of the prophet to know she would need a companion, especially since the three gentlemen would be too distracted with Company business to pay her any mind. *That* had been worth the wait.

The good news paled in comparison to the bad. While Isobel could join Aaditri as her guest at the Trowbridge residence, she could not travel with them to Reading.

To begin, Leila would not be joining her mother. Instead, she and her cousins would stay in Hampshire, as Jules's grandfather had invited them for a special visit. That, in and of itself, was not terrible but certainly disappointing since Isobel's plan had been to accompany Leila — she would also miss seeing Leila and hearing about the visit to Hampshire. Second, and more importantly, Aaditri had no plans to return to Devonshire until after the Company business concluded, at which time she and Mr. Owen would return home via Hampshire to retrieve Leila and the boys. To return to Devonshire first, only to double back the way they had come, was too far and would take too much time, and so they would proceed from Hampshire directly to Reading, leaving Isobel stuck in Devonshire without an escort.

Isobel retrieved a quill and penknife from her writing box. Once the quill tip was dutifully trimmed, she planned to dash off a reply to Leila, complete with a message for Aaditri. She would then begin the arduous task of writing to her mother with the news she would be accompanying Aaditri to the city.

Her scheme to accompany Alistair was intact. Victory!

But how were they to travel to Reading without the Owens as chaperones?

It was not out of the realm of possibility for her to stumble on a djinn, make a pact, and, for a small sacrifice, be granted the ability to fly. Knowing her luck, rather than a magic carpet, the djinn would cause wings to sprout from her back and then never remove them, thus fulfilling his side of the bargain of allowing her the ability to fly only to leave her disfigured with feathery appendages she would never be able to hide in a gown.

Sigh. There was nothing for it. She would have to disguise herself as Alistair's page.

Chapter 10

Outside the carriage, the landscape rolled past. Sunrays slanted through clouds, illuminating the distant hills as though heaven's window had opened for a glimpse of the world below. The hedgerows framed paddocks dotted with sheep shadowed beneath cloud cover.

Isobel could not turn away. Every building, every field, every stone wall fascinated her. Nothing was terribly different from home, not yet, but somehow, even the most staid church spire stole her gaze. There was a world to explore! What was life like in the village they had just passed? Did they have Sunday feasts at the local inn and literary society meetings? What about the next village? Would they have forest walks connecting a manor and farmhouse through which two lovelorn parties could wander?

When the carriage bumped and swayed over a bridge, Isobel clasped the leather strap to hold steady. Had the outriders checked beneath the bridge in advance of the carriage's crossing? Who was to say there were not brigands lying in wait? She could see it now.

The carriage would grind to a halt, sending her flying forwards in her seat and into Alistair's arms. Shouts would rent the air. The boom of a blunderbuss! Neighing of horses and stamping of feet, a rock of the carriage in response. A man with a kerchief covering his mouth and long, curly hair bushing about his face to frame the pockmarked cheeks would wrench open the carriage door, pistol aimed at the occupants.

"Jewels or your life," said the scratch of a voice, low, edgy, intent on frightening his quarry.

"No!" Isobel shrieked, clutching the pearl necklace at her throat. "Not my jewels!"

A shot rang out, and the villain dropped dead before Isobel's eyes. Gaping, she looked up into Alistair's face. With a grin that glinted in the sunlight slanting through the clouds, he set her back against her bench, revealing the dueling pistol in his hand — was that a smoking hole through his travel coat? Oh, Isobel was impressed! A deadly shot without the need to aim!

Voices surrounded the carriage: shouts, threats, gruff anger, a clamor of boots against the cobblestone. Alistair leapt through the open carriage door. Following, Isobel heard the clang of steel. *Clang, clang, clinkety clack.* Sword drawn in one hand, dagger in the other, Alistair fought three ruffians at once. She peered out the window to watch the glory. To help, she poked the air with her sword arm, simulating his moves.

Across from her in the carriage came a sniffle and a sob, then a frantic wave of a perfumed handkerchief. "Don't let them get me! My hair will be tousled! *Ohh-hhhohohoho nooooo!*"

Isobel unclasped her necklace and tossed it onto Lord Dunley's lap. "Hold this, please."

The viscount waved the handkerchief at her, cowering and sobbing.

Lifting the hem of her gown, she jumped out of the carriage. From her trusty traveling scabbard, she whipped out her shortsword. "To me, vagrants!"

Alistair, seeing his ladylove at the ready, sidled to her, holding the bullies at bay with a *clink clack* of his sword and *clonk clink* of his dagger, two-hand wielding. Together, they fought against the gang, no one a match for the two of them.

Between thrusts and parries, Alistair said, "Shame about the coachman."

"I'll take the ribbons from here," she replied with a wave of her sword at her adversary.

Tightening her grip on the hilt, she—

"Are we winning?" Came a distant voice from another plane.

Isobel blinked. Out the carriage window, she could see sheep grazing. Leather strap still in hand, she turned to Alistair, seated across from her, his back to the horses. He arched a brow, a knowing curve at the corners of his lips.

Resisting the urge to stick out her tongue, she said, "I'll have you know, we were. I could have fought the last brigand if you hadn't interrupted me."

"*You*? Was I aiding or cowering in the carriage?"

She flicked her head towards Lord Dunley, who sat next to Alistair.

"Ah. I understand," Alistair said with a chuckle.

Hetty turned to eye Isobel askance. "What *are* you on about? Who is cowering? What brigand?"

Isobel shrugged. "Oh, nothing important. Mr. Trowbridge merely wished to enquire about the novel

I'm reading and if I had progressed to the chapter with the, um, sword fight."

A small, sleepy voice to the other side of Hetty questioned, "Wha-wha? What's this about swords?" Grumbling, the voice added, "Not a word that ought to leave a lady's lips if you ask me."

Lord Dunley narrowed his eyes at Isobel. "Quite right, Mother. The delicacy of your sex ought to be respected."

Trying not to roll her eyes, Isobel turned her attention back to the sheep, wishing Alistair had been convinced by her master plan rather than accepting the viscount's offer. It would be a long few days with them cramped together in a carriage. Had they planned sooner, she was certain the viscountess would have insisted on taking two carriages for the party or having the gentlemen ride alongside with the outriders. On the bright side, they had respectable travel companions.

Lord Dunley wafted his handkerchief as they passed a field with loudly bleating sheep.

Early that evening, they descended the carriage steps with mouths agape and knees knocking. In truth, Isobel was likely the only one to descend in that manner, but she paid no heed to anyone else to gauge if their mouths were as cavernous or their knees as misaligned and clanking. Before her stood a haunting Jacobean mansion, one constructed from the ruins of a dismantled abbey. An evening fog shrouded the stone, rising from the courtyard's rain-soaked gravel.

The travelers approached the front door. Heavy oak framed with studded iron barred their entry until, with a creak of hinges, it swept ajar by an unseen hand. Isobel swallowed, sparing a glance at Alistair.

He leaned in her direction to say discreetly, "This is when Count Deimos steps into view, terrifying you into a faint with his scarred face before carrying you to the dungeons."

"You would let him carry me off? Just like that?" Isobel scoffed.

"I would have no choice, my damsel, for with his evil eye, he would cast a spell, bewitching me. My feet would turn to stone. I could do no more than hurl curses. I am mortal, after all."

Isobel eyed him head to toe. "Mortal? I'm not convinced."

He smiled. Was that the sparkle of the sun against his teeth? *No, Isobel, do not be silly, for the sky is overcast, and the glint was only from the imaginings of earlier.* Her gaze darted back to him a few more times as they ascended the front entry steps, just in case she might catch a real heroic spark.

Isobel and Alistair took up the rear of the party, Lord Dunley and his mother at the front, Hetty in the middle. A butler greeted them in the vestibule. He and a myriad of busts poised on stone pedestals.

With a bow, the butler said, "His Lordship awaits you in the drawing room."

Lord Dunley's cane clicked against the marble flooring as he followed the butler.

A footman surreptitiously interrupted Isobel's progress with an invitation to escort her to her room. Rather than be affronted at the subtle deflection from following the viscount to meet her host, she was relieved. With a reassuring, if not apologetic, smile to Alistair, she followed the footman.

They would only stay here for the night. Lord Dunley refused to sully his high heels by overnighting at inns. Only the residences of his friends and acquaintances would do, the few not yet in London or with no intentions of attending the Parliamentary Season. It was Isobel's fortune Hetty and her mother-in-law would be attending the social scene, for otherwise, she would not have been able to secure passage in the Dunley carriage. Hetty had whispered to her before they set out that she and Lady Dunley had been invited to join him only because it was the first Season since the marriage, and thus it would be expected he bring his bride. Poor Hetty must curtsy before the queen and whatever else was required of a new viscountess. Isobel did not envy her. Quite the contrary. She pitied Hetty. Maybe there would be enjoyment in the venture for her friend, no matter how horrifying it all sounded to Isobel.

The only disappointment of the journey was they would be going directly to Reading. Isobel had hoped they would take the route northeast to stop at Jules Knowlton's family home so she could see Leila and the twins and hopefully ride with the Owens the remaining distance. Alas, not only were the Owens ahead of arrangements, set to arrive at the Trowbridge residence two days before Isobel and Alistair, but Lord Dunley refused to detour, even if it would mean ridding his carriage of the company sooner.

At least the journey had not been unpleasant thus far. Cramped, with Isobel, Hetty, and Lady Dunley sitting elbow to elbow, but not unpleasant. Lord Dunley still appeared taken with Alistair, devoting his waking moments to striking up a conversation with his carriage seat companion.

With luck, her portmanteau would await her in the guest room. She had packed her writing slope and could not wait to write the next scene of Comte de Corentin's story. The poor Frenchmen had been neglected lately, and this majestic, if not malevolent, palace inspired her next scene.

Chapter 11

After several days on the road and evenings at one stately home or another, Isobel was ready to reach their destination. It was not the traveling that bothered her. It was the company. Lord Dunley and his mother made for sour carriage partners, never wanting to stop and explore, never taking joy in the scenery they passed. Even the long barrow Isobel had spied from the window had been passed without a care. But what of the wraith haunting the barrow? There must be one, and Isobel wanted to meet her! Alas. With a sniff, Dunley dismissed her pleas.

How different would this journey be with only Alistair sharing the carriage? Should all work as planned and they wed, and should he and his father kindle a relationship, they may well make this journey many times in the future.

Lord Dunley coughed daintily. "Not long now, Mr. Trowbridge. My carriage will not linger. I shall bid my farewell upon arrival, but I say now it has been my pleasure. My desire for your company has not been sated. I wish for us to meet again. Should you find yourself in London…"

Isobel turned her attention back to the window, ignoring the viscount's obsequiousness. How differently he would see Alistair if he knew the change of circumstances to come. But then, if Alistair did not share his circumstances of no longer being a governor in India, no one would question he wielded power and influence. He exuded it in his every movement. The noble brow, the piercing gaze, the firmness of his chin, and the strength of his shoulders all professed greatness. She recalled the first time she saw him. He had been in traditional Indian attire, each finger ringed in gold. No one would have convinced her he was not the Nawab of Bengal, not with so regal a bearing. Circumstances would not change this.

She flicked her gaze between Dunley and Alistair. How long was "not long"? Fidgeting, she searched her surroundings for signs of a country house, a village, something. Flat lands stretched to the horizon, not a hill or building in sight.

What sort of house did Mr. Trowbridge have? He was deputy chairman for the Company. Isobel did not know what that meant, not entirely, nor if he was *a* deputy chairman or *the* deputy chairman—were there many? But he must be wealthy. And his tastes must be extraordinary to have lived in India and married a Persian woman of what Isobel believed but could not confirm was of some importance, at least judging from the family jewels she had thus far seen, jewels that could purchase Alistair the grandest home in England if he so chose, not a humble cottage, much less the need to take up a trade. The jewels, to him, meant something different. She understood that and accepted it without question. But what of his father?

She fidgeted so much that Hetty elbowed her to sit still. How could she sit still when they would arrive soon? Alistair and his father's reunion was imminent! Isobel meeting the father was imminent! The house coming into view was imminent!

Any minute now, she would feast her eyes on the Trowbridge abode. She would wager it was a castle with a forbidding but crumbling curtain wall. There would be much to explore, of course, an endless maze of drafty hallways, circular stairs into tower rooms with overlooks and arrow slits, priest holes in which to hide, and secret passageways to traverse. Isobel was positively giddy at the possibilities. Would it be haunted by the warriors of the past? Would suits of armor creak to life in the dead of night?

She could see it now. She would be creeping along a gallery — no, the armory! — innocuous armor poised to either side, lining the perimeter, still and silent. But what was that? A faint creak, not unlike a hinge needing oil. Out of her periphery, she would catch the glint of steel. Just in time! As she leapt aside, a longsword would slash within inches of her shoulder. The suit of armor from *The Castle of Otranto*! There he would be, facing her, both hands gripping the sword to raise it overhead, ready to strike. Isobel would stumble backwards. The suit would stagger forwards. A step back. A step forwards. She would pivot to run only to hear the clash of swords. A glance back would reveal the suit in combat with Alistair, his shamshir making short work of the plated spirit.

A nudge at her foot disrupted her fantasy. She blinked. Alistair, seated across from her in the carriage, nodded towards the window.

With a gasp, she realized they were no longer in the countryside. An endless row of terraced shops lined a bustling street. The carriage slowed amidst the traffic. Horses, pedestrians, sedan chairs, and carriages of every shape and size traveled up and down the street to the melodious cacophony of horse hoofs, rattling coach kit, squeaky wheels, shouts, and general hubbub. A haze of dust dulled the colors, but not so much that Isobel could not admire the rainbow of parasols and walking gowns of the women.

"Are we in London?" she asked, unable to disguise the awe and wonder from her voice.

Lord Dunley sniffed. "Hardly. We're in Reading." He pronounced the word with displeasure as though he were inconvenienced by its existence.

Oh. The landscape of the teeming market town was a far cry from her atmospheric castle. If this was only Reading, what must London resemble?

With a bump and a lurch, the carriage turned into a courtyard and stopped. Isobel peered out again to see a chaotic innyard, hostlers running to and fro, the scent of sweaty horses almost overpowering.

Lord Dunley said, "This is where I leave you."

Isobel turned to Alistair in alarm.

Before she could question the situation, Hetty clasped her hand tightly. "I'll write to you as soon as I'm settled at the London house."

Brisk farewells and parting words of gratitude were exchanged to the accompaniment of Lady Dunley's soft snores, and then Alistair climbed out of the carriage, offering a hand to Isobel.

As she descended, he said, "Apologies, *aroosakam*, my doll. Of convenience, we are to meet Mr. and Mrs. Owen here, then continue to the house."

"Oh," was all she said, chagrined she had not recalled since he had likely told her of this plan already and she had not paid attention.

She could not deny the relief, not only to be rid of Dunley but to be reassured they were not being booted out at a random inn. A short distance away, she recognized the Owens' carriage. Grooms were busy transferring her and Alistair's traveling trunks from the Dunley's luggage carriage to the top of the Owen family carriage.

Alistair directed her attention to Mr. and Mrs. Owen, then said, "I'll be but a moment. I wish a word with my valet before he joins the coachman."

Arms outstretched, Isobel raced to greet Mrs. Aaditri Owen.

Isobel could do little more than laugh quietly as the Owens' carriage left the innyard in Reading. Mrs. Aaditri Owen's voice overlapped with Mr. Owen's, the two competing to be heard over each other, excited about absolutely everything, from Isobel's arrival to the Company election at the April meeting. Aaditri directed her chatter to Isobel while Mr. Owen aimed his at Alistair.

While Aaditri was heard to say, "We ladies must band together. So fortunate am I to have you with me in a house full of boys," Mr. Owen's voice drowned out the last with his, "Good to be in Trowbridge's company again, my boy. I'll forever be in his debt for introducing me to Aaditri, she being a friend of your mother's, but then you already knew that. Of course, you did."

She exchanged a knowing glance with Alistair, he as amused as she. Neither dared interrupt the enthusiasm of the Owens. Only when they turned down the road leading away from Reading did Isobel look at Aaditri with questioning eyes.

"The house is in Burghfield, the distance from Reading not unlike our Sidvale from Sidbury." Aaditri's voice both soothed and enlivened Isobel.

It was a voice she had known since childhood, one that always set her at ease, the wise voice of Mrs. Owen with its East India tones, softened by her years of living in England. By that same token, it enlivened Isobel to think of their arrival at the house and the similarities of locales.

Continuing, Aaditri said, "We will spend at least one full day in Reading, *azizam*, a shopping day to remember. If it is only us ladies, we can walk to take in the scenery, but if the boys join, we may take the carriage. Oh, but we'll have packages, will we not? From all the shopping? We should take the carriage with or without them."

As she rambled, Isobel tugged her bottom lip between her teeth to keep from grinning.

Mr. Owen rattled on, as well, to Alistair, neither Owen tiring of their monologue.

Isobel watched as they left the busy town behind, the landscape flattening again into farmlands. Not a soul passed them. The route was south, a different road from which the Dunley carriage had taken. Isobel could see why they had met in Reading rather than carrying on to Burghfield. Had the Dunley carriage taken them all the way to Trowbridge's house, it would have added two hours, including backtracking, to their journey to London.

Although the distance was little more than five miles from Reading to Burghfield, the journey took them an hour, but a more pleasant hour Isobel had not spent since leaving home. She knew they were drawing closer when the endless fields were interrupted by redbrick houses lining the road, at first detached and then terraced, and finally, they had reached the center of a village no larger than Sidvale. The carriage rolled past not one but two inns. White-walled with friendly, swaying signs that read, to the right, The Hatch Gate Inn and then, to the left, The Old Lion. Rather than continue down the main road towards the common, they turned down a private driveway. Slowing to a crawl, the coachman navigated the lane to the best of his ability. It was almost too narrow. They bumped along, kicking up so much dust that the windows were nigh impossible to see through, although it would not have mattered, for tall trees and a stone wall covered in part by greenery and overgrown bushes blocked views to either side.

Isobel gripped the leather strap, not that it helped. Just when she thought she would succumb to carriage sickness for the first time in her adult life, the road smoothed, the horses stepped up their pace, and the trees and wall cleared into the wide-open lawn. So vast did the lawn stretch that it appeared deceptively rural. They could not be but five minutes walking distance to the two public houses. Had they not just left the village behind them, Isobel would be hard-pressed not to believe they were back in the countryside. Grounds lengthened as far as her eyes could see except for a lone tree dotting the green.

As they continued down the endless drive, she sat up straighter, craning to see more, for almost within view was a formal garden. She could not yet see the house. It must be perpendicular to the drive, straight ahead and thus blocked by the horses. Mr. and Mrs. Owen had not stopped talking yet, although she had forgotten to listen some time ago. She gave a little bounce, flashing an eager smile to her companions. Alistair returned her smile with a grimace. She reached over to pat his hand. He was nervous. An understatement. He looked positively peaky.

How thoughtless of her not to realize he would be suffering an increasing inner turmoil as they drew closer. How long had it been since he had last seen his father? Had their relationship already been strained when his father made the journey to India, or was it only the stretch since their previous reunion that added to the tension? Regardless, that tension would be compounded by the announcement he carried. As she pulled her hand back, she thought she had better add *announcements*, plural, to that, as he had more than Company business to share. There was also his broken betrothal and new courtship to address.

So intent on trying to convey her concern to him with her eyes in hopes of also eliciting a response, she missed the carriage circling around a wide courtyard. Only when Mr. Owen was handing down Aaditri from the carriage did Isobel realize they had come to a halt. Oh dear. This was the moment. All her excitement lodged in her throat. She gave Alistair's hand a squeeze before he ducked out and descended the steps.

For the briefest moment before she accepted his hand, she held her breath in anticipation. A castle? A tower? An abbey? A priory?

She stepped down to survey Mr. Trowbridge's domain.

Oh.

A modern, redbrick, five-bay Georgian house greeted her.

So much for her imaginings of secret passageways, hidden towers, priest holes, and the like; there was nothing to disappoint her, though. It was a pretty little house, she supposed. And this trip was not about her gallivanting ancient ruins. It was about Alistair. This was Alistair's journey to face his father and pave a new path for his life.

Turning a bright smile to him, she nodded additional encouragement.

His stomach fluttered, and his chest tightened. From the distance between the carriage to the door, Alistair worried he would disgrace himself by casting up his nuncheon meal. All about them, the courtyard bustled with activity, grooms and footmen tending to the luggage, the carriage, and the horses. Before them, the front door stood open, the interior shadowed. His father awaited him inside. Alistair could not see past the door, not with the sun in his eyes, but he knew.

Would his father have changed in comparison to the man of memory? Alistair could not honestly say when he last saw his father. Ten years? Five? It felt like a lifetime.

With mature awareness, he knew his father was not to blame. If one must blame anyone, it could be argued his mother had been the one to split the family. After all his father's vying for promotion in the Company to move them to England, she had stubbornly refused to leave, not wanting to release her dream of returning to Persia. Her closest friend, Aaditri Owen, had already moved to England. Nothing kept her there except that cursed dream. Why had she not told his father she would not move so that he might never have sought after promotion?

Then, Mr. Alexander Trowbridge had not been forced to accept the promotion. He could have stayed in India in his current position. For as long as Alistair could remember, he had blamed his father for abandoning them. He resented being left behind. The constant written pleas from his father had made it all worse, for each plea to his son to join him in England drove another wedge between the family, as if the man wished to separate Alistair from his mother, leaving his mother behind in favor of the father. With only Mr. Owen to call on Shahrazad periodically, Alistair had needed to stay with her. *He* was her protector. He was the defender of the family, the man of the house, when his own father chose the Company over his family.

But mature awareness bit into his gut. With travel from England to India taking as long as six months, who could blame his father for visiting only rarely?

As his feet dragged towards the door, time slowing with each step, he could sense the Owens holding back, Aaditri Owen wrapping an arm around Isobel's shoulders, the trio allowing Alistair to enter the house first. If he could run in the opposite direction, he would.

And *he* was Isobel's hero? He was no better than a coward, a boy afraid to face his father. He stopped before the threshold, closed his eyes, and breathed in the fresh air, allowing it to fill his lungs with life-giving strength. He was Isobel's hero. He was his mother's protector. He was Aršama.

Pulling his shoulders back and holding his head high, he stepped over the threshold into the darkness.

As his eyes adjusted to the dim lighting in the reception hall, his father's form took shape. Had he expected an old man, stooped and greying, leaning heavily on a cane, he would have been sorely mistaken. His vision blurred as tears pricked the corners. With arms outstretched, his father stood before him. Tall, lean, powerful. Aside from Alistair's darker complexion, he might as well have been looking in a mirror right down to the misty eyes.

Alistair bowed low. "*Pedar.*"

"*Pesar,*" his father replied in the deep, thunderous voice of Alistair's memories.

Crossing the entry, Alistair embraced his father and said in nought but a whisper, "*Bâba.*"

His father's arms were strong, heartening, and welcoming. Alistair lingered, blinking rapidly to dismiss the tears he knew would shine if he backed away too soon. The embrace felt good. It felt right. The resentments of old did not melt, but Alistair knew peace.

At last, Alistair released his father and retreated. No further words were exchanged. The Owens filled the entry with their competing voices, all vying for Alexander Trowbridge's attention.

Alexander raised staying hands and nodded to the stranger at Aaditri Owen's side. "Is this your companion, Aaditri? Come all the way from Devonshire?"

Mrs. Aaditri Owen presented Isobel, both hands clasping Isobel's shoulders. "This is Miss Lambeth, Leila's friend and nearly a second daughter to me. I am so pleased she's come to keep me company."

Alexander took in Isobel with a cursory sweep of his gaze, offered a curt nod, then said, "I've little doubt the ladies will require their rooms before dinner. Geoffrey, show Miss Lambeth to hers. Gentlemen? Join me in my study for port?"

With a firm pat on Alistair's arm, the host led the way. Allowing Mr. Owen to follow first, Alistair met Isobel's gaze with a silent promise to catch her alone at his first opportunity.

Chapter 12

Mr. Trowbridge mistook Isobel for a servant. It was the only explanation Isobel could see. After the brief introductions, Aaditri took Isobel up the main stairs to show her the first floor, which consisted of the primary apartments, the guest rooms, and a parlor. The house had two wings at each end of the center block, making it larger than it appeared from the front, one wing being for Mr. Trowbridge and the other for guests. Aaditri, Mr. Owen, and Alistair would be staying in the guest wing. The butler, Geoffrey, had waited patiently by the main stairs to show Isobel to her room. The main stairs only went to the first floor, Isobel soon discovered.

Escorting her back to the ground floor, they followed a hall to its conclusion, three doors at the end, one leading outside, one into a billiard room, and one a jib door for servants, flush against the wall and paneled to seem invisible. The jib door opened into a stairwell to the second floor, bypassing the first floor. Isobel's guest room was the door immediately facing the servant's stairs. When Mr. Trowbridge had called her Aaditri's *companion*, she had not thought anything of it. Now she understood that was precisely what he thought of her. Not an auspicious beginning.

There was plenty of time before dinner. Isobel was too stirred to nap, so she went about unpacking her portmanteau, trying her best to press the wrinkles out of her gowns, washing herself of the day's grime, and then changing for dinner. It was still at least an hour before she would meet Aaditri in the reception hall. She eyed the book from Mr. Bradley. She was only on volume one of the three-volume set. Best explore now, then read after. Otherwise, she would lose herself in reading and miss time to explore.

Her room was pleasant enough. It was small but cozy. Elements of it, such as the decorative paper hangings, fireplace, four-poster bed, and chair, led her to believe this was not for a typical servant, most likely for a governess or tutor given the private entrance. Then, considering its easy access to the billiard room, it could be offered to a bachelor guest. Isobel was not insulted or displeased. This would suit her and offer ample opportunity to write.

There was only one window, a small dormer. The view was to the side of the house, presumably the shared view from Mr. Trowbridge's apartments. A three-tier fountain centered in a small garden was the main attraction. Was it like the fountain in *Vathek*? The fountain that never sated thirst?

In the distance, she could see a yew tree and what she thought might be a stone bench beneath. Something to explore. All else was lawn. The formal gardens she had spotted on their drive in must be on the other side for the guests to enjoy. The house may not be ripe for writing inspiration, but she rather thought she could find inspiration anywhere, even from a lone tree and fountain — assuming a djinn or

arch-demon did not disturb her fountain-side medi-
tations, as in *Vathek*.

Leaving behind her room for now, she decided to
explore the second floor. More to the point, that was
her plan until she realized there was little to explore.
Her door faced that of the stairwell, but beyond her
room was an ample sitting room, not unlike in size
to her great hall at home. It would make a perfect
nursery had this been a family home. As it was, the
room was sparsely decorated but well-appointed, a
retreat to escape the hubbub of a busy house. Adjacent
was another guest room similar to her own, except
its window overlooking the front of the house. She
preferred her room, then, with its secret garden.

At the far end of the sitting room were three steps
onto a landing — what a perfect stage this would be for
playacting! — and then a short hall and another door.
When she tried to open it, however, it did not budge.
She gave it a firm push, then a tug, to no avail. Squat-
ting, she tried peering through the keyhole. Curious.
It seemed the key itself was blocking the lock. But
why would the key be inside where no one could
retrieve it?

There was only one logical answer. A warden
stood guard on the other side of this door, keeping a
watchful eye on the imprisoned maiden.

Or, illogically, it was haunted.

Isobel giggled.

Whatever the reason, there was nothing more
to explore. To bide more time, she returned to her
room, intent on reading some of the book that Mr.
Bradley had given her. She was not convinced yet
if she liked it or not. It was too much of a departure

from what she typically enjoyed, although she did find herself increasingly invested in discovering what would happen. A tyrannical character had imprisoned his own daughter to keep her from wedding the neighbor. Isobel was distrustful of some of the characters who tried too desperately to gain the reader's empathy. If she hazarded a guess, she would say they, too, were malevolent, hiding dark secrets of their past.

Moving her chair beneath the dormer window, she cozied with her book.

Oh dear. She ought not to have changed into her dinner gown so soon. It would wrinkle if she were not careful. Shrugging, she tucked her knees beneath her and set about reading.

Mr. Trowbridge looked from Mr. Owen to Alistair and back, his dinner a secondary priority. "We will be a force to be reckoned with, the three of us. A team to take the April meeting by storm."

Isobel listened to the conversation from her place next to Aaditri. While both Aaditri and Alistair spoke on occasion, it was Mr. Trowbridge and Mr. Owen who dominated at the dinner table, the two not so much talking business — not while ladies were present — as sharing in their gratitude to be in each other's company, especially now that Alistair had joined the ranks. Their host meant well, but Isobel could see Alistair's discomfiture every time the Company or the meeting was mentioned.

Mr. Owen said, "If all goes well with my election, I'll be taking advantage of your hospitality more often. Think of it — the two of us together again after all these years. It'll be like old times!"

"A pity my son can't stay longer," said Mr. Trowbridge, nodding to Alistair. "His position is too important to neglect, though. I shan't keep him longer than I must. The expansion from settlements into provinces will further strengthen our empire, providing a vital role for my son to fulfill. We must make the most of our time while we have it," he added the last with a look to Alistair. "I'm proud of my boy, following in my footsteps. Here we all are, together. Never thought I would see the day. Did I ever tell you, Josiah, of the time he hid in the room so he could attend a Company meeting? He was, let me think now… no more than ten years of age."

Mr. Trowbridge continued with his story, to the amusement of Mr. Owen, before launching into another similar story from Alistair's childhood. Isobel was as amused by the stories as everyone else at the table, but she did not fail to notice the common thread — they all involved Company business in one way or another, be it Alistair shadowing his father to watch the dealings with local laborers or sneaking into private meetings or variations thereof. Isobel's gaze flicked to Alistair throughout, curious to know his thoughts and reactions.

Aside from Mr. Trowbridge's preoccupation when it came to conversation, Isobel almost liked him. Yes, he mistook her for a servant, as Aaditri's companion. Yes, he stood as a potential barrier to Alistair's plans. But his bearing was so similar to Alistair's that Isobel could not help but fall under his spell. She hung on his every word, taken in by the timbre of his voice, the strength of his profile, his predatory posture. In so many ways, he was like Alistair. To say he was merely an older, British version would undermine all that made Alistair himself since so much of his charm, values, and uniqueness were rooted in his heritage and upbringing. And yet, the two gentlemen were remarkably similar. How could Isobel *not* like her host?

The contrast between Mr. Trowbridge and Mr. Owen made her host's potency to enthrall that much more pronounced. Mr. Owen, although handsome, was Mr. Trowbridge's opposite. Unlike his host, he was blond and blue-eyed with a weak chin but a jovial nature, all lightness and jest in comparison to Mr. Trowbridge's dark gaze.

As the conversation continued about some other antic from Alistair's childhood, Alistair interrupted to say, "The house is new."

Mr. Trowbridge answered in silence for the stretch it took Isobel to serve herself from the fish platter. He seemed first confused by the change in conversation, startled by the observation and then resigned to address the comment.

At length, he said, "Eight years new, in fact. Didn't have much say in it, to be honest. As soon as we saw what was on offer, it was too good to pass."

Before he continued, Isobel's ears perked. *We?* She looked around the table. No one else had seemed to notice. She shrugged off the tingle at the base of her neck.

"Seventeen acres in total. If anyone fancies a ramble, there's a small wilderness to be enjoyed at the far end, including a folly worth seeing. The folly was here when we secured the land, but the house was not. The claim to fame, you must know, is the Cedar of Lebanon tree within sight of the formal gardens. Not to be missed."

Alistair questioned, "The house was not here?"

"The former rectory was here instead. Couldn't live in that, could I? Everyone knows rectors are greedy fellows, persuaded only by the tithes. The rectory was in sore shape, the old rector having spent his fortune on... er... more earthly pleasures. The living changed, as did the patronage, following his death, and now we have a vicar, his residence further afield in a vicarage of far better condition than the old rectory. I couldn't see living in the old place, either, once purchased. Demolished it to build what suited our needs. Many a Company dinner I've hosted here. Stone's throw from London and all. Not as grand as your place — eh, boy? — but it's my slice of heaven."

Isobel wished to ask many questions, not the least of which included asking about the locked door on the second floor, but knowing her voice would not be heard, not as a mere companion, she kept her head bowed and listened.

By the end of dinner, Isobel's eyelids drooped. It had been an exhausting journey east and a long day. Thus, Alistair's next words were music to her ears.

Mr. Trowbridge asked as dinner wound to a close, "Shall we proceed to the drawing room? Make an evening of it? Ample conversation to be had, cards, tea, could go a round at the billiard table later."

Alistair said, "Many apologies. Travel has worn me. I think I am not alone in the wish to retire early. Miss Lambeth?"

Isobel blinked rapidly, startled out of a head lull. "Yes, yes, a tiring journey, I would —"

"Let us end the evening early," Mr. Trowbridge said, interrupting Isobel. "It will do you good to regain your strength after the journey, son."

And so, they each bade the other a good evening and dispersed for their rooms, only Mr. Trowbridge and Mr. Owen staying behind to share port and cigars.

As Isobel passed the main stairs, Aaditri caught her arm and guided her into the hallway towards the billiard room. "I have written your mother, *azizam*, thanking her for allowing you to travel." In hushed tones, she added, "I will not keep from you my disappointment. So special a time for you but Mrs. Lambeth does not see. I told her about our Alistair. I told her he is taken with you and what an honor this is." Aaditri raised open palms in a helpless gesture. "I will overindulge you, *azizam*. You are my second daughter, and I will coddle you. You'll see." She pulled Isobel into a hug. "The courtship is proceeding?"

Isobel spied Alistair in her periphery, loitering around the reception hall as though admiring the ornamentation. "Oh *yes*, Mrs. Owen. It is everything and more. *He* is everything and more."

"An understanding, is there?" Aaditri nodded with vigor.

"Not as such, no, but we do *understand* each other and *understand* there will be an understanding soon if you take my meaning. He wished for his father and me to meet first, and there's their reunion to consider, and —"

Waving a hand, Aaditri said, "Very well. I know you will be made happy soon. Until then, leave the pampering to me." With that, she headed up the main stairs, leaving Isobel alone in the hallway.

Not long did Isobel have to wait for Alistair to wish for a peek into the billiard room — and who should he coincidentally bump into in the hallway?

"Ah, *nazanin*, a vision of loveliness for my tired eyes." He cupped her cheek in his palm. "Thank you for accompanying me on this journey. I think I have not the strength for this without you."

Isobel's stomach fluttered at his tender touch. "And? How are you faring?"

"Better than if you had not been here. You are my strength, my fortitude. I will talk with my father on the morrow. There is much to say. I think he will not like the news, but I hope you will be pleasing to him, knowing I have found happiness with you."

"Wait!" Isobel pressed her hands against his waist-coat. "Give him time before you mention me. You haven't talked to him about Leila yet, much less about your decision with the Company. Wait until he's had the chance to mull those over."

"You're correct." He leaned a shoulder against the wall, his expression weary. "We had agreed to that. I had forgotten. I wish for this time to end quickly, for us to be announcing our intention, for us to be plan-ning. This waiting hurts my heart. To see my father speak over you hurts here." He pressed his hand over his heart, clasping her hands beneath his in the move-ment. "I dislike the coming confrontation, knowing I will disappoint him. He will not be pleased with what I have to say."

"You said that with me, and I did not so much as flinch, did I? I think your father will be far more accepting of your decision than you think. From everything I've seen so far, I believe him to be a father who wishes to make peace with his son and rekindle a relationship he feels he's lost. All he could talk about over dinner was *you*, the you he recalls from your childhood, but still you. I think he'll surprise us both."

"I hope, my sweet. I hope."

With a kiss to her temple, as soft as a spring breeze, he bade her a good evening, leaving her to retreat to her room. What she had said to Alistair had not been untrue. She only hoped it was more true than she believed it herself. His father was more preoccupied with the son of memory than the son before him, as well as the son who wished to work for the Company like his father rather than a man of his own right with dreams of his own making. She did not wish to share those observations with Alistair, though, for fear of disheartening him.

So exhausted, she did not bother lighting a candle in anticipation of nightfall. The book remained in the chair where she had left it. The writing box sat untouched. It took all her remaining reserves of energy to ready for bed. Her eyelids weighed heavily as though under a sleeping spell. With a sigh and mumble, she climbed into bed, smiled to realize it was featherdown, and then drifted into the sleep of the dead.

Chapter 13

"Nothing makes sense, son." Alexander paced in front of his study window, the backdrop a serene formal garden, so juxtaposed to the mood in the room. "First, you denied me the chance to be a father when it most mattered, and now this. It's deliberate to hurt me."

"This is not about you," Alistair began, his arms crossed over his chest from his post by the hearth. "It has never been about you. I never denied you. You denied yourself by leaving. I could not leave her. My desires mattered not. If we are to use the past to explain the present, this will be a short conversation."

Halting, his father clasped his hands behind his back and scrutinized Alistair. After a lengthy perusal, he resumed his pacing. "I already knew about Miss Owen, of course. Josiah broke the news. He was on the cusp of having the banns read for the time of asking when you refused. All my visions of you and the Owens arriving together and us preparing for a wedding, a union of families, a reunion for us. What happened instead? Josiah arrived with his wife, and neither you nor my future daughter-in-law with them. And why not? Their daughter is meeting her *other* future in-laws. Explain this. I can't understand it."

Alistair watched the back-and-forth march of the pacing. He had come to the study expecting the worst. So far, all met expectations. The temptation to leave rose in his throat, constricting his swallowing and shallowing his breathing. A quick word to the butler, and he and Isobel could be on their way back to Sidvale to start whatever life they could with his current purse. The April meeting was unimportant. Reconciliation with his father was unimportant. He needed neither and owed nothing to either.

"The reason is my own. You need not understand."

"I can't begin to understand. This union was not only a family dream long in the making, but it was also one of mutual benefit, an alliance the Company would have rewarded ten times over. After all this time, have you no understanding how the Company functions, what it values, what it rewards? This match—perfection itself. Set aside your position and think as a man, at the least. You can't deny the girl's beauty. I simply cannot understand your choice. Nearly six months of travel to meet, marry, and collect your bride only to reject her within two weeks of courtship? It makes no sense, son."

Alexander stopped, his back to Alistair. He combed a hand through his short-cropped, black hair and growled low. "And now this other nonsense. I won't dignify it with a response."

"You will," Alistair said, taking the carrot in hopes they could leave the conversation about Leila behind.

For so long, his father remained silent, staring out the window; Alistair almost gave into temptation and left. As he uncrossed his arms, ready to depart, his father finally spoke.

"I had a different vision for this reunion. So different. I have... something of my own to share, something... not without challenges." He hesitated as though about to explain. Instead, he said, "But this news, all of it, is too much. Where did the boy go who admired his father, who wished to follow in his footsteps?" His voice turned gruff, his pace slowing. "You blame me for leaving. You resent me. Now you throw into my face all I've done for you, a way to punish me."

"No, Father," Alistair said, his tone harsh. "This is not about you. This is about me. I wish to make my own footprints. I wish to live as a true English gentleman, to live in England."

"Think of the name you could make for yourself working up in the Company as I have." He turned to face Alistair. "You could be in my chair one day. Think of what the East India Company is accomplishing. We're expanding the British empire across the globe, bringing civilization to natives who have only known poverty and heathenism. We're doing *good*, son."

Alistair uncrossed his arms to hook an elbow over the fireplace mantel. He ran a hand over his face, readying himself to address these points and refute them as appropriate.

Waving his hands to stave off Alistair's would-be reply, Alexander continued, "No, listen to me. I do not like your decision to resign from your current position, but I can accept it. The new governor-general is spineless. We need someone like you there to keep the peace, to form the armies, to continue our goals, now more than ever, but I can accept your not wanting to be there. After all, I made the same choice, did I not? What I cannot understand is resigning from the Company rather than taking a new position in England. I can arrange whatever you'd like. A director position? It's yours. Say the word. *This* I could understand. *This* I could support."

With a shake of his head, Alistair said, "I do not wish to be a Company man, Father. I do not deny I am grateful for all you've done, for the man I've become and the position I've held. What I want now is different. This is a long time in coming, after deep thought and ample planning. This is not a desire of the moment. Nothing binds me to India. My position was good for India and good for *Maman*. Now, I wish to be of my own. I do not need your approval nor your assistance, but I would ask for both."

"You have it, son. You need not ask. All that is mine is yours if you would but take a position here. Is director not to your liking? There are others. With the right words at the General Court meeting in June, I can have a new position created to suit you if nothing else is appealing. I have this power, you see. Power you, too, could wield in time. Whatever house you desire in England is yours. I'll front you the means now. An estate to rival the wealthiest aristocrat? It's yours. A modest manor with admirable gardens? It's yours."

Alistair covered his eyes with his hand. "You do not understand, and I cannot explain the reasons for my dream. What more is there to say? We are at an impasse, Father. I shall prepare to leave. It has been good to see you. I thank you for dinner."

Pushing off the mantel, he offered a deep bow, then turned to leave.

"Please, don't leave. We've… we've so much time to account for. We have lost each other, son. I don't know you, nor you me. Must it be that way? Stay. We'll speak more when we've had time to think. Please, stay, think over my proposition, and in the interim, allow us to know each other as we used to. There are things I want to tell you, so many things, things I *must* tell you. Give us more time?"

Not wanting to rush the answer, Alistair considered his options and the request. It sounded genuine enough, but he could feel the pull of the strings, his father's hope of him accepting another position. This was not time for Alexander to think over what had been said; rather Alistair to consider changing his own mind. And yet, he could not bring himself to turn down the invitation. Some small part of him wanted to make peace with his father, even if there remained a point of contention. Some small part of him refused to leave until he had announced his intention to wed Isobel, his ladylove on his arm, as his equal, not as Aaditri's companion. Some small part of him wanted to know how his father had led his life all these years.

With a curt but not impolite nod, Alistair said, "I will stay."

Hand over heart, Alexander took to the nearest chair. "We will… we will talk. Not of this, but of other things. Of your life in India after I left. Of your mother. You've become more like her than me, I feel. We'll talk. Of… of everything."

"In time," was all Alistair said in response.

She hummed a tuneless song, her fingers trailing through the water. Isobel's thoughts were far from the serenity of the little sanctuary, the trickle of the fountain mesmerizing. She ought to rewrite the scene with Comte de Corentin's rescue of his lady fair. The stairway duel had sounded adventurous when she first planned it, and his being trapped in the tower had seemed dramatic, but upon further reflection, a sword fight along so narrow of stairs was unlikely — she had tried a shadow duel earlier in the servant stair across from her room, and though it had straight stairs rather than spiral castle stairs, it had been too confined. Additionally, she did not like that he would be so unaware as not to realize someone was behind him to lock him in the tower.

A glance at her window shook away all thoughts of Corentin.

A shadow looked down at her from her bed-chamber window. She could feel it more than see it. A chill ran down her spine. No, wait, that was not her window. Hers was the small dormer. That window was beyond the locked door. Someone, or something, lurked there.

The soft rustle of steps against grass stole her attention. Alistair approached. She glanced back at the window. No shadow. Not even a waft of curtains. *Foolish imagination*, she scolded with a shake of her head. Or, in her defense, it was most likely a trick of the sun's rays through the heavy clouds, which portended rain.

Turning her attention to Alistair, she stood from the edge of the fountain, an overeager smile curling her lips despite her efforts to hide it and appear non-chalant — on the chance someone *was* watching. He must have been looking for her high and low to think about this side of the house.

He did not bother trying to hide his smile, wearing it proudly as he drew near. "You are as an angel. My soul is yours, should you wish to take me."

"A morbid compliment. My favorite," she crooned. "Does that mean you've been reading the *Sicilian*? Are you ready to swap books?"

"Ah, no. I confess I have neglected reading. It is good to distract my worries, and so I will begin again today." He reached the fountain at last and rocked heel to toe and back as though tempted to embrace her.

She said in warning, "If I'm not mistaken, your father's apartments overlook the fountain."

"You have read my mind." He waited only long enough for her to wave a hand to the edge of the fountain, and then he joined her at a respectable distance.

"A good thing you're not ready to swap books because I'm only on volume two of this Caleb fellow. I need to read faster because I want to know your thoughts. I can't tell who is a villain and who is a hero. They all teeter on the edge of villainy, I think."

Ignoring her talk of books, he said, "I wish you had chosen the forested folly. I would take you in my arms and — "

"Hush!" Isobel felt her face redden. "I can't hide my reactions! Oh heavens. No talk of arms or... or...

eek!" She hid her face and tried to breathe through her dueling embarrassment and excitement.

It did not help that he had taken extra care with his appearance today, his long hair tied neatly at his nape with a fine riband that matched the deep blue of his suit. After days of travel, he had turned scruffy into sleek, weary into primal.

"Another time, then," he promised, his voice low. "Seeing you now has my heart beating, your smiling beauty. Oh, but no more. I shall save my adoration."

Inching a hair's breadth closer, Isobel inhaled the sweet spices of his cologne, so familiar and titillating. She closed her eyes to savor the moment, the feel of him nearby, the sound of his tender voice, the memory of his kiss.

"I have spoken to my father," he said, the words tugging her from her reverie. "It was as unpleasant as I knew it would be."

Succinctly, he told her what was said. It did not take a genius to fill in the details of what he omitted. Even his expression had altered from adoring to pinched. Sensing his tension, she abandoned any thoughts of playful flirtation.

"I will give him time, Isobel, a few days because I know that is your wish. I cannot say we will stay until the meeting."

He paused, looking into the fountain's depths, but his hesitation only seemed to be to collect his thoughts rather than await Isobel's reply. She held silent.

"Attending April's meeting is important to me. I am a Company governor with great responsibility. My resignation should be in person, accompanied by a full report and guidance. I should like to advise on my replacement." He leaned towards her, his hand raising as though he meant to take her hand, but with a frown, he dipped his fingertips into the water instead. "My father brings out the angry boy in me. I wish to run away, not face him or the Company. The man in me can't do this, but the boy in me wishes it. It is a challenging contradiction. Rather than feeling as a responsible man wishing to begin a new chapter in life, I feel as an ungrateful boy. Will you be my reason? Will you guide me and tell me what I ought to do?"

No one had ever accused Isobel of being a voice of reason. Had the conversation not been serious and Alistair not been pained, she would have laughed at playing the reasonable role. She? The whimsical and irrational? *He* needed her, though, and he believed her to be more than fluff and fantasies.

Organizing her words, she offered, "You already know what to do. You just said it. You will give him time, and you will attend the meeting to apprise them, advise them, and resign. But what I think is most important, for you anyway, is to give yourself time. You may have planned all this well before leaving India, but you couldn't know in advance how you would react emotionally. You've seen your father for the first time in *years*, Alistair! This is more than a resignation. This is your father. Have you thought about what you want, if you want him in your life or if this is a 'thank you but goodbye'?"

His head drooped before he angled his gaze to her. "You are my guiding star."

Isobel looked down at her hands, blushing with both embarrassment and pleasure to be taken so seriously.

Without warning, he rose from the fountain's edge. "Aaditri has been asking about you. May I escort you to the drawing room for tea?"

Looking up at the dark clouds, she said, "I suppose tea is in order. I had planned a tour of the grounds but only made it this far. Now it looks like rain. Some companion I am. I've left Aaditri to entertain herself."

Alistair offered his arm.

After a lingering look at the empty window, she accepted.

Chapter 14

When Isobel and Alistair arrived at the drawing room, only Aaditri sat waiting, already preparing tea.

"*Azizam*," Aaditri greeted Isobel, her expression aglow. "Sit with me." She patted the arm of the chair next to her before turning her attention to Alistair. "You're joining us, yes?"

"I would never decline. You brew the best tea, Aaditri *khanoom*."

Pleased, she preened as she began to pour.

Isobel sat, tugging at the skirt of her walking gown and hoping tea would remain between the three of them, safe and comfortable company. With these two, she could be herself. "Oh no, you don't," she said, nodding to the cup. "I know that's hot as brimstone. I enjoy being able to taste food and drink without a scalded palate."

Aaditri shook her head pityingly. "It's no good otherwise. If you wait too long, it'll lose its bite." She handed Isobel the teacup and saucer.

Alistair accepted his teacup, and the madman did exactly what Isobel knew he would — savored a sip of the devilish brew, so hot the steam billowed, shrouding his visage.

Isobel scoffed. "Superb. Now the two of you will team up against me, determined that I never taste food again."

"If it is Mr. Bradley's tea on offer," Alistair began, "you will be fortunate not to taste it."

Isobel snorted over her cup of lava as Aaditri said to her, "He's not wrong. You see, we look after your best interests. Now, drink while it's hot."

The drawing room door opened, stealing the attention of the occupants, both Mr. Owen and Mr. Trowbridge entering mid-conversation. Isobel's shoulders drooped in disappointment. She had so hoped to enjoy the company along with the tea. Now she would have to be the meek companion, blending into the sprigged wall. It was not that she aimed for that role; rather, it was the role in which Mr. Trowbridge was determined to place her. She bowed her head to stare into her teacup.

Their host joined them, saying, "There is no happier sight than a tea connoisseur filling teacups. I hope we're not late. Josiah has been entertaining me with tales of the trip from India. Not a journey I relish. Never was fond of ships."

"Thankfully," Mr. Owen said, "I need not make it again any time soon, if the election goes well. You know how desperately I wish to be home." He eyed Aaditri with a flirty grin. "But of course, you do! How could I not with a daughter soon wed and grandchildren to look forward to? Apologies for leaving you on your own for the return trip, Alistair. But then, who is to say you won't have a lucky lady accompanying you, eh?"

Isobel's attention shot to Mr. Owen, his brows waggling at her. With a darting look between Alistair and Mr. Trowbridge, she calmed to see her host busy adding milk to his tea, paying no attention to the conversation. Alistair, meanwhile, maintained composure, unperturbed by references to a return to India or lucky ladies. So close did he hold his cards she could not discern if he was tense around his father after their talk. He must be. His calmness was a veneer, so convincing that she was almost fooled.

Aaditri, not to be outmaneuvered by her husband, said, "One lucky lady in the room is me to have so devoted an almost-daughter that she would travel from Devonshire to keep me company. I've planned a shopping day in Reading next week, a chance to overindulge Miss Lambeth as we take in the sights and sounds."

Alistair exchanged a knowing glance with Isobel. "Is this to be a 'ladies only' day, or may I press upon you both my company? There is a rumor I am skilled as an escort."

Aaditri insisted, "You must join us! What fun shall it be for the three of us to explore. You may help me pamper Miss Lambeth, yes?"

"I would like nothing better."

Mr. Trowbridge wheezed over his teacup, clearly not expecting it would be quite so hot. Hoarsely, he said, "I'm pleased you'll have a companion and escort for your outing, Aaditri. You've my leave to take the carriage if you would rather not use yours after so much traveling lately."

"Oh, but you do not wish to join us?" Aaditri looked from her husband to Mr. Trowbridge and back.

"Shopping? No, I already suffer my fair share when—" He coughed violently, raising his teacup as though to blame the temperature. Once recovered, he said, "The, er, decoration of a new home takes a personal touch, you see."

Isobel's ears perked. A glance around showed no one else any wiser. Absently, she tipped the teacup to her lips and then blanched. Good heavens. Eyes watering, she fought to swallow the scalding brew. It burned a path down her throat.

Mr. Owen shrugged. "That's what wives are for, Alexander. And housekeepers. At the very least, the steward. Never tell me you waste time poring over paper-hanging samples. It's a good thing I'll be staying in England — we hope. You're in need of reformation, my good man. Masculine company will keep you away from paint colors and furnishings."

Alistair chimed in with, "I would consider it an honor to make choices for my own home. Empty rooms to make my own. This is not for women but for anyone wishing to take pride in their abode. At Raj Bhavan, all things belong to the Company, not unlike a gentleman who inherits a house from generations previous. I could make a change or two, yes, but it is not *mine*. I should like to decorate my home."

Mr. Trowbridge coughed again, this time with a different timbre, one of wanting to avoid this line of conversation, or so Isobel imagined. But was it the talk of Alistair living elsewhere and all that implied, or was it the talk of home decoration and shopping that he wished to avoid?

Not sensing tension, expressive coughs or otherwise, Mr. Owen cheerily said, "You're living the dream, Alistair. No time or resources wasted, no burdens. Almost a shame your promotion will come with landownership — Raj Bhavan will be your responsibility while the Company continues to make use of it."

No one spoke, but before the silence could be described as awkward, Aaditri offered to refill cups — to which Isobel all but hissed at her as she waited for her cup of magma to cool enough to be considered drinkable.

Still nudging the teapot towards Isobel, Aaditri asked, "Will we enjoy another theatrical from you? Performed by you and Alistair, perhaps? Here in the drawing room?"

Mr. Trowbridge answered on Isobel's behalf. "What's this about a theatrical? What are you on about?"

"Miss Lambeth is a novelist," Aaditri explained, "and a rather good playwright. Is she not, Josiah?"

"But of course, she is! Any friend of my daughter's is bound to be skilled at writing. My Leila writes poetry, you know."

Mr. Trowbridge waved a dismissive hand. "Embroidery, painting, or music would be a keener pastime, but it is not my business how young ladies spend their time. So long as Miss Leila Owen isn't seduced by those demonic novels. Keep a watchful eye, Josiah. You know the ones, full of horror to confuse impressionable women, lead them astray from virtue, convince them towards vice."

With a tilt of her head and an expression of bemusement, Aaditri argued, "I believe my Leila would not be confused between wrong and right, not from a book. Besides, Miss Lambeth here writes gothic novels. I'm certain you don't mean those. She is an exceptionally skilled writer."

Isobel paled as Mr. Trowbridge's gaze turned full on her. She felt the calculating stare, his taking her measure for the second time, this being to determine if she was under the persuasion of "demonic novels." Try as she might, she could not muster a smile. Instead, she remained as an insect beneath his quizzing glare.

Alistair spoke, shaking Mr. Trowbridge's attention away from Isobel. "*Maman* favored the gothic above all others."

His words were said innocently enough, a continuation of the conversation, but Isobel sensed a sort of challenge in his tone, as though daring his father to speak out against the memory of Alistair's mother.

Mr. Trowbridge chose that moment to sip from his teacup, then just over the rim, said quietly, "Explains everything."

Isobel flicked her gaze between Alistair and Mr. Trowbridge, concerned tea was about to take a sinister turn. When no one said anything, but before silence stretched too long, Isobel raised a timid voice to offer, "I think, Mrs. Owen, we shall have enough to look forward to with the Reading outing. What little I saw of it was most exciting. Are you familiar with Reading, or will this be your first time shopping there, as well?"

Taking the bait in stride, Aaditri said, "Let me tease you of the fun we shall have!"

As she listened to all about Reading, Isobel took another sip of her tea. Tepid. She hoped her disappointment did not show in her expression. After all, the temperature should have been perfect for her palate.

After several attempts earlier that day to draft a letter to the solicitor helping with his property search, Alistair had set aside the task for later. He hardly knew where to begin. He could not offer any direction as to whether he could afford a modest cottage or a country manor with farmlands. His frustration had mounted with each quill stroke.

The frustration, he knew, had nothing to do with the house search.

Why had he agreed to remain here?

His father had spent the day with Mr. Owen, not obviously avoiding Alistair but not open for conversation, either. Had it not been *he* who had begged Alistair to stay so they could better know one another?

Thus, Alistair had spent his day rereading Radcliffe's novel. Isobel had been right to choose it, though they had both already read it. It was a needed escape.

The late evening supper proved no more productive than the rest of the day. Mr. Owen did most of the talking. Aaditri offered her words of wisdom periodically, the two keeping the conversation afloat. Alistair was grateful to them both. While they did not know Alistair's intentions to stay in England and resign, they did know a great deal and were, in their own way, supportive of all of Alistair's dreams.

Although Mr. Owen and Alexander Trowbridge had been long-time friends, Aaditri and Alistair's mother had known each other longer, sharing deep bonds. Aaditri would always stand by him, he knew. In addition, Alistair and Mr. Josiah Owen had worked side by side in India for years, Mr. Owen the one to call on Alistair and his mother in the absence of Alexander, and Mr. Owen the one to guide Alistair through the intricacies of Company liaisons. He had never been resentful or otherwise negatively affected when Alistair was promoted as a Company governor over him. If anything, he had acted relieved, for his plan had been — and remained — to win a director position and relocate to England with his family, not stay in India as a governor. It had been a plan long delayed and still remained in the air until the April election. Alistair could not see him losing the election, though. Not this time.

Yes, Alistair was grateful to the Owens for many things, two people who understood much of his situation and were, above all, happy with his choice of Isobel.

It should come as no surprise, then, that as the family gathered in the drawing room that evening, the Owens tried to persuade the situation. Aaditri and Isobel partnered in a card game against Mr. Owen, leaving father and son to find their own entertainment, although they offered ample invitation for the two to join by teaming together. Alexander claimed a preference for observing rather than playing. More than once, Aaditri remarked on the view of the formal garden, even by moonlight, as if to convince them both to walk that way. Neither accepted.

Alistair's concentration slipped throughout their game. A half-hour passed.

His attention fell to his father time and again. If he moved to the window, would his father follow? Did he *want* his father to follow?

There was no time to answer the question, for Alexander stood with a nod to the Owens and crossed the room to look out the window. Invitation or escape?

Alistair thumbed a button on his waistcoat.

One glance at Isobel directed his next move. Her expression was both a command and a question, accompanied by a nod towards his father's retreating back. Those beseeching eyes of hers beguiled him. How could he disappoint her?

With a flick to the button, he said softly to his companions, "If you'll excuse me."

His steps dragged. His thoughts raced.

When he reached his father's side, he said nothing and simply looked out the window. The moon hung bright in the sky, illuminating the formal gardens with eerie beauty, the blooms colorless at night.

His father spoke first. "I didn't know. About your mother, that is. Her..." He circled a hand in search of the words. "...reading preferences. She always loved to read, but it seems her tastes changed."

Replies by the dozen swam through his head, but none passed his lips. Alistair continued to admire the garden in its shades of grey.

"It is difficult for me to speak of her, but I suppose I must, *we* must." Alexander, too, kept his gaze on the garden. "I will never stop loving her. She was my everything. With each of your letters apprising me of the life I was missing — you were a prolific letter writer in your youth, if you'll recall — I felt a widening breach. I questioned everything. Had I been a means for asylum, nothing more?"

Alistair was surprised, shocked, really, as well as moved by his words. This was not the opening conversation he had expected.

Angling towards his father, he said, "I cannot speak for my mother, but she spoke of you with the voice of worship."

"And yet what you said this afternoon... After all these years of loving her as I remembered her, she was like a stranger to me. How could I not know that about her?" He hesitated as though on the verge of saying more but then sighed instead.

Prepared to continue the discussion, however unexpected the direction, the place, and the time, Alistair was further taken aback when his father patted his arm, then excused himself for the evening, leaving the party without his company. To Isobel and the Owens' expectant and confused expressions, Alistair had no explanation.

For another hour, he partnered Isobel against the Owens, determined to enjoy what remained of an otherwise glum day.

When the shadows grew long and the card game lulled, Aaditri asked him, "Did you not say you were a skilled escort?"

He was slow to understand, but when he grasped her meaning, he said, "Ah, yes, it would not do for a young lady to walk alone so late at night. Miss Lambeth, may I escort you across the hall?"

Isobel snorted a laugh. "It is such a *long* walk. And I would *so* hate to become frightened. You are kindness itself to think of my safety."

The Owens dipped their heads with teasing comments to each other, leaving Alistair to tend to his love. They slipped out, both grinning to have a few minutes to themselves.

As they ambled through the reception hall, Isobel said quietly, in case the walls had ears, "Don't leave me in suspense. What did he say?"

"Only a little. About his surprise to learn my mother favored the gothic."

"Disapproval, more like."

Alistair guided them down the hall towards the second-floor staircase. "Perhaps. He spoke more of disappointment not to have known. Isobel, I do not know how to proceed. It was always to be difficult but now there is the barrier of my choice. How to surmount this? What is it worth? We could leave and put him behind us."

"No. It's been one day since you first clapped eyes on each other and a handful of hours since the disagreement. I will encourage you every hour of the day if you need it, but—"

The jib door opened, and Alexander stepped out, lost in thought until he nearly collided with Alistair. Stuttering an apology, he shuffled away without noticing Isobel.

Isobel stammered, "*What* was he doing on the second floor? *My* room is there, and only my room. He knew we were all in the drawing room."

Alistair could see what she was thinking—that his father had been rifling through her things. Inexplicably defensive over a man he had moments ago wanted to leave behind, he accused with an edge of harshness, "Your imagination has turned

an innocent man into a villain from one of your
stories."

Mouth agape, she said, "Alistair! Retrieve both
your insult and insinuation. If I didn't know you
were tense and emotional, despite appearing calmness itself, I would take offense."

He dragged a hand down his face and took a
moment to compose himself. "Many apologies."
Embarrassed by his outburst, he tried again with,
"Perhaps he is a secret lover of the gothic and wished
to read your work?"

Although this elicited a laugh, they both shared
a look that seemed to question again just what his
father had been doing. Then, if his father had mistaken her for a servant....

"The second floor," he questioned, "Is it servant
quarters? I will not accept this. You must be moved
to a proper guest suite."

"Oh no, I like my bedchamber. It's not servant
quarters, really, rather another wing of guest rooms."

He mulled, not entirely satisfied, but said, "I
need your assurance your quarters provide comfort."
When she nodded, smiling her assurance, he accepted,
but his mind returned to his father's presence on the
second floor. Alistair refused to believe his father had
been in Isobel's bedchamber, but if not there, where?

Chapter 15

However muddy the lawn from the evening's rainstorm, Isobel did not allow it to deter her from exploring the grounds as thoroughly as she could. Aaditri had joined for the formal gardens, of which there was a terraced garden overlooked by the drawing room and then, down stone steps, a sunken parterre garden. Once Isobel set out to walk the perimeter — her destinations including the Cedar of Lebanon tree with its purported spicy aroma, the woodland at the far end of the property, and then the yew tree she had been eyeing from her bedchamber window — Aaditri had made her excuses, not wanting to lose a half-boot in the sludge masquerading as a lawn.

With the sun bright, the sky cloudless, and the earth sloshing beneath her feet, Isobel adventured.

There was nothing *not* to admire. She would have enjoyed a walk through the woodland, but she wanted to wait for Alistair to join, if they could arrange to be alone for a walk. Her thoughts wandered to when he had asked her about her ideal home. It was not something she had entertained before. As beautiful as the park, she thought it a waste of good land. Could this not be more useful? Granted, the setting allowed for exquisite views, but she would prefer more woodland, hidden follies, gardens within the woodland, designated paths for riding, and certainly farmland.

Just how many acres was she thinking with this vision? She did not *need* any acreage. It was merely how she would have used *this* land differently. More trees. A larger farm. More riding paths. There. Now, what would *she* want for a house? In a way, she thought the less, the better. Something simple. The more natural light, the better; also, that way, she could save on candles, but then, given the window tax on the number of windows, would having more natural light be a purse saver compared to the expense of candles, or would it work against her rather than in favor? Things a young lady ought not to concern herself with, but things Isobel considered, nonetheless. The newer the home, the better, for less upkeep, or at least sturdy enough construction not to need much upkeep.

Did she fancy having live-in staff? That thought had never crossed her mind, either. In many ways, it would be a delight. Even a lady's maid sounded divine. She did not need one, had never had one to need, but how wonderful to think someone who knew what they were doing could arrange her hair, choose her clothes, mend and adjust her gowns as they became tighter or looser, aid her in all daily efforts that she now saw to herself. In many ways, staff seemed unnecessary, at least for her present living situation, but in the future, she might like to have live-in servants, even if only a few.

She had rounded the property in her walk and was a stone's throw from the yew tree. A narrow, stone bench awaited beneath it, but there was something else, something in front of the bench. Isobel quickened her steps.

Gnarled branches of the ancient yew stretched overhead as though reaching for something unattainable, a few sweeping the ground, searching. Beneath the canopy was a lacework of limbs, spidering a web that cocooned visitors. It shadowed the sky with false evening, the world beyond a halo of light.

The bench was cold to the touch, sending a shiver up Isobel's arm and down her spine. In response, the needle-like leaves whispered in the wind. Bracing for the chill, she sat on the bench. She could hardly see the house from here. The tree was in clear view of the house, though a distance away, but the branches enclosed her from the outside world. Oh! She had forgotten her urgency to arrive. The strange something that had caught her eye. No more than a few steps away was a smooth stone lying in a bed of old yew leaves and soil, a placard of some sort, perhaps with an estimated age of the tree.

Rising, she covered the few steps and knelt before the stone. There was no need to wipe it clear of debris. Its face was clean, pristinely clean, obviously well looked after.

Upon its face read: "Blessed are the pure in heart: for they shall see God. Matthew 5:8"

Isobel's first reaction was to recoil. This was not a tree placard. This was a gravestone. Her next reaction was to weep. This was a child's gravestone. No, a baby's. The size. The scripture. The winged soul effigy. Touching a hand to the stone, she apologized for her initial shock.

Had this not been an old rectory before Mr. Trow-bridge purchased the land? Yes, that was right. This must be a carryover from the rector's time. But the little grave was exceptionally well maintained. Little to no signs of wear, moss, or passage of time, the etchings sharp. Whoever lay here was much loved.

Resuming her seat at the bench, she took in the sanctuary, her thoughts on the baby. She hummed tunelessly. There was no sense of time in this place. All stood still, eternal peace.

A prickle at the back of her neck crept into her meditation. She had the curious sensation of being watched. But out here? There was not another soul in sight, simply the soft whisper of the tree leaves, punctuated with occasional birdsong. Yet she could not shake the feeling.

With a shiver, she took her leave of the gravesite and headed back to the house.

The drawing room was the place to be before tea, Alistair discovered. Isobel had set up her writing box on one side of the room; her view was the Cedar of Lebanon tree. Aaditri had monopolized her husband's attention by convincing him to go another round or five of cards with her. The only person unaccounted for was their host.

This was a promising opportunity to sequester his father. To say what, he was unsure.

He should have brought his book. At least he could appear occupied by the book while he mulled over conversation starters. Instead, he watched Isobel writing, her quill moving fluidly between paper and inkpot. A dip, a dab, a scribble. The quill danced across the slope desk, then back. A dip, a dab, a scribble. Back to the paper, it pirouetted again.

Decided, he excused himself to all in the room, his destination either his father's study or Geoffrey the butler, whichever he encountered first. He did not have to walk far, for no sooner had he stepped into the reception hall than his father stepped out of the study.

"Son," Alexander said, his tone curiously welcoming. "Change into boots and walk with me through the garden?"

Alistair nodded, then took the main stairs two at a time, not wanting to keep his father waiting lest the man change his mind or mood.

In short order, he had changed attire, not wanting to muddy or sweat in his silk. The evening's rain had invited warmer temperatures, at least for England. In a peculiar way, he felt responsible, as though he brought the Indian sun with him. Taking the steps at an angle to quicken his descent, he found his father much in the same place as he had left him.

The two set out.

As they rounded the house, Alistair glanced at the window he knew would display Isobel hard at work. With the glare of the sun, he could not see beyond the glass pane, but he was positive she watched him, perhaps with a grin to see father and son together.

Hands clasped behind his back, Alistair took one slow step in front of the other, admiring the herbaceous borders of the terraced garden before his father guided them to the sunken parterres. There was no denying the beauty of the gardens. Was this a requirement of an English gentleman's home? Alistair thought them frivolous. Beautiful, yes, but frivolous. Would the land not serve better with a purpose? A deer park, perhaps, with an impressive kitchen garden. Certainly riding paths. What was an estate without farmlands, either for one's income or to lease for the additional benefit of tenant profits?

"Is this a whim?" his father asked after they had walked the length of the garden. "Did you arrive on English soil, become star-struck by the aristocracy, and decide you wished for a different life?"

Alistair's first reaction was to take offense, but after two deep breaths, he chose to assume his father's question was genuine, an attempt to understand his son's desire to resign. "No, Father. This has been a long-time plan. It began with Company mandates. I thought myself in a position to right wrongs, to help the people, to turn bad decisions into good, but as time passed, I felt not like a man of power but like a — what is the word… marionette? — yes, a marionette pulled by strings. *Maman* wished me to be a Company man, like you, but after she chose to walk with God, I decided the time had come for a change."

Shaking his head, Alexander harrumphed, then *hmm*ed, then harrumphed again. He took his time before replying as if weighing his words. "But to live as a gentleman without employment? All the prestige you have with the Company will be lost. How are you to support yourself and your family?"

"I am skilled at many things, Father. I can enter into trade if needed, but my vision is to be an English gentleman, one who presides, one who lives by his own cunning rather than the use of his hands. It is no different than my role in India, merely repurposed. I can make the lands work for me. From parklands to farmlands, I can lease, I can profit. I am the marionettist, not the puppet on strings."

"This is not a desire to search for lost youth? To live the London life of late nights, gaming, dancing — the life of youthful indulgence?"

Alistair stopped walking and turned to face his father, his shoulders back. "Look at me. Do you see a *roué* standing before you? A libertine?" Under his father's scrutiny, he said, "Your influence and persuasion have made me the man I am today. That man wishes to wield more than Company commands. I want my own empire, one to prosper under my word, even should that empire be smaller than your lands here. I want *my* empire."

Alexander resumed their walk, Alistair falling in step with his father again. They turned the far corner of the garden and doubled back to weave through a narrow path between parterres. The lines of green were crisp, exacting, boxing bountiful colors, each trimmed with precision.

"I have long wanted you here, son," Alexander said. "Every year, I hoped something would change; your mother would see reason. So long have I waited for you to join me, especially after her death, I hardly know what to do or say now that you're here. I don't wish us to be strangers or at battle. On the contrary, I want to ensure my son's happiness, so long as what brings happiness is in his best interest. I believe I have the experience to determine without prejudice."

"I value your insight. I hope, in return, you will trust in my judgment."

The two paused in the center of the garden, each eyeing the other, each taking the other's measure. Alistair could not read his father's expression, his eyes shuttered, his lips pursed in contemplation, but he hoped this was the beginning of an understanding between them. It was difficult to become familiar with a man who was resistant to all his son said and wanted, a man who did not seek his son's company to open conversation. Every moment of tension incited Alistair to run. If they could reach a truce, at least long enough for casual discussion of all they had missed in each other's lives, he would not be so eager to leave, to cower from confrontation.

Alexander draped a hand over Alistair's shoulders and turned him in the direction of the house. "We've left our guests to their own devices long enough, do you not think?"

The walk to the house was a quiet one, but Alistair felt a pang of hope. His father, after all, had said *we*.

Chapter 16

The next day brought a rare opportunity for Alistair to speak alone with Isobel. With their host needing to confer with the butler after tea, Alistair invited Isobel and the Owens to repair to the terrace. While the lawn had not sufficiently dried by Aaditri's estimation, Alistair managed to persuade them to tour the small, private garden with the central fountain on the opposite side of the house from the drawing room and, conveniently, the study.

The Owens, in their wonderful way, became engaged enough by the fountain to allow Alistair and Isobel to slip away in the direction of the woodland.

As they set out on their own, Isobel's hand on Alistair's sleeve, he asked, "You do not mind I keep you distracted so my father can rummage in your room?"

Isobel turned her head with wide, startled eyes before she laughed aloud, the sound pealing with a delightful ring. "I almost believed you."

"As you should. If my father knew of your talent, he would beg to read your novels." Askance, he admired the blush stealing across her cheeks. "How is our French count? Has he been beheaded yet?"

Aghast, she said, "I do *not* make a habit of beheading my characters, I'll have you know. Besides,

Corentin is too fine a gentleman to lose his head. Honestly, I rewrote the tower rescue scene. It was too melodramatic, even for my taste, and I thought it made Corentin look a right numpty. While he's not reached the tower in the rewrite, he's *inside* the castle and searching out his nemesis in hopes of facing him first."

Alistair listened, enthralled, eager to read. He had liked the original and not found it outlandish, but the bravery to face the villain was more appealing.

"When may I read the new scenes?"

"Two conditions must be met. First, you must swap books with me so that I might have a turn at the *Sicilian* and you can make sense of silly Caleb's tale. Even after finishing it, I'm not certain what to make of it. It's wholly dissatisfactory, in my opinion. The heroes were villains, and the villains were double villains, and *oof*, what a dreadful mess."

"Second?"

"Hmm? Oh! The condition. Yes. Second, you must tell me about your talk with Mr. Trowbridge in the garden. I watched the two of you pacing up and down the garden, back and around, to and fro, in and out; good heavens the two of you made me dizzy with all the walking—keeping in mind, I could only see your shoulders and heads bobbing about once you took the steps down—so naturally, I've been biting my nails to know what was said. No wink, no frown, no note through a discreet footman: nothing. I'm in utter suspense!"

They reached the edge of the woodland, but rather than enter the narrow path, they turned back, neither wanting to risk being out of sight of the Owens— their matchmaking only went so far, after all. Isobel waggled her eyebrows and nodded her head to the distant yew tree in the opposite direction.

Slowing his strides, his eyes on the ground before him, he said, "A beginning, I hope. Nothing more. Nothing less. He questioned my reasons and goals, but with interest, not accusation. We have one week before departing for London. I must confront him before then to know the way forwards. I think I will wait a few days; then I will insist he chooses to stand with me or against me."

He listened to their footsteps before saying more. A soft swish of each step. The grass smelled of mossy earth, not unpleasant like a humid bog, but rather like fresh morning dew with its promises of a new day.

"When I confront my father, I will express my intentions towards you. I want nothing left unsaid, no secrets untold. Now that you've met him, seen from what stock I am bred, seen my cowardly behavior beneath his brow, how do you consider my intentions?"

"You're not cowardly. At least not to me. Never to me." Removing her hand from his sleeve, she looped it under his elbow and clasped his arm snuggly. "I'm more determined than ever to proceed."

He waited for her to say more, and with each glance at her, it seemed she was on the cusp of making a joke, perhaps about him being her most devoted reader, or having seen how he might age, she did not want to miss out, or whatever possible tease she could say, but instead, she left it, and he rather thought it was perfectly said as it was.

"Pleasing words," he said in response. "I will not know what to write to the solicitor until I have my father's answer, but if we are hopeful, I can express an interest in the manor with tenants or the larger estate, however overbold."

He could see the pucker of her brows even from this angle.

"Not to sound daft, but… of *what* are you referring?"

"The properties I've viewed."

Her steps slowed to a stop. "You've been *house searching*?"

"Of course. I had found my bride, and so I knew we must then have a house. What else could I offer you except my name since my estate would not be mine much longer?"

"Wait. When I met you, you were betrothed to someone else. We've only been courting, not officially, for less than a month — no, it would be two weeks if we don't count this week with your father. You had yet to tell me of your plans to resign. We're not betrothed. But you were *house searching*?"

He shrugged, a bashful smile playing at the corners of his lips. "I knew I would have you as my wife, so I saw no reason not to proceed."

She laughed, the sound on the edge of hysterical. "But you had no way of knowing I would say *yes*! I haven't said yes, for that matter. You've not asked."

Chagrined but still confident, he said, "I know you will say yes. I would not ask if I did not know this."

Throwing her head back, she laughed heartily, so heartily, he could feel the tips of his ears burning with an embarrassment he did not often feel.

"How is it," she said between bouts of raucous laughter, "I manage to fall for the most arrogant man in all of England? You, sir, would out-arrogant the prince himself."

Alistair's cringing smile deepened into a smirk. "Ah, you see. You admit you have fallen for me. There can be no doubt. You will say yes."

Isobel tossed her gaze heavenward, then tugged him to the yew tree. "I want to show you something."

They ducked beneath the centurion branches, the leafy canopy a shield. Alistair made for the bench, then took a seat after Isobel had found comfort. Laying his hand over hers against the cold stone, he laced their fingers.

"Did you find a house?" she asked, sober, although her voice still smiled in remembered laughter.

"Several, but none were for us."

She hummed in response so quietly he did not think she was aware she was doing so.

When she did not reply, he ventured, "There was something said I have not understood. Something the solicitor said. At one property, he warned that 'my kind' might not be welcomed. Because I'm Persian?"

"Oh, that was rude of him."

"He meant it as a kindness, to forewarn before purchase."

Isobel squeezed his hand. "Was it an estate?"

"Yes. An abbey with ample acreage and existing tenancies."

"Ooh. An abbey. That sounds inspiring, doesn't it?" Her tone was wistful, and her expression glazed with a dream-like quality. Then, wrinkling her nose, she said, "I'd wager the upkeep is terrible. No, maybe not an abbey."

Returning to her humming, she stared back towards the fountain where the Owens were sharing quiet conversation. Although her expression was so distant, he did not think she saw them.

With an *Oh!* she said, "I beg your pardon. I forgot to answer your question. I lost myself wandering an imaginary abbey. In answer, I don't think it had anything to do with you being Persian. In fact, because of the East India Company's expansions and affiliations, you would be quite the sensation here, as everyone would assume you were some sort of influential nawab, and thus they would wish to know you — you must realize the country is full of sycophants. No, I think he meant because you *worked* for the Company. I assume you told him? If you didn't, then I'm mistaken, but — "

"Yes, my beauty, I told him."

"Right, then, there you have it. The locals would assume anyone who took possession of a property like that to be a gentleman, so to have a *working* man take possession, well, it would not be the thing, would it? But you *will* be a gentleman soon, assuming all goes well with Mr. Trowbridge. If not, I don't mind if we live in a one-room cottage with a dirt floor and only drink watered-down tea that tastes of mule dung and hay, the Bradleys our only guests."

He chuckled. "I think you *would* mind, although you may think you would not, but I appreciate the sentiment. I am also at ease with your words about the solicitor. I had not thought of the Company. In India, to work with the Company is a great honor and a garnering of respect. One says proudly their position with the Company."

"Not here. Mind, I don't consort with anyone like that. It reminds me of how surprised I was about

Viscount Dunley's reaction. I can only assume he misunderstood your position, thinking you a high-powered figure in India liaising with the Company rather than employed by it. You certainly won his affection."

He thought about this and about what the solicitor had said. Not wanting to waste their time alone, he tucked the thoughts into the back of his mind. Leaning close enough for his arm to rub against hers, he angled his head low and pressed his forehead to her temple, inhaling the subtle scent of rose water.

"You've shown me a trysting place, *nazanin*. Yet we have not taken advantage of the privacy."

"Oh!" She jolted away from him. "No, look. *This* is what I wanted to show you."

Pulling him off the bench, she dragged him towards a ground stone and knelt before it. He followed suit.

To his surprise, it was a small grave. So unexpected, he forgot to be disappointed at his stolen moment.

Isobel looked from him to the grave. "It looks new."

"Impossible." Alistair shook his head. "Must be from the rector's living."

"Or a servant. What if a maid found herself in the family way, then something happened, but since your father is *not* a villain, he did not turn her away but rather offered this burial for the baby? In this way, the maid can visit the gravestone often."

He did not know his father well enough to say if the man would be so magnanimous. It was not likely a servant would share the news with an employer, rather would try to hide the condition for as long as possible, but he could say nothing with certainty.

"Or," he countered, "It is from the rector's living, and the gardener wishes to maintain it from kindness."

"Oh, you're probably right. That makes more sense than my unvirtuous maid, although it lacks drama."

With a quick kiss to her temple, he said, "Shall we rejoin the Owens?" Standing, he offered a hand to help her rise.

After church service at nearby St. Mary's, Mr. Trowbridge invited Alistair for a ride. Isobel was positively giddy. For them to have more time together would mean so much to Alistair, even if he would not readily admit how much he wished to know his father. Isobel hoped this boded well. Not only for their getting to know each other better, but also for Mr. Trowbridge's acceptance of his son's plans.

With Alistair and Mr. Trowbridge out, Mr. Owen offered to busy himself with business and correspondence, leaving Isobel and Aaditri to take tea together.

Aaditri nursed her teacup. "All is proceeding well with our young man."

"Yes, I think he and his father only need more time together."

"I was referring to *you*."

"Oh." Isobel blushed, peering into her teacup, unable to hide the grin.

"You will like India. I will miss you, but you will like it there. You will be hostess to his parties and have much to keep you occupied. I have friends you will want to meet, although you'll make your own in time."

Her grin waning, Isobel all but whispered, "I won't be going to India."

Aaditri's teacup clattered against its saucer. With trembling hands, she set it on the table. "Is it an argument? Something he said? Something not to your liking?"

"No, no, nothing of that nature," Isobel hastened to clarify. "*We* won't be going to India." She chewed on her bottom lip before confessing, "I ought not to say anything since it's currently a point of contention between him and his father. I hate to hide anything from you, though. Could we wait to tell Mr. Owen until Mr. Trowbridge has accepted Alistair's decision? You see, Alistair has decided to stay in England."

Hand to her heart, Aaditri's eyes watered. "He *and* Josiah will be with us at last. It is a sacrifice. His estate is bountiful, his position notable."

At least three biscuits later and a refill of tea, they had lightly talked of Aaditri's move to England and life apart from Mr. Owen, her pleasure over her daughter's choice with Mr. Knowlton and how pleased she was by his family, and Aaditri's memories of Alistair's mother.

The teapot empty, Aaditri looked out the window as though eager to walk the garden. "A lovely view from my window. One can better take in the sunken garden from the first floor. A pleasing parterre design. Oh, but you can't see it from your window, can you? How thoughtless of me."

"Not at all. I have the view of the fountain and, in the distance, the yew tree."

"Oh, yes, that's right. I did think the little garden was a perfect oasis, so private. Let me see, the only windows overlooking would be Mr. Trowbridge's apartments and your window from the second floor. I'm happy the view is not wasted."

Isobel hesitated, her thoughts on last night. "There's another window that overlooks the garden, just past my room. Only, I can't say what's there, as the door is locked. Not that I was snooping," she added with a laugh.

Aaditri raised her eyebrows. "If I had to guess, I would say the second floor is the bachelor wing, being with easy entry to the billiard room. I've not been there. Is your room pleasant? Warm enough? Cool enough? Comfortable?"

"Oh yes, perfectly! It's a perfect snug for this writer. Yes, simply perfection." Another hesitation, and then, "You'll think me silly, or possibly nosy, but do you know what's behind the locked door? More rooms, perhaps? I ask because there's a lovely threshold before it, and I thought it perfect for performing, if not before an audience, then in acting out a scene or two while I'm writing only I would hate to disturb anyone or they think me mad if there were servant quarters beyond there." Her rambling drifted as she realized she was, in fact, rambling.

The explanation was innocent enough and not untrue, except the question sounded rude to Isobel's ears. What business of hers was it to question locked doors? It was likely the door to the attic, or as she said, servant quarters or storage, or as Aaditri had suggested, guest rooms for bachelors, only unused and thus closed off for now.

Aaditri shook her head and, with a dismissive air, said, "I've many locked doors at Nasrin, including in the kitchen where we keep the tea."

That settled it. Isobel felt and looked like a ninny. Any thought to mention she had seen the key in the keyhole, locked from the inside, would make her sound barmy. Clearly, she had misremembered and seen a keyhole cover, not a key.

Only, well, last night, she could have sworn she heard voices. Hushed, whispered, so faint it could have been the wind. Then, if the door led to the attic for storage, the servants would use it any time they needed, most logically when the family was abed so as not to disturb them. So vivid her imagination that she had not thought of the most logical explanation at the time. Thank heavens for the light of day.

Chapter 17

Alistair refilled his teacup. Across from him, his father ran a finger around the rim of his own cup. Early that morning, his valet had nudged him in the direction of his father's study, following an invitation to break his fast there. However good had been the ride the day before, however increasingly comfortable he was becoming in his father's presence, he thought it too soon to confront him about the resignation. They had until Saturday, after all. Saturday, they would leave for London. As eager as he had been to demand acceptance, after the ride, he discovered he was enjoying Alexander's company too much to break this new spell.

His father.

They were novel concepts: he and his father in the same room, he and his father learning about each other, and he and his father sharing a laugh.

What required a reminder was his father was *not* a storybook villain. He had not abandoned his son and wife, no matter how it felt for so many years. Alexander only wanted his son to make decisions he would not regret, allowing his heart to overrule his head. Alistair would do well to remember these points.

And so, he made free to enjoy his father's company, exchanging anecdotes over breakfast.

Alexander tipped his cup towards him, then reached over to the teapot to refill. "Aaditri enjoyed the confections we brought yesterday. Your quick thinking to bring gifts has increased my standing with my guests." He chuckled. "Kind of you to think of the companion, as well."

Meeting his father's eyes, Alistair saw the opening he needed. He had not planned to discuss Isobel until after the resignation had been revisited, but....

"About Miss Lambeth," he began, setting his cup down and straightening his posture.

Alexander stood, turning his back to his son to look out the window, his teacup and saucer in hand. "I beg a moment, son. We've almost polished the tray, and yet I've not spoken what's foremost on my mind. I fear if I don't say it now, I'll lose heart."

Leaning back, Alistair propped an elbow on the chair arm.

When his son did not reply, he said, "I understand your choice. I don't agree with it. I think it foolhardy if you must know. To rely on one's own estate for income, to set aside a lucrative and powerful position... it's... it's illogical. But I understand. Where I'm most torn about your decision is if you come to regret it, my hands may be tied such that I cannot secure you a return into the Company." He waved a hand, his back still turned to Alistair. "Don't mistake me. I maintain considerable control. If I want something done, it will be done. But there is more than one's desire to take into account, and to find you a new position after resigning from a joint-stock Company, well, it would not be without challenges."

Alistair sat still, afraid to breathe lest his father change his tune. Even now, Alexander was discussing Alistair's return to the Company. Approval was not needed. Alistair could resign without attending the meeting. He could afford a place of his own, however humble. He did not need his father's approval. For reasons he could not voice, he *wanted* it.

His father drank from his cup; the only sounds were the clink of cup to saucer between each sip and faint birdsong outside.

At length, he turned around. "I will stand by you at the meeting when you resign. You will want, of course, to apprise us of the situation abroad, especially of the new governor-general, and offer recommendations for your successor. You've served your role admirably, and it's not a father's pride to say the Company will bemoan your loss. I should like, if you're amenable, to discuss shareholding options. It would ease my mind about your financial security. Now, to a more pressing point. If you've no objection, I would value investing in your future in so far as you'll allow. Do you have an eye for an estate already? They do not come available often, so have you considered leasing in the short term?"

Alistair closed his eyes, his head spinning, overwhelmed with possibility and promise. His father supported his decision. *This*, above all, was what he wanted. Nothing was impossible now. A *family* was not impossible now. A relationship with his father was not impossible now.

He wanted nothing more in this moment than to dart out the door, find Isobel, and share the good tidings.

Unable to hide the pleasure from his expression, he leaned forwards in his chair. "Thank you, Father. It means more than words can convey to have your acceptance. I did not wish to stand in opposition to the man I have so admired."

Alexander returned to his chair, setting his empty cup on the tray. "We'll need to share the news with Josiah before leaving. A shame he's running for a director position rather than vying for promotion in India. I would motion for him to take your place. Alas, this will be his fourth attempt to run as a director, and I will not allow him to lose the election. The way of the Company is a curious thing, me winning my first election all those years ago only to learn the win non-retractable once your mother informed me she would not be joining me, and yet Josiah has fought all these years for a return to England while his family lived apart in anticipation of his arrival. It's in my power to ensure his wish is granted."

Although Alexander's point had been about Josiah, the words of Alistair's mother caught his attention. "Why did she stay?" He knew her views as she had shared them, but was there more? Did he want to know if there was more?

With palms out in a helpless shrug, Alexander offered, "I've asked myself that every day since I bid her farewell. We were happy, you understand, as far as I knew. She never gave any indication of wanting to be apart from me. There were even promises of us united again, as though she would join in the future." He drummed his fingers against his waistcoat, deep in thought. "I don't wish to lessen your mother's memory, as she was my first choice, my first love, my first wife, but, you see, son, there comes a time in life when we must move forwards, when we realize the life we had intended was not to be. We must make way for a new life, new opportunities."

Believing he knew where his father was heading in this discussion, he seized his chance. "You're correct, Father. I'm pleased you see from my perspective. It was not to be with Miss Owen, but by rejecting the arrangement, I was able to open my heart and mind."

Alexander's fingers stilled as he stared at his son, at first with furrowed brows and confusion, as though not comprehending a shift in conversation. As dawning enlightened, his hands moved to the arms of his chairs, his fingers furling around the wood.

"I intend to offer my hand to Miss Isobel Lambeth."

Spluttering, his father questioned, "The *companion*?" He pushed himself out of the chair to pace behind it. "If you've got a servant in trouble, son—"

Alistair sat up straight and said with force, "I will not hear filth. Miss Lambeth is not a companion. She is *my* guest and a friend of the Owen family."

"Then what the devil is she doing serving as Aaditri's companion? If I was made to believe she was a servant so you could bring your doxy—"

Alistair stood, his fingers curling into his palms. "She is a gentleman's daughter. *You* mistook her for a servant. Aaditri introduced her as she was, a friend of Miss Leila Owen. As a gentleman's daughter, she's more respectable than anyone in this house, and I will not have you speak foul words about her."

Alexander crossed his arms over his chest, but his pacing stopped. He considered Alistair's words before echoing, "A gentleman's daughter?"

"Yes," was all Alistair said.

Resuming his seat, Alexander leaned forwards to rest his forearms on his legs. "An impressive dowry, no doubt. With her father to introduce you to other gentlemen, I suppose. I can see your interest."

"You're mistaken." As the heat of the moment passed, Alistair, too, returned to his chair, but he remained on his guard. "Her father is taking tea with *Maman*. Miss Lambeth has no dowry."

"You threw over my friend's daughter for love? The match of the year, son—all so you could follow your heart." He shook his head. "If I hadn't done the same, I wouldn't have you sitting in my study. Well, it's your heart, your choice. I've not had a proper look at the girl. Things will change now that I'm to understand she's to be my daughter-in-law. Why didn't you introduce her? Why not write to tell me? A gentleman's daughter. I won't deny I'm relieved. Forgive my initial shock."

"I would have written about her, brought her as my intended, but we had, I believe, more pressing matters before us."

"For pity's sake—she didn't bring a lady's maid, and I've not provided one," he said, ignoring Alistair's reply. "What must she think of me? No, don't answer. I'm ashamed to be a poor host." As the conversation lulled, Alexander said, "I have more to say, confessions that need to be made, long overdue, but I believe, once I've made them, you'll understand the secrecy. I don't think now is the time. This is about you, not me. Let us make plans for your future, and you can tell me more about this Miss Lambeth who has stolen your heart."

"We have spoken of me, Father. Please, say what is on your mind."

"No, no. It'll keep. Shall we ring for a fresh pot, or have you had your fill of tea?"

Alistair laughed at the ridiculousness of there being too much tea.

By the time Isobel needed to change for dinner — said dinner being held later than usual given how distracted her host had been all day — she had only seen Alistair from a distance, he and his father spending most of the day together. Unless she was mistaken, Alistair had smiled a time or two, the tension ebbing from his shoulders. Mr. Owen had not been left to his own devices for long, as he joined their ranks before tea, leaving Aaditri and Isobel to take tea alone. It was just as well since this would be their lot once the gentlemen proceeded to London — Aaditri and Isobel to serve as the ladies of the manor in their absence, or so the two jested.

Her writing box tucked under her arm after an afternoon of writing, she headed for her room to refresh. The path down the hall and through the jib door was becoming familiar, her private retreat. The stairs up were narrow but not dark or pokey. There was nothing artistic about the staircase, unlike the engraved wood of the main stairs, but a high dormer window invited natural light during the day and moonlight during the evening, at least when there was moonlight to be had.

Opening the top stairwell door, she stepped out to the second floor. A hand to her bedchamber door, she leaned towards the sitting room to eye the locked door at the far end. Wind had whispered past her door more than once last night. Curious how wind could throw its voice to sound so much like it came from *inside* rather than outside.

With a shrug, she pushed open her door. No more than one foot into the room, she shrieked and shielded herself with the writing box. Standing in the middle of the room was a young woman.

The stranger bobbed a curtsy. "Ever so sorry, miss. Never wanted to startle you."

Isobel blinked, taking in the young woman. A maid. Yes, Isobel could see that now. A sweet-faced maid.

With a tight smile that Isobel hoped was not as awkward as it felt, she said, "No apologies needed. I wasn't startled. Merely, er, not expecting someone to be in the room."

"Mr. Trowbridge said you're to have a lady's maid, miss, seeing as how you didn't bring your own. I hope I'll do. However you've managed without your own is anyone's guess, but I'll not disappoint you. I've already chosen a dinner gown and all."

Isobel blinked again. A *lady's maid*? She had never had a lady's maid in her life. What did one *do* with a lady's maid? Her evening attire had already been chosen? She stood in the doorway, writing box held tight, waffling on what to do or say. Why had Mr. Trowbridge insisted she — *oh. Oh! Oooh.* Her stomach knotted. Alistair must have told his father.

The maid watched her, still and expectant.

"Thank you," Isobel said, taking tentative steps further into the room. "How thoughtful." At a loss as to what more to say, she gave another half-smile, then set her writing box aside.

"You'll be wanting to rest, miss. I've prepared your toilette if you wish to wash first, warmed the sheets should you wish to nap after, and set out all you'll require for dinner. I have the perfect styling in mind for your hair now that I've seen it. Shall I help you undress?"

Overwhelmed, Isobel chortled nervously. "I don't even know your name."

"Julia." She dipped another curtsy.

"Right. Well, then. You know what's best. I'm at your command."

Julia eyed Isobel with curiosity before taking control of the situation. Isobel found the lady's maid a curiosity of her own, quite bossy, really. As unnerving as it was to have someone else in her suite, especially for changing and washing, it did not take long to loosen her tension and allow Julia to apply her skilled ministrations. In fact, as awkward as it *should* have been, the maid knew what to do so that everything seemed natural and efficient, so much so that by the time Isobel slipped off into a short nap, she could not recall how she had managed her whole life without Julia's expertise.

After dinner, they gathered in the drawing room. Isobel hoped no one noticed her hand repeatedly touching her coiffure. She had never had braids before, never ribbons interwoven. The feel of the silken strands against her fingertips brought a grin to her lips with each feathered touch. A pity her gown was still an old one that refused to fit correctly. Of the selection to choose from, Julia had done admirably better than Isobel would have, but one could only do so much to make a sack attractive.

What she hoped would steal everyone's attention was not her hair or her dowdy gown but Mr. Trowbridge. Pride in his son was written in the lines on his face. There could be little doubt the two had come to some sort of understanding.

Alistair's gaze flicked often to Isobel, his eyes conveying all she thought he wished to share. She could only guess the meaning in each glance.

Mr. Trowbridge had dominated the conversation through dinner and now again in the drawing room, unusual to his reserved behavior before today. He laughed considerably more, punctuating most of his anecdotes with a hearty chuckle. Given Mr. Owen was perpetually jovial, the two made quite an entertaining pair.

"Shall we all venture into Reading tomorrow?" Mr. Trowbridge asked.

Aaditri's expression shone with delight and surprise. "*All* of us? Together?" She reached a hand over the arm of her chair to clasp Isobel's forearm. "We shall have far more to do and see with the gentlemen joining, *azizam*. I think I will not be the only one pampering you tomorrow."

Isobel was both quizzical and eager at the twinkle in Aaditri's eyes. Just what did she have in mind when she said "pampering"? Sparing a glance at Alistair deepened the mystery. He shared the twinkle.

Alistair teased, "Untold treasures await you, Miss Lambeth."

"Miss Lambeth." Mr. Trowbridge turned his attention to her with an intensity that straightened her posture. "Mr. Owen tells me you've been his daughter's friend since childhood."

Isobel looked from face to face at the table, unsure about being the center of attention. "Yes, she's my closest neighbor. Once we discovered our love for books, we were inseparable."

Aaditri's voice brightened to be discussing her daughter. "Leila took to our Miss Lambeth far earlier than that. When they were only babies, Mrs. Lambeth was on several committees, of which I, too, was a member, and still am, although of one I'm now committee president, but point being, she brought her daughter, and I brought mine." Turning to Isobel, she asked, "Do you not remember?"

Isobel laughed. "How good do you think a baby's memory to be? My earliest of Leila was the two of us tugging at a book, each wanting to read it. I can't recall when we met or what came before, but we would have been friends earlier than that memory, I'm sure. By that point, we were old enough to read."

"You were often at our house." Aaditri said. "Mrs. Lambeth was a good neighbor and loved her committee work, but then, she changed. That is not a conversation for now, though, is it?"

Mr. Trowbridge had been listening intently, Isobel could see, not missing a single vowel. He cleared his throat and said, "Mr. Owen mentioned some kind of sewing society you and Miss Owen participate in together."

Cringing, Isobel chided, "Embroidery is the bane of my existence, as Mrs. Owen will tell you. I couldn't thread a needle without her help." Isobel almost clamped a hand over her mouth. Perhaps airing her weaknesses when it came to a lady's accomplishments was not in her favor. Hiding her embarrassment with a shy smile, she hastened to add, "Oh! But Mr. Owen remembers so well what Leila and I enjoy. It is indeed a society, but a literary one."

"My Leila is a poet, I'll have you know!" Mr. Owen exclaimed with pride but also a dawning as though only now remembering that fact.

"Just as Mr. Owen said," Isobel continued, "she's a poet, and you've already discovered I write those dreadful gothic novels. Yes, we're part of a literary society, nothing fancy, only the four of us in Sidvale. There's Leila, of course, and me, and then two of our friends, both of whom have publications releasing within the year."

Was she talking too much? Was she rambling? She tried to still her hands from wringing in her lap.

Aaditri offered, "Tell Mr. Trowbridge about the retreat." Before Isobel could do just that, Aaditri said to their host, "Mrs. Randall hosted a writing retreat recently. The girls attended. I believe it was inspiring, yes? Leila returned with many new poems written, and Isobel had caught an itch for playwrighting, which led to no end of fun. Is that not so?" She looked at Alistair.

A glance at his father, he said, "We playacted in a home theatrical, you see. I was, I think, heroic, but in hindsight, I might have been written as a villain. I cannot say."

Isobel blushed as Mr. Trowbridge's eyebrows rose. Indeed, Alistair *had* been the villain, but she had not the heart to write him as such, so despite Leila's pleas to make Mr. Knowlton the hero and Alistair the villain, Isobel had written two heroes, albeit of different motivations.

Mr. Owen chimed in with, "I fancy myself of actor material. I would cut a dashing figure if given a chance. Shame we're not planning a theatrical." He eyed Isobel in invitation, as though wanting her to say she would plan that very thing.

Aaditri said, "Isobel was telling me about a little stage on the second floor we could use."

Mr. Trowbridge stood, saying hastily and gruffly, "No one will disturb the peace of the second floor. Now, let us all take advantage of the night air and retire to the terrace, shall we? We can further plan our Reading outing. Can I tempt everyone with promises of a bookshop in town?"

What could have been the end of the conversation metamorphosed into further discussion as they took to the terrace garden, the night air the right combination of warm with a cool breeze.

Alistair said, "I believe, Father, you will lose us — that is, Miss Lambeth and myself — in a bookshop. We enjoy exchanging our reading experiences. Presently, we are sharing thoughts about two different novels, one being by Radcliffe."

"Is that so?" Mr. Trowbridge looked from Alistair to Isobel, likely not the least interested but doing a fair job of feigning it, so much so, that Isobel could not resist the bait.

"Oh, yes, Mr. Trowbridge. We've each already read this Radcliffe novel, but we're reading it again. It is a delicious tale where the father turns out to be the villain. He's imprisoned his wife, if you can believe that. But there's so much more — "

Alistair added, "Don't forget the poison."

" — there's even a poisoning! And all the dreadful horror one expects from these tales."

Alistair added, "Miss Lambeth finds inspiration within the pages."

"But not of poisoning!" she clarified hastily. "Currently, I'm writing a story about a French émigré. I assure you, no one dies in my book's plot."

Mr. Trowbridge leaned against one of the stone statues on the terrace, the candlelight from inside the drawing room reflecting on his face to reveal sheer amusement at the conversation. Isobel could not deny her relief, given the last time the topic had arisen, he had expressed distaste for the genre, not to mention judgment.

A glance at Alistair, he asked, "And you enjoy these novels, son?"

"I do. Not all of life is business meetings and politics. Tell him, Miss Lambeth, of Julia's plight. Perhaps we can tempt him to become a reader."

"Julia? How did you know my — Oh! The heroine of *A Sicilian Romance*! What a curiosity that is. Julia also happens to be the name of my new lady's maid. I must share this with her and see if she's as amused as I am — but I've not thanked you, Mr. Trowbridge."

By the time the Owens joined the conversation after their turn about the terrace, Isobel was feeling confident, exuberant, only a touch self-aware that she may be rambling, but Alistair and his father both continued to goad and prompt with more questions, encouraging her chatter. If she were rambling, they would change topics, would they not? And so, with the smile of a sunny day and with braids in her hair, she stole the stage, happy at last not to be thought of as a companion.

Chapter 18

Isobel awoke with a start. The dark of night engulfed her. No light shone by which to adjust her sight. A moonless night. Tugging her bedsheets beneath her chin, she nestled against the feathered mattress to resume her dream — the next scene of her Corentin story, if she correctly recalled.

Creak.

Her ears perked.

The groan of leather?

She strained to listen.

Scratch.

A pencil against parchment?

Groan.

A floorboard?

Scuffle.

Footsteps?

Yes. Footsteps in the adjacent sitting room. Erratic, slow, ungainly. A step, then a moan — a protesting floorboard or a disgruntled ghost?

Isobel clenched the sheets. Was that whimpering she could hear?

Scrape.

Something drew closer. She squeezed her eyes closed, afraid to open them, afraid she would see more than darkness, afraid she would see nought but darkness.

A whisper, faint as an August breeze, exhaled from beyond her bedchamber door.

Clink.

Isobel awoke with a start. Her eyes darted around the brightly lit room, the morning sun streaming through the window. Beside the bed, Julia dragged a tray across the table.

"Oh!" Isobel cried in alarm.

Julia blanched. "Ever so sorry, Miss Lambeth. It seems I'm determined to startle you every which way." With a wave to the tray, she added, "Cup of chocolate to greet the morning. I've chosen the perfect gown for your journey into Reading, when you're ready, that is." Dipping a curtsy, she bowed out.

Isobel sat up, eyeing the tray and steaming cup. What had she been dreaming? *Had* she been dreaming? Surreptitiously, she glanced askance at the bedchamber door. It held its silence, secretive and reserved.

The scent of chocolate took precedence. Rubbing her hands together, Isobel fortified for the day's adventure.

Some time later, wearing a worn pair of half boots that pinched her heels and squeezed her toes, a freshly ironed walking gown, and her best bonnet, Isobel watched out the carriage window as the landscape changed in reverse of her journey to Burghfield from Reading. Now, she headed into the borough, an eager smile on her lips and an elevation to her pulse.

As the houses sprang into view and the number of horses on the road doubled, she looked from the window to Aaditri and back, so animated, Aaditri laughed with her every glance.

Both Aaditri and Mr. Owen teased her for much of the drive. She loved every second. After all, it was not every day a young lady had the pleasure of touring so large a place as Reading. It may not be London, but since she had never been to London, Reading might as well have been just that to Isobel. Alistair and Mr. Trowbridge rode alongside the carriage. Mr. Trowbridge had offered the excuse of not wanting too cramped of quarters, but Isobel suspected he wished more time with his son. She hoped she was correct. When the road was wide enough, Alistair paced her window, stealing glances with flirty eyes. As the road narrowed, he disappeared from view, he and his father either ahead or behind the carriage; Isobel could not say with certainty.

The road straightened for long stretches, flat farmland, paddocks, and empty fields of green scenery, but each turn and curve brought a new cottage or farmhouse to admire. After one particularly wide curve, she could make out a coaching inn along marshy flats. It was busier than she would have expected. Before she could take a good look at it, the carriage turned another corner and then came to a rather abrupt stop.

Isobel looked again from Aaditri to Mr. Owen. Outside, she could hear shouting. She could not discern what was said over the whinnying of horses, creaks of the carriage as it rocked, and wheels over rough-hewn stone. The shouts did not sound alarming or unfriendly. Someone laughed in the distance. Craning, she tried to see past the horses, but all she could see was a line of trees to either side.

The carriage rocked into motion, but with care, moving so close to the tree line, Isobel could have plucked the leaves from the branches had she opened the window. Horse hoofs clippity-clopping, wheels turning, a carriage groaning, and then *whoosh* — past the opposite window to Isobel's seat flew another carriage heading to Burghfield. Her carriage picked up pace, and before she knew it, they were crossing a stone bridge, a river flowing below. She pressed her face to the window to take it all in. Fishermen lined the banks. She waved at one stout fellow who watched their passing over the River Kennet.

The view disappointed after that, at least until further afield. The sides of the road were overgrown with trees and hedges. They had to make room for another passing carriage, but otherwise, she only saw trees and more trees until... *Reading*! They must be soon to arrive! Trees gave way to cottages, each at increased intervals until the housing was terraced and fairly lined the road straight into... oh, not Reading. Not yet. They stopped at a tollgate, then carried onto a turnpike. The road widened, and the traffic increased, the houses becoming aged trees with arching, gnarled branches. Just when she thought they had arrived, they seemed farther away than ever. Her excitement did not dim.

However tempting to sit back against the bench and let the carriage roll its way while she carried on a conversation with Aaditri and Mr. Owen, she could not keep her eyes from the rolling landscape, her thoughts on the lives of each person she spotted, each house she passed, each horse that cantered in the opposite direction. The few who stayed in view long enough earned brief tales. In one field, she spied Mr. Evans tending to his chattel, his thoughts on that evening when his daughter and wife would return from London after a grand day of shopping for a new gown for her upcoming nuptials — his surprise gift to her after a particularly successful market day. Oh! And in that field must be Mr. Davies, the father of the bridegroom, obviously, the two being neighbors and all.

Isobel flashed a smile at Aaditri and Mr. Owen, the two deep in conversation about something that kept Aaditri giggling. Isobel had not been listening.

When she turned back, she was surprised to see houses again. Happy terraces lined the road. Traffic steadily increased as carriages, people, horses, and sedan chairs turned from one direction or another, first one or two, then five or ten. Their carriage had to slow to a crawl as the road populated.

And that was when she knew they *had* arrived.

As they reached a wide and muddy crossroads of chaos, the carriage pulled to one side and stopped. Isobel did not know where to look next. The red brick buildings? The wattle-and-daub timber frame buildings? The stone buildings? The tall castle-like structure she could spy hiding behind the line of buildings? The sedan chairs whizzing by? The parasols twirling in a rainbow array? Before she could decide, the carriage door opened.

"Well, well, I hope we won't be a bother." Mr. Trowbridge ducked inside to squeeze next to Mr. Owen.

Aaditri joined Isobel on her side of the carriage in time for Alistair to shoulder his way next to his father, angling so all three gentlemen could fit on the seat, albeit crammed and looking downright uncomfortable.

Alistair's eyes sought Isobel's. His grin spoke of missing her for the past hour, wishing he had been part of whatever fantasies she had weaved along the way and promising her an excitement-filled day.

Everyone was talking at once, so Mr. Trowbridge had to raise his voice to say, "Thought we'd take a roundabout way to complete the tour. Coachman's going to take us south down Seven Bridges, then back up London Street, where he'll drop us off at Broad."

Without awaiting a reply, he racked the roof of the carriage, and it lurched forwards into the traffic. Isobel swayed with the motion, her heart in her throat, her palms perspiring in her gloves. A glance out the window. A glance to Alistair. A glance out the window. A glance back to Alistair. He chuckled.

Mr. Trowbridge demanded attention with his voice of authority and... enticement. "Reading is the place to live. I anticipate you'll all move here once you see what it has to offer." He waggled his eyebrows at Alistair and Isobel. "Ironworks, brewers, cheese fair — what's not to love?"

Mr. Owen said, "Traffic."

Just as he spoke the word, the carriage jolted as a pair of sedan chair bearers darted in front of it, followed by a string of shouting and cursing not fit for Isobel's ears.

Mr. Trowbridge was undaunted. "All part of her charm, Josiah. She's a major coaching route now. Even traffic along the rivers, what with the Kennet Navigation open. We can thank Parliament for moving to London, at least. Otherwise, we would have *that* to contend with, as well. Did you know that, Miss Lambeth? Parliament met in Reading once upon a time."

Isobel shook her head.

"The plague moved the lot to London."

At her widening eyes, he laughed.

The plague? She could sense a story forming already. A visiting noble, Italian, perhaps. The threat of plague was nigh. Parliament was in session. Oooh, she could see it all now.

Mr. Trowbridge had already moved on to talk of other things. "Turn away from the unsavory parts. It's been nearly a decade since the Act of Parliament to pave the streets, enlist night watchmen, and light the town during the evening, but nothing has come of it. The streets teem with poor after dusk. More tenements than ever over the past year, overcrowding at every corner."

"Yes," Mr. Owen began with a guffaw, "I can see why we would all want to move here. Charming, isn't it?"

"Just you wait, Josiah. Don't hold muddiness against her. She's a beauty at the right angles."

Isobel turned back to the terraces lining the street as they inched their way down Seven Bridges from Castle Street. There was no rhyme or reason to the buildings, all different heights and colors, each presumably built during a different century, all wedged together, not quite fitting seamlessly.

"Here we have the Simonds Brewery." He waved a hand past Alistair towards the window opposite Isobel.

She could only just make out a tall brick wall, obscuring whatever she was supposed to see.

"Moved from Broad. Still under construction. The house is finished, at least. The most expansive and impressive brewery complex you'll have ever seen, I should think. I wager they put Sowdon Brewery out of business before the year ends."

The brick wall ended with a fanciful flourish to open into the brewery yard. Isobel gaped at the house, situated dead center of the entry. Brick with four huge Ionic pilasters with stone capitals. It was remarkable and grand. Behind it, but somehow not overshadowing it, rose another massive red brick building, and to the side, along the bank of the river, more red buildings. Before she could take it all in, the wall loomed again and blocked her view.

Rather than slumping against her seatback, she sat up straighter, for just after a little bridge was a medieval church. Small and quaint, but Isobel itched to see it. Alas, the carriage trundled along, turning past the church only to turn again in the direction from whence they had come, along a new street with a different line of never-ending terraces. Just as varied but more artistically, Isobel thought. From honeyed colors to red, some three stories, some two, some four, arched windows, square windows, tall windows, squat windows — what a curious little town!

"To the right," Mr. Trowbridge indicated, "is Dr. Addington's surgery, or rather *was*. A greater loss in Reading, I don't know. So devoted, he worked gratuitously. He saw our good king back to health, I'll have you know. Worked with those who would have seen the inside of an asylum if not for him." He shook his head. "I've little respect for the profession, but he was a man to admire. How different life would be if he were still with us."

Isobel had little interest in a doctor's surgery until the mention of *asylum*. He was one of *those* doctors, then. She must feature a character based on him. Not for Corentin's story, as she had no one mad, nearly mad, or even slightly mad in that tale — should she? A dart of her gaze to Alistair gave her pause. As if reading her mind, he shook his head. Well, it was not a *bad* idea to feature madness somehow, was it? She would present her case in favor the next time they exchanged thoughts on the *Sicilian*. All the best gothic novels possessed some element of madness, after all.

The carriage crossed another bridge. Just as with the little stone bridge on the way into Reading, fishermen lined the edges, poles in hand, but rather than along the banks, they leaned against the bridge railing. Along the banks were washerwomen hard at work.

As they inched farther, one slow wheel rotation at a time, Isobel grew increasingly agitated, her toes curling, her fingers tapping, her head turning from one window to the other. There was so much to see. Too much. And yet, she wanted to explore it all. Would the carriage ever stop?

Mr. Trowbridge was carrying on, oblivious to Isobel's mounting anticipation. "They call it the 'Reading Flying Machine' because it can make it from Angel to Bolt and Tun Inn on Fleet Street, then back again all in the same day. I wouldn't recommend we use it, gentlemen, despite it being surprisingly roomy and well-sprung."

His voice had been captivating at the outset, but now it was an irritating buzz. Isobel curled her fingers into her palms to keep from swatting the air. Angel? What was Angel? Where was Fleet? She only cared about setting her half-boots to earth and racing from one end of town to the next to take in all the sights. Would this silly carriage ever—

With a lurch that had her grasping for the leather strap, the carriage came to a stop.

"Welcome to Angel!" Mr. Trowbridge exclaimed.

Isobel pressed her face against the windowpane. Wood-engraved letters in red and gold boasted the name above the door: Angel Inn and Brewery. Was she smiling like a loon? Most likely. Before she could catch her breath, they were one by one descending from the carriage. Alistair handed her down, his palm warm, firm, and steadying. His eyes were intent on her as she at last set boots to ground.

She inhaled a deep breath to speak, only to grimace with revulsion, hoping she would not cough. The pungent odors of manure, sweaty horseflesh, and she dared not guess what else invaded her senses, tempting her to pivot back into the safety of the carriage. Instead, she stepped closer to Alistair to inhale the spicy scent of his perfume instead.

He leaned in to whisper over the hubbub, "Not tempted to move to Reading?"

With a slight shake of her head, she watched their carriage rock into motion, leaving them all on the inn side of the street, in point of fact, the broadest street Isobel had ever seen, muddy and dusty but thriving. Every building looked to be another inn or brewery or both, coaches and horses and ostlers and grooms, splashing mud puddles and billowing dust clouds and —

Alistair waved a handkerchief. She looked from it to him, quizzing him with raised brows.

"It's scented, my lovely." He tucked it in her hand with a wink before leaning in again for more whispered words. "Lovely as a blossoming rose. You are a vision of this loveliness today. I am a man honored to be chosen as your escort."

She wanted to laugh at his foolishness, but his tone was so sincere, his voice so silken, she could only blush with a bashful dip of her head. Holding the handkerchief to her cheek to hide the pinkening evidence, she sniffed to realize how divine the linen smelled. Oh! Delightful! She sniffed again. Little more than rosewater, but there was something extra she could not identify, not unlike the spice of Alistair's perfume.

And then they were on the move, heading in the direction of — *oh, what majesty*!

Town Hall should have been impressive, especially with it hosting the assizes and quarter sessions, but Alistair's attention was fixed on St. Laurence's church as his father discussed the newly built Town Hall next to it. It was not so much the church itself but rather that Isobel was fixated, and thus, so was Alistair, his eyes following the path of hers.

In a low enough voice not to disturb Alexander Trowbridge's history lesson, Isobel said, "I'm positive it's haunted by mad monks. They're bent on rewriting history to prevent the destruction of the abbey."

As Alistair leaned in to reply, lips parted, he stopped short. Isobel's expression had adopted what he thought of as her woolgathering gaze, his storyteller caught in her own world. He loved these moments when she was dazed since it allowed him an uninterrupted opportunity to caress her face with his eyes. The spark of creativity lit in her pupils, and one corner of her lips lifted in the tell-tale grin of a writer at work.

He followed her hazy gaze as it shifted to spy new inspiration—the Abbey Gateway. What did she see beneath the gateway's arch? A daring sword fight? A dramatic rescue of a heroine in distress? A ghostly monk?

His father's voice filtered through his thoughts, continuing the Reading tour as they headed south down King Street. Alistair heard little and saw less, his attention on Isobel. Walking the streets of Reading with her by his side differed from walking through Sidvale. Here, no one knew them or their story. For all they knew, he toured the town with his wife.

Mmm.

His wife.

He liked the sound of it, the feel of it, the pride accompanying it. Who amongst the passersby could boast of so clever a wife, one quick to laugh and smile and inspire the same?

Again, his father's voice interrupted, this time stirring Isobel as well. "Did you not say your story featured a French émigré, Miss Lambeth? Don't be surprised if you see him walking the streets with us." Lowering his voice, he explained, "The gateway has been housing French refugees since January. Look lively."

Isobel looked about her, as though expecting to see her character standing on a street corner.

She did not have long to look, though. Before they turned onto Minster Street, Alexander ushered them into a shop, their first of the grand outing. In the time it took for Alistair's eyes to adjust to the dark shop interior, he took in the scent of leather mixed with the odor of dissipating turpentine.

Alexander rested a hand on his son's shoulder. "Did I choose rightly for our first stop? I've not been here since it opened."

Alistair turned to Isobel as she turned to him. Their gazes locked. A bookshop. Her lips formed an *Oh* of awe. This was a far reach from the little library of The Tangled Fleece. *This* was a proper bookshop. No one in their group needed prompting to explore. The Owens drifted one way, Alexander another, leaving Alistair and Isobel to walk the stacks.

It did not take much effort to distract her with a few volumes so he could have a private word with the bookkeeper.

Alistair did not doubt Isobel would live for days on the exhilaration of the outing, the sights, sounds, and scents, perhaps finding ways to incorporate the experience into her stories. For his part, the outing did not hold his attention, not as much as plans of pampering Isobel, be it private purchases and orders of his own machinations or whispering conspiracies with Aaditri on how she might do the same.

Once they ventured west on Minster Street, the main thoroughfare for shopping, the group split ways, Aaditri taking Isobel to a dressmaker's shop while the gentlemen explored James Noon's Glove Shop — known more for its fine breeches than gloves, curiously — followed then by a stop at the jeweler.

It was at the jeweler's when Alistair's unformed thoughts about his father began to surface into cohesion, although he was uncertain what to do with the thoughts once formed. He could not put a name to these thoughts. Curiosities? Confusions? Questions? Idiosyncrasies? Contradictions? Whatever they were, they had been nagging Alistair since his father's quick turnaround to accept both the resignation from the Company and the courtship with Isobel. These were two points his father had been adamantly against. After the briefest period of contemplation, Alexander had accepted his son's decision. Then, after a gentle mention of Isobel's lineage, he had accepted her into the family, as well. Acceptance was what Alistair wanted, of course, but the turnaround struck him as peculiar. He dared not question his luck, not when it worked so well in his favor.

Besides, what did he know of his father? This could be the man's way, quick to change his mind after reflection.

His father pointed him to a few bobbles in one of the displays, gold pieces encrusted with jewels. "That would look fine on Miss Lambeth, don't you think?"

Alistair hesitated to reply. Should he point out they were not yet betrothed, and so such a gift would be improper? Should he mention his mother's jewels? The latter contradicted the former, as well as danced with a delicate subject — his mother. By the time he thought of an adequate reply, his father had transferred his attention to a pendant. So engrossed was Alexander with the jeweler about this pendant, Alistair did not wish to interrupt, and so he joined Mr. Owen, who was eyeing a pair of earrings for Aaditri.

For whom would his father purchase a pendant?

The thought struck him only after they left the shop. Another enquiry he did not pursue but one he tucked into those same thoughts that had now surfaced and were demanding attention he did not wish to give.

"Have a care!" shouted two fellows with a sedan chair, weaving their way through the traffic. "By your leave!"

Alistair searched the crowd for Isobel. Ladies caught his glance from all sides, many taking in more than his visage with a sweep of appreciative gazes. Hooded lids, fluttering lashes, waving fans. Their attentions were not lost on him. It was not arrogance that accustomed him to their behaviors, for he knew an appreciation of one's physique was a far cry from the deeper attraction that formed a lasting marriage. Never would he search for hooded lids or fluttering lashes, only for Isobel.

Disappointed not to see her at a window or flitting from one shop to the next, he ducked into Snare's Bookshop with his father and Mr. Owen.

As he had done at the jeweler, Alexander sidled next to Alistair and said, "This is the best shop for paper, son. I daresay Miss Lambeth would appreciate more for her writing." He nudged Alistair in the direction of the shopkeeper.

The reply on Alistair's lips was to remind his father how critical he had been of gothic novels until that sudden turnaround to accept Isobel as a future daughter-in-law. Ah, those thoughts again. Only now that all proceeded as planned did Alistair's mind dip into doubts. Nonetheless, Alistair did exchange words with Mr. Snare about more than paper. Following their turn around the shop, they visited the perfumery next door, and then headed to their final destination. Alistair's breath caught, and his pace quickened as they drew closer to the end of the street.

Standing at the entrance of Rose Inn, Isobel and Aaditri awaited the gentlemen. Alistair's pulse skipped a beat, seeing Isobel's shy smile. Her wit, her authenticity, and her humor all shone through that smile. She fairly glowed.

Had Aaditri succeeded, then? Alistair would have to anticipate the answer.

Describing the day as the best in Isobel's life would be an understatement. One surprise after another tantalized her into a euphoric stupor. What divinity!

Shortly after returning from the Reading outing — which Isobel thought should be a novel title, something along the lines of *The Terrifically Horrid Case of a Young Lady Lost, then Found, in Reading* — she had raced up her private stairs to her suite, champing at the bit to see if the gowns had arrived ahead of them, and if so, could she take a turn about her room in each one, at least twice.

Had the troupe returned to the house directly after shopping, the gowns would not have arrived in time, but as it was, they had enjoyed luncheon at Rose Inn, toured at least three more shops, one with an admirable Elizabethan fireplace surround at the back of the shop — tucked out of sight from all but the most curious — then taken in the Oracle Workhouse. The Oracle was as imposing as it was remarkable. Above where the Holy Brook streamed, it loomed: a Dutch-gabled entrance to the front and, from the niche above the archway, a sentinel John Kendrick statue overlooked the central courtyard. Mr. Trowbridge had much to say about the Oracle and its respectability.

Immediately following, they strode quick-stepped past the County Gaol on Castle Street, which was, Mr. Trowbridge had explained, one of three gaols in Reading. This particular one had recently closed, but rather than the building being demolished or repurposed, it had been left to ruin. Dilapidated walls inspired Isobel to imagine a prisoner still trapped inside, chipping away at the stone in hopes of passing a note to the outside in a plea for rescue.

Their adventure had ended with a return to Angel on Broad Street. However much Isobel was still keen on seeing Friar Street beyond, her feet ached from the pinching half-boots, and Mr. Trowbridge reassured that while Friar had once been the primary street, all shops worth seeing had moved to Minster. And so, they returned to the house.

Ample time for her gowns to have arrived.

What awaited her was more glorious than any gown. Perched atop her writing slope was a sizable and stupendous package with missive tucked beneath bow-tied twine. Fingers twitching to tug at the twine, she took steadying breaths to unfold and read the missive first. She did not recognize the hand, likely written by the shopkeeper, but she knew the words to be Alistair's.

Someone else in Sidvale may wish to read the library edition.

It was cryptic until she opened the package.

Even as her cheeks wet with tears, her lips parted with laughter. The two-volume set of *A Sicilian Romance* looked up at her from its wrappings. Her first personally owned book. Not borrowed, this. No, this was *hers*. With trembling hands, she lifted the first volume, afraid to spoil its beauty while wanting nothing more than to leaf through every page and touch every letter. She raised it to her lips and closed her eyes. Inhaling deeply, she dizzied at the aroma of *book*. The speckled calf binding was soft beneath her fingertips. The green and black goatskin spine with gilt ornamentation kissed each of her fingers in turn, textured, cool, promising.

She had not known her eyes could ache so pleasurably. By the time she set the two volumes back atop the writing slope, her lids were puffy and itchy, her throat scratchy and raw. Oh, but that was not the only gift that awaited her. This was too much! Isobel could burst from it all — and there was a most unladylike thought, but who cared what was ladylike when there were treasures to unearth!

When she turned towards the dressing room to ring for Julia, she saw another package on the side table, next to a vase of fresh flowers. No note this time, only the package.

Exhaling her final breath in time with the tug of twine, she died a heavenly death, her soul escaping past chapped lips, free of its earthly confines.

How could anyone deny this? Isobel had surely died and ascended to heaven.

The four-volume set of *Mysteries of Udolpho* enchanted her, casting its spell.

What had begun with her first book in two volumes ended with her second book in four volumes. She practically had a library of her own! Imagine them lining the walls of her little parlor at home — *divine*! Isobel spun in circles before flinging herself onto her bed. The sound that followed could not be described as a shriek or a snort but more of a gargle or giggle or all the above combined into a delirious laugh interrupted by racking sobs.

First Aaditri's motherly kindness for a daughter not her own, and now not one but two gifts from Alistair that were beyond her imaginings. It was a good thing she would not find the slim package beneath the *Sicilian* until later that evening, a package from the bookshop containing ample writing paper, courtesy of Mr. Trowbridge, the missive would read, bringing Isobel to tears yet again. Yes, it was a good thing she would not find this until later, for if she had found it now, she may well have expired after all. There was only so much delirious happiness Isobel could handle at one time.

By the time Isobel collected herself and Julia attended her, those puffy and swollen eyes were redder than before. Dinner was an hour yet: time still for Julia to work magic. One would have thought it was the lady's maid receiving the gowns for all the excitement she showed, cooing over their arrival and selecting the perfect one for Isobel to wear for dinner.

Gowns of Isobel's own!

Aaditri had shocked Isobel straight down to her blistered heels when ushering her into a dress shop. The shop in question was not of a modiste, and these were not to be tailored gowns; rather, they were ready-made, but that fact did not lessen their beauty, for Isobel had never had a new gown in her life.

Aaditri and the shopkeeper fussed over Isobel, holding up this gown and that, comparing this color and that, trying this cut and that. The shopkeeper had known they were coming, much to Isobel's confusion. She measured Isobel in every possible way, promising it would be the work of a moment to adjust hems and bodices, all gowns to be delivered *prontissimo*.

Isobel cast frantic looks between the woman and Aaditri. "But *Aaditri*," she pleaded, although she could not put words for what exactly she begged.

At first, she had misunderstood, thinking the bill would be sent to her mother. The horror was too great.

Aaditri pressed her cheek to Isobel's. "You are as good as my daughter, *azizam*."

Then Isobel understood. The bill would not be sent to her mother. Aaditri, or Mr. Owen rather, was responsible. Embarrassment and the deeper horror of beholden sentiments tinted her cheeks pink for the remainder of the fitting. Plea after plea, Isobel was ignored.

"How striking you are!" Aaditri exclaimed more than once, followed by variations of "Fortunate my Leila is betrothed, or you would steal her beau — *oof!*" and then giddy laughter to tease Isobel's cheeks pinker.

Gowns selected, order placed, and Isobel rubbing where the fitting needles had pricked, Aaditri guided Isobel out of the shop and on to the next, for she was not finished with Isobel yet. There were shoes, stockings, gloves, stays, chemises, bonnets, and so much more to accompany the new, albeit modest, wardrobe. Isobel's emotions tumulted — glee, guilt, excitement, fluster.

Tugging Isobel into another shop, Aaditri said, "A pity Mrs. Lambeth is the most selfish creature, or she could enjoy seeing your happiness as I am now. I won't apologize, however disparaging."

Isobel caught words of defense on the tip of her tongue and held her peace. Her mother was not unkind, never unkind, merely... absent.

Aaditri continued as Isobel was fitted for new shoes, one of several pairs. "I would have done this years ago, *azizam*, if I had the right, but it has never been my place. Now is different. Now, I claim you. You are to marry our dear Alistair Trowbridge, after all." She placed two fingers to Isobel's lips to shush any protests.

After a day of pampering by all and sundry, Isobel thought she understood what it was like to live as Leila Owen. Oh, what a glorious life!

Chapter 19

After two days following the Reading outing, Alistair was still awestruck at the change in Isobel. Her confidence shone in her bearing. She moved with an elegance and grace he had never witnessed from her. Everything she did was exaggerated, as though she performed a theatrical, only she was so convincing in the role that he was completely taken in by it. However much she humored herself with her feigned airs, Alistair saw only a woman realizing her potential — and oh, so potent was that potential.

He wanted nothing more than to pull her into his arms, express his affection for her in an endearing kiss to end all kisses, and then propose. His hesitation was in not wishing to appear shallow. Her mirror must tell her what he saw. She had transformed, swan-like, from untidily frumpy but pleasantly plumpy to cravat-tighteningly curvaceous. What had been mistaken for curves of overindulgence proved in well-fitting gowns to be curves of *woman*. For all Alistair's admiring — in truth, he could not tear his eyes from her — he did not wish her to think him lustful or vain. He loved her untidy frumpiness. It was part of her beauty, in his eyes, a beauty that extended from her soul outwards. He loved everything about her and all versions of her.

Still, he wished to continue with his plan to wait until after the London meeting to propose, wished it now more than ever, so she would not think him besotted by her figure alone.

They gathered in the drawing room after dinner. Aaditri and Mr. Owen busied themselves with a card game. His father had excused himself, promising to rejoin them shortly. Alistair did not think he would notice when or if his father rejoined. His attention was riveted on Isobel. They were attempting a card game of their own, but she had won every hand since he could do little more than gaze upon her, a lamb enthralled by her divinity.

He played a card without so much as a glance at the card table. "To upset your mother, this I do not wish. I must meet her approval before we are to progress."

Isobel studied her cards with care, glancing from the table to her hand and back. "About that." Furrowed brows softened as she chose her card and laid it on the table. "I've been giving it a good deal of thought, and while I don't want you to consider me disrespectful, I believe a letter will suffice." She glanced at him from over the fan of cards. "Don't look so aghast. I told her about you. I begged her to come home so you may court me. Aaditri begged her, as well. Is it our fault she did not believe you were serious? The truth is, Alistair, if we wait for her approval, we'll never progress. A letter will suffice."

He tossed a random card. "But I wish not to seem a blackguard. She will think poorly of me. Is not the correct way for me to seek her approval? I will dispense of letters and go to her directly if I must. Tell me where your aunt resides. I will go to her after the London business concludes. She will not think me a 'whim' then."

Staring at the card he had played, Isobel canted her head, brows furrowed once more, then resumed her study of her hand. "No. I'm finished playing the forgotten daughter. I'm ready to live my life. I'll write to her. As to whether it's before or after a wedding remains to be seen. I am, after all, beyond my majority and no longer require her permission, regardless of whether I *want* it or not."

"As you wish, *nazanin*. I have expressed my displeasure. I do not wish to make an enemy of my mother-in-law-to-be." Alistair forfeited, laying his hand aside. "I am selfish, however, and wish to offer for you soon. If you grant me permission to break this rule, I will only protest with a light heart. Before we wed, I *will* go to her, and that is where my foot must come down."

Isobel collected her winnings with a giddy bounce, then reset the counter for a new game.

They shared silence as cards were shuffled and cut. Across the room, the Owens flirted, their game mostly abandoned as far as Alistair could tell. His father had still not returned. When he turned his attention back to Isobel, his hands stilled mid-deal. Her gaze had lowered. Her cheeks had reddened. And she was fidgeting with the edge of her open robe, running a finger up and down the length of the hem. She glanced up to catch him staring and averted her gaze anxiously.

Was it his mention of offering for her? They had spoken of this many times since arriving at his father's house. It was not a subject about which to be bashful. He quirked a brow to quiz the top of her head, her eyes attending to her lap rather than him.

"Alistair…" She drawled the word, then let the last syllable hang in the air between them.

"Isobel," he said in a mimic drawl.

She drew her bottom lip between her teeth.

When she said nothing else, he completed the deal and readied his hand for the next round.

"Alistair…" she started again, shifting in her chair. "I was… wondering…." Moving her hand from her hem to the tokens on the table, she fiddled with them absently. "Did you, um, well… last night. You know. Was it you?"

He folded his cards into a neat stack, using their edge to scratch his cheek as he stared at her, trying to decipher what she was asking. Last night? Was it he who… *what*?

Urging further, she said, "*You know*. Um, the spying of my ankles." Her voice cracked on the last word. She had yet to look up at him.

Spying of her ankles? Hmm. He had certainly done his fair share of admiring throughout the day and far more than trying to glimpse her ankles, but he was not about to admit that aloud. Instead, he said, "I profess innocence, my delicate flower. Only if it would please you would I gaze upon your ankles in worship and adoration."

Rather than laugh, as he would have expected her to do, she frowned at the tokens. With hushed harshness, she emphasized, "*Through the keyhole*."

"Ah, you refer to being locked in the tower, sweet damsel."

"No." Edged with an increasing annoyance, she asked, "Did you… try to… *open my door* last night?"

He dropped his cards as though singed. He did not answer immediately. He could not. What she was implying was... well, it was beyond the pale. It was roguish. It was sinful. It was insulting. Alistair could not determine if he was furious at this accusation, curious if it was a veiled invitation, or concerned about her safety. She would not ask so vulgar a question as a riddle or jest, he was certain.

"Explain," was all he could bring himself to say.

Her eyes darted around the room before braving a glance at him. "My door. My *bedchamber* door. Last night. Someone tried to open the door. I'm certain of it. I... thought it might..." She did not finish, her face already crimson.

"I promise I will never compromise you, Isobel. I will never force my attention."

With a curt nod, she asked her wringing hands, "Then *who* was at my door?"

He thought in silence, on the edge of fury, that someone would be at her door, that someone would attempt to compromise her. Grounding himself in reason, he rationalized no one in the house would dare do that. His concern for her safety was paramount, but could there not be another explanation, something obvious they were not immediately seeing?

After enumerating the possibilities, he offered aloud, "A maid? Wishing to stoke a fire, empty the grate, exchange the basin, yes? A maid not so skilled at stealth."

Isobel shook her head. "I thought so, too, but I have Julia now. She sees to everything. No maid would dare enter the room. It's Julia's domain."

His most pressing concern now was, "Do you feel unsafe, Isobel?" He would... he would what? Move rooms to serve sentry? Instruct her lady's maid to stay with her? Demand she be moved to the guest room next to Aaditri? There were possibilities, each as eyebrow raising as the next, but he would not have her feel unsafe.

She lowered her gaze. "Not unsafe, no. To be perfectly honest, it could have been my imagination."

Staying his desire to come to her rescue, he asked, "Do you think it was a dream? You dreamt of a ghost maid haunting you in the night in search of escaped dust she forgot to clean?"

She was slow to respond, but when she did, she began laughing, too, joining him in the joviality of the ghost maid. "You must be right. How foolish of me. *Of course*, I was dreaming! I had stayed awake far too long reading the *Sicilian* — I'll have you know, I awoke with it still in my hands — and so I must have dreamt the whole silly affair." She covered her face with her hands to smother her humor. Peeking between her fingers, she mumbled, "I can't believe I asked if you had… Oh, bless!" Her fingers tightened to hide her eyes.

He leaned closer to the table and waited. As soon as she lowered her hands, he waggled his eyebrows. With a fling of her hands back over her face, she squealed, drawing the attention of the Owens, who merely looked on with teasing winks.

If only she had not extinguished the candle. Mere chapters remained in the *Sicilian*, pages she could surely finish reading within an hour or two, allowing her to start *Udolpho* on the morrow. After her long wait for Mr. Bradley's copy to arrive, she need not wait any longer — she possessed her own copy now. Drumming her fingers against the bedcovers, she stared into the pitch black around her, unable to sleep. She should have started *Udolpho* this evening. She had already read the *Sicilian*, after all, no need to finish it, but she could not bring herself to stop reading so close to the end. It was one of her favorite stories. How could she abandon the characters? No, *Udolpho* could wait a little longer.

Isobel hummed to herself.

Tomorrow — or was it already today? — was Alistair's last day at the house before the London trip. The gentlemen would carry on to London, leaving Isobel and Aaditri to entertain themselves. They would only be gone for a week at most. A pity she could not tempt Hetty to join her. The distance was not great, and Hetty must be bored to tears, but then, tearing her away from the neediest mother-in-law on earth was not likely.

Why had she extinguished the candle? With care, she should be able to spark flint and steel. True, it was the dead of night, and there was not so much as moonlight by which to see, but with a steady hand, determination, and patience, she ought to be able to light the candle. Lying in bed, sleepless and agitated, was a waste of time. In the *Sicilian*, she had reached one of the best parts — when they discover the hidden wife locked in the castle by the malicious villain, a wife thought deceased.

A sound from the sitting room silenced her thoughts.

She stilled. Her fingers flexed.

Shuffling footsteps, unmistakable, as though feet dragged across a rug. A slow gait. One step, and another, then another.

The sound did not move closer. It repeated, ad nauseam, for so long Isobel's guard lowered. There was nothing terribly frightening about the sound. Perhaps a maid dusting. Although, Isobel could not see candlelight beneath her door. All remained dark. The ghost maid? The promise of the supernatural tempted Isobel to rise from the safety of her bed and step into the sitting room in hopes of catching the ghost unawares. To see a real ghost!

Paralyzed from a fear she could not acknowledge, even while lightening her mood with humor, she remained in bed, her body still, her fingers flexed.

Faint, so faint, a whisper, incoherent, soft as a sigh.

Isobel's pulse quickened.

Sssss sounded the whisper, so subtle it could be a hiss, but beneath was words. Whisper to mutter, and then…

Humming?

Yes, Isobel could distinctly hear humming from the sitting room. Each shuffle of a footfall accompanied a tuneless hum.

This was silly. Isobel shook sense into herself and flung off the bedcovers. There was a person out there, a maid, no doubt, who would be all apologies for awakening one of the guests. After a short exchange, all would be well. Isobel would have peace of mind. She lowered her legs to the side of the bed. With deep breaths, she slid until her bare feet met the cool, plush rug beneath. Standing, then with palms against the bed, she, hand over hand, walked herself towards the door, not wanting to trip or lose her sense of direction.

Just as her fingertips slipped away from the bed-post, she heard a giggle. She stilled. Her fingers flexed. The giggle was... unnatural. There. Again. High-pitched, frantic.

Isobel stepped back, reaching for the bedpost.

The shuffling tread beyond her door quickened in pace, matching the frenzy of the giggles.

She wrapped her fingers around the post and squeezed, taking another step backwards.

The footfalls outside began a slow crescendo, shuffle to stride.

In two of Isobel's own steps away from the door, she realized the echoing steps in the sitting room were not increasing volume so much as moving closer, moving towards her door. She clutched her night rail, eyes widening, legs trembling, breath shallow-ing. Whoever, or whatever, was outside crossed the sitting room, the footfalls stopping only when they reached the bedchamber door. Isobel's eyes darted in the darkness, not knowing where to look, unseeing in the black.

Silence met her straining ears. No shuffles, no steps, no whispers or hums or giggles. Silence.

Fear caught in her throat. Isobel dared not move.

Silence stretched for an eternity. One minute became five. Five minutes became ten.

Her toes tingled. Her heartbeat slowed. She wanted to laugh. It had all been in her imagination! All her thoughts of ghost maids, villains, and damsels locked in castles had all created sounds beyond her door that simply were not there. Heavens, she could even be dreaming now. Had she dreamt it? Was she now in a dream? She pinched her arm. *Ouch.* Not dreaming, then, merely imagining. Then, if she *were* dreaming, would she not think the pinch hurt if it did not? Hmm.

Feeling silly, she climbed back onto the bed and began tucking herself beneath the covers, tempted to laugh aloud at herself but not wanting to test fate.

As she settled in, a bemused grin on her lips, a soft scratch scraped at the door. Low, rumbling, punctuated with a snarl, came a growl, animalistic, nefarious.

Chapter 20

Before dusk, Isobel and Alistair walked along the terrace. This was their last chance at a private conversation before he and the gentlemen were to leave for London in the morning. The Owens remained in the drawing room, watching the two stroll but permitting privacy. Mr. Trowbridge had absented himself for the day. Although the sun had not yet set, it might as well have. The evening sky weighed heavily with grey clouds.

Alistair's voice droned.

She wanted this moment together before their week-long parting, but her mind wandered. It had done so all day. An endless ramble, skirting a feeling more than a thought: the sensation of paralysis. *That* was more frightening than any beast, ghost, or villain. Fear of fear itself.

The inability to move when faced with fear — was it a normal reaction?

"You're certain?"

No, she was not certain it was normal, not at all certain.

"Isobel?"

Who?

"Second thoughts about staying behind? Or reluctant to see me leave?"

Only when Alistair stopped walking did Isobel jerk her attention to the present. Oh dear. Had he asked her a question? She had been miles away, tucked beneath bedcovers, unable to move.

Turning to him with a titter, she asked, "Will you ever forgive me? I didn't hear a word. A scene came to me. Just now. Vivid. Corentin's next scene, of course." The lie sounded unconvincing despite her airy tone.

"Ah, I thought you to be distracted. Yes, this explains it."

"What were you saying?"

He nodded towards the sunken garden for them to continue their ramble. "As you have said sagely, this will be good. More time with my father. Opportunity to fulfill my role with the Company before walking the new path. But I worry you will miss me," Alistair teased her. "You are certain you do not wish to join us in London?"

"No, not this time. Aaditri and I will entertain each other."

They descended the steps into the garden, the air more humid than on the terrace. Isobel glanced at the sky, darkening, leaden. Was there no escape from darkness? It was one thing to read about characters roaming dark tunnels and hidden passageways, chased by ghouls, quite another to be trapped, a frightened hare paralyzed by fear.

Oh. Alistair was talking again. She had forgotten to listen. What a dreadful companion she was today and on his last day at the house of all days.

"Alistair," she interrupted.

Perhaps she should say something else. Perhaps she should ask about London. He had been in a cheery mood all day, ready for the adventure. To say what she wanted, what was foremost on her mind, would shadow that excitement. Besides, she did not want to appear a coward. She was a gothic novelist for crying between book pages!

"Alistair, I was wondering something." She hesitated, wringing her hands at her waist.

With infinite patience, he waited, guiding them back around the parterres in the direction of the terrace.

"Is there, um, a mad maid in the house? Or, no, not mad, but maybe someone like Benji? You know, Mrs. Thomas' son, the one who has been ill, who helps around my mother's house?"

"Yes, I recall Benji. But I don't follow your question."

"Oh, you know what I mean." She waved a careless hand, as though this was inconsequential. "Anyone amongst the servants who might fancy a lark on the guests."

He shook his head, his expression perplexed. As they took the steps back up to the terrace, he reflected, "The ghost maid? Has she called on you again?" Brightening at having realized what Isobel was about, he offered, "You are haunted by a ghost maid, yet you have not initiated conversation? Now is your chance! Interview her. Ask what life is like beyond the veil. Or do you suppose she cannot see the living? Ah, Isobel, do not lose this chance!"

His smile and laugh, encouraging her to engage with the ghost, made her stomach knot. It was not that he made light of this or that he might be right. How could she explain the *fear*? This was not a ghost, she did not think. Nor was this a dream. Then... what if

Alistair *was* correct, and she was to lose this opportunity to come face to face with the supernatural? She liked that. She liked thinking his words wise rather than dismissive. She liked thinking she had control over the situation and encounter, a friendly ghost, nothing demonic or intending her harm.

Meeting his smile with her own, she said, "You've guessed it. You're correct, of course. I should fling open my door and introduce myself. Foolish of me not to have done so already." She held her smile as the memory of paralysis shivered down her spine.

As they reached the drawing room doors, he stopped and turned her to face him with a nudge of his fingertips to her elbow. "You do not feel unsafe in my father's house, do you? You would tell me if you do."

"Without hesitation! All is well. I'm being silly about ghosts and shadows — *me*, the lover of all things mysterious! I've been burning the candle too long, reading; that's all it is. But in the event it *is* a ghost maid, I shall exchange words with her about the dust needing her attention."

Her answer seemed to satisfy him. However distracted she was for the remainder of the evening, he carried on with confidence; none the wiser, an unseen hand choked her words.

Chapter 21

Isobel turned the page. After a dramatic pause and a glance at Aaditri, whose hands were busy with embroidery but attention riveted on the story, Isobel continued reading aloud from the first chapter of *The Mysteries of Udolpho*. With luck, they would finish all volumes before the gentlemen returned. How envious Alistair would be to know they had read it first! She could not wait to tease him.

Aaditri was not terribly interested in novels of any variety, gothic or otherwise, but she had begged Isobel to read aloud, wanting the two to share in the fun. Their first day without the gentlemen, and they had already read five chapters of Isobel's story and half of the first chapter of *Udolpho*, walked the garden twice, written a letter each to Leila, and played a card game. Not too shabby for two ladies in want of entertainment.

"Go on," Aaditri prompted. "How did St. Aubert respond?"

Isobel looked at her companion, her brows pinched. "So sorry. Away with the fairies, was I? Well, no matter. Now, where was I… ah, yes, here." She continued reading.

The chapter was not without interruptions. Isobel had to explain points to Aaditri, namely, who might prove to be an important character and who might not. Aaditri, bless, had thought the father was to become the main character and hero. Interruptions aside — no, rather perhaps because of those interruptions — Isobel enjoyed their time more than she could express in words. Never had her mother asked Isobel to read anything aloud. Her heart swelled at all Aaditri did to show affection. Not for the first time, she felt a pang not to have a mother-in-law in her future, especially since Alistair had been so close to his mother. She resolved to convince Alistair they *must* live near Sidvale to maintain walking distance to the Owens, although she might not have to do much convincing since he seemed already of the same mind, at least according to the secret house browsing he had admitted to.

That thought brought a smile to her lips. Aaditri cast her a curious glance, but Isobel kept reading, keeping the reason for her smile to herself.

They read for the better part of an hour and would have continued to do so had Isobel not experienced a curious tickle along her spine. The hair on the back of her neck fairly stood on end. Nothing touched her — that she was aware of, at least. But… She glanced around the drawing room, searching for… what? The prickle on her skin whispered that she and Aaditri were being watched. Not another soul was in sight, though. Unless… Isobel turned to glance out the window. All she saw was their reflection basked in candlelight, the garden beyond already dark.

She shrugged off the sensation. Likely a footman out for fresh air.

Really, she needed to take hold of her silly night-mares, now more than ever, if they were affecting her waking hours. Last night, she had heard nothing, dreamt nothing, proving the previous occasions had been dreams or her imagination misinterpreting the sounds of a maid, nothing more. Vividly, she recalled the fright she had felt, everything sounding so real, but during waking hours and in Aaditri's presence, Isobel could not account for her silliness. If there was anything sinister in the house, others would have noticed. Even Alistair had made light of the sounds she heard.

There was no danger. She was in Alistair's father's house. Safe. Despite Mr. Trowbridge's peculiarities, extended absences, and occasional lurking about servant doors and the second story, he remained Alistair's father, not a storybook villain up to mischief. Over the past week or so, he had become so accepting of his son and of her; she should be ashamed to think his house anything but safe, and he anything but the perfect custodian of the house and all within. No, there was no danger, only her imagination.

She rubbed the back of her neck, trying to flatten the pesky hairs so determined to deceive her.

With another glance at the window, she closed the book, the first chapter completed.

Aaditri said, "Poor Madame St. Aubert. I don't suppose she'll recover?"

Isobel shook her head. "This *is* gothic, after all. No one recovers in a gothic. Besides, we need to orphan the heroine to thrust her boldly into her journey. All the best heroes and heroines are orphaned. That's how these things go."

"*Orphan* her?" Alarmed, Aaditri dropped her embroidering needle. "Not her papa, too!"

"We must wait to see, but if I weren't a gentle-woman, I would wager his time is short."

"And you *like* these stories, *azizam*?"

"By the time we're knee-deep into the plot, you'll be a lover of Radcliffe. First, we must empathize with the heroine; otherwise, what would we care of her journey?"

Aaditri sighed with resignation but shook her head. "I would rather empathize with you. Are you enjoying your gowns? You're so pretty in them, *azizam*. I know our dear Alistair agrees." She teased Isobel with a smirk. "He can't take his eyes off you! Not that he ever could, but now more than ever."

Pressing her hands to her cheeks, Isobel balked, "No, don't tell me these things! I shall hide behind a screen if I think he's paying so close of attention." As an aside, she added, "I do love the gowns. I feel regal in them."

Less than an hour later, Isobel mounted the servant stairs up to the second story. Although her mind had wandered, she had been no less enthralled by the first chapter of the novel. Inspired, her fingers itched to write a new chapter of Corentin. Normally, she would write in the drawing room with Aaditri present since the light-ing was better, but Aaditri had wished to retire early.

As Isobel reached the last landing in the staircase, the door to the second story only steps away, she paused. Beyond, whispers warred. Two voices argu-ing, but in tones so hushed, Isobel could not make out the words. Were they in her bedchamber? The sitting room? Before the door? She strained to hear. It was rude to eavesdrop, but she was unsure what else to do—she did not wish to open the door and interrupt them lest they think she was intentionally eavesdropping, but walking back downstairs to wait was too silly for consideration. She took a step closer, then another, stealthy in her movements, ears perked.

Try as she might, making sense of the words proved hopeless.

Isobel waited a short while longer until the dueling whispers lagged. What she did not want was for someone to open the door and find her standing there. Best to pretend she had been unaware of anyone's presence.

Taking the last couple of steps with not-so-ladylike enthusiasm — hoping they would hear her approach — she swung open the door to the second floor, her eyes on her bedchamber.

A slight gasp in the sitting room invited Isobel's attention. Affecting surprise, she turned. Two maids stood facing each other, both bowing their heads in deference to Isobel. Without a word to each other or to Isobel, they scurried past her and down the stairs, pulling shut the door behind them.

Isobel's mind wandered through the dark forest of her imagination. It was not impossible *those* were the sounds she had heard at night or even the inspiration for those sounds if she dreamt a variation of what her sleeping self heard.

See? Nothing to fear. Only two maids arguing!

Exchanging her ink-soaked quill for a fresh one, Isobel dipped the tip into the inkpot, desperate to continue her sentence before she lost it.

'Nevermore will you keep my lady trapped in a tower, your prisoner. What did you think to gain? Her submission? My wrath?'

Quill to inkpot.

'My dear, Comte de Corentin, I've gained precisely what I desired. You.'

The maniacal laughter shivered down Corentin's spine.

Quill to inkpot.

His nemesis continued, 'Did you think no one would recognize a Frenchman disguised as an Austrian? My dear, I would know your stench anywhere.'

Quill to inkpot.

It struck Corentin — his nemesis was stalling. The authorities would be upon them, ready to transport him to France to face the guillotine. No! He had come too far.

Blast. She was being too heavy-handed. Ink had splattered. The last sentence smeared. The tip of the new quill was already softening. Isobel emptied the quill end, tossed it aside, and leaned back in her chair to reread what she had written thus far.

Blinking heavy lids, she rubbed away sleep. Determination would not win this battle. She yawned, stretching her arms to the heavens. Her eyes itched. Could one's sight actually ache? Well, if it could, her sight ached from straining in the dim candlelight too long. She dared not enquire the time. She had been writing for hours.

Satisfied with the direction of her story, she began packing away her implements, humming to herself as she did so. Tired as she was, she fancied hearing an echo, an answering hum, the harmony to her melody.

Double blast. She was low on pounce. Tomorrow — or in a few hours after sunrise, rather — she would beg for some from the butler. Hating to blot but having little choice unless she wanted to leave the page atop the writing box to dry, which she did not wish to do, she reached for the blotter and rolled it across the page, one section at a time. Not that anyone would enter her room except Julia. And not that Julia would wish to pry by reading the paper. And not that Isobel cared if anyone read it. But... well... blame it on a writer's idiosyncrasies. Isobel could not bring herself to leave out the story.

As she tucked the page into the writing box drawer, it dawned on her she was *not* humming, yet the echoing continued. Drawer agape, her hands stilled, trembling slightly. Listening, straining, and focusing, she tried to pinpoint the sound. Singing now, not humming, soft, melodic, a lullaby — from the window?

Isobel rose with care, cringing when her chair creaked. She followed the siren's song. Yes, the window. In tempo, she swept aside the edge of the curtain, parting enough to spy the garden below. All she saw was the reflection of her own candlelight.

Inching back to the table as though a single creak of a floorboard might interrupt the tune outside, she crept to her candle. Raising the douter, she snuffed the flame. Darkness and acrid smoke enveloped her. Hand outstretched, she made her way back to the window for a second look down to the garden below.

The singing had stopped. So had Isobel's visibility. Even without the reflection of her candlelight, she could see nothing in the darkness beyond the window.

Isobel tossed and turned, fighting Corentin's enemy, saving the lady trapped in the tower, nursing Madame St. Aubert back to health, warning her husband of his impending demise — for all the best heroes and heroines must be orphaned, she explained to Aaditri. Bedcovers were tossed aside in a fit of night sweats, then wrenched over her head again as she tried to block light, desperate to sleep, desperate to save the trapped lady, desperate to expose the villain.

She awoke with a start.

Glancing around the bedchamber, short of breath, Isobel tried to orient herself. The black of night still surrounded her. For a confusing moment, she thought herself at home, then realizing this was not her bed, panicked. *Alistair, Mr. Trowbridge, the house.* She inhaled deeply, slowly. How long had she slept? What had awakened her?

Isobel sat up.

The curtains were still parted, she realized. And there was — *a light*?

A faint glow shone from the far side of the lawn near the yew tree. It floated, faintly swaying, not unlike a will-o'-wisp. In only a few moments, it would be out of sight from her vantage point as it moved towards the house.

Making short work of it, she clambered out of bed and darted to the window. Yes, there it was. An orb of light carried by a breeze danced its way towards her. No, not towards her, to the fountain. As it drew closer, Isobel could hear singing, the same lullaby from earlier that evening. The orb swayed. The light shifted colors: yellow, then green, then yellow, then... *white – a woman in white*. A ghost! Isobel knew it as assuredly as she knew she was not dreaming. An apparition in a white gown, faceless, a lantern swaying at her side, hovered gingerly at the edge of the garden before approaching the fountain. The song continued.

This was it! Isobel was not afraid. She was giddy! *This* must be her evening caller. It explained everything! The house was haunted, and this was proof. Isobel had never seen a ghost before, but she had always suspected the supernatural was real. Proof! Being a ghost, it could not harm her, could it? No, surely not. But, perhaps, the ghost could communicate. Or not? Oh, Isobel had no way of knowing.

Hopping from one foot to the other, she searched with growing frustration for her dressing gown and slippers. Then she opened the tinderbox and felt for the flint and steel. Rubbing one against the other, she tried to create a spark. Under her breath, she cursed in frustration.

Her hands stilled at the sound of soft laughter. The hair on the back of her neck stood on end. Isobel dropped the flint and steel back into the tinderbox to return to the window. No light. No ghost.

The floorboard outside her door creaked.

Isobel gasped and flung herself against the wall, shaking.

Chilling laughter, almost a cackle, a witch's cackle, preceded rustling that moved from Isobel's door through the sitting room. She followed the sound as it receded towards what she thought must be the locked door at the far end of the sitting room.

She could not stop trembling. Even if hard pressed, she would not be able to distinguish between the tremble of excitement and fear. She rubbed her hands against her arms. Beyond her bedchamber, silence stretched. Only when her nerves calmed did she climb back into bed.

Isobel needed a plan. She was *not* going barmy. There was a genuine ghost haunting this house. She was *not* mad.

There was only one way to prove her sanity — face the apparition.

Chapter 22

The next day proved one of the longest of Isobel's life, not because she was carrying on with only a couple hours of sleep, but because she could not wait until night arrived again. There could be no guarantee the ghost would make another appearance. Nevertheless, Isobel would be ready if she did.

Aaditri had assumed her to be distracted by Alistair's absence. Isobel had not corrected her. It was not the thing to confess to ghost sightings, after all. They tried a walk around the grounds, but Aaditri tired quickly of Isobel's investigation of the fountain and desire to linger longer than necessary. They tried reading until Isobel reread the same paragraph three times in succession. They tried a card game until Aaditri wearied of prompting her it was her turn. They tried writing letters, but by the end of the time, Aaditri had four letters to show for her efforts and Isobel a blank page.

The table clock received most of Isobel's focus. *Tick tock. Tick tock.*

As dusk fell, she made a hasty excuse to retire and raced to her suite. She wanted to practice.

The stairs were the trickiest, but she wanted to be prepared. The stairwell held wall sconces so servants would not need to traverse it in the dark, and there was a dormer window at the top to allow for moonlight. The problem Isobel foresaw was there would not be ample moonlight for at least another week, and she did not think this stairwell was used enough by the staff to be kept lit throughout the night. Either way, Isobel could not take the chance. Sure, the ghost could be civilized enough to meet Isobel in the sitting room for late-night tea and biscuits, but again, Isobel could not take the chance.

Thus, she walked up and down the stairs by sunset glow, counting the steps to each landing and then pacing the landing with smooth, controlled strides. Once confident, she tried it with her eyes closed. Again, and again, and again.

At last, evening fell. Isobel readied herself. Isobel, Ghost Hunter Extraordinaire.

In a chair before the window, she waited, her eyes searching the darkness, an ever-long vigil. A sensible person would have kept a candle burning rather than plan to find her way to the garden in pitch black, not that Isobel was insensible; rather, it made more sense to her to sit in the dark. The candle would affect her sight. The candle would make it difficult to see outside. The candle would only burn for so long. The candle might frighten the ghost.

And so, Isobel waited in the dark.

Why had the ghost chosen to reveal itself to her? Or was it that Isobel possessed some uncanny ability to sense the supernatural? What did one say to a ghost?

Scenario after scenario, she planned her first words. The whole theatrical played through her imagination, Isobel at first stunned by the ghost's ethereal beauty, and then, once collected, a humbled curtsy, low and regal…. Isobel's head bobbed as though on a hinged spring. Good heavens. Had she nodded off to sleep?

Shifting her position, she tapped her feet, drummed her fingers, and hummed. So silent the house and surroundings, Isobel could hear the breeze rustling distant tree leaves. Perhaps the ghost would not show herself this evening. Not every evening had Isobel heard noises, and those few times she had were only recently, almost like an escalation, a restless spirit needing to be set free of her confines. What if she did not appear until tomorrow or the next day? Isobel could not wait up every night. She yawned at the thought.

Was Alistair enjoying London and the time with his father? Was he anxious about the meeting? Would he propose the first day of his return or wait until they returned to Sidvale? Oh dear — would he return to Sidvale? Or decide to stay here with his father?

Her chin bounced against her chest.

Oh goodness. She had dozed again. Tea before bedtime would have done the trick. Why, for heaven's sake, had she not thought of that? Even as she thought of tea, she stifled a yawn, shaking her head to dispel the heaviness from her eyelids. The lids had other plans. They drooped. They fluttered. They closed.

Soft snores marked time, a metronome to the lullaby, each cadence carried on the evening breeze.

Hovering out of the chair, leaving her corporeal form sleeping, Isobel floated out the window to follow the melody, following it to the fountain where the spirit awaited her. *I have been waiting for you*, sang the ghost within the phrases of the lullaby. Isobel marveled at her, a pulsing light, vibrant, with only a modicum of transparency. *Me?* Isobel thought this rather than said it, for she could not instruct her mouth to move, not when she had left her body in the house. The ghost nodded in understanding. Without explanation, she hummed, a wisp of a hand guiding Isobel's attention to the window. As Isobel followed the pointing finger, she felt the scream rather than heard it, seeing not herself in the window but the ghost; that beautiful guiding light turned sinister. Isobel fought to return to her body before the ghost possessed it. Her senses slipped. Her awareness slipped. She clawed at the air, desperate to save herself. The humming, the humming continued, the same blasted song. Isobel slipped, slipped away, slipped —

Her temple knocked against the window casement, waking her.

Shaking herself, Isobel looked around, her breath short. She had fallen asleep. Again. With vigorous strokes, she rubbed her arms, then patted her cheeks. She really should have ordered tea.

Then she heard it. The lullaby. *That* was not a dream. Leaning forwards in her chair, she scoured the tiny garden. Her pulse raced when she saw the ghost sitting at the fountain's edge, the lantern beside her. Isobel pinched her arm. *Ouch.* Definitely awake. Definitely seeing the apparition. Now was her chance! No time to question her decision. Time to act. Time to initiate her plan.

Counting her steps, her hand outreached for safety, she headed for the bedchamber door.

Her breath hitched. Her pulse raced. Her palms perspired. With each step, she worried. A maid or footman could intercept her despite the late hour. The ghost could disappear by the time she reached the little garden. A forgotten rug or unseen rock or divot could trip her along the route. Worries or not, she refused to be cowed. Also on her mind as she counted the steps down the stairs—one, two, three, four, five. First landing. One, two, three. Top step. One, two, three, four, five—was worry over the ghost herself. *Could* ghosts see living people? If so, were ghosts afraid of the living? Did the ghost *know* she was a ghost?

So many questions, so little time. Last set of steps. One, two, three, four, five. Ground floor. Fingertips tracing the wall, she felt for the seam of the jib door. Once in the hallway, she pivoted to face the door to outside. Counting resumed. At the precise number of steps she had anticipated, her hand met the door. Had it not been dark, and had there been a maid or footman present, they would have witnessed her grin. How clever she was! Never bested by the darkness! Not this Ghost Hunter Extraordinaire.

Thankfully, it had not rained that day, not the slightest drizzle. Overcast, yes, but no rain. The ground was dry, sturdy, and cooperated with her counting. No sloshing, slipping, or sliding for these feet to miscount.

Not that she needed to count. As soon as she stepped outside and turned to face the garden, she saw the candlelight. The faint glow haloed the figure, one side dark, one side illuminated. The ghost had not moved, her attention on the fountain pool, her face lowered. As Isobel drew closer, she could see the lantern had multicolored panes, a sort of stained-glass mosaic adorning the sides, sending shades of green and yellow and red over the fountain tier.

Isobel enumerated her questions for the ghost, assuming they could communicate. Question number ten was to ask about the lantern. Presumably, elements of the supernatural did not require candle-light. Was this a carryover from her life, a burden or responsibility, maybe a task to light the way? Per-haps *she* was the will-o'-wisp, only in human form. Or maybe she was an angel, prepared to light the path to heaven.

Running her palms down her dressing gown, Isobel tried to ease her nerves and dry the sweat sheathing her skin. The closer she drew, the more anxious she felt. Controlling her breathing was increasingly more difficult. She did not want to startle the ghost by sneaking up on her, but more importantly, she did not want the ghost to have enough warning to vanish before Isobel had a chance. Silent, undetected, Isobel crept. Ahead, the woman sat unawares, clad in a white night rail so pristine and unblemished it could have been new.

The lullaby of yesterday evening ebbed and flowed on a wave of sound.

Isobel tugged her bottom lip with her teeth. Ever closer, she slinked, creeping like an earth-bound vine.

The ghost dipped a hand in the fountain water, then fanned her fingers to and fro.

Isobel halted. She was close enough now to take fair measure of the ghost. Attention riveted, Isobel could see skin not so much milky white as almost translucent. It was the hands that gave her pause, that caused her fright, that had her questioning the rationale of facing a spirit of the astral plane — what if this was not a ghost, not an angel, but a…. Isobel did not complete the thought. She could not. She was standing too close now to turn around.

The woman's fingertips were red and raw, the skin peeling around the nails.

This was not right. Ghosts were not *grotesque*. Were they?

Isobel took a tentative step forwards. Then another. Her heart thumped its way into her throat. Her breathing shallowed. Her lips parted, preparing the greeting.

The lullaby stopped. The fingers stilled in the water. Head raising, the ghost lifted her face to Isobel. The woman stared but did not seem to see Isobel, looking straight past as though Isobel were not standing feet away. The eyes were bleary, vacant.

It was not the ghost's gaze that struck Isobel with horror.

The prepared greeting was never articulated. Instead, Isobel's mouth fell open in a silent scream.

The horror! The horror at the fountain's edge. Slack-jawed, gaping, drooling, the woman's chin dripped with saliva, the front of her night rail drenched. Unprepared for so ghastly a sight, Isobel took a step backwards, hand to her pounding heart, her heavy tongue swallowing against fear.

With a croak, Isobel managed, "I… beg your pardon. No wish to disturb."

The creature snapped to attention jolted from her daze. Eyes pinpointed Isobel, red-rimmed and watery, pinning Isobel to the spot. Features contorted into confusion, then fear, then rage. The raw, peeling fingers reached up to claw at pale cheeks, the ghost turning its outrage on itself. Before it could scream, lunge, or lash out, Isobel launched herself towards the house, fleeing in fear and helplessness.

She stumbled. She whimpered. She cried. Counting steps was beyond her ability. Hands grasping for familiar textures, she found the door, found the hall, found the jib door. She tripped up the steps, bear crawling to safety. Once she reached her bedchamber, she fumbled about the desk for the key, grasped it, dropped it, rammed it into the keyhole, struggled, then locked the door. Flinging herself on her bed, she burrowed beneath the covers.

It had seen her.

It had been angry.

Illogical or not, Isobel felt *touched* by the creature, affected somehow, *seen*. She dabbed a shaking hand to her chin. No drool. She felt the tips of her fingers. No peeling skin. She was Isobel. Only Isobel. Unaffected. Untouched. She was not becoming a wraith.

Chapter 23

Isobel awoke with a jerk, nearly toppling out of bed. She sat up, eyes darting around the room. The curtains had been pulled open. Rather than the warm sun streaming through the window, inviting Isobel to walk the garden, a dark sky shadowed the room, obscuring the time of day. In contrast, a cheery cup of steaming chocolate sat at her side table. She inhaled the sweet aroma. Beneath her palms, she could feel the bedlinen, damp from sweat but soothing, reassuring her she was awake, not trapped in another dream of sitting at the fountain's edge. So lucid were the dreams, each featuring Isobel as the ghost rather than the ghost hunter. She shivered.

"Julia?" she called, hoping her lady's maid was in the dressing room.

Julia popped her head into the room. "Good morning, Miss Lambeth!"

Isobel could have laughed at the liveliness. If only she could feel the same, but not after the ghostly encounter and endless nightmares, the lost moments in time and disorientation.

"Don't laugh," Isobel warned, "But I've had so wretched a night's sleep, I can't recall the day." How many days since Alistair left for London?

True to form, Julia did not laugh or appear fazed by the question. "Saturday, and a gloomy one at that, but we needn't let rain spoil the day."

Saturday? Alistair had left on Tuesday.

Had Isobel lost days? She hoped her confusion did not show in response to Julia's kindness. The lady's maid plumped the pillows as Isobel sat up to retrieve her cup of chocolate.

If only she could sleep without nightmares. If only she could stop checking the window each night, ever watchful for the ghost's return. If only she could stop from jumping at every little creak of a floorboard. If only she could rid her memory of the ghastly face.

Oh. It was raining. She would not be able to walk to the fountain today.

What was she to do if she could not walk to the fountain? Had she not done so every day since that dreadful encounter? She *needed* to sit at the fountain. She was compelled to, mesmerized to do so. As the edge of the cup rested against her bottom lip, the steam of the chocolate tickling her cheeks, she fretted, the mad obsession with reliving the encounter sending her mind into a frenzy, however placid her demeanor as she sipped the chocolate.

"Julia?"

The lady's maid again leaned into the room.

"Have you ever seen a ghost?"

With a half-suppressed laugh, Julia said, "Can't say I have. My great-aunt swore on her deathbed her cat was curled by her feet—long dead was that cat, mind, Miss Lambeth, and I never saw anything at her feet. Don't suppose that counts as a ghost?"

"Ghost cats sound more plausible than human ghosts. I don't mean to ask so absurd a question. Ignore me."

Julia watched Isobel finish the chocolate before asking, "A ghost in your book, is there?"

"Yes, of course. You've perceived exactly." Isobel set aside the cup.

Time to face the day, rain and all.

However determined to be present without a wandering mind, Isobel caught herself going through the motions of dressing, of breaking her fast, of greeting Aaditri, of sitting in the drawing room. Her glances fell to the terrace. Her nerves frayed with each movement of a maid or footman. The hair on the back of her neck stood on end at every sound.

"*Azizam*," Aaditri said after a long stretch of silence. "You are unwell. I'm a mother. I know these things. Are you not sleeping? Writing all night? Or is it Alistair you are missing?"

Isobel fidgeted with the hem of her open robe. "Would you be disappointed if we waited to read more from *Udolpho*?"

Her companion raised her eyebrows. "You're not enjoying the story?"

"It's not that. In fact, it's better than I expected. Only, I—" How to explain she worried her imagination was working against her? "As you said, I've not been sleeping. Yes, some writing, but also a good deal of worrying over the story. Without it on my mind, I might sleep better."

Even to her, the excuse sounded silly. Worrying over the story? *Pssh*. They had not read anything remotely gothic in the book yet, no suits of armor coming to life, no apparitions, no villains or damsels in distress, nothing. But she knew *something* was coming—this was a Radcliffe novel, after all!—and she did not want to fuel the fire of her fear, a fear etched with a gaping jaw and drooling mouth. She shook the image from her mind.

"So worried over St. Aubert you can't sleep? I understand." Aaditri reached over to pat Isobel's hand. "We've not read far enough that we can't start from the beginning when the gentlemen return. Although, I think we'll wish to return home soon after."

Isobel bowed her head, hoping Aaditri would not tease her about wedding plans, as she had done at least three times this week. As exciting as the prospect of the long-awaited proposal and all it entailed, Isobel was not in the mood, not with the more pressing matter of being haunted weighing on her conscience.

"And your story?" Aaditri asked. "Will we continue reading your progress, or will you lose sleep knowing you must write faster than we can read?" She tittered.

"Oh, well, I don't wish to stop writing, but I think it might be a good idea to consider a respite from both reading and writing. To clear my mind."

Nodding sagely, Aaditri said, "I won't deny I'm disappointed not to hear what your Corentin does next, but you do need sleep. I do, too, I think. How do you enjoy these gothic tales without the running away of fantasy?" Lowering her voice, she said, "I would swear, but only to you, *azizam*, I saw Madame St. Aubert from *Udolpho* entering Mr. Trowbridge's suite yesterday evening. My imagination only, of course, for there is no one here except us, and the lovely lady is a fictional character. So finely was she dressed that she could not be mistaken for a maid. A trick of the mind, yes? I almost asked my lady's maid if there was another guest, someone not introduced to us, but then I thought better of it, in case it was, indeed, the imaginings of Madame St. Aubert."

Eyes widening, Isobel clarified, "You *saw* someone? Someone *in* the house? A woman?"

"Of course not!" Aaditri laughed. "My mind made a fantasy. I only thought I saw someone."

"A person?" Isobel pressed. "Or a... a *ghost*?"

Tilting her head, Aaditri studied Isobel before tittering again. "No slipping the idea into my head! Next, you'll try to convince me ghosts are real, and Mr. Trowbridge's house is haunted. No, no, *azizam*, you cannot fool me. There was no one. A shadow at the corner of my eye. I blame our St. Aubert in *The Mysteries of Udolpho*, the poor widower that he is now. I cast my thoughts back to my old friend, to Alistair's mother, and how Mr. Trowbridge must have suffered to mourn alone. With thoughts as these, how could I not imagine the shadow of a woman entering his suite? And no, don't say it was her ghost. It looked nothing like Alistair's mother!"

Isobel gaped. Aaditri had seen *her*. There was little doubt it was Isobel's ghost. But then, why was the ghost well-dressed? Isobel did not think ghosts changed attire throughout the day, and Isobel had only ever seen her wear a night rail.

One thing was for certain. Isobel had not gone barmy.

Chapter 24

Monday greeted Isobel with an unexpected letter from Alistair. She could not break the seal fast enough, eager to devour every word. Rather than large and looping, his handwriting was straight and even, the few flourishes elegant. As she scanned the letter, she heard the words in his voice. Her heart thumped a little louder. It would be a week tomorrow that he had left for London. So enraptured by her mystery woman, Isobel had not realized how much she missed him, from the headiness of his cologne and seductive smiles to his teasing jests.

His task was complete, his letter explained. He had recited his report, which was well received and offered ample fodder for discussion on how best to proceed with the new governor-general, and then he offered his resignation. It was both the easiest words he had spoken and the most difficult, but he was confident about their future and what he could offer her when he returned from London.

The return, if all went to plan, was Wednesday.

She captured her bottom lip between her teeth. Wednesday. She would see him again soon. His proposal was imminent. She would be an engaged woman *to Alistair*. Would they marry in a month? Would they wait? What about a double wedding with

Leila? Would her mother believe the news or think Isobel a fibber, weaving a tale as though she were a child prone to lies? So much to think about. So much to prepare! And what had she been doing all this time instead of planning for the life ahead? Ghost hunting. Of all the silly... *Oh!* She had only until Wednesday to solve the mystery. She could not very well follow around will-o'-wisps in her dressing gown with the gentlemen present, could she?

Letter in hand, she excused herself from the morning room to change into half-boots and a walking dress, then headed outside, wanting to reread Alistair's words and think beneath the yew tree. Once nestled on the bench, she enjoyed the letter thrice more in private, her only company that of birdsong.

The walk to the garden had been muddy from two days of rain and drizzle, but beneath the yew tree was dry, a sheltered oasis from the world. Of the terrace and sunken parterre garden, of the lawn and tree of Lebanon, this simple stone bench beneath the ancient yew was her favorite hideaway. Then, she was not truly alone, was she? Her gaze fell to the little gravestone.

Good heavens. The gravestone. A thought struck — what if the ghostly woman was not *haunting* the house so much as searching for her baby? What if the little one lying beneath the yew belonged to the woman? This was not a gothic story, then, but a love story, one between a mother and her child.

Isobel had not seen the ghost since that dreadful night. The shame of her reaction weighed her shoulders into a slump. The woman had not been angry and vengeful, some frightful wraith out to harm

Isobel, but rather a scared lady needing help. The face branded in Isobel's mind was horrific, but then, it had been night, only the lantern glow illuminating the woman's fear, and Isobel had arrived believing the woman supernatural. What if what she saw was not what she thought? If she had stayed a bit longer or if she had tried to help somehow.

Aaditri had seen the woman. This was *not* Isobel's imagination. Was the woman a ghost or real? Was she stricken by madness? Was she a guest here, hidden away from prying eyes, a relative of Mr. Trowbridge, or was she being held captive, driven mad by the loss of her child and the lock and key that bound her? Oh, there was the gothic novelist talking again, Isobel scolded. If the woman was being held captive, she would not be wandering the garden. But if she was free, why wait to wander by the cover of darkness?

Isobel had until Wednesday to discover the truth and offer aid as best she could.

That night, Isobel readied herself for the woman to make an appearance. She remained dressed, candle within reach. She did not want to scare the woman, after all, by sneaking up on her in the dark, as she had done previously. Isobel waited by her window, listening for floorboards to creak, watching for a glimpse of lantern light. Earlier temptation had her wanting to ask the butler outright about the locked door on the second floor and the mystery guest, but she decided against it, not because she feared him thinking she had gone mad but because whoever this was, if not a ghost, did not intend to be seen, either by her own volition or that of her keeper — or should that be *captor*. The woman's presence was kept secret.

However ready Isobel was to follow and confront the woman, it was not to be. In the wee hours, with no sway of a lantern, Isobel slipped off to sleep in her chair, waking the next morning to a bright sun and a crick in her neck.

Tonight, then, was the final night. The gentlemen would return tomorrow. Isobel worried the woman would remain a mystery. She could see it all so clearly. The gentlemen would return. Alistair would propose. And back to Sidvale they would return to confer with the vicar and prepare for the reading of the banns. Life would move forwards, and Isobel would always wonder at the woman's identity and if she ever reunited with the baby beneath the yew.

The day lingered, the sun inching its way across the sky in slow time. Each glance at a table clock had the hands standing still or clicking backwards. Would night ever fall?

A turn about the terrace, conversation and tea, a needle pulling thread, a chapter of a cheerier book read, and… at last, dusk cloaked the drawing room in shadows. Isobel excused herself early. Aaditri did not seem to mind, for she was as eager for evening as Isobel, ready for the morrow when the gentlemen would return, bearing gifts and stories enough to entertain the ladies.

Isobel prepared for her vigil. Tonight was the night. Tonight was the final night.

Seated in the chair before the window, a candle lit and several others at the ready, she waited and watched. Close to midnight, her eyelids drooped, and she wondered if she ought to do something productive while waiting, anything to keep her awake and not feel the time wasted. No matter what she chose, she would not be bright-eyed and well-rested for Alistair's return, but her pleasure at seeing him again and on his new path to becoming an English gentleman and all that entailed should have her smiling wide enough to fool anyone into thinking she had slept well.

Head nodding, she snorted herself awake with a snore. What had she been thinking? Oh, yes, something productive.

As she turned to eye the desk in the corner where she kept her writing box, she heard a floorboard creak. Isobel stilled. Her hands gripped the chair arms. Another creak right outside her bedchamber door. So loudly her heart pounded, she almost missed the gentle *thud* of the stairwell door closing. This was it! This was her chance!

Isobel snatched her candle. Cupping her hand in front of the flame to keep it from guttering or extinguishing as she moved, she left her room to follow the mystery woman.

The stairwell was dark and empty when she entered, but she heard another *thud* below — the jib door. Quick steps took her down the stairs to the ground floor. She opened the jib door and peered into the hallway. Darkness peered back. The garden would be the woman's destination. Isobel paused before opening the side door — unless Mr. Trowbridge's suite was the destination? Aaditri had seen the woman *inside* the house, not the garden. Well, Isobel was not going to traipse around the house, much less her host's apartments, so off to the garden she went.

The faint glow of the lantern swayed ahead. Isobel sighed in relief. The woman was slinking towards the fountain, her gait ambling, stumbling, shuffling, uneven. Isobel refused to be afraid. Chin raised and chest proud, she followed.

Even from this distance, she could see the woman wearing her night rail again, barefooted, no less. Free-flowing hair cascaded to her shoulders, dark hair, uncapped but stylishly trimmed and brushed — curious for a ghost and more so for a mad woman or captive. By the time Isobel drew close enough to initiate the much sought-after conversation, the woman had taken her usual seat at the fountain's edge and resumed the lullaby as though recreating their previous encounter. Although Isobel held her candle for all the world to see and did not tread quietly in her following, her presence had not been noted.

Now was the time. Isobel squeezed her eyes against the image of the ghastly face that had haunted her for days. Now was the moment.

Clearing her throat to draw attention but not startle, Isobel said, "Pardon the intrusion. I've no wish to frighten you. I only wish to introduce — "

As before, the woman whipped her head to stare at Isobel. And as before, drool coated the woman's chin and front of her fine linen night rail. Eyes fixed on Isobel, pupils dilating.

Isobel stood her ground, offering a weak smile of reassurance. "My name is Isobel. May I offer my assis — "

The woman hissed, spittle spraying.

Rather than continue, Isobel held her peace, at least for the moment. They studied each other, taking each other's measure. Of several things, Isobel was certain. The woman was assuredly not a ghost. A flesh and blood person sat on the edge of that fountain. The woman was also remarkably attractive, although a fair bit older than Isobel — she could not hazard a guess at the age because, despite the smooth complexion and pleasant features, there was unquestionably something *wrong*. Mad? Captive? *Drugged*?

Isobel's memory had not deceived her or played tricks. The lady's skin was so translucent as to appear veiny, her hands red and raw, the eyes hazy as they tried to study Isobel and make sense of this stranger holding a candle aloft. This was a damsel in distress, kept drugged somehow and held captive in Mr. Trowbridge's house. How she escaped her confines at night and why she did not run away, Isobel could only guess, but she suspected whatever drug was being administered kept the lady docile and confused.

Which meant — *Mr. Trowbridge was a villain?*

With a deep breath, Isobel said, "I'm here to help you. Will you come with me?"

Her companion whimpered. Then, with a darting gaze, she seemed to realize she was in the garden after midnight, dressed in nought but linen and about to be touched by a stranger. She shrank from Isobel, hissing again. Isobel raised her hand to show an empty palm of friendship, but the woman panicked, scrambling along the fountain's edge and knocking the lantern into the water. The stained glass bobbed twice before it sank, the flame within extinguishing.

Shrieking, the woman ran past Isobel towards the house.

Swearing an oath beneath her breath, Isobel followed her, shielding her flame with her hand. By the time she reached the second floor, her bedchamber before her and the sitting room in sight, the woman had disappeared. Isobel narrowed her eyes at the door she suspected would be locked.

Who was she?

Chapter 25

Alistair breathed in the fresh country air. His father's house looked from the outside much as they had left it. They had only been gone for a week, but it felt like an eternity. He had not favored London. Not that he had seen much of it since they had done little more than attend to business, but what he had seen was enough to mark it as a place he did not care to frequent. Should Isobel wish to see it one day, it would be his pleasure to take her; otherwise, he saw no appeal.

Ah, but *this* house held an appeal. Isobel awaited inside, and that was all the appeal he needed.

Smoothing a hand through his hair, he followed his father and Mr. Owen into the house. If he could have a moment to wash the grime of travel, that would be ideal, but he could not wait so long to see his ladylove. To walk up the stairs to the first floor rather than to walk into the drawing room was counterintuitive to his desires. He had thoughts, eyes, and heart for Isobel alone.

The butler greeted them in the reception hall, exchanging words with Alexander. Alistair did not listen. His attention was fixed on the drawing room doors. Vaguely, he was aware of his father excusing himself. Alistair did not so much as turn his head. Instead, he marched to the doors, not bothering to see if Mr. Owen followed. A footman anticipated him. Without breaking stride, Alistair moved from entry into the drawing room, his gaze sweeping from right to — *nazanin*.

His lips curved. Oh, she was remarkable. Curious how a week away had blurred his memory. Throughout the trip, he had recalled the former Isobel with her ill-fitting gowns. What a surprise to return to the new Isobel — confident and *alluring*.

Mrs. Aaditri Owen and Isobel stood to greet him and Mr. Owen. They had been waiting. He saw no embroidery, no books, nothing except a tea tray. Had her pulse raced when she heard the carriage wheels against the drive? Had they sneaked peeks out the window as the gentlemen descended? Heaven knew *his* pulse raced now.

Moving ahead of Mr. Owen, he accepted Aaditri's outstretched hands and leaned in to exchange cheek kisses, three each. "*Salaam*, Aaditri *khanoom*."

"*Salaam*," she said, then turned her attention to her husband.

Alistair stepped to Isobel, taking her hand between both of his before placing it over his heart. "Isobel, *nazaninam*."

His grin deepened to see her blush. As he had done when stepping out of the carriage, he breathed deeply, inhaling the breath of fresh air that was Isobel.

"*Salaam, koshtip*," Isobel said, her words little more than an exhale.

He raised his eyebrows. "You remembered? I *am* impressed." He did not correct her awkward pronunciation, for it sounded music to his ears to hear so flirty of a compliment from Isobel's lips.

Had he not wished to inhale more of her rosy scent—oh, yes, he could tell she had taken extra care today for his arrival, an effort that touched his heart as complimentary as her Persian words—she would have taken his breath away. Her gown, a shade of blue, the hue of a cloudless sky, became her. Blue was, most assuredly, her color. It somehow accentuated the pink of her cheeks, the arch of her dark brows, the depth of her eyes.

"Have you missed me?" He hooked her fingers over his and brought her hand to his lips so he could kiss the air above her knuckles.

Before she could answer, he released her hand and stepped away to include the Owens. He had made a spectacle of himself with the greeting, but he did not care. She was his, and he was hers, and the Owens knew this already. Yes, it was good to return to her side.

Aaditri swatted at Mr. Owen's coat, as though knocking the dust from the journey. All theatrical, of course, for they had traveled in the carriage, not horseback.

"I see our host has absented himself," she said, "as usual, but I cannot fault him. He is wiser than the two of you."

Mr. Owen chuckled. "On the contrary, madam. We are wise enough to see to our ladies first."

"In *this* condition?" Aaditri scoffed. "Oh no, no, no, Mr. Owen, I prefer my husband to greet me in pristine form. Off you both go. We'll ring for a fresh brew—ours is cold now, and only hot will do—and await your return. Off with you! I want to enjoy the scent of pomade and cologne, not of horse. Shoo!"

Her teasing elicited a wink from her husband, but he obeyed, as did Alistair, the two taking their leave of the ladies, but only for an interval. Alistair, for his part, could not return fast enough. He took the stairs two at a time.

He gazed over the brim of his teacup at Isobel, making love to her with his eyes.

They all rejoined in the drawing room, his father included. He allowed Alexander and Mr. Owen to lead the conversation, regaling them with stories after offering gifts. Alistair bode his time, awaiting the opportunity to sequester Isobel. Had she begun to read *The Mysteries of Udolpho* yet? How had she devoted her time this week?

He felt his father's gaze before he turned to meet it. Alistair set his teacup in its saucer and arched a brow.

Alexander had been as supportive as Alistair could have wished, more so even, and now, he was eager to see all settled between his son and Isobel, but Alistair had yet to pinpoint why his father's acquiescence of all things bothered him when it was what he wanted. From opposed to all things to accepting of all things. The London trip offered no hints as to why the sudden change of heart. It had left Alistair with more questions than answers, as his father had taken him aside several times and hedged at wanting a private word, each tête-à-tête ending with a vague exchange of nothing remotely private, such as Alistair's plans for requesting an audience with Mrs.

Lambeth, or his thoughts about his father's house, or the weather. Alistair suspected his father wanted to talk about Shahrazad, but there were never any hints to the direction of his thoughts.

Alexander looked from Alistair to Isobel and back. "You should have seen him in action, Miss Lambeth, when he took the floor with his report. The Company has lost the best province governor it could have wished for, but all is done now, the resignation made."

Isobel turned to Alistair. "Did they offer any resistance? Beg you to stay?"

Alexander answered on his son's behalf. "They would have offered him the moon if they thought it would secure what they wanted. No, my son was firm, composed, and suggested his successor should they wish to consider his recommendations, which I daresay they will. Even in his farewell, he had them eating out of the palm of his hands. You should be a politician, my boy. Maybe," he waggled his eyebrows at this, "you could consider running as an MP in the future."

A rapt audience though she may be to Alexander's answer, she turned her questions again to Alistair. "How do you like being one step closer to becoming an English gentleman?"

His father made to speak for him once more, but this time, Alistair set his teacup and saucer on the tray and stood. "It would please me to invite Miss Lambeth for a turn on the terrace. Does this suit?"

No one objected, and Isobel accepted, at last providing Alistair the opportunity he wished to converse with his rose blossom without the ears of all and sundry, although he had no doubt their eyes would follow the couple's path from one end of the terrace to the other.

Escorting Isobel outside, he smirked as soon as the terrace door closed. "Now, I may shock you with pretty Persian words about my longing to kiss you."

He did not need the Persian words after all.

Isobel gasped, then hid her expression behind clasped hands. "I'm not well rested enough to handle allusions to naughtiness. *Behave*."

"Not well rested? What has—"

With a wave of a hand, she began the promenade across the terrace. "I want to hear about London, about the meeting. No, I don't. I want to hear about *you*. No second thoughts? No regrets? Does this mean you'll never return to India, not even to say goodbye to those you left behind?"

"All is at peace. I am free of burdens. I do not deny I enjoyed my position in the Company, but now I am my own man and am ready for my own land, my decisions my own, my everything my own. All farewells I wished to make, I did so when leaving with Mr. Owen. I had no intentions of returning, with or without my father's support. There are people I will miss. Friends, neighbors, the laborers I had come to know. There is a pain *here*." He held his hand to his chest. "All I've ever known I have left behind. But it is a good pain, one which tells me I have known a good life with good people. Now, I am fulfilling all my mother wanted for me, but in my way."

He glanced towards the drawing room, wishing its inhabitants were not behind the panes of glass. His arms ached to draw Isobel into an embrace. Soon, he would say the words that would bind them. It could not happen soon enough. He had waited until the London business was at an end. He had waited long enough.

Isobel said, "Your father seems pleased. All his posturing, and he's so supportive now. Were you able to talk more in London? Become better acquainted?"

"Yes and no. He is supportive, yes, eager to see me settled and ready to do what is needed to help me fulfill my plans." He hesitated, wondering if he should voice his concerns. They sounded ungrateful and unfounded to him, but if he could not voice his concerns to his future wife…. "He has become exceedingly *biddable*. I have no explanation. I am pleased. This is in our favor, yes? But if I asked him if I should ride my horse backwards, I believe he would agree wholeheartedly. Do I make meaning?"

Her brows furrowed in thought. For the briefest of moments, Alistair thought she looked tired, not the tired of a young lady who had not slept in anticipation of her lover's arrival but one who had many worries on her mind. A shadow lingered under her eyes. He shook away these observations, for she was exquisite, nothing less.

Isobel said, "I admit, I thought similarly while you were away. He's become downright amenable. As you say, in our favor. But it does make me wonder. Is there, perhaps, something he is hiding? Something he doesn't want us to know?"

Alistair's pace slowed as they made their second turn around the terrace. "I do not follow."

With a hollow laugh, she said, "Oh, don't mind me. I'm being silly and turning the mystery of your father's kindness into a chapter from a gothic novel."

He would have joined in her laughter had her expression and tone not said to him she did not find her questions silly at all.

Chapter 26

That evening, Alistair entered the drawing room expecting gaiety and festivities. With them all together again, and with him being a free man ready to embark on a new path with his anticipated offer of marriage, the mood should be bright and airy. A card table was set up, along with a light supper tray. He rubbed his hands together, eager to partner with Isobel at the games table.

Mr. Owen's mood was as cheery as Alistair's, and Aaditri teased and flirted with them all. Isobel sat at the card table, her attention glazed—undoubtedly imagining a fictional card game with a blackguard being challenged for cheating or some dastardly plot of similar quality.

The host mulled in quiet contemplation, his shoulder propped against the window casement, his eyes combing the dark exterior of the terrace. His pensiveness was nothing new. More frequently than not, in London, he had slipped into these silent stupors, as though on the precipice of a great confession or simply lost in meditation. Alistair worried his father was displeased with him despite claiming the contrary.

Shrugging his concerns aside for now, he accepted the chair next to Isobel. With a cheeky grin, he whispered, "Has the rogue been caught with a cheating hand yet?"

Dazed, she continued to stare into the ether. Her imaginary scene must be splendid not to notice his arrival or hear his words. He waited and observed her loveliness while the Owens moved to join them at the table, his father continuing his study of the window. However lovely he knew Isobel to be, the shadows beneath her eyes caught his attention again, darker than before, worry lines creasing her brow.

Her expression spoke to him of more than her imagination-induced woolgathering. Something troubled her.

Leaning closer so the Owens did not hear him above their own conversation, he said to test his theory, "Isobel. Set aside your scene. The game soon begins."

She did not acknowledge hearing him, only frowned deeper. It was then he realized she was staring at his father with a troubled expression. Or at least her gaze was in that direction, although he could not be certain she *saw* his father, perhaps still imagining whatever plot played in her writer's mind. All the same, her eyes bore a hole in his father's back.

"Isobel," he said again, then touched her arm.

At the feel of his fingertips, she jerked her head to face him, her mouth forming an *Oh* of surprise. Looking about her, she flushed. He squeezed her forearm in reassurance, but she shifted away from him as though to discourage his touch. Had he said or done something wrong? What troubled her?

He turned his attention to his father. Coaxing him to the table required more effort. Like Isobel, Alexander was lost to his thoughts, seeming not to hear the calls for his attention, not until Mr. Owen retrieved him with a hand on a shoulder. At last, their game began, mingled with jests and stories and all the gaiety Alistair had hoped. Almost.

"Isobel, now is your turn," he said for the fifth time over the stretch of an hour. "Isobel," he repeated. "Isobel."

Another touch of his hand and another startled expression, then she was back in the game, returned to the land of the living, but still with the unhappy brow. Her responses to conversation were curt, and her responses to Alistair terser still.

Had Alistair not been in so stellar a mood, he would have found her behavior distressing. She did not seem the least pleased to be at the game table, her mind miles away, but not with her usual imaginary abandon. Was she not happy to see him? Had his week's absence not brought more fondness to her heart? She was, for all his flirty teasing throughout the evening, distracted to the point of *his* distraction. He would have assumed her plotting a scene, but there was an uneasiness about her, a distance he could cross, almost a coldness towards him. Was he imagining this?

At the first opportunity to speak more openly below the raucous conversation, he whispered to Isobel, "You are troubled. Did something occur while I was away? Will you not share your thoughts?"

Avoiding his eye contact, Isobel physically tensed. "Of course, nothing happened. Nothing at all. All is perfectly perfect."

"Then why are your knuckles white from gripping the arms of the chair? Set your mind at ease by sharing your troubles, my flower."

Snapping, she said, "Absolutely, positively, nothing is wrong."

Sleep did not come easy that evening. He would not have fretted had circumstances been different. Had he not returned only that day. Had he not been planning his offer. Had his reception not been met with mixed responses. She could not be having second thoughts about him, could she?

Alistair observed Isobel in the morning room as the family breakfasted. He observed her during the family's ramble outside to take in the brief spell of sunshine before a drizzling rain began. He observed her during tea. Aside from admiring her, as he was wont to do, he watched for signs of distraction, hesitancies, nervousness, anything to hint at possible second thoughts after his week's absence. She must know the proposal was imminent. They had spoken about this at length, that he would wait until after London. The time was nigh. Did that frighten her?

All his observations revealed her inattentiveness. For the briefest of exchanges, he resorted to repetition to catch her interest. Part of him wished to take Aaditri aside and ask if anything had happened or been said to discourage Isobel from his suit, but he did not wish to involve anyone in so private a matter.

As if her behavior were not troubling enough, his father was increasingly anxious and equally distracted, as though he wished to have his house to himself, although he said nothing of it. Their time as guests drew short. The Owens would want to return to Sidvale sooner rather than later, and following his offer, he would need to request an audience with Mrs. Lambeth, which was incorrectly ordered, but he would not wait for her permission since she had shown little interest thus far, and it was Isobel's choice, not her mother's. Yes, their time of departure drew near. But why was this happy occasion of his impending proposal turning sour?

After tea, his father took his leave of them for the afternoon, as did Mr. Owen. For Mr. Owen's part, he left the drawing room with all the bombast a newly elected Company director could muster, citing at least a dozen tasks he must complete in preparation for the June meeting — *director business*, he had winked half a dozen times. Mrs. Owen tittered and fawned over his every word, pleased her husband would be staying in England indefinitely rather than returning to India. After many years of lost elections, he had at last succeeded in his promotion.

With the gentlemen out of the drawing room, Alistair saw his opportunity to dote on Isobel. Aaditri busied herself with her embroidery, pretending to take no notice of Alistair's guiding Isobel to the terrace window, their view of misting rain.

He opened the conversation with, "Would a week be appropriate for our return to Sidvale?"

"Mmmm," she hummed, staring outside.

"A week would allow time for our… *conversation*… and a letter requesting an audience with your mother. It would provide needed time to confer with my father about our plans and arrange for the return travel. We will, thankfully, have the Owens' carriage for the journey."

"Mmmm."

Alistair's jaw tightened. There was much to be done, and only a week in which to do it, their entire future lying ahead of them, and all she could do was offer a noncommittal sound? His pulse drummed rudely in his ears. She could not show disinterest any clearer. If he went down on bended knee now, he believed she would reject his offer, or at least delay her answer. What had changed?

His tongue was dry and heavy when he tried to swallow. One week apart, and she had changed her mind. What was he to do without his Isobel? He had never met another woman like her and knew he never would again. He did not want another woman. How had he upset her — was it something he had done or something he had not done? The wrong gift, perhaps? Should he have written more letters? Fewer? Her distraction was one thing, but her complete lack of interest had him tugging at the edge of his waistcoat.

"Isobel?" He watched her profile for a reaction. "Isobel? Have you…" He swallowed again. "…a change of heart?"

"Mmmm." Then, her nose crinkled in thought. "Wait. What did you say? Oh, our departure. Yes. A week is good. Yes."

He shifted his weight to his other foot. "Now, we have time. Aaditri is not listening. Let us talk, yes? What troubles you?"

"Me?" She moved a slow glance in his direction, staring at him blankly. "Nothing. Why would something be troubling me?"

"I cannot resolve the problem if I'm not apprised of the problem. Something has created distance between us. Is it something I have said or not said?"

Brows rising high on her forehead, she angled to face him. "Whatever are you on about? All is as it has been."

"No, Isobel," he insisted, keeping his voice low but unable to curve the edge of his words. "Your thoughts are your own. If you cannot share them with me, what am I to think? You should wish to lay your worries at my feet, even if I'm to blame, especially if I'm to blame."

The more she denied, and the more erratic her mood changes and reactions, the clearer it was *he* was to blame, from last night's terseness to today's dismissiveness.

Isobel glanced at Aaditri's bowed head before slipping her hand into his. "I *do* have a secret, but I can't share it, not yet, and of all people, not with you. Please understand. If I share, you'll… you'll… well, I don't wish to learn how you'll react or what you'll think. I *can't* tell you this, not until I know more. If you must know, I'm protecting you with my silence."

He squeezed her hand but was more confused now than before. There was little he could do except afford her another day to be more forthcoming. How was he to offer for her if she harbored secrets she did not trust to share?

The mystery woman had not made an appearance or a peep since the return of the gentlemen. Isobel remained vigilant. Throughout the day, she watched for signs, some brief glimpse, eyeing maids' profiles at every opportunity lest one of them bear a resemblance. Throughout the night, she listened for creaks, groans, lullabies, anything. Any excuse she found, she returned to her room and the second floor so she could press her ear to the locked door and eye the keyhole. No luck, but she still had a week to formulate and initiate a plan.

Mr. Trowbridge was holding the woman captive. Of that, Isobel was now certain. On several occasions, she had encountered her host at the jib door, leaving the stairwell as she entered. More often than not, he showed no recognition of her, as though she were not there, his mind a million miles away. On two occasions, he was startled to cross her path, his face guilt-stricken as he mumbled an apology. There could be no other reason for him to go to the second floor than to ensure his captive was safely bound. For all his kindness, he was a villain fit for a Radcliffe story.

There could be other explanations. The mystery woman could be an acquaintance or servant, someone he knew who had lost the plot, and he was doing a kindness by caring for her. If so, then why keep the woman secret? Why keep her so medicated she could not escape? Or she could be an opium addict. Isobel had never met one to know the signs. But why would he allow an opium user to stay at the house? And why keep her a secret? Every alternative circled to the same question of *why the secret*. The secretiveness proved his guilt.

Isobel needed assistance if she was to help the woman, but it was not as though she could tell Alistair. One did not accuse the father of the gentleman courting her of holding women behind lock and key. Besides, Alistair would see the most logical action as confronting his father, which would leave Isobel vulnerable as the one who knew the secret. Next thing she knew, she could be behind the locked door, as well. There was also the concern that Alistair would think *she* had lost the plot. She had already confessed to him about hearing sounds. Now, to claim a woman was held against her will? He would think her mad. Alistair's own sanity must be considered, as well. After all this time, he had rekindled his relationship with his father. How could she ruin that, villainous father or not? Which was better, to know one's father was a villain or remain ignorant? She believed this would hurt Alistair too much for a confession. Best keep this to herself. But how to initiate another encounter with the woman if the door remained locked and Mr. Trowbridge on his guard?

Were she not so concerned about the woman needing aid, she would be suffering disappointment. This should be a time of celebration. She and Alistair should be bowing their heads together to conspire about their future, a future which should include his father, that supportive gentleman who trusted his son's choices despite his initial reservations. As it was, she needed to concentrate on the woman. Once she had helped the woman break free, she could then focus on herself and her future with Alistair.

The situation, every aspect of it, required delicacy.

Alistair thought otherwise.

He caught her alone the next day. She had been stepping into the ground floor hallway after another round of locked door listening when he spied her.

With a look to his left and right, he ushered her into the billiard room across from the jib door. For a heart-thumping minute, she thought he intended to kiss her. Isobel had been hoping for this moment since his arrival home but had been too distracted with the mystery woman to invite flirtation.

"We must speak," Alistair insisted, closing the door firmly behind them. He looked around the room to ensure they were alone. "We must speak with candor. I did not sleep for worry."

Isobel waved for him to sit as she did the same.

"You are angry with me," he said, leaning forwards to rest his forearms on his thighs. "I have erred, and you wish me not to offer my hand."

Taken aback, Isobel straightened her posture and mouthed her confusion.

"You are distracted, *eshgham*, my love, distant and dismissive. This was not the way before I left, yet I return to find a woman who can scarcely look at me. Where have I erred, and how may I make amends?"

Burying her face in her hands from embarrassment, she mumbled, "No. It's not you."

"Not me? You have had a change of heart, and I wish to understand why."

She dropped her hands and shook her head. "No, that's not what I meant. Nothing has changed. No change of heart. You're perfect and wonderful and all that I adore, just as you were before you left. I'm merely in the middle of something that has my full attention. I don't mean to ignore you. I'm merely, as you said, distracted. Forgive me."

When she began to rise, thinking all was settled, he clasped her hand and tugged her to resume her seat.

"Tell me, Isobel. What has your attention."

Shaking her head again, she said, "Let's forget my silliness and talk about your plans. Will you be staying with the Owens when we return to Sidvale?"

He sandwiched her hand between both of his. "I will not leave the room until you tell me what has distracted you. Your flights of fancy, they are endearing, until they are not. This, whatever it is, has stolen you from me. I'm not a jealous man, Isobel, but I would wish you to trust me if your feelings are unchanged."

She stared at the parquet floor, unable to meet his eyes. She could not tell him. She simply could not.

With a squeeze of her hand, he pressed, "This week should be ours to plan our future. Why do you not trust me?"

"It's not that," she muttered. "I'm *protecting* you. More to the point, it's not my secret to share."

A stolen glance had her wanting to trust him. If not him, who? They had arrived at this house as a team. Why should that change? Why should she allow his father to come between them? He deserved to know the truth about his father, and given how little he knew of the man, maybe this would not sting as much as if they were close.

The truth was she needed his help. It did neither of them any favors if he thought her affections had changed, and keeping a secret from him, despite the risks of confession, was proving impossible. She should have realized that from the start.

Heaving a weighty sigh, she asked, "Do you know where your father goes when he absents himself?"

"His study? It is not my concern." Alistair's eyes did not waver from hers.

"He goes to the second floor."

Searching her face for more information, he held his silence before offering, "To speak with you? To discourage you from accepting my suit?"

"No. Not that. He… he goes there to ensure what is behind a locked door is secure."

"Yes, that is the purpose of a locked door."

Isobel tugged her hand from his grasp so she could fidget with the embroidered trim of her open robe. "Do you remember the sounds I heard?"

"Your ghostly maid who forgot her dust?"

She nodded, focusing her gaze on the embroidery. "She's neither a ghost nor a maid. I… I don't know who she is, but… she's unwell. She's being hidden behind that door, and I believe drugged against her will." In a quiet voice she hoped he would not hear, she added, "By your father."

She felt his sharp intake of breath more than she heard it, as though he sucked the air out of the room. Her chest hurt, and her lungs burned. Had she really said that aloud? To Alistair? She could not now recall the words.

Alistair stood. "I ask for your trust. I beg the woman who would accept my hand to trust me. Instead, you mock my family. I admire you as a talented novelist, but not this. Do not weave tales to hide behind."

Standing and meeting his angry expression with one of her own, she said, "I *am* trusting you, and I'm *not* making a joke. I thought I was being haunted by a ghost, but it turned out not to be a ghost; rather, it was a ghostly sort of woman who I discovered was unwell." She took a deep breath. "But I don't think she's unwell because she's, well, *un*well, rather she's perfectly well, only medicated beyond comprehension and perhaps sanity," deep breath, "and *someone* had kept her hidden from all of us and a secret that no one, not even the servants, is talking about," deep breath, "and who do I see going to the second floor but your father, and so he *must* be a dastardly villain," deep breath, "and it is up to me to stop him because I'm the only one who seems to care a woman is in distress," deep breath, "*and* here I am trusting you, and you accuse me of *lying*." Inhaling deeply after her tirade, she crossed her arms and dared him to reply.

His eyes narrowed, and he studied her. "You accuse my father of villainy? And his household staff of being accomplices?" With a shake of his head, he said, "If you no longer wished me to pursue you, you should have said with bold, honest words. It would wound me, yes, but it is superior to this... this gothic rubbish. If you will excuse me, Miss Lambeth."

Without a backwards glance, he walked to the billiard room door. Isobel's heart thumped wildly, her breath short, her mind whirring and spinning. What had she done? Why had she admitted the truth? Oh, what had she done? She cried out for him, but he closed the door to the sound of his name.

Chapter 27

S aturday passed without Alistair needing to inter-
act with Isobel. He ensured others were present
any time they were to be in each other's company. Undeterred, she made several efforts to initiate
private conversation, which Alistair volleyed, not
wanting tempers to flare or to hear nonsense excuses
and hurtful accusations. When the company of others
could not be guaranteed, he made himself scarce,
inviting his father for a ride.

What he had hoped would ease his mind of
Isobel's claims left him with more questions than
answers. While out riding with his father, he did not
dare broach anything that might validate or refute
what Isobel had said, but he did make a concentrated
effort to slip his mother's name into the conversation,
hoping his father would speak his mind, as it had
seemed for so long he wished to do. Instead, his father
had spent the outing as distracted as Isobel had been
and with no shortage of moodiness and melancholy.
Whatever Alexander wished to share with his son,
nothing was forthcoming.

In truth, he did not know his father well. He did
not know the man at all, really. Yet he refused to give
credence to posits of captive damsels and villainy.

Yesterday, Alistair's mind had been so fraught with fears of Isobel's rejection that was all he heard from her words, a nonsensical tale inspired by Radcliffe's *A Sicilian Romance* to push Alistair away, his week's absence the catalyst to her change of heart. He had heard what he did not want to hear because it was what he had expected to hear — rejection. Upon the day's reflection, he realized what a disservice he had done them both. As with his father, something worried Isobel, and while her accusations were outlandish, Alistair did not think her capable of untruths. While his father would not speak his mind, holding his cards close to his chest, Isobel had been honest with what was on her mind, something that could not have been easy given it was about her future father-in-law. Yes, what was on her mind were fanciful imaginings but not lies. He also believed if she did not wish to continue their courtship, she would tell him unequivocally.

Part of him admonished the ease with which he wished to forgive her. Had she not accused his father of abducting a woman? The other part of him that prompted his rise to heroism spoke louder. His ladylove needed him, if for no other reason than to help her see reason and think logically. Here was his chance to play the hero.

Sunday morning, he joined the Owens and Isobel in the morning room, his father breakfasting in his rooms, according to the butler. Within a minute of his taking a seat, Isobel made and held eye contact. He did not look away. However she interpreted his response, the tension eased from her expression. They listened to Aaditri and Mr. Owen arguing over plans for after breakfast—attend service at the local church or walk the grounds.

Alistair was curious about the church service. He had expected them to be present every Sunday since arriving, but his father had discouraged attendance. For that matter, his father had discouraged calls from neighbors and calling on neighbors. It had not bothered Alistair before, but it did now in light of Isobel's theories. Why would his father not wish to introduce his son to everyone in Burghfield? There was no reason unless he had something to hide. From his understanding, his father was not a recluse and enjoyed the company of his neighbors. What was there to hide, then?

Midway through their argument, Alistair interrupted with, "I desire to walk Miss Lambeth to the yew tree." When everyone turned to look at him, he added, "To take in the good weather while it lasts."

Aaditri was the first to speak. "A splendid notion! Have I not been saying that is precisely what we ought to do, Josiah? Let us enjoy the day." She shushed her husband's would-be reply and looked to Isobel, who nodded with wide-eyed eagerness.

They left word with the butler of their whereabouts, in case Alexander wished to join them, and then proceeded from the morning room outside, pairing off soon thereafter.

Isobel walked silently at his side. Of all he could say, Alistair did not know where to begin. He allowed the silence to linger, hoping their companionship would be enough to balm the wound, at least to start.

When they reached the yew tree, the Owens winked and continued to the fountain in the small garden, leaving behind Isobel and Alistair. They likely thought the lovebirds wished to exchange poetical verses of affection. Regardless, Alistair was pleased with the privacy. It was, after all, his plan for the morning.

Before he had made himself comfortable on the bench, Isobel blurted, "I'm so sorry for saying what I did, and I know you can never forgive me — what a dastardly thing to have said, and about your father, no less — but I hope you can find some way to blame my overactive imagination and — "

He placed two fingers against her lips. "It is for me to apologize. I promised to trust but did not. Tell me about your ghostly maid, please."

Isobel furrowed her brows. When he moved his hands for her to speak, she said, "I would rather not. Let us pretend I never said — "

"Isobel, please. I wish to help. To help, I must understand. I will not react angrily again. It is my promise to you. Also my promise is to listen with intensity to all you say, never to accuse you of imaginings. I only wish to be your hero, yet when offered the chance, I accused you of dreaming, of imagining, of lying. I have failed as your hero."

"No, Alistair. You didn't fail. I did. I should have been forthcoming." She worried her lips, looking everywhere except at him. Her eyes fell on the gravestone. With a sigh, she said, "First, you must know I never meant to hurt you or distance myself or anything of the sort. I want your offer desperately, passionately, madly. Oh, I shouldn't have said madly, for you may have changed your mind now you've realized I'm unhinged enough to think — "

His chuckling stopped her mid-sentence. "I am relieved you can forgive my reaction. Relieved you have not had a change of heart. Beyond relieved. We will revisit this. For now, let us make sense of your mystery. You say there is someone staying on the second floor? A guest, perhaps? A servant who is unwell?"

"Yes." Isobel wrung her hands but took several deep breaths as though to steady her nerves. "Someone else is in the house with us. It's not a ghost. It's a real woman, flesh and blood. I've seen her several times now and tried to talk with her, but she's... ill. Aaditri has seen her, too. We've only seen her in the evening, although the servants must know about her; there's no way they couldn't."

"What has you thinking she is ill?"

Blanching, Isobel said, "Physically, she *looks* ill. Her skin, her hands, her vacant stares — something is wrong. She stumbles when she walks. But more to the point, she struggles to communicate with me or understand what I'm saying. The few times I've tried to approach her, she's become frightened. I don't know if she has the mind of a child or if she's being medicated. Laudanum? Opium? I don't know."

"And my father knows she's here. She is a great secret, then." He mulled over her words, listening to the rustle of the wind through the leaves, before offering, "Rather than my father as the villain, have you thought he is the hero? If she is ill, he could have cast her out or institutionalized her, be it in a lie-in hospital or asylum. Instead, he is sheltering her, caring for her, ensuring the silence of the servants."

"It's possible." Isobel eyed the fountain across the lawn. "I don't think she's a maid, but I don't know who else she could be. I've only seen her in a night rail, but Aaditri saw her in evening attire. Both our impressions are of quality. The night rail is new and very fine. Regardless, why keep her a secret? Why not share with us his efforts to help this woman? Ooooh. I'd never thought, but... what if... what if she's his sister?"

Alistair could not answer. He did not know. All he knew was keeping this a secret seemed a kindness to the woman if the illness was in her mind rather than her body, kinder still if she was a relation. Did he have an aunt? From his perspective, his father was keeping her safe from harm, be that harm to herself or from others.

"I do not think," he began, lacing his fingers in his lap, "my father would appreciate a confrontation, but the best course of action is to ask him, not accuse. I will first confer with Aaditri on her experience and speak merely of that, leaving your name from the conversation. I believe that if I ask him directly, he will not lie. We would then understand his motives and could support his efforts to help her."

"No!" Isobel rushed to answer. "No, please. It's not that I think badly of him, at least not anymore, or that I worry he'll be angry or... but... well..." She began to stutter and fidget. "If this has been kept a secret, it is not without reason. If we force an explanation he's not ready to make, it may strain the relationship the two of you have been building and compromise the mystery woman — what if *she* has begged for secrecy? We should respect that, at least in so far as we can assure her safety."

He thought over her words before prompting, "What if she'll confide in you? Then, it is her choice, and it does not disrespect my father's secret."

Isobel brightened. "Yes. Yes, that's perfect. Unless she cannot speak. I don't know. How do I initiate contact at least? I've not seen her since your return. The connecting door remains locked, so I can't barge in and beg her attention."

"Slip a note beneath the door?"

"Oh. Hmm. No, what if someone intercepted the — oh! I have it! At our last encounter, she dropped her lantern. I brought it to my room and still have it there. What if I slipped the note inside the lantern? I could then leave the lantern at the door. If anyone saw the lantern, they would surely return it to the woman, not knowing a note was tucked inside for her to read."

Chuckling again, Alistair said, "I think you could safely slip a note beneath the door or be brave and ask a footman — however startled he would be — to deliver the note for you. But if you wish subterfuge, I see no reason not to play the game."

"Yes, this is what I'll do. I knew you'd come to my rescue, Alistair. If she does not wish to confide in me, then it'll be her choice, and your father and the mystery woman may keep their secret. But we'll have offered the opportunity for honesty and assured her safety in the process. The note also gives her the chance to write if she can't speak, assuming she has writing implements, of course. I can see a dozen reasons this plan could fail, but if we assume she's *not* being held captive, this might work. Infinitely better than our continuing to play silly buggers at the fountain every few nights."

"If all fails, I will be heroic and break open the locked door to rescue her."

Isobel gasped, looking all the world like she believed he would do it and likely thinking it a grand idea. Alistair knew the moment she realized he was teasing her. Her neck flushed pink from her fichu upwards, painting her a lovely image in rose.

Chapter 28

Isobel waited until she dressed for dinner to enact the first part of her plan.

It began with a brief note. She mulled over what to say and how to say it for longer than she wished, but this needed to be perfect to elicit the desired result. A short introduction to start. Then an expressed wish to help in any way possible. Next came an invitation. Two, really. Isobel invited a written reply — ooh, she should include a piece of graphite in case the mystery woman did not have writing implements of her own — while also promising to be available in the sitting room on the second floor. With what she thought was a touch of genius, she promised to wait between eleven and one so as not to interfere with the lady's evening constitutional should she *not* wish for the interview. Isobel would wait there every night before making herself scarce at the one o'clock chime.

Isobel chewed the edge of her fingernail. Did the note sound friendly enough? Helpful? Trustworthy? She did not want to come across as pushy or nosy. The more innocuous, the better. The whole of this plan was farfetched, but she had to try. She had instigated this, and so she must try to finish it.

She folded the note as small as possible, then tucked it inside the lantern. Oh! The graphite. She had almost forgotten. Tugging open the drawer of her writing box, she made quick work of wrapping a piece in twine and nudging it into the lantern next to the letter. When one did not have a quill and inkpot and all the writing things, a pencil would do. Closing the lantern door and latching it, she patted the stained glass for safekeeping, and trundled out to the locked door.

Unable to resist, she leaned against the wood and listened. Silence answered. She lowered onto her haunches to peer through the keyhole. Blocked, as usual. With a shrug, she sat the lantern before the door. As she turned away to head to dinner, she halted, tapped a finger to her lips, then turned back to the door and rapped smartly.

In a firm voice, with a confidence she did not feel, not when her stomach was somersaulting, she said, "I'm returning the lantern. It's here before the door. I'm leaving now, should you wish to retrieve it."

Without awaiting a reply, she scurried across the sitting room and to the stairs. Who knew if anyone had heard her? The door most likely opened to an entire wing of guest rooms or possibly a suite of rooms or apartments, so whichever room the lady might be hiding in, she may not have heard Isobel. Whatever the case, the plan was in place.

The remains of the day dragged on. All Isobel could think about was the lantern sitting before the door. Would it still be there when she returned? Would Mr. Trowbridge discover it first? She watched every move he made, afraid he would excuse himself and then head for the second floor. At least she had not put anything incriminating in the note, like suspecting the woman was captive and naming the captor — how dreadful! Alistair had been the voice of reason on that point. She believed Alistair to be correct and was ashamed to have thought his father a villain. It made sense now that Mr. Trowbridge was helping someone, keeping the secret for her own good, perhaps at her behest.

Realizing Alistair must be correct and believing it without a shadow of a doubt was different. If asked under duress, Isobel would vow her continued scrutiny of her host's words and movements was to validate his kindness, not spy signs of guilt or malevolence — really, truly!

After hours of playing the tedious game of attentive guest while her eyes darted to the clockface, the time to retire finally arrived. About time! If her stomach somersaulted any more than it had since delivering the lantern… well, it was not a ladylike thought.

As soon as the jib door closed behind her, she lifted the hem of her gown in one hand, hoisted her candleholder in the other, and raced up the stairs. At the top, she flung open the door to the second floor and —

The lantern was gone!

Hand on the stairwell door, Isobel gaped, unable to respond. Someone had opened the door and taken the lantern. Had it been a servant? Had it been the lady? It had not been Mr. Trowbridge, as he had never left their company. A steadying breath was what she needed. Filling her lungs with said breath, along with a puff of uninvited candle smoke, she headed into her bedchamber. There was nothing to do now except prepare, then bide time until eleven.

After Julia attended her—how she would miss Julia once they departed for Sidvale!—she wrote a few letters, one to each of her friends, and then one to her mother about her return home—not because she wished to write letters this late into the evening by the light of a single candle, but she had to do *something* to occupy her mind while she waited—and then she paced the length of the room and back and forwards and back—a dozen times, at least—and then she made notes for Corentin's story, and then paced again—two dozen times this round, and frankly exhilarating for the health!—and then….

How had she lost track of time? Screeching, she darted to the bedchamber door, then doubled back to grab the guttering candle. Oh drats! She flung open a drawer, loose items knocking back to front, felt around for the candles she had shoved in earlier, then lit a new one using the last-life flame of her current one. What if she was missing her chance? Hurry, for heaven's sake, Isobel!

Set, she darted back across the room, flung open the door, and pounced into the sitting room.

Empty.

Her shoulders rounded. It was still on the early side of eleven. There was time. A written reply had not arrived at any point, nothing tucked under the door, nothing waiting on her desk, nothing lying around the sitting room pleading *Read Me* with inviting, penciled lettering. Heart lodged in her throat and pounding a tattoo, she made herself as comfortable as she could in the sitting room and waited.

And waited.

And waited.

Midnight came and went. Isobel fought sleep as her chin slipped from her palm, and her elbow from the arm of the chair.

The plan after the return home was tenuous. While Alistair did not desire a long engagement, he wanted to wait until he had secured their future home. The Owens offered use of the cottage on their property for as long as he needed, the same cottage in which he had resided when he had paid court to their daughter, Leila. He wanted the perfect home for their new life together, but he did not wish to hunt long for said house since each day was another day they would not be wed. He would be a man on a mission once they returned. He had slipped a whisper in her ear after dinner that he would write to the solicitor he had been working with to move along the process.

Isobel imagined their life together and those delicious literary soirees he had mentioned to Lord Dunley. To be his hostess — divine! She resolved to write more short plays for the express purpose of hosting salons.

Only when a soft snore awakened her did she realize it was approaching one in the morning, and she had quite nodded off to sleep. Pooh. No mystery lady. It took every ounce of resilience to convince herself to retire rather than wait in continued hope the lady would appear. After all, she had promised in the letter to make herself scarce after one o'clock in case the woman wished to go for a moonlit stroll in the garden. Gathering her candle collection, used and newly aflame, she returned to her room, trying not to be too disappointed.

The next day lingered with the same determined slowness as the day before. The marked difference between the two was Isobel would swear an oath on the Bible that several of the servants eyed her over-long. It *must* be her imagination, for why would they? But there it was again and again, that niggling sensation of the parlor maid studying her, a footman taking her measure, and the butler appraising her. They were all the same familiar faces and bowed heads she had come to recognize throughout her stay, but it was as if… it was as if *they knew*. Isobel imagined her note to the lady making rounds downstairs, everyone knowing what she said and speculating what she must be thinking. No, it *must* be her imagination.

With a yawn at the end of the day, Isobel wished everyone a goodnight and headed for her bedchamber with no less enthusiasm than the previous evening, but with heavier steps, discouraged and doubting steps. The mystery lady was most likely the housekeeper who had fallen ill, and so Mr. Trowbridge, being the kindhearted soul he ought to be as her intended's father, offered her aid during recovery, but then here came nosy Isobel to poke and prod where she did not belong and disrupt everyone's life with her flights of fancy. There was no ghost, no damsel, no one needing or wanting her help.

Carrying heavy steps, heavy heart, and heavy shoulders, she trudged to her bedchamber. Until eleven, she busied herself with a house wish list to give to Alistair. It was a silly list because she would happily live with him in a lean-to beneath the forest canopy if he asked. Still, it kept her distracted while time traveled forwards.

At last, at a quarter to eleven, she tucked away her work and readied her extra candle. A shame to waste quality candles waiting for something that would not occur. She would give her left arm for candles this quality at home. Needs must.

Making herself comfortable in the sitting room, she waited.

And waited.

And waited.

Midnight came and went. Isobel's chin slipped off her palm, jerking her awake. Wait. No. That was not what had awakened her. It was a click. The sound of a key turned in a lock. She sat up straight, looking about the sitting room. A squeak of hinges drew her attention forwards.

The heretofore locked door crept open with an eerie whine.

Chapter 29

Isobel's eyes widened, and her palms perspired. Pulse racing, her breath shallowed. How was she going to communicate with the woman, given the previous failings? *Could* the woman communicate verbally? What on God's green earth had Isobel been thinking to assume she was equipped to help someone? She sat up, hoping her fears did not show in her expression.

The door opened, and a smartly dressed woman stepped out.

Isobel deflated. This was not the mystery woman. A caretaker, most likely. How disappointing.

Surprise raised the woman's eyebrows high on her forehead. "Oh, it's you," she said, closing the door behind her.

Isobel tilted her head, perplexed. Then she spotted the hands. This smartly dressed woman held her hands at her waist, fingers laced, hands with red, raw fingers, skin peeling around the nails. Eyes darting from hands to face, Isobel tried to make sense of what she was seeing. The face… this could not be the same woman. But… yes, the face was that of Isobel's "ghost," however, there was no excess salivation and no vacant stare, but rather a curious and penetrating gaze. A stylish coiffure framed the face pleasingly. Before Isobel stood a beautiful woman.

Mouthing like a fish, Isobel struggled to reply. "You remember me?"

The woman nodded to the chair nearest Isobel for permission to join her. "Not precisely. I received your note, and while I admit I wished to ignore it, I thought it best not to. You are familiar, although I can't place why. I know we've met. I see your face and think, 'This is a friend, someone to trust.' I can't, I'm afraid, recall how I know you."

"We met at the fountain. Twice. I was abominably rude."

"The fountain?" The woman looked into the distance, deep in thought, then blanched. "Oh, yes, I see."

Isobel's plans frayed, not that she had established firm plans of what to say, but anything she might have said fell on a heavy tongue. This woman appeared, for all the world, *normal*. How could this be the damsel in distress? The ill, possibly mad woman Isobel had met? The cackling ghost that scratched at her door in the wee hours?

Hands trembling ever so slightly, the woman offered, "Despite the late hour, I suppose I must explain myself. I should have done so sooner. I should not have been a coward. May I beg of your discretion?"

Isobel nodded even while questioning if the nod was a lie — she could not withhold her discovery from Alistair, could she?

"Your note. You said your name was Isobel?"

"Yes, Isobel Lambeth, from Sidvale. That's in Devonshire, five miles north of Sidbury. I'm a guest of Mr. Trowbridge's. Unofficially speaking, I'm his son's intended. I hope you don't think me a Nosy Nelly. I thought... I thought you might need help, but I didn't trust talking with Mr. Trowbridge in case the kind of help you needed was, well, *from* him."

Startled, the woman shook her head. She made to speak, hesitated, then focused on stilling her shaking hands. After a time, she laughed softly. "On reflection, I can understand. But no, I do not need help from Alexander. You see, he's my husband."

The outline of the woman's face blurred as Isobel fought a fainting spell. *Her husband?*

"I see I've taken you by surprise. It's my fault. I begged him not to say anything, as I beg you now for your discretion. Forming a relationship with his son is important to him, and I knew if I was present, it would ruin everything. I begged him. He did not want to meet his son with a lie on his lips, but I forced his silence."

"But why?" Isobel had not recovered from the shock. Mr. Trowbridge had remarried, then kept his wife a secret—from his son alone or from everyone?

The woman pressed her fingertips to her temples and closed her eyes. "My apologies, Miss Lambeth. I... momentary dizziness, nothing more." Composing herself, she continued, "My name is Eleanor. I'm, as you've gathered, unwell. I would prefer to remain tucked here for privacy, kept secret from the other guests and especially my stepson, at least until I am better. I do not want my first meeting with him to make a poor impression. From all his father has told me, I understand he loved his mother to distraction, so how terrible it would be for him to learn his father remarried, and... to me. No, I want our meeting to be a happy one."

"But *why*?" Isobel repeated, feeling dimwitted.

"I am not well enough to play hostess. I cannot be in company with others, not until the... the rages are controlled." Eleanor clenched her hands, folding them, wringing them, balling them into fists. Their trembling worsened. "I hope to be on the mend soon. Once the treatment works."

Isobel leaned forwards, wanting to help, wanting to understand, wanting to know everything, but she did not know what to say or do to elicit trust.

"I see you have questions you're unable to voice. You must. Certainly, you must if we met at the fountain. I dare not think of my condition, what you witnessed." Sighing, Eleanor said, "You have troubled yourself over me. I owe you an explanation."

However dim the candlelight, Isobel could see her companion's features tighten as though recalling an unpleasant experience. Tears brightened her eyes but did not fall.

"The pain... the... I..." Eleanor grimaced. "You see, I was in the family way. To ease the more unpleasant symptoms as my delicate state progressed, the doctor prescribed me one blue mass pill per day. I dislike the blue pills. They make me feel so deeply ill, but I was a good patient. I never missed a dose. For the health of my baby and to relieve the sickness, I did as he said. Although I followed his instructions, I... we... my condition... it was too soon." She closed her eyes for a moment of silence. "We buried her beneath the yew. The unpleasant symptoms, the sickness, did not abate. It worsened. He was forced to increase my dosage. Two pills before bed. This should do the trick. I should be on the mend. I *am* on the mend. Maybe,

maybe, there's still hope for our little family, for a second chance."

Eleanor did not explain further, but Isobel believed she understood. This was all so much to take in. She had more questions, endless questions. Blue pills? What blue pills? What was wrong with her? Good heavens. Alistair had a stepmother. Alistair almost had a sibling. Isobel struggled to take it all in. What was wrong with Eleanor? As the not-so-mysterious-anymore woman opened her heart, Isobel tried to reconcile the memory of the shambling madwoman at the fountain with this composed, becoming lady.

Just as Isobel thought the last, Eleanor began to ramble. "If I'm not on the mend, he'll increase the dosage again. I don't *like* the blue mass pills. They're helping me. I must take them. They're the only way, he said. But I don't *like* them." Her words shifted, alternating between mumbles and almost frantic pleas, hasty and shaky. "I take them at night, before bed, but I never know what will happen. I may sleep like a log. I may have vivid, horrifying dreams. I may dream of sitting by the fountain while sleeping soundly to later realize I was not sleeping after all. The rages, the rages are the worst. Don't tell him. Please, don't tell him, but some days I don't take the pills. I take them when the pain, when the sadness, when the never-ending melancholy is at its worst."

Isobel had a peculiar feeling she did not have long before Eleanor would need... what? Assistance? To duck behind the locked door again and remain hidden? She could not say, but the composed lady was steadily losing her composure. Had she taken the little blue pills this evening?

Wanting to reach a hand to Eleanor but not daring, Isobel said in as soothing a voice as she could muster, hoping her own nerves did not give her away, "Alistair will understand. The Owens will understand. Will you reconsider? We leave soon, and I think it's important Mr. Trowbridge introduces you. It's important Alistair meets you. We're here for you and want to become acquainted. Don't let being unwell stop you. We can help."

Aghast, Eleanor shook her head, then gripped the arms of the chair as though she might swoon. "I… I must beg your pardon. I… I'm feeling faint and need to retire. Please, don't tell anyone. It is enough to see a friendly face, and now you may rest assured I do not require your help. A kind offer. Such a kind young lady. My stepson is fortunate. One day, we'll all meet, and I'll be well, and… and… I must…" Her words trailed off as she tried to stand, then stumbled back in the chair on shaky legs. "I need my… my blue mass pills."

Isobel rose and offered to assist. Taking her companion by the hand, she helped Eleanor to stand. Wobbly steps and an apologetic nod were all Isobel saw before Eleanor disappeared behind the door.

Alistair watched for an opportunity to pull Isobel aside for a private conversation. Throughout breakfast, she had cast him enough glances to give the impression the ghostly maid had appeared. This was not a conversation he wished others to overhear. His usual excuse to have her to himself was a walk in the garden, but rain stymied that possibility. He aimed to bump into her in the entrance hall and sneak her into the billiard room, as he had done before. Now, to find an opening.

His father did not join them in the morning room.

Mr. Owen took his leave halfway through Alistair's second cup of tea.

Sequestering Isobel may prove easier than he thought. There was only Aaditri to contend with now.

When Isobel rose to leave, claiming she needed to return to her room — a cue for him to follow? — he joined her at the door with an excuse of his own. Aaditri, not to be left alone in the morning room, thought it a grand idea to follow Isobel. Alistair had no choice except to go through the motions of mounting the main staircase as if to proceed to the first floor, allowing Aaditri and Isobel to pass through the reception hall without him. Foiled.

His next plan was to hover around the door of the billiard room, waiting for Isobel's return and possibly ducking into said room to avoid being seen loitering. And so, he positioned himself by the door and waited.

And waited.

And waited.

When the third footman cast him a curious glance, Alistair forfeited the plan. Getting Isobel alone should not be so difficult, but any witnessed attempt on his part would have the household believing he was declaring himself at last, and while that was on the agenda this week, he did not wish anyone to misconstrue his intention — he and Isobel had a mystery to solve first!

He busied himself until tea by writing a reply to his solicitor's most recent letter about property offerings, writing to Mrs. Lambeth a request for an audience, and writing to the vicar of Sidvale, Mr. Walsley, a request for an interview. Now that his resignation was final, it was time to do more than plant seeds. He needed roots, strong roots. That he had nothing to his name now except a modest purse would not keep him from offering his hand in marriage, but it did fuel his need to act swiftly in securing a home and setting into motion at least one way to generate income as a gentleman.

His father had assured him during the London trip that whatever he needed would be his, be it backing to purchase property, introductions to society, or otherwise. Alistair had no intentions of being dependent or indebted to his father, but accepting modest aid would make a difference between having to purchase a cottage without foreseeable income or property with income potential. All he would need was at least one tenant to start or a workable farm, ideally both, no matter how small. While helping Isobel solve her ghostly mystery, his mind was grounded in the reality of building their future. He would not disappoint her.

Teatime arrived at last. Another opportunity to catch Isobel alone. He arrived in the drawing room before anyone else, hoping Isobel would think to do the same. They did not need long to talk, he did not suspect. Long enough for her to share any news of the ghostly maid.

An empty drawing room greeted him. He shrugged and made for the garden view while waiting. It was so misty, with a low-lying fog shrouding the terrace and parterres beyond, that one could hardly see the drizzling rain. Atmospheric weather for hunting ghosts. Ah, hindsight struck him. Now would have been the opportune time to loiter at the jib door. It was not too late. Only a few strides across the entry hall.

The drawing room door opened to the sounds of Aaditri's lively chatter. Alistair welcomed her but grunted to himself for not returning to the billiard room door sooner. Isobel arrived soon after Aaditri, her expression telling Alistair she had much the same hope of being the first to arrive for their chance to talk. Mr. Owen joined with apologies on behalf of Alexander, who had pressing business to see to and would join them for dinner. After tea arrived, Aaditri played mother and prepared the teapot and filled the cups, conversation lively, a mixture of London stories Mr. Owen had saved to share, plans for the return journey to Sidvale, and the reading aloud of Miss Leila Owen's most recent letter to her mother, Aaditri doing the honors.

Alistair heard little and conversed less. His eyes remained fixed on Isobel, wishing they could communicate silently somehow. Her expressive eyes shared endless stories. If only he could understand them.

As the teapot emptied and the kettle cooled, Alistair saw his chance dwindling yet again. So simple of a task to speak alone with her, yet impossible without noteworthy importunity. He arched his brows in her direction. She waggled hers.

He cleared his throat. "I have a wish to exercise. The rain disagrees. Would Miss Lambeth desire exercise, as well, by taking a turn about the room?"

She nodded with characteristic enthusiasm.

This was not what he had wanted, as the Owens would be present and could overhear if they wished. He had wanted privacy. Talk of clandestine meetings with ghosts and damsels in distress was not for the ears of others. Alas.

Alistair guided Isobel to the garden view for the start of their promenade in largo. Wasting no time, he bent his head and said as low as he could without whispering, "Have you met your ghost? Did she reply?"

Isobel eyed the Owens as she said in return, "Last night, yes. She braved a meeting. I have more questions now than answers, but the plan worked."

"And? Does she require our rescue?"

Rather than laugh, Isobel chewed her bottom lip. Not quite meeting his eyes, she said to his chin, "In part, you were right. Your father *has* played the hero and is helping her recover from illness. I think she is still in danger, although not the type I had thought. I think she needs more support from friends… and family. It is family she needs now more than anything. Trusting family."

"How may we help her? I will be the gallant knight if it is your wish."

Abusing the poor lip again, she tucked it between her teeth. They ambled their way to the other side of the drawing room by the time she answered. "I think the best we can offer at present is for you to speak with your father."

Alistair slowed his gait. "My father? And I'm to confess your conference with the damsel?"

Isobel shook her head. "No, I think you should do nothing more than initiate conversation. I believe your father has much to tell you but is hesitant to do so. I have it on good authority that he wishes to strengthen his relationship with you but is afraid to say too much lest you not wish the same. There are things he wants you to know, but those things involve promises that have tied his hands, so as much as he wants to be honest, he is sworn to silence." She paused and said, "As am I."

Full stop, Alistair stared at her, searching her face for answers. "You speak in riddles. My father wishes to tell me what he cannot? I do not understand."

With a light touch to his arm, Isobel said, "Please, talk to him today. Just talk. About anything. Father to son. Talk about your plans for the future, our plans. Talk about where you see your father in our future — will we call on him often? Will he be invited to stay with us? Talk about anything and everything personal. I think it'll help."

Continuing their walk around the perimeter, Alistair nodded. "I will do as you say. This is an invitation, not a command, something I want even if my father holds his silence. And your ghost said this?"

She looked at him with a wan smile. "As much." Their walk about the room complete, they pivoted to return to the Owens, but first, Isobel added, "Should he confess nothing, give him time. Should he open his heart to you, listen… and know I'm a stone's throw if you need to talk with me afterwards, as I suspect you'll want to do."

Alistair needed no more incentive than Isobel's nudge to confer with the butler that he wished to see his father whenever the gentleman was available.

Less than an hour later, Alistair sat with his father in the study, sharing port and plans.

"Do you think me touched by madness?" he asked his father.

"Not in the least. It's ambitious, but not beyond your capabilities, son. What does Miss Lambeth think?"

He cradled the glass in his hand. "I've not shared it with her yet. I'm of the mind to surprise her. It could go poorly. I have an alternative property in mind if she rejects my surprise."

"Brave move." Alexander raised his glass in salute. "From what I've come to know of Miss Lambeth, I think your idea is a stroke of genius, and it is a surprise she would favor. Or so I hope, for your sake. Now, tell me more about this folly you built for your mother, the one to inspire this gesture for Miss Lambeth."

Slipping into a conversation about his mother was easy, familiar, and heartening. For so long, he had wished to exchange words about Shahrazad, but his father had tiptoed around her, discouraging any mention. To have him speak of her, ask about her, even if by way of a garden ornament, had Alistair leaning forwards in his chair, hoping this would be the connection he desired.

After two glasses and ample tales, enough to bring laughter and tears to Alistair's eyes, his father said, "I'm a blessed man to have my son before me. After your mother died, I struggled. I lost more than my wife. I lost my self-respect, but more importantly,

I thought I lost you, or rather lost my chance to know you."

Alistair's hands stilled the swirling of his glass. He said nothing, merely studied his father from beneath furrowed brows.

"I wasn't there. She needed me, and I wasn't there. You needed me. I knew she was ill, but daft that I was, I thought it fleeting, a passing chill, nothing serious. As her condition worsened, I set in motion plans for the journey, but it's not a quick or direct trip, as you now realize. It takes months, the better part of a year. Are these excuses? Perhaps they are. She didn't want me there. She made it clear. She didn't want me there. I was going anyway. Before the journey began, it was too late. You sent word, and with it, you washed your hands of me and refused my aid and my invitation and everything I had to offer." Alexander set down his glass none too gently and buried his face in his hands. "Now you must think I'm blaming you. I'm a failed husband and father, and you see the truth of it."

Of one point Alistair was relieved; that his father had not said these things upon his arrival to Burghfield. At that time, he would have agreed. He would have blamed his father, accused him, and unleashed the years of pent-up anger. Now, he knew his father better, accepted the man into his life, and believed the situation he had seen through his youthful eyes was far more complicated than he could have imagined. He did not need to know those complications. They were between a man and his wife. It had been all too easy to side with his mother on everything when that was the singular perspective he knew. Now? He did not need to know his father's perspective to understand it was as worthy as his mother's had been.

His father cradled his head in his hands, saying nothing more.

Alistair ventured, "*Pedar*, I'm here now, as are you. All else is spilled water. As *Maman* used to say, a new language is a new life." He set down his glass and rested his forearms on his thighs. "She did not want you to see her. It was not you, *Pedar*. It was not as you think. She wanted you, but she did not want you to see her. Her illness… she…" He circled his hands, searching for the words. "She was dependent, bedridden, not mending but weakening. It pained her enough for me to see, but never you, never you of all people. You were to know her as strong, spirited, the Persian wife you loved."

Alexander dragged his hands down his face and looked at this son from over his fingertips. "You refused me. You were angry. You blamed me."

"I did. But I did not." Alistair shook his head. "I had lost my everything. I needed someone to blame."

"You were right to blame me. Don't you see? I was her husband. I was the one who should have been there and ensured she healed, hired the doctors, and pressed her to adhere to the treatments. This was *my* responsibility. I failed her. I failed you. She died because of my negligence."

"*Ghamet ché rang varangé.*" Alistair reached out and clasped his father's hand, squeezing it hard enough his father winced. "Your sorrow has many colors." Moving to the edge of his chair, he pulled his father closer, pressing forehead to forehead. "*Ké dar afareenesh z'yek goharand*. Do you understand?"

Alexander's voice cracked when he said, "For in creation, from one soul, they came."

Alistair held their position until his father's breathing steadied. When he leaned back, he nodded to his father, his voice firm and strong. "Now, we walk the same path."

Rubbing his eyes with his thumb and forefinger, Alexander stood. He looked down at his glass, half-finished on the table, then turned to stride to the study window, his back to Alistair. "I need you, son. I need you, but I don't think you'll agree when I confess my burden. The only apology I can offer is this was not entirely my secret to share."

He stared at his father's back, recalling Isobel's riddles at tea.

"Bravery eludes me," his father said, head bowed, attention on his feet rather than the garden mist outside. "All this time, I've blamed myself for your mother's death. If I had but been there. Call it life's morbid sense of humor, my punishment for your mother, or a second chance to correct my mistake. Call it whatever you wish, but I find myself now in a similar situation, and I'm... I'm as helpless as I was before but without the burden of travel to blame."

Alistair's jaw clicked as he clenched it.

Alexander turned to face Alistair, tucking his hands into his waistcoat pockets. "I never intended to keep this from you. Never. Only this morning have I been released from the promise I made. It is a burden once relieved, immediately replaced." Rocking from toe to heel, he cleared his throat once, then twice. "Is there room on the path for one more?"

With a cock of his head, Alistair quizzed his father between narrowed lids, trying to work out the meaning before he answered.

It struck him without preamble. The damsel. The second chance. He knew. Like a foot to the chest, he fought to breathe. His struggle was silent, still, stoic, as he refused to show a reaction.

In an even, controlled tone, Alistair asked, "Daughter or wife?"

His father paled, then said, "Wife."

The word hung between them.

Alistair's emotions waged war. That single word, the reality of it, should have stung. It should have stripped him of any respect he had for his father or any sorrow over the guilt Alexander had confessed. The man had abandoned his family for another. Strangely, though, Alistair believed none of this. Instead, he felt hope, the promise of the new path and the family to walk along it. He closed his eyes and inhaled deeply. Praise be that Isobel had prepared him. When he opened his eyes, he saw his father's face stricken with fear, regret, and that faint hint of hope Alistair himself felt in his breast.

"I wish to meet her," Alistair said.

His father's shoulders softened. "That could prove problematic. I want you to meet her, and she is as eager to meet you, but she is not well, hence the secrecy." His words were low and soft. "I think she believes she's dying. The doctor, however, is hopeful, as am I. But she believes it so strongly that she did not wish you to know. Read into that what you will. I was sworn to secrecy, and I could not betray that."

"You need not explain. I leave in a few days. I hope to meet her before then. Will you express my hope?"

Sharing with his son a half-smile, he said, "With all my heart."

Chapter 30

I sobel could not say with certainty what had been shared between Alistair and his father, but she knew whatever happened had altered their relationship and brought them closer. Throughout dinner, the two were inseparable in conversation, no matter how inconsequential the topic. In the drawing room that evening, Mr. Trowbridge had stayed for the card games and company, taking the seat next to his son. Everything Isobel saw brought a smile to her lips that would not fade. She did not have a chance to speak with Alistair, but he did manage to pull her into his arms and press his cheek to her temple for all of five seconds as everyone made for the main stairs to retire.

The evening should have brought a sound sleep. She knew who was behind the locked door. She suspected Mr. Trowbridge had confessed to Alistair about his second marriage. All her worries were resolved. Sleep, however, had other ideas. It teased her thoughts with the myriad ways she could try to convince Mrs. Eleanor Trowbridge to meet everyone, namely Alistair. So determined, Isobel had to fight the urge to write another letter in the dead of night and slip it beneath the door, a letter enumerating all the reasons Eleanor should make herself known.

In the end, Isobel fell asleep counting those reasons rather than sheep.

The next morning brought the promise of a beautiful day. A shame Eleanor would remain locked indoors when there was sunshine to enjoy, never mind the muddy lawn that made slurping sounds with every step Isobel took during her stroll after breakfast. After all Isobel and Alistair's attempts to talk alone the day before, today offered a plethora of opportunities, including the slippery stroll, but Alistair had promised himself to his father for much of the day. Was she disappointed? Not if her never-ending smile was any indication.

She did not see Alistair all morning, not until teatime. Aaditri was already in the drawing room when Isobel arrived, but not far behind her were the gentlemen. So deep in conversation, they did not stop to pay the ladies any heed, merely chose their chairs and shared in laughter.

As Aaditri prepared the tea, she leaned closer to Isobel and said under her breath, "Our host shared a secret with Josiah and me this morning. A secret I'm to understand that you know."

Isobel nodded, relieved Aaditri now knew.

"Fancy our seeing her," Aaditri continued. "Do you suppose she caught me spying her entering Mr. Trowbridge's suite? She must have done. I am so pleased he has found love again. Men do not do well without a wife. They need us." Leaning a little closer, she added, "I was all astonishment, but Josiah did not fool me for a minute. He must have known. The cad never said a word to me!"

Her teasing tone and titter told Isobel that Aaditri was not the least upset about Mr. Owen keeping their host's secret. Aaditri passed Isobel a teacup and saucer before turning to the gentlemen.

The drawing room door opened, and the butler stepped inside. They all turned.

Mr. Trowbridge, laughter still in his voice from whatever he had been saying to Alistair and Mr. Owen, asked, "Yes, Geoffrey?"

"Mrs. Eleanor Trowbridge," he announced, then stepped out of the way of the door.

The room fell silent, so silent the sound of Isobel's teacup clinking against the saucer reverberated like the peal of a bell. Into the room, stepped Eleanor. Isobel started in surprise. With the elegance and grace of an aristocrat, Eleanor met her guests' stares. She was, if possible, even more beautiful than she had been during their midnight meeting. It was not so much her visage, although that was attractive as well, as it was her deportment, her bearing, her presence.

Setting her teacup and saucer down, Isobel made to stand and go to her new friend, but before she could, all three gentlemen rose, Mr. Trowbridge being the one to go to her. His wife showed none of the unsteadiness she had the other evening. Her strides were sure. A footman rushed forwards with an extra chair, readying her a seat while Mr. Trowbridge did the honors of introductions.

"May I present our guests, Mrs. Trowbridge?"

They each had a turn to greet Eleanor, no one remarking on the unusualness of a complete stranger and secret wife appearing to join them for tea. Everyone welcomed her as though they had all known she would join, had known she was their host's wife all this time, and had merely been missing her company due to an extended holiday.

When the introductions reached Alistair, whom Mr. Trowbridge saved for last, Isobel would swear everyone held a collective breath.

"It is with a full heart I introduce my son, Alistair," Mr. Trowbridge said as his hand clasped Alistair's shoulder.

Eleanor's lips curved into a deep smile. "At last. I've wanted to meet you for so long."

Alistair bowed deeply, reverently, but Eleanor stepped closer and offered her hand instead. He accepted without hesitation. "Your servant, Mrs. Trowbridge."

Her reply chimed with happiness. "Eleanor, please. We're family. At least, I hope we are."

Alistair saw her to her chair and nodded to Aaditri for another teacup, one which had been added to the tray by unseen hands during the introductions. Aaditri, so enraptured by the proceedings, had not seen it appear. She made quick work of readying the cup.

Eleanor looked at each of them, a shyness settling in now that she had joined the party. "I'm here for more than introductions. I owe everyone an explanation." Words collided as everyone spoke at once, all to reassure her, but she held a staying hand. "Please, allow me this opportunity. I have been the most abominable hostess. Although it should provide for a memorable visit since I do not believe it common to have a hostess you do not know exists."

So unassuming was her laugh, so honest the tease, they were all put at ease. Isobel settled into her chair and savored her tea. This would be a memorable afternoon, indeed!

Without preamble, Eleanor launched into her tale, removing any and all blame from her husband's name, as he had been eager to share news of his marriage and had wanted nothing more than to introduce his son to his new wife and beg for his son's blessing, but she had forced his silence, too cowardly to be seen until she was well again.

As she said all the things Isobel already knew, Isobel noticed the tremble of her hands, much like before. Otherwise, Eleanor appeared in control of her faculties. For all intents and purposes, she looked well. There was still an unmistakable delicacy about her, but the gown she wore was long-sleeved, hiding what Isobel knew would be the almost translucent skin. She did not wear gloves to hide her fingers, but with the gown being a rosy pink, they were not noticeable, or at least not startlingly so. Isobel recognized those subtle signs, but she did not think anyone else did. Her confidence swelled at this, for underlying her nerves was an almost defensiveness for this kind but curiously ill woman.

"We were so eager to have the family together at last and for me to meet Alistair," Eleanor was saying before lifting her teacup to her lips, not wanting to neglect her tea. "If I'm not mistaken, I fell ill round-about the time you," she nodded to Alistair, "and Mr. Owen set off from India."

Aaditri asked, "How fortunate Mr. Trowbridge has been with you since you fell ill, or were you unwell before the marriage? So kind is our Mr. Trowbridge to tend to your health."

Eleanor looked into her teacup, her smile faltering. "I fell ill after…" She paused with a flick of her eyes to Alistair before returning her attention to her teacup. "After I found myself in an interesting condition."

Aaditri leaned forwards with interest while the gentlemen shifted in their chairs.

"I fell ill and did not improve. Time passed, and I worsened. Alexander was so attentive. I don't know what I would have done without him. But it became too much for me to bear, and I begged him to send for a physician. At first, we tried bloodletting. It seemed to work for a fortnight and eased the pain. He came twice a week to help balance my humors. But then it all worsened again. I shan't spoil our tea with the details, but the pain was enough for him to believe the humors needed more than balancing, rather a complete cleansing from whatever was poisoning them. We tried a dose of quicksilver to purge me, and then we followed that with a weekly dose of calomel and then with the blue pills."

She stopped for a moment, long enough to finish her tea and for Aaditri to refill cups and offer slices of cake. No one spoke as though afraid to interrupt the story. Eleanor's composure remained strong, but her voice had begun to weaken, not from exhaustion but rather from what Isobel thought was the crux of her illness — losing her unborn child.

When Eleanor continued, her timbre softened, and her tempo slowed. "My… condition… changed soon after. My… condition arrived to its natural conclusion too soon, much too soon. After the loss, melancholy replaced the pain. Endless melancholy." Her words drifted into nearly a whisper.

Mr. Trowbridge placed a hand on the arm of her chair. She momentarily covered his hand with hers before returning her attention to her heretofore ignored slice of cake.

Isobel glanced at Alistair but could not read his expression. Had his father told him about Eleanor being in the family way, or had he just received a shock? She wished she were sitting closer to him, but he sat on the other side of Eleanor, waiting for her to continue.

"The best treatment, the physician explained, is to continue the blue mass," Eleanor said, fiddling with the handle of her teacup. "One pill every evening will resolve my melancholy over time, purge whatever illness affected me during my condition and lingers, and balance the humors. At first, it did improve my sleep and energize me during the day. A miracle cure, he calls it. And I believe him. Only, it isn't lasting, for whatever reason. My humors refuse to be purged. Just before you were all to arrive, he increased the dosage to two pills. They must be working, for I can *feel* the pills trying to purge the sickness."

Isobel's memory whirred with all she had seen and heard since arriving, all the sleepless nights because of Eleanor's so-called purging pills.

"I knew," Eleanor continued, "I was not fit to be hostess, not yet. There have been, oh, I don't know what else to call them, bouts of rage as the mercury in the pills fights against my illness, working to cure me. While I think I'm on the mend, I could not risk any of you seeing me so unfit as a wife. I wanted to wait until I was cured. You can understand?"

Everyone was still, listening intently, cakes and tea forgotten. At the prompting, heads nodded, but no

one spoke. Isobel knew what Eleanor did not voice —
she did not want her guests to see her in that state
and think her mad. Madness was not like physical
illness. One was understandable, forgivable, curable,
the other….

After a length of silence, Aaditri said, "If the treatment is not working, you should reconsider your
physician. It sounds to me the treatment is not this
miracle cure if he must increase the dosage."

"Oh, but it *is* working. You see, everything is
worse after I take the mercury pills in the evening.
That means they're working. They're drawing the
illness out, cleansing whatever ails me."

Aaditri scoffed. "Your physician is a man. What
do men know of women's needs? Doctors have no
business at our bedside. I'm not embarrassed to share
that our Leila lost a sibling, one she knows nothing
about." She cast a knowing look at Isobel. "Like you,
I suffered a melancholy. But this was when we still
lived in West Bengal. Life was different. Women know
about women. Ayurvedic remedies for melancholy
are what you need. Ashwagandha and Brahmi, this is
how I will treat you. You are my patient now, *azizam*.
We care for our own. I will mix them into our tea, and
we shall share a brew."

Eleanor looked taken aback by the offer at first,
glancing between Alexander and Aaditri.

Alistair spoke up for the first time since meeting his stepmother. "*Khanoom* Aaditri is correct. My
mother's illness was incurable, but I mixed the roots
in her tea to brighten her spirit. Without, she would
have lost her will. With the tea, she stayed active until
near the end, sharp as a nail."

Mr. Trowbridge set down his saucer and rose. Drawing a hand through his hair, he paced behind his chair. "I should have known this. *I should have known this.* If I had been there, if I had... I should have known, then I could have... we never would have needed the physician. I should have—"

Alistair and Eleanor spoke at the same time, stopped to look at each other, and then each nodded for the other to speak first.

After several attempts to urge Eleanor to speak, Alistair relented. "You know now, *Pedar*." Turning back to Eleanor, Alistair asked, "Will you try our remedy? Set aside the doctor's treatment for now and try our method. If it does not help, you still have these blue pills of yours to return to. Will you try?"

Isobel thought the offer not without challenges, for here was a group of strangers suggesting remedies from foreign shores. What had any of them done to earn Eleanor's trust?

Eleanor angled in her chair to see her husband.

Mr. Trowbridge had stopped pacing. "It is what I would have suggested to you, my dear, had I but known. I am ashamed not to have remembered what I once knew so well while I lived in India, more ashamed not to have known how my beloved was treated during her final days."

Patting the arm of his chair, Eleanor waved him to return to his seat. "If you'll stop blaming yourself long enough, you'll realize not everything is in your control. Sit. Eat your cake." With a lift of her chin, she said to no one in particular, "Hope is Heaven's greatest gift. Without it, we have nothing. I had begun to think all was lost. Then Miss Lambeth came into my life and helped me find my way to all of you. And now, all of you welcome me as a friend and tell me there are other treatments to try, ones you offer with confidence and smiles, not the doom and gloom of the physician. Hope, this is what I have now." She reached a hand to Alistair and clasped his forearm. "I've also gained a son. This is the happiest day I've seen in a long time."

Chapter 31

The next two days were steeped in normality, Mrs. Eleanor Trowbridge joining them throughout the day. Aside from exhaustion and weakness when standing, she appeared to all observers full of life, health, and happiness. One of those days, Isobel spotted her hostess walking the parterre garden with Alistair. Her heart sang at the sight. Alistair had arrived at this house with anger and resentment towards his father, but now he wanted nothing more than to build a family, be the rock anchoring them — and there was a mixed metaphor if ever Isobel heard one. Was he a rock or a carpenter?

This was exactly what she deserved for avoiding her Corentin story for so long. Now that her life was not a gothic story in the making, she could settle back into her pattern of reading Radcliffe and writing daring tales.

Writing was precisely what she was doing when a knock resounded at her bedchamber door. Served her right to turn a quick change of clothes from her walking gown to her tea gown into a writing session, too distracted by the call of the quill to return to the ground floor, at least not yet. The middle of a glorious day, and she had sequestered herself in the bedchamber, scratching her goose feather across the paper.

"Come," she called from the desk, not pausing her quill to look up.

The door creaked, and then a squeak of a maid's voice said, "You're wanted in the drawing room, miss."

Thinking she had lost track of time and was abysmally late with everyone gathered around the tea things waiting for her, Isobel shrieked and jabbed the quill into its holder over the inkpot. With a quick glance at her hands and face in the little mirror to ensure she was not wearing ink, she hoisted the hem of her gown and darted past the maid and down the stairs. How late was she? What must they think of her? An abominable guest with no manners!

Careening to the ground floor, she raced towards the entrance hall. Before she reached the main stairs, she ground her heels to a halt. To either side of the drawing room doors lined her companions, forming a swordless sabre arch. What in heaven's name? She cocked her head and frowned in question. The Owens stood on one side, facing the Trowbridges. No sign of Alistair.

Oh.

It dawned as brightly as the morning rays.

Isobel's knees knocked, and her head swam in the swoony, vaporish way of novel heroines. Slow steps, one in front of the other, hoping her knees would not give way, she approached, a cavalcade of one.

Aaditri squeezed Isobel's hand as she passed. Eleanor touched Isobel's arm, nodding encouragement. Mr. Owen winked.

With a look to each side as she processed forwards, Isobel flushed, shy and flustered.

Mr. Trowbridge was closest to the door and stopped her progress with a clearing of his throat. In a low voice, he said, "I'm in your debt, Miss Lambeth. You have emboldened my wife, fortified my son, and heartened me. What is mine is yours."

Having duly ingratiated himself, he stepped aside. Isobel did not see she had done any of those things, but she found comfort in his words, a familial acceptance she had not anticipated. Two footmen, one to each side, opened the drawing room doors in regal fashion, bowing as she passed, as though she were of noble lineage.

Directly in the sightline of the drawing room doors and positioned between two garden windows, stood Alistair, dressed in fine evening attire, ready for a ball, never mind it was only teatime, only family, and in this instance, only her. Her heart raced and thumped and bumped and pulsed so erratically that she was unsure she would make it much further into the room without fainting. That was when she noticed he was not alone — metaphorically speaking.

On every surface of the drawing room, be it table-top or mantel, bouquets of flowers adorned. Even the wall sconces and candelabras held some bit of floral fluff instead of candles. No, on second look, the buffet held more than flowers — a tray of confections punctuated each vase along the length of the table. She wanted to laugh, cry, perhaps both, but all she could do was stare, eyes wide, in awe of the romantic splendor. Oh. Oh dear. Oh no. There was more.

She swallowed.

Stacked around the hearth were boxes, so many boxes, endless boxes. She knew without asking they were the myriad gifts he had been dying to give her throughout their courtship, the gifts that a betrothed gentleman could present to his intended. This was too much. This was... *Were those flower petals?* Covering the chairs, sofas, settee, and even the settle at the back of the room that no one used, were flower petals.

Heart skipping a beat, Isobel's eyelids fluttered. Her arm arched, and the back of her hand met her brow, just as her knees gave out. In a flurry of muslin, she swooned.

With the reflexes of a panther, Alistair launched himself forwards and caught her in his arms. Swift but gentle. Even with his arms wrapped around her, the hold was ever so awkward, leaving him with two choices — manhandle her to lift her up or lower her to the rug. As she slipped from his grasp, he chose to cradle her as he knelt, lowering her to the floor.

One arm around her waist, one palming her head, he looked down at her. Isobel could feel his breath on her cheeks, enjoying the scent of minty freshness. Risking a peek with one eye only, she stole a glance between parted eyelids before squeezing them closed again.

Alistair shifted closer, pressing his cheek to hers, his words tickling her ear. "I saw that, *zendegim.*"

Try as she might not to give herself away, a snort of laughter escaped.

In response, he pulled her against him, cupped her cheek, and kissed her.

Both eyes flew open in surprise before fluttering closed again, for this was not a chaste kiss, but rather a kiss to end all kisses, a deep, passionate, toe-curling kiss with parted lips, a moan from him, and a sigh from her.

When he leaned away, his eyes told her the kiss was not finished, only suspended long enough for him to say, "*Asheghetam*, Miss Isobel Lambeth. I am in love with you. You are... you are *nafasam*, my breath, *zarabaaneh ghalbam*, my heartbeat, *jigaram*, my liver — "

"Your *liver*?" Isobel sputtered.

"Shh. I am waxing poetical, *nazanin*. Where was I? Ah, yes." He caressed her cheekbone with his thumb, then traced the curve of her face with his fingertips. "Now is *khastegaree*, the asking of marriage ceremony. *Dooset daram, ba-ham ëzdevaj mikonee*? I love you; you are marrying me?"

Isobel simpered. "And I love you, but do you not mean, *will you marry me*?"

One corner of his lips curled into a mischievous grin. "It is for me to ask, not you."

"Wait, that wasn't... oh, never mind. Just kiss me."

Arching a brow, he touched his lips to hers but did not pucker. Instead, he asked, "May I take this kiss as an emphatic *yes*? Your English rules prohibit me from kissing a woman who is not — "

Isobel clasped the front of his coat and tugged, shushing him with the completion of their kiss.

Her moan drowned out the sound of the drawing room doors opening, but she nearly leapt out of Alistair's arms at the cacophony of overlapping voices that followed.

"We're here to wish you happy!"

"It's official?"

"Shall we celebrate with cake?"

Shortly followed by:

"Oh my. What is happening?"

"I hope it's official because…"

"Did she faint?"

As smug as a pirate hiding his loot in a cove, Alistair helped Isobel to rise, both having been caught kneeling on the floor in a shockingly lurid embrace. And that was a reality Isobel had never thought could happen to her, not in her wildest dreams.

Chapter 32

Two months later

F lower petals showered Mrs. Isobel Trowbridge as she raced from the Sidvale parish church to the awaiting barouche. Alistair's arm linked with hers, his strides longer but his pace slower. Behind them, Mr. and Mrs. Jules Knowlton followed suit but headed towards their own awaiting carriage, the double wedding having concluded with the peal of bells.

The barouche pulled away from the crowd with a lurch seconds after Isobel had secured her seat — for all the good securing her seat did since she was thrown against Alistair in what must have looked like wanton flirtation but was quite unplanned on Isobel's part. Alistair draped an arm around her shoulders and kissed her cheek to the musical accompaniment of cheering and clanking, the carriage dragging behind it an assortment of old pots, kettles, and kitchenware. The noise was brutal, doubly so, given Leila and Jules's carriage dragged much the same.

As the noisy train of carriages made its way through the village and towards Nasrin Manor for the wedding breakfast, Isobel tried several times to speak but could not be overheard above the din. She gave up and contented herself to wave to all who peeked out their doors and windows to see the fuss.

When they reached the crossroads with Nasrin Manor to the left, the barouche traveled right. Isobel looked behind her to see Leila and Jules carrying on to the left. Isobel's carriage was going the wrong way! She quizzed Alistair, but he shrugged, his smug grin deepening.

Searching the landscape, she could not understand where they were going or why. This was the road to Sidbury, and the only thing worth seeing this way, aside from Sidbury itself, was the Stanbury estate. For a hand-clenching moment, she thought that was, indeed, their destination and that Alistair had done something dreadful like purchase it from Mr. Stanbury, and this detour to the wedding breakfast was him revealing their marital home — the manor. Only when the carriage turned down a narrow path a quarter of a mile from the manor's gatehouse did she release the stranglehold on her wedding gown. Whew! That had been too close for comfort.

Alistair had teased her for weeks about a wedding present and had feigned ignorance about where they were to live following the nuptials. It did not require an Enlightenment scientist to hypothesize what her wedding surprise would be, but the *Stanbury estate*? She had been to the manor once when she was a wee girl. She had accompanied Papa to call on Mr. Stanbury, a bushy-browed gentleman who lorded about the place with his fowling piece slung over his arm, grumbling about poachers. The manor, as she remembered it, had been grand. Too grand. The thought of being mistress to *that*. Well. It did not bear thinking. A shiver ran down Isobel's spine.

She eyed Alistair with a narrowed gaze, darting brows of suspicion. He continued to shrug at her glances.

The barouche bumped along, hitting what felt like every rut in the road, the terrain worsening the longer they traveled the pokey drive. A part in the trees ahead gave Isobel a glimpse of... *something*. Too many branches still obscured her view. They drew closer, and she could see several men walking along a roof. One of the men knelt, then raised his arm to hammer. Quirking a brow, Isobel sat in silent contemplation.

At last, the carriage pulled to a stop. Alistair descended first, then helped Isobel do the same. A good thing because she was too busy taking in the curiosity before her to mind her step. They had stopped in front of... a coach house. A partially roof-less coach house, no less. Was the carriage to stop here while they walked to their destination—*in her wedding gown?*

Alistair remained the silent, stoic type, his one reveal an obnoxious smirk that told her nothing.

The area teemed with workers, on the coach house, in it, around it. A few turned to wave, but most paid no heed. The structure obviously belonged to the Stanbury estate with the same architecture features as the manor, at least of what she could remember. It was a two-story, long and narrow, rambling building with arched entries all along the wall facing her, the carriage entry nearly the full two stories in height. Perpendicular ran the stables. One did not need to be a genius to see the whole of it had been abandoned for some time, but that did not detract from its stone and timber-accented glory. A stately coach house and stables, to be sure.

She cast her unasked questions to Alistair. He waggled his eyebrows.

Isobel turned back to the structure. And then she saw it.

A sunlit dining room with a two-story, arching window — no, make that a library. Yes, a library with the desk in the middle, looking out the old carriage entry. The two arches next to it would lead to a parlor, and next to it, the drawing room, and… *she could see it*. Running through the house would be their children, all seventeen of them — well, perhaps not that many — shrieking and howling in play.

"Yes?" came Alistair's voice from afar.

"Yes," she said. "Oh, *yes*."

He exhaled a *whew* and laughed heartily. "It was a gamble. We will, in the interim, stay in the Owens' cottage if that pleases you. We will be the only family in England to live in a converted coach house. Unusual, yes, but it will be reconstructed to suit our needs. I will show you my plans so you may agree and disagree as appropriate."

Clapping her hands and squealing, Isobel said, "Just wait until Hetty hears we're moving into a *coach house*. She will *die*! Once she sees it complete, she'll realize it's far superior to Dunley Manor. Oh, and my mother. My mother will have the vapors! She'll be the first person I tell at the wedding breakfast — but *I* must tell her. If you tell Mama, it will spoil everything. You are infallible in her eyes, of course, well, except for your taste in brides." Isobel swatted at the pesky wetness of her eyes. "Oh, Alistar. This is beyond delightful! Whatever gave you the idea?"

"Necessity met ingenuity, *nazanin*. To avoid mortgaging the estate, Mr. Stanbury decided to sell parcels. Ours is the coach house and stables, as well as the immediate surrounding farmland. I have in mind to let the farmland, enough for three tenants, more if I divide the land further. As an alternative, if you're disappointed in the coach house conversion, we could instead choose a farmhouse on our new land. Although I had intended the one I bear in mind to be let, it would make a perfect home."

With a shake of her head, she said, "No, *this* is *perfect*. But you know what would be even more perfect?" She batted her eyelashes. "Not being the last to arrive to our wedding breakfast."

Epilogue

"We now end our last Ladies Literary Society meeting of the month, to resume next week." Lady Hetty Dunley, née Clint, rapped her knuckles against the table in The Tangled Fleece.

Mrs. Abbie Randall, née Walsley, tucked the draft of her latest manuscript into a worn leather satchel. "May I be the first to express my eagerness for our next meeting? It'll be your turn to read, Isobel, and we won't allow you to leave the meeting without telling us what the publisher suggests to make this as bestselling as your first novel — no more secrecy!"

Isobel blushed. "You're not really interested in how Lord Rhys rescues the damsel. Confess. You hated his arrogance the last time I read. Imagine if I tell you my publisher wishes him to be *more* arrogant."

"Did I say I was looking forward to hearing about Lord Rhys?" Abbie grinned ruefully. "What I'm eager for is the verisimilitude you promised. You're a world traveler now! You vowed atmospheric authenticity based on those travels, and I expect to see the sights vicariously."

Mrs. Leila Knowlton, née Owen, helped Isobel rise from her chair with a hand tucked in the crook of her elbow. "Personally, I prefer Lord Rhys. He has charisma. Swoonier than the bucolic scene you read today."

Abbie harrumphed. "I was not aiming for *swooning* readers. How can they read if they're swooning?" She hoisted Isobel's satchel over her free shoulder.

Isobel rubbed a hand over her swollen belly. "*Abbie*, you're not going to carry both our satchels. Give me."

Ignoring Isobel, Abbie led the way as the four friends left The Tangled Fleece, waving a hand to Mr. Bradley, the innkeeper, as they departed. A cart and mule waited. Leila helped Isobel climb onto the back of the cart before joining her, legs swinging over the back of the cart. Abbie climbed in front to guide the mule forwards. They waved farewell to Hetty as she headed in the opposite direction to the Dunley Manor.

As they traveled through the village towards home, Isobel said, "Let me be the first to offer sage advice. Do not travel abroad with children under the age of five. Dreadful nightmare. Can you imagine it? A babe on each hip as I'm trying to climb castle stairs? Alistair is of little use, with his hands full, as well. No, save the world travels for *after* the children are old enough to make their own way up a stone spiral."

"No plans to travel next year, then?" Leila asked.

"We have so much to see, but we'll wait at least five years before setting off again. He wants to focus on his campaigning for Member of Parliament, and I'm, er, indisposed at present." She pointed to her belly and made a face.

Abbie turned the cart down the widened drive-way, passing beneath a stone arch engraved with the word *Pardez*, or Paradise. "I'll thank Papa for the use of the cart, shall I? I can't believe you wanted to walk home after the meeting, Isobel."

Isobel grinned, swinging her feet as they approached the house. Running amok around the courtyard were giggling and screeching children. A horde of goblins, from Isobel's perspective. Oh, wait, not all were giggling. At least one was crying, but she could not spy which one in the chaos of clamoring feet and flailing hands. Chasing them — or was this an attempt to herd them? — were three gentlemen and two young men, namely Alistair, Abbie's husband Percy, Leila's husband Jules, and Leila's twin cousins Anik and Anil. The children led them in a merry dance. No one would suspect the gentlemen began their day finely dressed, for now, their cravats were twisted askew, their breeches dusty, and one husband was missing his coat altogether.

Leila watched her twin daughters Clio and Eleni, trying to drag Isobel's eldest daughter, Beryl, into their game, Beryl being the one who was wailing tears of upset. "I suppose it'll be our turn next. The gentlemen deserve an evening of manly port and cigars or whatever it is they do when we're not around."

Isobel wrinkled her nose at the thought of cigars, but said, "It's their own doing. Rafe, Everard, and Beryl's grandparents are inside the house doing stuffall, for heaven's sake. Why not leave the children inside with them? No, I wager it was Percy's idea to bring them all outside to play."

Chortling, Leila said, "And I wager in return they're regretting that now."

"Good heavens." Abbie pulled the cart to a stop. "Where is Percy's coat?"

Leila pointed. "Edmund is wearing it."

Abbie groaned, especially when she saw her daughter Emma had lost her shoes and torn her stockings.

Alistair broke from the group to help Isobel step off the cart while her friends and their families headed inside the house for nuncheon, the ladies all smiles, and the gentlemen none the worse for wear.

Hoisted on Alistair's hip was his two-year-old brother Tobin. "We began to lose hope you would return." Tobin tugged at his brother's cravat. "*Help*," Alistair pleaded, his once perfectly pomaded hair now frizzed from children's curious hands.

"I recall, when you were courting me, *you* wanted to be *my* hero. Made quite a fuss about it, if I'm not mistaken. Changing your mind so soon?"

"I will scale a wall for you, *nazanin*, but when it comes to family, I need you to rescue me."

She stood on her tiptoes and kissed his cheek before ruffling Tobin's hair, then turned to wave their three children inside Paradise.

Flash Fiction

Lord Weatherby Arrives Home

E lwood dismounted, handing the reins to an attentive stableboy. The ride from London had not been
unpleasant, but it had been long. Intentionally so.
At every village, no matter how large or small, he had
stopped to allow the horse to graze and himself to
delay the inevitable.

The closer he had drawn to his own parish, the
more frequently the memories intruded. A black-
haired beauty. A kissing bough. Whispered words
of love. All superimposed on reality. Flashing and
slashing were the darker memories, the ones that
drove him to join the British Army. His brother newly
arrived from London. A party. A compromising kiss.

His brother Henry had been wild. A rogue, they had
called him. For the first time in years, Henry had come
home, giving their parents a reason to celebrate; the
prodigal son returned. At the party, it was not any girl
Henry had been caught kissing. It had been Elwood's
girl. From the moment the pair's fathers had announced
a marriage between her and Henry to right the situation, Elwood had left, never to return. What man would
want to see his love on the arm of his brother?

Standing now on the lawn of the ancestral home,
Elwood felt his stomach knot. *Never* had come too soon.

Inside the house awaited his brother's widow.

How could he face her? How could he live with her? She was his felled albatross.

Eight chimneys. Fifteen bays. Fifty-eight plodding steps he took to the Tudor manor. This was a home he did not want, a reminder of his brother's passing, a reminder of his father's passing, a reminder of an inheritance that should never have been his.

Heavy-hearted, he opened the front door without knocking.

Rather than the gloom he expected to find, the feel of dark mourning, he was greeted by the shouts and giggles of children running back and forth along the upper-floor balcony overlooking the entrance hall.

"Girls! Stop running *now*!" shouted a voice from the past.

Chasing after two girls was a woman clad in grey. Not the young girl of his memories anymore, but rather a grown woman, a mother, a widow. She had not seen him enter. He did not announce himself. Instead, he watched. Back and forth they chased, the girls screeching, the woman scolding.

His heart hammered.

Oh, he could not do this. He could not take up the mantle of his father or his brother. He could not become the caretaker of the woman who had betrayed him. He could not. The blood pumping in his veins urged him to take flight, to run where no one would find him.

A crisp voice spoke from the other end of the entrance hall, the old butler. "Lord Weatherby. You've arrived." He bowed reverently.

Elwood winced at the appellation that should not be his. Mr. Elwood James was his name. Plain Mr. James. Second son.

Ignoring his queasiness, he nodded to the butler, donning the cloak of Lord Weatherby as he must. "Donaldson."

"The Countess of Weatherby requests I direct you to the study upon your arrival. Is that your wish, my lord?"

The Countess of Weatherby.

Elwood closed his eyes and took a deep, steadying breath. "I had hoped —"

He was interrupted by the squeals of the two girls as they raced down the staircase.

"He's here! Uncle Elwood is here!"

Uncle Elwood. A curiosity. He had not known he had two nieces, not until receiving the notice from the family solicitor about the inheritance, yet they knew him, or of him at least. A curiosity indeed.

Uncertain, he smiled at them.

A voice from the top of the staircase, *her* voice, called down, "No running!"

If the girls obeyed, Elwood did not notice, for his eyes followed the banister to the top to behold Lady Weatherby. His brother's widow. Elwood's lost love.

When she saw him, she halted, teetering at the edge of the top step and gripping the banister as though her life depended on its strength, and perhaps it did. Her eyes widened. Her cheeks flushed. A trembling hand tucked a stray strand of ebony behind her ear.

Every action, every flicker of movement, every breath, Elwood observed.

True to her nature, she was plainly dressed for a countess, even for one in mourning. Grey wool, simple lines, hair bagged at the nape of her neck.

"Ah, you're here," she said, her words soft.

The door to his right opened. He paid it no mind, his eyes locked with hers. Did his eyes convey the pain of years gone by, the regret of not marrying her before his brother visited, the betrayal of her choosing his brother instead? Did they convey his turmoil now, the joy of seeing her, the loss of losing first father and then brother while he fought on the Continent, the reluctance to be here now?

Whoever had opened the door said brusquely in echo, "Ah, you're here. I expected you this morning."

Elwood broke eye contact to turn to the speaker. A haughty young woman bedecked in a black veil, crepe, and jewels stared at him from down the length of her nose, never mind that he was now the Earl of Weatherby. With disregard, she swept her gaze over him, head to toe.

Eyes trained on him, although not speaking to him, the woman said, "I gave strict orders for them not to leave the nursery. Disobey me again, and you'll see what it's like not to have my husband's protection."

Elwood raised an eyebrow.

"Yes, my lady," Rachael said from the top of the stairs.

He snapped his head back to the stairs. Rachael held open her arms, and the girls scampered upstairs into her embrace before the trio disappeared around the corner.

The woman next to him said, "Pity is never a good reason to hire a governess. I'll see to a new hire as soon as our business is concluded today. Donaldson will show you to the study."

Governess? The word took a long time to sink in, long enough that the cheeky woman had returned to the parlor to the right, leaving Elwood in the entrance hall with the butler. When the word registered, he wanted to take the stairs two at a time, burst into the nursery, and demand answers.

Instead, he turned to Donaldson. "Show the governess to the study and see that we're not disturbed."

The butler nodded, making no attempt to walk Elwood to the study, for they both knew he was well aware of its location.

The governess.

He paced the room that had been his father's, his brother's, now his. He paced, trying to make sense of what he had witnessed. No more than five minutes passed.

Rachael entered, her head bowed, her hands clasped.

He forgot himself. Struck dumb, he stood still and stared at her. *The governess.*

His opening words were not flattering. "Are you not the widowed Lady Weatherby?"

She looked up, surprised, then shook her head.

One step forwards. His palm itched to reach for her.

Rachael studied him, then said, "Lady Weatherby is in the parlor. I'm the governess."

He ached to touch her. His fingers twitched at his side, recalling the softness of her cheek.

"He eloped with her the day after you left," she said.

One step backwards. Elwood stumbled, breathless.

"I stayed with my father until your brother posted a governess position. He took pity and hired me. No one else would have me, not after the scandal." She bowed her head again. "I know it doesn't matter anymore, but I've wanted to say it for ten years. Think of me what you will, but I did not permit him to — " She sucked in a breath. "I never loved anyone but you."

Elwood reached a hand for the desk behind him, steadying himself, his heartbeat erratic.

"Say something, Elwoo — Lord Weatherby. Tell me I'm to resign because your wife would not want me in the house."

Leaning against the desk, unable to stand on his own two feet without his legs shaking, he said hoarsely, "I've no wife. I've loved only you."

They looked at each other through a haze of tears. He skipped seconds in time, unsure how he had moved from the desk into her arms, but when he next opened his eyes, he found his lips to her cheek and his arms about her in a tight embrace. Elwood inhaled the scent of jasmine that had kept him alive for the past ten years.

He asked, "If you can ever forgive me for abandoning you, for not trusting you, then is it too late to ask you to be my wife?"

"I would consent even if you had waited twenty years."

Peppering her face with his lips, he said with a laugh, "I can't wait that long. Elope with me?"

"I thought you'd never ask."

Miss Connelly Misses the Valentine Ball

Fifteen more miles. Or was it twenty?

Trudy watched their progress from the carriage window. The snow-covered scenery, with its blinding reflection of the setting sun, made it difficult to gauge the remaining distance to Lady Oswald's country house.

Trudy squinted. How could serenity *look* cold? The inside of the carriage was warm, cozy even: a hot brick at her feet, her hands tucked into a muff, her cloak about her shoulders, a few blankets next to her.

For two weeks, she had looked forward to tonight: Lady Oswald's Valentine's Ball. Traditionally, this was the most auspicious ball of the year, for one lucky young lady always found love at the ball. Would she be the lucky one this year?

Aunt Gertie had promised to accompany her, to introduce her to everyone who was anyone. Over their morning meal, Auntie had winked with promises of love. During nuncheon, she had teased about a spring wedding. Early that evening, she had tittered over who might win Trudy's affection.

After all the ribbing, Aunt Gertie had slipped while descending the stairs, turning her ankle.

Despite Trudy's insistence to stay and look after her aunt, Auntie had the last word.

The warmth of the carriage chilled without her aunt sitting across from her, regaling her with tales of potential beaux, plotting the best introductions to persuade an invitation to dance.

A jolt flung Trudy's shoulder against the side of the carriage.

Righting herself, she rubbed at the smarting arm and looked out the window. All at peace. The carriage trudged along. If her shoulder from top to elbow did not throb, she would think the jolt her imagination. The wheels must have slid on ice. Nothing to worry about. Mr. Coachman was the best of drivers.

Another mile. Snow flurries began to fall. The sun dipped behind distant hills. Trudy shivered deeper into her cloak and muff.

Would Mr. Sunderland attend the ball? Mr. Wilkerson? Sir Teddy? She would not mind a dance with them, all kind gents, all neighbors of Aunt Gertie.

Another jolt knocked Trudy sideways onto the carriage seat, then tossed her with a jerk in the opposite direction. The carriage slid back and forth before slowing, steadying, then returning to its pace, drawing ever closer to the Oswald family home. How many miles remain? Far more than she cared for if the carriage wheels continued to slide every so often. A strand of hair had already slipped from its pins, and her wrist echoed the ache of her shoulder. Her faith in Mr. Coachman did not waver. She only hoped she would not arrive disheveled.

Setting the muff atop the extra blankets, she tried to pin the loose lock.

Crack. Her elbow slammed into the wall as the carriage slid again. She grasped for the leather strap to keep herself upright as the carriage fishtailed. Back and forth. Back and forth. Her stomach churned. Another *crack*, this time from beneath her. The leather strap imprinted on her palm as she gripped it in fear. A groan, a bump, a jolt, then the carriage tipped backwards, tossing her into the corner. The brick at her feet slid against the side with a *thunk*.

When the world stopped moving and her head stopped spinning, she knew all was not right. The carriage was tilted, the bench across from her staring down at her. Releasing the leather strap, she pushed against the carriage door until it opened. Before she could sit up or lean out, the door slammed closed with a sharp gust of wind. From outside came the sounds of horses snorting and the coachman cursing, followed by the carriage groaning and shuddering.

Trudy stilled, wide-eyed.

More noises followed. A lurch of the carriage, creaking, grating, more cursing.

"Miss Connelly?" The coachman called to her.

Exhaling from her cheeks, she steeled herself. One foot against the cushioned bench, she crouched to reopen the carriage door. This time, she braced her shoulder against it. It swung open with ease. A crisp wind whipped at her exposed cheeks and cut through her cloak, shivering her to the bone.

By standing on the bench, she could angle halfway out of the door to look around. She was in a ditch. An empty creek bed, to be precise. Behind them was an arched bridge. Mr. Coachman had already unlatched the carriage from the horses, both of which stood at the icy road, clouds of breath mushrooming from their nostrils. They appeared disgruntled but unharmed. Dusk had settled, but the sky remained bright, reflecting the white dales.

She ought to panic. It would not be sensible, but it would be expected. Even now, her breathing shallowed, and her heart pounded. From the angle of the fall, the carriage would take far more than one man to raise it from its earthy grave. Likewise, she would not be able to gain purchase to escape and reach the road. Even if she did, what would she do? Leap on one of the horses bareback and ride on to the ball?

"Miss Connelly?" Repeated the coachman. "Are you injured?"

He stood at the edge of the ditch, looking down at her. It was not a far distance, merely icy and out of arm's reach.

"It would appear not," she said, her voice strong and steady despite the tremble of her fingers clutching at the edges of her cloak.

He sighed in audible relief, his breath pluming in a white cloud. Slipping a hand into his greatcoat pocket, he pulled out a flask and swigged deeply, warming himself against the cold. "We're not far from the Sword and Cross. I'll take a horse to find help."

Without further explanation, he mounted one of the horses and trotted in the direction whence they had come.

Trudy watched him cross the bridge, and then she huffed herself back inside the tilted shelter. At least her brick held warmth. Mostly.

She tidied the space and made herself comfortable while awaiting his return. It would not be a long wait, she told herself. He would return in minutes with five or so laborers who would be able to hoist the carriage to safety and send them on their way to the ball.

Ah, the Valentine's Ball. Would Mr. Mercer attend? He had always been kind.

The brightness shining through her window was deceptive. She knew it was after dusk. She knew the sun had set behind the hills. She knew, and yet the world appeared light. Time ticked. The brick cooled. The air in the carriage sharpened. Trudy shivered and tugged one of the blankets onto her lap.

Her ears perked. Horse hoofs. Was it not?

Tossing the blanket aside, she reached for the door, then paused, palm to fabric lining. It had to be Mr. Coachman with help. But what if it was not? What if it was a highwayman? She shuddered at the thought but then dismissed it. This was far too remote a road to attract the likes of thieves.

She popped out of the carriage door, eager to greet Mr. Coachman and his helpers.

Only, it was not Mr. Coachman coming over the bridge. From the opposite direction, heading to the bridge, was a man in a donkey-led farm cart. Next to him sat a young girl who must be his daughter. When they spotted her, they pulled to a stop.

The man said, "Fine state you're in."

Trudy swallowed the affront that he did not even ask after her well-being, much less ask if she might need help or if she could use a ride to the inn. "Yes, it would seem I'm stuck. My coachman has gone to find helpers to right the carriage. We're for the Oswald's house."

His daughter sniffled and drew her shawl more tightly about her shoulders.

"Fine estate." He whistled. "Right cold this eve. Hope your coachman finds help soon."

With that, he tipped his hat, flicked the reins, and left Trudy standing halfway out of the carriage.

There was nothing left to do but return to the inside of her box. She wrapped the blanket over her and tried to draw her knees close to her chest, but her ballgown restricted her movement. The window light began to darken, the deceptive daytime coming to a close. She would not be scared. Mr. Coachman would be along soon.

Ah! There he was. Unmistakable sounds of horse hoofs against the snow and ice.

Once more, she popped out of the carriage, ready to greet him, her body trembling from the cold even with the blanket cocooned about her. It was brighter outside than inside the carriage. Approaching the bridge, heading in the same direction she had been bound, were two men on horseback. At first, she could not make out if it was Mr. Coachman and a helper, but as they drew closer, she realized it was, yet again, not Mr. Coachman. Her hope sank to the pit of her stomach.

The two gentlemen wore impressively caped greatcoats, their ball attire visible even from her home in the ditch. She was one part relieved that they were not highwaymen and one part excited that they were heading to Lady Oswald's ball — they could send help her way!

They both stopped at the edge of the road but did not dismount.

"I say," said one gentleman, "quite the rut you're in."

"Yes, yes it is," she answered, her voice trembling with her limbs. "My coachman is seeking out laborers to save the carriage. I'm waiting for him. Are you bound for the ball?"

"We are," said the second gentleman. "Late at this hour. Pity." His eyes trained not on her face but on her bosom, despite it being well covered with the blanket.

When she shuddered this time, it was not from the cold. A stab of fear lanced down her spine. Never had she felt so defenseless. She should not fear two gentlemen; they were her equals, after all. Yet she knew only fear. Her request for them to aid her or at least send help died on her tongue.

"We wish your coachman well," said the first gentleman.

"Stay warm," said the second with a malicious grin.

Off they trotted without a backwards glance.

She would be outraged if she was not so relieved by their departure. Once she settled back into the carriage, she questioned her reaction to the two men — foolishness on her part, was it not? Why would she ever feel fear at seeing two peers? They could have been her dance partners had the evening not turned sideways.

However much she convinced herself she was silly for reacting as she did, her whole body tensed when she heard the approach of horses again. Only when she recognized carriage wheels crunching along the snow did she rise from the door, ready to greet her next possible savior. With a carriage, they could hoist her out of the ditch and take her to safety.

Darkness had settled. Lanterns swayed, lighting the way for the carriage. Worried they would not see her, she dropped her blanket onto the bench and waved her arms. The carriage passed without slowing.

Trudy slumped back onto the bench. If Mr. Coachman did not return soon, she would be hard-pressed not to try climbing out of the ditch and riding the poor remaining horse barebacked back to town. The trouble was, she knew she would not be able to get out of the ditch, not as icy as it was, not in her dress slippers. She did not know her way to the Sword and Cross, nor did she have a means to light her way. The reflection of the night sky against the snow did add an element of brightness, but there was no denying evening had arrived. The best she could do was keep warm until help arrived.

She arranged her blanket, adding the second blanket over her for additional warmth, and waited.

Resting her head against the side of the carriage, she tried to sleep. Never had she been so exhausted. Bone-deep exhaustion. Every breath drew in sharp air that dried her lips, stung her tongue, and made her teeth ache. Every exhale puffed out as a cloud. Gooseflesh covered her skin. She shivered, her toes curling in her shoes. Time passed. Wind howled. The carriage creaked and groaned. The cold had seeped into her blanket and cut through her ballgown, chilling her from the inside out. Against the constrictions of her gown, she pulled her knees to her chest and buried her face against the blanket. She could not stop shaking. Would he ever come?

When Trudy finally heard again the sound of horse hoofs, she could not convince herself to move. The carriage door was too far. The air too cold. Her limbs limp and trembling beyond her control. She remained where she was and waited for the hoofs to pass by.

Clip clop clip clop clip clop.

Trudy awoke with a physical jerk as the carriage door wrenched open.

Startled but too frigid to be frightened, she looked up into the masked face of a gentleman. A scarf covered his nose and mouth; a tricorn adorned his head; all other notable features were lost to the darkness of night.

"Are you injured?" asked a deep voice, one of concern rather than curiosity.

Her voice croaked and scratched. "No. I'm well. I'm for the Valentine's Ball. My coachman has gone to find help."

The man looked around behind him. "I see neither coachman nor help. Allow me to escort you back to town. It's far too treacherous to ride yourself, so ride with me on my horse. I'll tie the gelding to my saddle, and we can bring him with us."

Her mind moved sluggishly. Droplets kissed her face, pinpricks of coldness. Was it snowing?

The wind knocked the carriage door against its side in a succession of bangs.

It took her ages long to realize he was standing *on* the carriage. He had made it into the ditch and *onto* the carriage. Could he get out of the ditch now?

Could he save her? Oh, but how tricky, for she could not very well be seen riding into town in the middle of the night on a shared saddle with a gentleman. She would be ruined! But if she stayed here…

"I thank you, sir," she said at last, "but my reputation would be at stake. If you wish to help, please find my coachman and the helpers he's bringing. They must have gotten lost along the way."

"If you stay, you'll freeze to death. Your reputation is not more important than your life."

"Oh, but it is. It is better to die virtuous than to live ruined." The argument made perfect sense in her cold-addled brain.

She wet cracked lips with a dry tongue.

"Forgive my impertinence," the man said, "but that is nonsense. I don't deny society can be cruel, but your life is more important than rumor."

She shook her head. Or she thought she did. She could not feel anything aside from her shivering.

"I must wait for my coachman." Oh! She tugged at the second blanket. "Could you take this and cover the horse? I'm worried he's cold."

As if to prove her point, another whoosh of wind filled the cabin and rattled the door, a heavier snow than before falling past the stranger's head and into her shelter.

Snow was a curious element. She thought it might melt as it fluttered onto her blanket. It did not.

"The horse is fine," he said. "You're not. Are you coming with me?"

"Please, could you find my coachman?"

He cursed under his breath, something profane that ought to have offended her, but she was too tired to care. "If you won't allow me to pull you out and take you to safety, then I'm not leaving until your coachman arrives. I'll guard the carriage and keep watch."

"That's unnecessary but appreciated. Please close the carriage door. It's frightfully cold."

With a harrumph, he shut the carriage door. She listened to the thumping his boots made against the side of the carriage, then to a scrambling sound as, she assumed, he climbed out of the creek bed and back onto the road. Would he truthfully keep watch? The thought brought her peace. She was not alone.

Curling into a tight ball on her tilted bench, she nestled back into an almost sleep. The wind picked up, whistling around the carriage.

A voice rose above the wind. "Broken axle, from the look of it."

In a moment of confusion, she wondered who had spoken. Oh, yes, the man, the stranger keeping watch over the carriage.

"Is it?" she whispered inaudibly.

"Snowstorm's coming. Looks like the Valentine's Ball guests will be staying overnight."

"A fine estate," she mumbled.

"Do you attend every year?"

"Every year." The back of her eyelids warmed her eyes.

"Miss?"

They would laugh and say she knew nought about snow. They did not know the truth. They did not understand.

"Miss? I need you to answer me."

She smiled at the voice. A kind voice, full of concern.

With a start, she awoke to find the man sitting next to her on the bench *inside the carriage*. Trudy shrieked. Or thought she did. She could not be sure she had actually made the sound. Her body shook.

"Miss," he said, "Please, allow me to take you into town. Your life is not worth your reputation. Not that it means much coming from a stranger, but I assure you I'll marry you if that will bring you peace of mind."

She stared at him, wondering what he looked like behind the scarf. Her eyes stung from the cold. Although she tried to process what he had said, she could not make sense of it. A snowstorm? Had he mentioned a snowstorm? Yes, that was it.

"You mustn't wait outside," Trudy said. "It's too cold. There's a snowstorm coming. The inside of the carriage is warm. We'll wait for Mr. Coachman in here."

Tugging her second blanket loose, she draped it over him.

He helped turn the blanket longways, but rather than wrap it around himself, he tucked a corner beneath him, then wrapped it back around her, pulling her scandalously close to his side. She pushed against him in protest.

"Your reputation is only at stake if we're seen. In case you haven't noticed, no one is here but the two of us. Come. It's warmer next to me."

It was. She could feel his warmth along her side. Instinctively, she nestled against this complete stranger, unconcerned with what he might think of her. Nothing mattered except warmth.

His voice was soothing, full of hope and promise. "Shall we talk until the coachman arrives? Your name would be a good place to start."

Her arm snaked around his waist, and she buried her face on his chest. So warm. "We've not been intro-duced, sir."

"Yet we've already reached an alarming level of intimacy, wouldn't you say?"

"Miss Connelly. Miss Trudy Connelly."

"Ah, yes, Lady MacGregor's niece."

He knew her? The fact was not as surprising as was the warmth she felt nestled next to him. Though her toes had numbed long ago, her torso soaked in his warmth, tingling to near normalcy.

"How do you know me?" she asked.

"I know all the guests at the ball."

She listened to his heartbeat as his chest rose and fell against her cheek. Just as she was about to ask how he knew all the guests, he sat up, moving the blanket to cover her. She, too, sat up, startled and confused.

He held a hand to her arm. "Horses."

Without further explanation, he climbed onto the bench, opened the carriage door, and hoisted himself up and out. The door closed behind him after a pile of snow and freezing air swooped into the carriage. She brushed away the snow, trembling anew, bereft of his warmth and company. Then she heard the hoofs. They were still a distance away, but the crunching, clopping, and snorting sounds increased as they drew closer.

Voices. Shouts. Scuffles.

Her heart raced. Had those two gentlemen returned to harm her? Was the stranger in danger? Why had he not stayed in the carriage? Her reputa-tion be dashed! He was safer in the carriage than out there in danger! There was nothing she could do to help him, but in a frenzy, she tossed aside the blankets, stepped with wobbly legs onto the bench, and flung open the carriage door.

The night was lit with dozens of swaying lanterns. Men bustled around, horses pawing the frozen earth.

"Miss Connelly!"

The voice she had expected to hear was not the voice that called out. Rather than the stranger's voice, it was Mr. Coachman's voice. He stood at the edge of the ditch and looked down, his silhouette outlined by the snowy night sky and the lanterns.

Through the heavy snowfall and sharp wind, she waved at him, hot tears pooling in her eyes.

But then there he was. The stranger. He leapt, light as air, from the road onto the carriage's side and held a hand to help her out of the cold coffin. She slipped her hand into his. His grip was strong and sure. With force but an unexpected gentleness, he pulled her high enough to be able to wrap an arm about her waist and lift her. Back in his warm arms again, she did not want him to release her. She held on to him even when her feet were firmly on solid ground, or rather, the side of the carriage. With a mumbled apology, he hooked an arm behind her legs and lifted her like a babe; then, in a mighty step, he leapt from the carriage onto the road, two men waiting to clasp his arms should he slide on impact.

While at least a dozen men worked to pull the carriage out of the ditch, broken axle and all, the stranger carried her to an awaiting farm cart. He did not release her until he could set her safely into the cart.

"It's not as fine a riding gig as your carriage, but it'll see you safely to town. Your coachman says there's a room at the Sword and Cross waiting for you. On the morrow, I'll see you to the Oswald estate myself, if you'll allow me. It is too late for the Valentine's Ball, but there will be a grand breakfast in honor of the guests who were trapped overnight."

He turned away from her, and she reached out to grasp his arm, afraid to be without him — a foolish thought since they had only been in each other's company for an hour at most.

"Stay with me," she pleaded.

He smiled. She could not see the smile behind the scarf, but she could feel it — more foolishness she would blame on the cold.

"Miss Connelly, I'm not going to leave you. I'm merely going to help with the carriage. My offer still stands, you know. Your reputation is untarnished. No one saw me inside the carriage with you. But the offer of my hand remains."

Had he offered his hand before? She could not recall. The most important and honorable offer he could make. How had she missed it?

Although he could misinterpret the length of her silence, the pause was only from her realizing she did not know his name or even his face, only his voice, his kindness, his honor, and his warmth. Even now, her face longed to be against his chest again, her side pressed to his. There was something *right* about being with him that went beyond safety and survival.

After the longest silence of the year, Trudy said, "You are under no obligation to marry me, sir. As you said, my reputation is untarnished. If you're sincere, however, then I accept, although I don't even know who you are. I know only that I don't wish to be without you."

Removing the scarf and hat, he revealed the smile she had known he wore. A handsome face with dimples that caused her breath to hitch greeted her.

"Lord Oswald. Harry to my family. My mother had to host the ball without me this year, as I was delayed in London. She'll forgive me when I introduce my bride." He took her hand in his and bowed over it. "Thank you for the honor, Miss Connelly. Despite circumstances, the evening has smiled on us. You know what they say — someone always finds love at the Valentine's Day Ball."

Sir Tristram Invites a Scandal

From atop his horse, Sir Tristram inhaled the spring air. Birds chirped. Sunrays touched his tricorn brim. Daffodils swayed in the breeze. To think, he had given up kicking his heels in London for *this*.

He was more than satisfied. He was elated.

After a decisive survey of the meadowland on the outskirts of his village — home sweet home — he nudged his horse to the edge of the greenery. It was Sunday. His family would be in church. *She* would be in church, sharing the family pew. He could delay his arrival for the sake of flowers.

Yellow trumpets heralded the sun. Ah, daffodils. Knowing his family, not to mention his valet, would suffer from vapors if he arrived with meadow stains on his Sunday best, he dismounted, set his steed to grazing, and ambled into the field. He had not lain amongst flowers since his youth. Tristram was giddy at the idea of doing so now. Responsibilities could wait. Duty could wait. *She* could wait.

One deep breath. Two deep breaths. Three deep breaths. His lungs filled with a sweet yet spicy aroma. He had not recalled daffodils carrying a scent. Decidedly sweet with a playful spice, full of promises, vows of a spring lark and romance. Four deep breaths.

He stood far enough in the meadow not to be heard from the road but still in sight of his horse.

To the daffodils and their promises, he spoke aloud. "Ye of abundant beauty, I have fallen. In love, that is, with your bountiful sweetness. With the curve of your cheek brightened by the sun. Would you do me the honor of being my bride? Of facing life's uncertainties with a cheerful disposition? Of remaining by my side through all the seasons?"

Just as he was about to sit amongst the beauties, the daffodils answered him. "Oh! This is so sudden. Marriage? We've not met in two springs, yet you're in love?"

Startled though he should be, he laughed. What were the odds of talking daffodils?

From a short distance, disguised by greenery and sheltered by the flowers amongst which she lay, rose a young lady. She did not stand, merely sat up to be seen. Leaning back against her arms, she cast him a bright smile at perfect ease with both her surroundings and the gentleman. Bold of her. Improper, too.

Tristram returned her smile. Who the deuce was she?

"Smitten, yes," he said. "Is that enough to base a marriage?"

She tapped a finger to her chin to intimate deep thought. "Only if you tell me one true reason why I should marry you."

This was an absurd conversation. She must surely know he had not realized her presence.

Although…

"One true reason you shall have," Tristram said. "Once I arrive at the church, I shall have to marry a gentlewoman I have no desire to marry."

She dipped her head to one side. "Is today your wedding day?"

"The noose is not so tight, my lady. My family has their heart set on my marrying a family friend, one whose own heart flits from one lover to the next. It would be an advantageous marriage for her and one of convenience for my family. There's only one solution — bring home a different bride."

"Me?" Her smile brightened.

"Do you object?"

The conversation had slipped from absurd to frighteningly real. However hot under the cravat he should feel, his shoulders lightened, his burdens relieving.

Daisy. Was her name not Daisy? A flitting memory from the shadowed recesses of his mind.

"You're a man of your word, I see," she answered. "I requested a truthful reason, and you've given it. I've no objection. Your timing is impeccable if I'm truthful in return. I've avoided church for the same reason. My family wishes me to marry someone I don't wish to marry. Today was to be the reading of the first banns." She reached out a hand for assistance standing.

Tristram stepped towards her, then faltered a hair's breadth before clasping her hand. For a heartbeat, his memory deceived him. He thought for half a heartbeat the family friend might be *her*.

What a coincidence that would be! Too much for old Tristram.

On second look, his memory jarred. The family friend was dirty blonde. A flirty blonde with batting eyelashes to match. He had met her only once two years ago, but once was enough. In contrast, his daffodil was yellow-blonde. A distinct difference to the discerning eye, to the eye of a man who also recalled meeting *this* beauty at the spring fête two years ago and asking her to dance. Twice.

"Daisy?" he ventured, tucking her hand in the crook of his arm.

She beamed. "You remembered."

He had been smitten with her at the fête but promptly forgot about her when his family informed him of their arrangement. Off to London, he had fled. His return now had been resignation. Cowardice? Which was more cowardly: running from an arranged marriage with a woman he had not liked or not having the courage to tell his family no?

Her voice, full of spicy sweetness, promised both lark and romance. "Shall we cause a scandal?"

"Yes, my lady. Let's cause a scandal."

East Meets Westerton
to Offer Well Wishes

The coin flipped into the well. Rather than peer into the depths to see where it landed, the young lady squeezed her eyelids, presumably to make a wish. Ronald watched her through the window. Every day, she had visited the well, but today was the first time she had tossed a coin. He knew this because he had watched her for two weeks, spending an hour each day in the private parlor of the Green Dragon Inn for the sole purpose of hoping to see her.

Miss Samantha was her name. The youngest daughter of one of the wealthiest tenants. To his advantage, the barkeep had a loose tongue.

That same barkeep set a plate before Ronald and said, "Avert your eyes, Mr. East. Her papa has his hopes she'll marry the baron's steward."

Ronald jerked his head from the window. "The steward? Not with his reputation, surely."

"The steward indeed. Seeing as how he acts on behalf of the baron, who's the real villain?" The barkeep leaned down and said, "With Miss Samantha as a bride, the steward is sure to find a way to save us from Dragon Westerton. A cunning man is the steward."

Ronald did not reply other than to thank him for the meal.

When he looked out the window, Miss Samantha was gone. Pulling the letter with its creased edges from his waistcoat pocket, he unfolded it and reread it for the hundredth time.

According to the anonymous letter sent from a tenant, if he had to judge from the quality of paper and writing, the steward had increased rents, lowered wages, and harassed the villagers who found themselves in arrears, all done by the mandate of his employer — Baron Westerton. How cruel of the baron to think so little of the people? How thoughtless of him to use a good man like the steward for his evil doings? The letter did not ask the baron for help against the steward; rather, it pointed a finger, accusing him, shaming him.

From all Ronald had heard in his two-week visit to the village, the letter's accusations proved true.

But what to do about it? Even if he fired the steward, which he most certainly would do posthaste, there was still the trouble of the misplaced blame. The steward's behavior had not come from the baron's mandate; rather, the baron had requested, after seeing the prosperity of the accounts, a lowering of rents and raising of wages. As if the villagers would take *his* word for it. They had never met him and did not know him.

For five years, Ronald had held the title of Baron Westerton. For those five years, his grandmother in the north needed him by her side, delaying his move. With a good steward in place of the new estate, there had been no cause for him to rush. The letter revealed his error. The villagers who frequented the Green Dragon Inn had confirmed this error.

As the friendly Mr. East, villagers were all too happy to share with Ronald their toils over a pint. The friendly Mr. East, they had been told, hoped for an audience with Lord Westerton, the baron rumored to be soon traveling to his estate at long last.

Ronald's deception may be held against him when discovered, another notch against his name, but it was necessary from his perspective. No one would divulge the situation to the baron himself, after all, not when he was the blackguard and the cause of their woes.

Now, how to proceed?

On the first day of his third week in town, Ronald admired Miss Samantha not from the window of the inn but from the bench across from the well.

When she first approached, unaware of his watchful gaze, she pulled another coin from her petticoat's pocket.

Before she could flip it into the well, Ronald stood and said, "Allow me."

Her hand to her heart at being startled, she took his measure. She would find him well turned out, a gentleman with a trustworthy smile. He had taken great care with his appearance to portray the right balance of friend and gentleman.

Assessment complete, she looked to his outstretched hand — in it, a coin. "How kind of you," she said. "But I have my own. You should save yours for your own wish."

"Very well." He tossed in the coin. "I'll wish to know you better."

"Oh dear. The wish won't come true if you speak it aloud." Her smile teased.

Closing her eyes, she tossed in her coin. After a stretch of silence, she opened her eyes, smiled again, then nodded as she departed, leaving him at the well, less one coin.

On the second day of his third week in town, Ronald again awaited her arrival at the well. They exchanged a brief greeting, nothing more, another coin denied.

On the third day of his third week, they met again, her eyes telling him she expected him this time. She accepted his coin with a shy smile.

Ronald allowed a moment of silence to pass for her to concentrate on the wish. "I have the advantage of knowing you're Miss Samantha, daughter of Mr. Warbler."

Miss Samantha said, "I know who you are, too."

"Do you?"

"Mr. East. The gentleman who hopes to call on Lord Westerton when he arrives. It's a small village. People talk." She shared a knowing glance before nodding her departure.

It took three more days of not-so-happenchance meetings before Ronald braved, "Permit me to escort you home?"

After a curious perusal of his person, she nodded and waited for him to offer his arm.

From the corner of his eye, he spied the barkeep, sweeping the doorway of the inn, watching them. Ronald winked as they passed. The barkeep returned the wink.

Once they reached the edge of the village, Miss Samantha said, "You've waited some time for Lord

Westerton to arrive. I'm surprised you've not decided to return at a later date."

"My business is worth the wait." He hesitated a moment before venturing, "I've heard quite a bit about Lord Westerton. If you'll excuse my saying, he sounds diabolical."

"But I thought you knew him? If you don't know him, why have you come to call on him?"

"Business," was all he offered, unable to think fast enough when in proximity of her long lashes.

Her voice was sweet, honeyed tones with an alto softness. Up close, he could see a row of freckles he had not spied from his vantage point at the inn's window. She smelled faintly of rose water.

Satisfied enough with his answer, she said, "I don't know for certain, but I don't think you have anything to fear from Lord Westerton. Although I may be the only person in the village to say this, I hope he arrives soon."

Ronald raised his eyebrows as they slowed their pace at an idyllic stone bridge. He believed he would enjoy living here once he settled. The sheep-dotted fields and stone cottages were picturesque.

"You see, Mr. East, I believe it's the steward who is diabolical, not the baron."

"Revolutionary words. What has you in opposition to everyone else?" He paused their progress at the hump of the bridge and leaned an elbow on the stone, awarding her his most solicitous expression.

Trust me, his eyes said.

"The new baron only inherited five years ago, but the steward has been here ten. He was under the thumb of the previous baron, but he was never a kind person. I have reason to believe he cannot be trusted."

Ronald waited for her to explain, but she did not. Recalling the words of the barkeep, he wondered for how long her father had angled for her to wed the steward.

She gazed at the creek bed, more rock than creek, and said, "I have an intuition about these things, Mr. East. I feel you're a good man, someone in whom to confide. If you have business with Lord Westerton, you could be the one who helps us."

He wondered if it would be better to reveal himself now or later. Now seemed too early, for he wanted to ask to court her before the knowledge of his true identity tainted her perception. Later seemed too late, an inexcusable length of time to deceive someone. Knowing her an ally and knowing he needed to secure her hand before her father could barter her to the steward, he realized it was time to act.

One week passed in which she did not see Mr. East. Her heart ached each time she approached the well to find it devoid of the handsome stranger. Silly to mourn the departure of someone she did not know, but she could not deny an attraction to him and a suspicion he was equally attracted to her. Had he not waited at the well every day for her?

The beginning of the next week brought three surprising pieces of news. Lord Westerton had returned, although no one had yet seen him. The steward had been seen leaving the village with bags packed. An invitation for Miss Samantha to take tea with the baron, Mr. East, and a chaperone arrived at the Warbler residence. Which of those bits of news was the most shocking, she could not say. Perhaps the knowledge she would see Mr. East again.

The next afternoon, Samantha stepped down from the baron's private carriage, sent to convey her and her lady's maid to the estate. However unusual it was to invite her rather than her father or even without her father, she assumed it was to do with Mr. East and the intuition with which she had entrusted him.

The butler saw her to the drawing room.

When she and her lady's maid stepped inside, it was to find Mr. East standing with his back to the window, his expression welcoming. Her heart fluttered to see his friendly eyes and broad smile. A quick glance revealed he was alone. The baron had not yet joined them. Behind her, the butler bowed and closed the door.

Before Mr. East spoke, the truth dawned on her. She could not say how she knew, but she *knew*. The immaculateness of his dress? His ease in the setting? The anxious paleness of his knuckles as he gripped his embroidered coat? Whatever it was, she *knew*.

Dipping into a curtsy, she said, "Lord Westerton."

The surprise in his expression proved he had not expected her to guess, at least not until he spoke the words that could be his undoing.

"How did you know?" he asked.

"I told you. I have an intuition about these things." To dispel his worry that she would be angered by his deception, she grinned.

He offered her a seat. "Then you must already know in addition to my confession and asking for your help in gaining the villagers' trust, I plan to ask permission to court you."

Her cheeks flushed. "No. I hadn't expected that."

"Oh." He grimaced before recovering with a sheepish smile. "It's what I wished at the well if you'll recall. To know you better. If this is too sudden, I'll understand."

"Not too sudden," she reassured. "In fact, it would seem both our wishes have come true."

He raised his brows in question.

"I had wished that a brave knight would come to vanquish the dragon. While many thought the dragon to be Lord Westerton himself, I suspected it to be the steward, and here you are. The vanquisher of the dragon."

He chuckled. "I'm not a knight but rather a baron, and I wouldn't say the steward breathed fire. You, for that matter…" He paused, tapping a finger to his lips. "I wouldn't classify you as a damsel in distress."

"Perhaps not, but I'll award you the accolades of dragon slayer if you'll award me the title of baroness."

The shocked pleasure of his expression turned to laughter. "Consider our wishes granted."

Baron Conover Attends a Fete

B aron Conover left the inn with a skip in his step. Today was an important day. No, correction. Today was not *an* important day. Today was *the* important day. *The* day he would meet his beloved's family, immediate, extended, and neighborly.

It had been three months — what ought to be three years for as long as it felt — since he had met her at a mutual friend's wedding breakfast. According to her letters since their parting, she had told her family about him, and they were ecstatic to meet the man for whom their Adelaide's heart pounded.

The village green thundered with excitement. The summer fête was fast underway. Children romped with kites. Villagers wandered with ices. Flags fluttered atop tents. A perfect, sunny, breezy day for family, fun, and folly. Inhaling a deep breath of fresh country air and exhaling his optimism for the day, he stepped onto the green and scouted the crowd for his beloved.

Meeting the family at the fête, she had written, would be the most sensible. He agreed. Far from the tension of meeting in a stuffy drawing room of manners and etiquette. Yes, this was more his speed — a meeting over lemon custard and a tankard of ale.

Not far did he have to walk into the frolicking fray before he felt eyes upon him. The eyes of the villagers.

Heads turned to watch him. Children pointed at him. Fans hid whisperings about him. They were all curious, he suspected, of the newcomer, the one dressed in London finery. He nodded, smiled, or waved as appropriate.

When his searching gaze could not spy Adelaide in the crowd, he headed for the archery stall—no, not to participate in the contest, although he was known for a straight and sure arrow, rather to head for a robust fellow who looked by stance, poise, and attire to be a man in-the-know, the village rector by all accounts. As he approached, the supposed rector caught his gaze, waving a sausage-fingered hand to the guest.

Grasping the fellow's iron—if not a little sweaty—grip, he introduced himself. "Baron Conover, my good man. A pleasure to attend the fête and be in amiable company."

"Donald Grubbes, vicar." The man drew back his shoulders. "The pleasure is ours. It's not every day we have so distinguished a guest attend our humble green."

"Not so distinguished, but I appreciate the hearty welcome, Mr. Grubbes."

"You'll be wanting to find Miss Adelaide, then?"

Surprise, no doubt, reflected in Baron Conover's features. "Why, yes, but how did you know I have an acquaintance with Miss Adelaide?"

Mr. Grubbes laughed, his chins, all three of them, jouncing. "We're a small village, more kin than not. There's not a soul here who doesn't know Miss Adelaide's gentleman is calling today. We've been anxious to meet you. Here at last!" He pointed to a copse of trees, the only shade in the square. A bevy of parasol-twirling ladies eyed him from under the branched greenery.

With a nod, the suitor followed the vicar — what a fine fellow! — to the long arms of the beech trees.

None of the ladies awaiting his arrival were Adelaide. Aunts? Sisters? Cousins?

Mr. Grubbes flourished a hand in his direction and said to the awaiting matrons, "I have the pleasure of presenting Baron Conover, Miss Adelaide's own."

Fans fluttered as the ladies tittered, looking from one to the other.

An older woman stepped forward and raised her hand for him to kiss. "How fortunate we are to make your acquaintance. My niece has spoken of little else, although she kept your identity a mystery. Naughty girl." When he released her hand, she added, "I believe you'll find her by the maypole. She's organizing the dance. I hope to see more of you, Baron."

Taken aback by her familiarity, he made every attempt to school his features and bow to her and the other ladies. He followed Mr. Grubbes to the maypole.

On the way, he was introduced to neighbors, friends, and family, all intrigued to meet Miss Adelaide's mystery gentleman. He did not think himself any great mystery, but then, perhaps not many new faces visited their village or courted their daughters. All were friendly and welcoming, and that was all he could ask for, really.

As they drew closer to the maypole, one person stood out from the crowd: Adelaide. She had not yet seen him, her profile to him and her attention on a woman perhaps thirty years her senior but sharing in likeness. Her mother? He thought so. Adelaide was as he remembered — striking, charming, and all smiles. The older woman, however, was austere and not a little intimidating. He gulped. The family he knew from Adelaide was respected, landowning, and wealthy. Not for the first time did he question if he would meet their approval.

Simultaneously, all heads turned in his direction. Adelaide, with her bright smile and wide eyes, lost all sense of decorum and elbowed her way past the onlookers.

She reached for him with outstretched arms, taking his hands in hers for a gentle squeeze. "You're here!" Tossing over her shoulder to anyone who was listening — everyone — she said, "He's here!"

The woman who shared her likeness joined their happy party, her arched brows looking to Mr. Grubbes.

The vicar flourished the hand for the fifteenth time in as many minutes. "Baron Conover, may I present to you, Mrs. Fletcher." Turning to the statuesque woman, Grubbes said, "I don't mind saying your daughter has found a most distinguished gentleman. What a welcome surprise she's brought to our humble village! Baron Conover, as I live and breathe."

Mrs. Fletcher studied her daughter's suitor.

He smiled in return. "I'm pleased to be here, Mrs. Fletcher, and to meet Miss Adelaide's family."

The corner of Mrs. Fletcher's mouth twitched as if to smile. "My daughter teased me about your being the son of a solicitor. How delightful to learn the truth."

Turning to Adelaide with a wink, he said, "I *am* the son of a solicitor, after all."

Mrs. Fletcher chortled. Mr. Grubbes and the onlookers joined her.

What else was there to do but laugh with them?

From his periphery, he saw an older gentleman approaching, just as formidable as Mrs. Fletcher, a quizzing glass held to his eye as he inspected Adelaide's suitor.

Mrs. Fletcher welcomed the gentleman first. "Your timing is impeccable, as always. Mr. Grubbes has introduced us to Baron Conover. *The* Baron Conover."

"Good heavens," said the man, his left eye magnified by the quizzing glass. "*The* Baron Conover? Well done, Adelaide." A hand thrust forward. "Mr. Fletcher, at your service."

Ah. The father. Yes, he had suspected.

Taking the proffered hand, he shook it with firm assurance. "Plain Baron Conover, sir. Couldn't say I've earned a reputation worthy of an honorific *the*."

More chortling. More laughter.

Mr. Fletcher released his quizzing glass, letting it swing from its ribbon. "Adelaide has shared stories aplenty about you. Claimed you were the son of a solicitor. I can't say I'm not relieved to learn you're from better stock since you plan to pay court to Adelaide. You must dine at the hall this evening."

"Thank you, sir. I'm honored by the invitation." The suitor's smile dipped at the corners. "I *am*, however, the son of a solicitor."

Whispers and giggles circled the surrounding crowd. The Fletchers, however, fell silent. The quizzing glass' ribbon swung as a pendulum, marking time.

At length, Mr. Fletcher said, "Be that as it may, your connections have spoken for you. Family ties are the most important, and it cannot be denied, despite your father's profession, blue blood flows in your veins, my lord."

His smile curved into a full frown. "There's been a misunderstanding, sir. I'm plain Baron Conover, son of a solicitor and gentlewoman."

"Nothing *plain* about being a baron, Conover. Newly inherited, then?"

"No, sir, my father lives and thrives, still, in his offices in London. Perhaps you've heard of him?" He cleared his throat and recited, "'Lost composure? Facing foreclosure? Call on Nero Conover!'"

Mrs. Fletcher gasped. The crowd fell silent. Mr. Fletcher grasped his quizzing glass.

"Mr. Baron Daniel Oliver Conover, sir, of London proper."

The vicar broke the silence with raucous coughs. "You're not a baron?"

The suitor shook his head. "I don't have the pleasure, no. *I'm* Baron."

"Then, you have no connections?" Mrs. Fletcher said, a hand to her heart.

"Well…" He thought for a moment. "My third cousin's husband's aunt—my third cousin twice removed, that is—married a baronet. Sir St. John Simpson, if memory serves."

The quizzing glass fell once more, swinging in time with the syncopated sighs.

Mr. Fletcher clasped Baron's hand and said, "A welcome relief, Mr. Conover. A welcome relief, indeed, to know you're so well connected. *The* Sir St. John. Yes, it's an honor to meet the kin of so great a personage as a baronet."

The whispers and giggles returned to the crowd, along with nods of approval. Mrs. Fletcher twitched her way to a smile. Adelaide beamed.

Baron swiped a bead of sweat from his brow. Given the happy turn of events, he thought better than to add that his third cousin's husband's aunt — the third cousin twice removed, that was — had married a highwayman, baronetcy notwithstanding.

Dante Bakerton
Wins His Prize

Much to the delight of the picnickers, the sun shone overhead, nary a cloud in the sky.

Mr. Dante Bakerton propped himself on an elbow, stretching his long legs to the side. He hooked a forearm over bent knee and surveyed the guests. Only one deserved his focus: the pretty blonde seated three picnic sheets away. His lips slid into a cunning smile. Without question, he would win a kiss from her before the end of the picnic.

She caught his gaze and then jerked her chin in the opposite direction.

Coy minx.

Sharing his groundsheet were several widows who had been eyeing him with lascivious intent, one such widow being the hostess, a bosom bow of his aunt and the only reason he had secured an invitation. It was not the food these ladies had in mind, but he paid them no heed, his attention sold to the pretty blonde.

One of the widows leaned towards him, the scent of lemon and something floral wafting uninvited into his nostrils. She whispered for his ears only, "I spy your gaze, Mr. Bakerton. She's not for you."

Instead of responding, he rumbled a chuckle.

The widow added, "The daughter of an earl has little to offer someone like you. You need *experience.*"

Under his breath, he said, "The daughter of an impoverished earl."

He did not inform the widow — who attempted to entice him with her assets as she reached for the plate of berries — that he knew a great deal about this particular young lady. No dowry. Inattentive parents. Dreams of a fairy-tale romance. This was not the first time he had seen her, after all. Two years had passed, but he remembered every freckle on her face. The question was, how well did she remember him? Her refusal to meet his stare across the lawn led him to believe she remembered him very well indeed.

Pit pat.

Dante flinched.

Pit pat, pit pat.

He looked to the ladies sharing his picnic blanket. They looked around at the other guests, as startled as he by this unexpected turn of events.

Pit pat, pit pat, pit pat.

Fat, rogue rain droplets splattered against the plates. One here. One there. Reconnaissance droplets determining whether the location was ripe for rain.

A solitary cloud mocked the picnickers. With only the handful of drops for warning, the deceptively blue heavens opened above them and unleashed a downpour so fast and so heavy Dante almost lost sight of his prey. The guests shrieked and scrambled, holding tight to bonnets and hats as all ran for the nearest structure, a too-tiny folly that would never fit everyone.

With a fraction of a second to make his move, Dante Bakerton darted past guests to reach Lady Lina.

He took the liberty to wrap an arm about her waist and say, "This way."

For a breath, he thought she would protest. Something in his expression must have elicited trust, however. She pressed into his side as though he would provide shelter from the rain, allowing him to guide her into the trees rather than to the folly.

In the panic, no one would see their detour. He smirked.

The rain drummed overhead, but the canopy of leaves shielded them. Releasing his arm from about her person, he laughed aloud in victory. Lady Lina ignored his humor, turning about her in slow revolution, the dawning of their situation readable in her expression. He knew she realized he had sequestered her from the other guests.

Before she could react, Dante closed the space between them, cupped either side of her face, and kissed her with all the passion two years of anticipation had built. Her body stiffened, her lips tightened, and she made to move away, but when he combed her scalp with his fingertips and traced the seam of her lips with the tip of his tongue, she relaxed into him.

Just when he thought he had won, she pushed against his chest. Not for long was he bereft from her touch. With the crack of thunder, Lady Lina's hand met his cheek.

It was as much as he deserved, he thought ruefully, palming his smarting flesh.

"Foul villain," she said.

What could he do but grin? "Too right," he said with a bow.

"You are unpardonable." She crossed her arms over her chest, an action that enhanced the cut of her bodice.

"Guilty as charged," he said, making his admiration of her pose unmistakable.

"*Oh*! You rogue!" Lady Lina turned her back to him.

"Should we announce our nuptials to the hostess now or later?"

She spun back to face him. "How dare you! How *dare* you!"

Leaning against a tree trunk, he shrugged before waggling his fingers for her to come to him. She huffed, pouted, huffed again, then launched herself into his waiting arms, this time kissing him with two years of restrained passion.

He lost track of time and circumstance, knowing only the pitter-patter of rain on leaves above and the softness of his wife's lips.

When she leaned away from him, she half-heartedly pounded fists against his chest. "*Two years*, Dante. *Two*. Not a single letter. A clandestine marriage, a promise of love, then *two years* without word. When you said you would bring home a fortune, I thought you meant a few months, not *years*."

He tightened his embrace and nuzzled his still-stinging cheek against hers. "You'll likely receive my letters a year from now when we're enjoying an alfresco meal on the terrace of our grand estate. Mail from India is deplorably slow, I'm afraid."

Her voice softened. "You wrote?"

"You know I did."

Then her eyes widened. "What estate?"

"Whatever estate you want, my darling. The investment was a success. We're as rich as Croesus!" He swept her into a spin and then pinned her against the tree trunk. "I believe that fact will soften the blow when we admit our elopement to your family. Shall we start with the hostess and her guests?"

Lina shook her head, her eyelids drooping. "Not yet. It's raining, remember? Kiss me until the rain stops."

For the length of the rainstorm, he kissed her like the rogue she accused him of being — and then for at least an hour after.

Garrett Receives a Proposal

As he guided his horse past the gatehouse and onto the main road, Garrett's thoughts turned to his task, one mixed with pleasure and unpleasantry: calling on tenants.

For not yet a month, he had resided at Mable Hall, his dream of land ownership realized at last. Days into nights, he had poured over ledgers, leaving no figure unturned. Thankfully, the steward kept meticulous notes.

In Garrett's pocket was a list of tenants in arrears. A short list, to be fair. Only two names. But the details and exact rent due were noted. He doubted he would have time to call on all tenants in one day to introduce himself and invite a return call, but he would not miss a visit with the two listed tenants. Mr. Little would be first, his farm being closest to the hall, then Mr. Lowe. After, he could see to the remaining rounds.

Fields to the left, forest to the right, Garrett breathed in the scenery. This was his home now, his and his descendants. One day, he would ride down this lane alongside his wife. Beyond, he would ride it with his children, teaching them about the land, the people, the pride and responsibility of ownership, and the importance of dreams. He had only to meet the right woman now that he had the perfect home.

Woolgathering was not a pastime a gentleman ought to partake in while riding a horse, he realized, when a scruffy dog no larger than a horse's hoof bolted out of the woods. The scraggly puffball barked and pranced. Not brave enough to attack but determined to warn the horse and rider this was his territory, he yipped and yowled, darting forward then shuffling back.

Garrett patted his horse's neck to calm him. Old Brutus was not concerned. He flicked an ear in response to the dog, nothing more. A quirk of Garrett's eyebrow had no noticeable effect on the canine guardian of the road. The yipping continued. With a chuckle, Garrett admitted defeat and dismounted.

If he had expected the pup to go for the riding boots, he would have been disappointed. The moment his heels met ground, the dog bounded forward, not for the leather boots but for the buckskin breeches, and not with teeth bared but with tongue lolling and tail wagging. The dratted scoundrel pawed with muddy pads and leapt up for more leverage, the barks turning to whimpers in an ungentlemanly display of begging.

"I hope you're not Mr. Little, however apt the name," Garrett said, reaching down to pick up the mutt.

In answer, it licked the air and paddled its legs to get closer.

"I'll make a memorable impression on my tenants with mud on my waistcoat. Thank you very much."

A stir from the woods perked the dog's attention. After a moment of stillness, the dog strained against Garrett and jumped out of his grasp, launching itself between two trees. The prize for the effort was a young lady. She stepped out of the woods and picked up the puppy with stern words.

Garrett was too arrested by the woman to pay heed to whatever she said to the dog. Out of breath, hair disheveled, and cheeks flushed, she stole his attention. Once he ascertained if she was married or not, he might admit she stole more than his attention, namely his heart.

He made to speak.

She did as well.

Their words overlapped. Their laughter collided.

They tried again. The result the same.

He nodded for her to speak first.

Hugging the dog to her bosom as it struggled to return to Garrett, she said, "I can't express how unpardonably rude Hercules acted. Normally, he has better manners. My apologies, sir. If Hercules could talk, he would beg your pardon."

The dog thrashed against her, tongue lolling, beady eyes trained on Garrett.

"Apologies are unnecessary, however appreciated. He took the liberty of introducing himself. We're already beyond an acquaintance and can be considered good friends."

Her shoulders relaxed. Hercules — not the name Garrett would have chosen, but somehow appropriate nonetheless — felt the change in his lady's posture and took advantage of it. With a kick of spindly legs, he leapt free to return to Garrett, sealing their new friendship with a fling of dirt and drool onto the boots.

"Pardon me for taking liberties of my own," Garrett said, "seeing as there is no one except Hercules to formally introduce us. Mr. Norris." He followed his bow to the young lady with a pat on the mutt's head.

"Oh! You're the new owner of Mable." She curtsied. "Miss Barchester, sir."

He grinned. She said *Miss*. "I'm for the Littles presently. Shall I change course to see you safely home?"

She laughed, a honeyed sound, sweet to his ears. "Thank you, but I have Hercules to guard against brigands. Besides, I don't live far. We walk this route every day. It's his favorite, you see."

The knowledge that she did not live far and frequented the lane overcame his disappointment at not having an excuse to walk her home. With a reluctant farewell, Garrett parted ways with Miss Barchester and a whimpering Hercules.

Onward to the Littles, his reins signaled to his horse.

Not that he would be able to concentrate on his day's tasks with the vision of Miss Barchester's flushed cheeks branded into his memory. Which home was hers? Would he see her again today? Was she the daughter of one of his tenants or a neighbor with a passion for walking?

The Little residence, he soon learned, was teeming with activity. The eldest son of the family of fourteen had married in June, introducing into the household a new bride and her two younger brothers, not to mention a host of confusion as to whether they had paid their rent or not. The wife, with hands on hips, refused to leave the room when Mr. Little wanted to talk about money and insisted to the noble Mr. Norris that they had indeed paid their rent, so the steward must be cracked in the head if he had noted otherwise. Mr. Little shook his head at her tirade. He stuttered that he could not recall if he sent Esther to the hall with the rent. Esther, or rather Miss Little, had shrugged a shoulder and buried her nose deeper into a novel when pressed as to if she had completed her errand.

It was a noisy affair with a great deal of bickering, children shrieking, and nappies waving — the latter from a toddler who was not receiving the attention he thought was owed to him. Introductions complete and rent sorted at last, he left for the Lowe farm with only the slightest of megrims.

His intention had never been to question the finances of the two listed tenants. The topic had been broached by Mr. Little himself. Garrett hoped to handle his meeting with Mr. Lowe with more finesse. Today was about introducing himself, nothing more.

The vision of a certain pair of reddened cheeks lingered as he turned his horse into the Lowe farm. He had noticed more than her cheeks, but his heart pitter-pattered at the near-perfect circles of pink her dog-chasing exertion had caused.

She was, by way of speech, dress, and carriage, a woman of quality. Yes, her hair had been disheveled. Yes, there had been mud along her hem and on her half-boots. Yes, there had been a tiny branch caught on the sleeve of her pelisse. All those denoted a spirited woman unafraid of nature and devoted to her dog. Those factors did not veil the tailored fit of her attire, the eloquence of her tongue, or her ladylike composure. His mother would approve.

Such were his thoughts as he approached the Lowe home and dismounted Brutus. Only peripherally did he note the unshorn sheep still grazing in an unfertilized field.

Faint barking ghosted a smile on his lips. What would his mother make of Hercules? She had wanted a dog with the new house, although he suspected she had meant something fluffy and obedient. The barking increased. Garrett looked about him, wondering if Hercules came from a large litter, a sibling for each tenant.

There was little time to explore this line of inquiry. Before Garrett had stepped away from Brutus, a tangled mass of dirt and caked mud barreled at him, catapulting into his arms.

None other than Hercules himself greeted Garrett.

Garrett was too busy trying to persuade man's best friend to walk on his own four legs to wonder why the dog was at the Lowe residence. It took a single knock at the door to learn why. Miss Barchester answered.

Handing her the puppy, he said, "You may be the last person I expected to see, but you're the only person I wished to see."

Only after the words left his lips did he realize what he had said. By the roses budding those plump cheeks, she had not mistaken his meaning.

An awkward exchange of pleasantries later, Garrett was shown into a small parlor to meet Mr. Lowe, elder and younger. Mr. Lowe, the elder, did not rise from his chair. The man, a farmer, was pale with a pained expression. He grimaced when he spoke, lines framing his mouth and etching his forehead. The younger Mr. Lowe was around ten years of age, a quiet boy bearing the tan his father should have worn.

Mr. Lowe bared his teeth in an obvious effort to smile. "You've met my niece, Gwendolyn, then."

Garrett stole a glance. Miss Barchester's eyes met his cravat.

"I have had the pleasure, yes," Garrett said. "She saved me from a vicious beast earlier today."

A bark protested from outside the closed door of the parlor.

Mr. Lowe nodded to his niece, who appeared to understand an unspoken message, as she left the room without taking her leave, the only words spoken being to Hercules as she scooped him into her arms before shutting the door behind her.

Once the door shut, Mr. Lowe said, "We wondered if you'd come yourself or send a messenger."

"I apologize for waiting so long to introduce myself. I hope to meet everyone by the end of the week."

Mr. Lowe waved an impatient hand. "Don't mince words, Mr. Norris. We know you're here to evict us. I can't pay, and that's that. If you've a heart, give us until my sister arrives."

Taken aback, Garrett hoped Mr. Lowe would excuse his rudeness for sitting without being invited to do so. "Be free to speak honestly. I wish to understand what has happened."

Mr. Lowe bowed his head. "No point now. What's done is done." Next to him, the boy sniffled and shuffled his feet. "T'aint your fault, boy. 'Tis mine."

For no longer than ten minutes did Garrett stay in the parlor. Try as he might to inquire, his tenant would offer no explanation and merely insisted he be held accountable as he was responsible for the farm's condition. Garrett offered to return in a few days after conferring with the steward.

He saw himself out. On his mind was not only Mr. Lowe but the complication of Miss Barchester. Evicting her uncle was not an auspicious start to an acquaintance he hoped to lead to a courtship. He could not allow the attraction of a moment to cloud his judgment as a landowner, though. Mable Hall relied on tenants. Still, was there not more he could do?

A hushed voice said, "Please, don't leave. Not yet."

He turned to find Miss Barchester standing next to his horse. Hercules sat at her feet, his tail thumping. Garrett squatted to welcome the dog into his arms, dirty paws and all.

Miss Barchester clasped her hands at her waist. "He's a proud man, my uncle. He's reluctant to ask for help, considers it a weakness."

Scratching the dog's head, Garrett said, "I assume he's injured?" An easy assumption to make given the man had not risen from his chair, even in the presence of his niece.

"His leg. He was making repairs and fell. He thought it would mend if he gave it a little time, but it's getting worse every week."

"Why didn't he notify my steward?"

"My uncle worried the steward would turn him out if there was a chance the injury would affect his work. No place for lame farmers, he said. He refused to listen to my mother's reasoning and only accepted my help because I wouldn't take no for an answer. Since he thought it would heal before anyone noticed, he had my cousin Braydon doing the work in the interim."

Garrett inhaled through his teeth. "The boy in the parlor?"

"Yes, that's Braydon. He tried. He sheared more than half the sheep himself and even tried taking a few to market, but it was too much for him. Now, there'll be nothing for harvest." She looked down at her hands. "I must beg your pardon for speaking so freely. Only… after what you said earlier…"

Despite the circumstances, Garrett smiled. "Impertinent of me to have said what I did, however true. I'm relieved you took no offense."

She looked up, their eyes meeting. It took thirteen heartbeats for her to return his smile — he knew because he counted them. The corners of her lips inched upwards as if to show she welcomed his attention. As if to show she trusted him despite only having met him.

"Thank you, Miss Barchester, for being forthright. I'll send a physician posthaste and several of my home farm's field hands. The timing is late, but not too late. Trust in me."

With a final scratch behind the ear to a contented Hercules, Garrett set the pup down, bowed to Miss Barchester, and was soon on his way to set all to rights.

It took three days to make the arrangements, but in three days' time, Garrett returned to the Lowe farm to escort the physician and ensure the field hands had arrived. More to the point, he returned to exchange pleasantries with Miss Barchester — while coddling Hercules, of course.

Two days following, he arrived laden with sweets and savories from his cook, who took it upon herself to heal Mr. Lowe through her cooking. Did Garrett save his favorite pie to share with Miss Barchester? Why, yes, he did.

Four days passed, each longer than the day prior, before Garrett called on the Lowe's family again. How shocked was Garrett to find Mr. Lowe in the field, barking orders at the field hands? Even if the man leaned heavily on a cane, his son's arm at the ready to help, he was on the mend. Not one to miss an opportunity, Garrett invited Miss Barchester to walk about the field — Hercules needed to stretch his legs, after all.

Was it only two days later when Garrett thought of a new reason to visit the Lowe farm? He believed it was. He could not very well invite Miss Barchester by letter to the dinner party he was planning for the tenants, not when he could do so in person.

One full week passed following the invitation. It felt like a century. Each day, he had to talk himself out of finding an excuse to see her. His worry was unfounded, but after he counted the number of times he had called on the Lowes in the past two weeks, it niggled a worry into his mind. Was Miss Barchester accepting of his attentions out of politeness? Did she feel beholden to him for helping her uncle? If only she would give him a hint of mutual affection for him to be certain, something beyond cordiality.

The next Wednesday — he would not soon forget the day of the week — he led his horse past the gatehouse and onto the road into town. He breathed in the summer air and surveyed all around him. His home. One day, it would be the home of his wife and, sometime after, the home of their children. The vision of a pair of wide brown eyes flashed into his mind — had she thought of him in the week of his absence?

His questions were answered not by Miss Barchester but by the yipping of a ferocious beast charging towards him down the lane. He slowed Brutus and dismounted. Hercules nearly tripped over his own tongue, trying to jump mid-run into Garrett's arms. The smile Garrett wore was not for the stinky pup but for the young lady he knew would not be far behind, and sure enough, she came faltering mid-sprint out of the woods, her hair in disarray, a twig or two branching from her coiffure, and a rumpled hat waving in her hand.

"Oh, I'm so sorry, Mr. Norris. Hercules is determined to ruin all your best waistcoats."

"My waistcoats were made to be muddied," he said, scratching the dog just behind his ears where he liked it best.

He made to speak again.

She did as well.

Their words overlapped. Their laughter collided.

She nodded for him to speak first.

Setting down Hercules, he said, "I'm for the Walton farm today."

If she looked crestfallen, it must be his imagination, for what would be disappointing about his visiting the Walton family?

Absently, she rolled the edges of her bonnet in her hands. "Aren't you going to ask if you should change course to escort me home?"

His heart skipped a beat. "I recall you declining my previous offer since you already had a great defender."

"Yes, I did. I've walked this route every day, hoping to remedy that decision."

If his pulse beat any faster, he may well faint—what a helpful escort he would be then! "I shall be pleased to see you home, Miss Barchester. You don't mind that we haven't a chaperone except Hercules and Brutus?"

"That does present a predicament. It wouldn't be proper, would it?" She turned the hat in circles, thinking with audible *hmms*. Then, with a gasp, she said, "I have it! The perfect solution. But you might not like it."

"Go on."

"If we were betrothed, we wouldn't need a chaperone." She beamed a smile.

Hand to heart, Garrett stepped back, struck by Cupid's arrow. "Are you proposing to me, Miss Barchester?"

"I am if you say yes. If you say no, what a merry lark we shared."

"Then, by all means, let us walk the lane together." He offered his arm. "So there's no confusion, my answer is yes, but only if Hercules approves."

Together, horse at his side and dog at hers, they walked arm in arm, breathing in the scenery and envisioning all future mornings of sharing their walk together.

Tangled Attraction at The Knotty Sheep

E linor bustled to and fro about the courtyard of
The Knotty Sheep.

Banners hung from the building. Signs
swayed in the breeze. Today marked not only the
busiest day in the tavern's history but also the grand
opening of the tea garden. A year in the making, this
had been her father's grand plan to turn their sleepy
village into the next metropolis.

She circled about the new pond, dodging guests
and geese, ducking under sapling branches, then
traversing the teeming bowling green, a game of
lawn bowls underway. Her destination? The tables
of spectators, each crowded with quizzing-glassed
gentlemen, cheering on their ladies who dipped and
bowed to roll their bowl onto the green.

The tray she carried was laden with tea things,
bread, cheeses, and her mother's best cake. Weighted
though it may be, Elinor gave it not a second thought,
not with the watchful eyes of Mr. Nolan Walsh upon
her. From her periphery, she could see him seated at
a table with his sister.

Her gaze never wavered, focused only on the posh
toffs. With an unacknowledged smile, she relieved her

burden: a plate of bread and butter at this table, tea at that table, cake at the near table, cheeses at the far table. Done. Back to the tavern she headed, ever aware of the hazel eyes of Mr. Nolan Walsh following her.

Inside the tavern, nary a soul tarried, not even old Mr. Byrne, who ghosted the corner table with his favorite mug. The attraction today was the garden, the tea, and the baron's house party guests. Elinor's father knew how to time a grand opening. Grabbing a new tray from the bar, she nodded to her father and made for the copse of trees that marked the new wilderness walk, the path lined with benches and tables ready for a tray of sweet and savory delights. She knew she would find Mr. and Mrs. Sullivan at the first table, eager to savor the syllabub.

"Elinor!" called a voice to her left.

She spared only a glance. Ah, Alexandra. Elinor smiled but carried on her way until she reached the overhang of the magnolia's flowering arms, her father's prized tree. Always with a kind word, Mr. and Mrs. Sullivan accepted their treat. This time, before returning to the tavern, she angled right. Her best of the best, Alexandra, waited at one of the outdoor tables.

For a moment, Elinor collapsed into a chair next to her friend. "Do you think it's a success?"

Alexandra grinned. "If you would call a king's coronation a success. This is history in the making, Elinor! I've never seen so many people here before, and all smiles and compliments. When are you joining me?"

"As soon as Ray arrives. She's running late, as always."

"What are sisters for other than to run their littles ragged?" Alexandra leaned in to whisper, "Did you know Jacob is courting Christina?"

Elinor nodded. "Only because the two have been exchanging notes all day. Through me, mind. A slip of paper under the tea towel for C on my way from J's table, then a subtle nod from C as a returning note finds its way into my apron pocket on my way past J's table. All day. Wish they'd meet in the wilderness walk and leave me out of it."

"Everyone knows you're the messenger, El. Wouldn't be The Knotty Sheep without you."

Elinor harrumphed, then made her way back inside the tavern for the next tray.

She would walk past Mr. Nolan Walsh's table for this errand. Her heart skipped a beat at the thought. Hazel eyes and leather perfume, strong hands and long limbs, boots of the finest quality framing shapely calves. Mr. Nolan Walsh was a sight to behold. A man to make any woman weak-kneed, especially Elinor, specifically Elinor. Thank the heavens, he did not know the effect he had on her. Lovesick and unrequited was not how Elinor wished to be seen by her neighbors.

Around the pond, past the geese, over the green, Elinor traveled with a tray of tea and biscuits. Mr. Walsh, or rather Nolan, the Adonis of Pickleberry Village, hunched in conversation with his sister, the two in a heated exchange. Elinor kept her chin high and her eyes forward, trained on the biscuit-craving table of nobs. She caught a whiff of leather as she passed Mr. Walsh. Her pulse quickened.

The table. The tray. The biscuits. The nobs. The smile. Elinor turned back towards the tavern.

His sister had risen from the table and was heading for the tavern. He was drinking his tea and facing the green. With a tug at her apron, Elinor marched forward, determined not to breathe until she had cleared the lawn.

She was not but two feet from his glistening boots when he cleared his throat. She gulped a gasp, thankfully silent, not so thankfully filled with his personal perfume of heavenly hide. She would never again smell another pair of boots without thinking of him.

She braved a glance.

His eyes remained on the lawn bowls. With his forefinger, he traced the rim of his cup. With the tip of his tongue, he wet his lips. With a lift of his wrist, he sipped from the porcelain.

Eyes forward, Elinor quickened her pace.

"Elinor!" called a voice to her left.

This time, the voice was Mr. Walsh's sister. Elinor caught up to her and walked in time towards the tavern, the sister slipping her hand into the crook of Elinor's elbow.

"Do me a favor?" she asked. "Nolan wants me to deliver this letter discreetly, you know, but I'm in a dreadful hurry for the *you-know-where*, and besides, everyone knows you're the messenger." Without awaiting a reply, she slipped the note into Elinor's apron pocket and skipped ahead.

As if Elinor's heart had not already taken a beating today from passing his table at least five times in the hour, it somersaulted in her chest and thumped wildly. A note! From Mr. Walsh! Without losing stride, she retrieved the slip of paper and turned it over in her hands.

Across the tightly folded letter read the name *Ms. Alexandra*.

Ah.

Chin up, shoulders back, feet in step with the laughter filling the tea garden she made for her best of the best. A smile haunting her lips, Elinor slipped the note into Alexandra's hand.

"What's this?" Alexandra questioned, turning the letter over.

"A letter for you."

"So I gathered. From whom?" With a tug at the edges, the letter unfolded.

"Mr. Walsh," Elinor said, her voice steady, not a crack or crinkle to be heard.

"*Walsh*?"

Elinor heard the name behind her as she continued into the tavern to collect the next order.

No one would think her heartbroken. All anyone would see was the tavern keeper's daughter helping make today the best of all days in Pickleberry, the day The Knotty Sheep opened The Knottiest Tea Garden. She delivered the trays with an unseen smile and collected the plates shorn of their sweets. She avoided the watchful eyes of Alexandra and Mr. Nolan Walsh.

It was on her sixth trip to the green that Ms. Walsh linked arms with Elinor again. "This is the fourth time I've been asked to pass a letter, and this is the fourth time too many. Why can't they ask you? Everyone knows you're the messenger. Be a dear and bring this to my brother?"

"Oh, but I don't have a tray for—"

Elinor's words died on the breeze as Ms. Walsh walked away towards the gaming tables, a fierce game of loo underway from the look of it. Tossed onto her tray and impaling a piece of cake was *the letter*. She had no choice. She could not deliver the tray to its recipient with a corner of a folded missive sticking out of the dessert. Swallowing her pride, she approached Mr. Walsh.

His eyes widened when he realized she was heading straight for his table. He sat straighter and brushed his hands over his waistcoat.

When she set the tray on the table, his brows knit in confusion. She addressed the knitting brows by saying, "Your cake, sir."

"But I —"

Elinor cut short his reply by setting the plate with cake and letter next to his teapot and cup. She collected his sister's teacup and saucer onto the tray and left without desiring a reply or the sight of him reaching for the missive.

The poor chap who had ordered cake would have to wait for her next round.

"Elinor!" called a voice to her left.

She turned to see Alexandra waving a fan to get her attention. *Sigh*. Tray still in hand, she joined her best of the best.

"*Elinor*," emphasized Alexandra. "You *must* join me in the wilderness walk. I won't take no for an answer. Hand that tray to Ray — she's here now, you know — and *come with me*."

From the glint in Alexandra's eyes, Elinor suspected what would be said. Had she the stomach to hear it? The trouble with small villages was one had no choice, did they? Everyone knew everyone. Everyone neighbored everyone. When one's secret love courted one's best of the best, the only option was to smile.

Ten minutes it took for Elinor to return the tray, speak with her sister, beg for another piece of cake for one of the baron's guests, which thankfully her sister would deliver, and return to Alexandra, who tapped a half-booted foot with impatience.

"*Come*," Alexandra goaded, tugging Elinor's hand.

It was good to be without apron at last. She had worn her favorite dress that day. It was not a dress for an assembly, but it was a loved sprigged muslin embroidered with sunny yellow flowers. Free of the apron, her dress could be seen, and the breeze was better enjoyed. These were her thoughts as Alexandra led her into the wilderness path, for any thoughts were good thoughts that did not involve Mr. Walsh.

Oh, Mr. Walsh.

He sat on a bench a fair distance into the walk, tugging at the bottom of his waistcoat.

Elinor bit back the welling of tears. She would not let either of them know she was disappointed by their choice to be together. She would only let them know how happy she was. Happy tears welled.

Upon seeing them approach, Mr. Walsh stood in greeting. Alexandra giggled in response and squeezed Elinor's hand. Then she fled.

Not Elinor. Elinor remained rooted in place, staring at Mr. Walsh. Alexandra fled, her laughter lingering in her wake.

Mr. Walsh's hazel eyes met Elinor's. "I hope you don't mind my involving her," he said. "I didn't know how else to get you alone. To be honest, I didn't know if you would *want* to be alone with me. I had to be sure."

Elinor said nothing, afraid she was misunderstanding the moment.

He continued, "Now that I've my own cordwainer's shop, no longer an apprentice, I'm of a state to ask your permission. I daren't before, not when I had nothing to offer. May I? Have your permission, that is? To court you?"

She answered his myriad of questions ten times over, screaming them to the heavens, but all in the silence of her own thoughts. Outwardly, she could do no more than stare in wonder.

He clenched his hands, wringing them. "I didn't think you had ever noticed me," he said. "I've noticed *you*. For so long, I'm ashamed to say. I didn't know if you noticed me in return until I found the courage to ask your friend."

Reaching for similar courage, Elinor found her voice. "You wrote to Alexandra to ask her if *I* noticed *you*?"

He replied with a sheepish grin.

"But I'm just the messenger."

"Not to me," he said, reaching a hand to her, palm up, open and waiting. "To me, you're everything. Could you be happy with a humble cordwainer, Ms. Elinor?"

Nolan's face blurred as her vision teared. She grasped his hand in both of hers and said, "Yes, a thousand times, yes."

The grand opening of the tea garden ended not with an unacknowledged smile but with Elinor's very own piece of cake, a wilderness walk with Mr. Nolan Walsh, and the knottiest of kisses.

Cedric Whittles Resolve

Dear Journal,

I survived the evening. Remains to be seen if I will survive the week. I was made to sit across from him at dinner. Every time I looked up, he looked back, chilling me to my slippers with his furrowed brow, sharp gaze, and perpetual frown. Dinner was not the worst of it. Mama insisted I play the pianoforte so he could turn the pages for me. Silent stares, not a word spoken. How am I to endure this? He is all reservation and no spark. I can't marry him. I won't.

Aimee

Peter,

Cedric here, reporting as promised. She is, as I feared, haughty. I'm uncertain if she's conceited or displeased with me as her intended. I warned Father nothing good would come from an arranged marriage. I will not disappoint him by leaving as a rejected suitor with head hung low, but I know not how to woo her. Wishing well to you and yours, the new babe, &c. Your humble friend,

Cedric

Dear Journal,

I rushed to tell you. I could not wait another minute without writing. He was there. In the morning room. Alone! I sat at the opposite end of the room, for I did not wish to encourage him. What sort of gentleman agrees to an arranged marriage? Mama says he will propose within a week, two at the most, and that I must accept. Who is this strange man? My quiet morning was shattered by his company, badgering me with questions rather than the silence of last night. Do you enjoy mornings? He asked. Do you favor a morning constitutional? Where's best to walk in the mornings, the woodland or the lake? He did not once smile and was all dull reserve, frowning deeper with each question. We will never suit.

Aimee

Peter,

All the best to you and yours. Thank the wife on my behalf for extending her advice to encourage the young lady to discuss her favored pursuits. My own endeavors for conversation thus far have failed. All questions have been met with monosyllables. Arranged marriages are never easy, but I aim to make the best of the situation if she would give me the opportunity. I met by chance one of her neighbors and am renewed in hope by the positive character given of my intended. I am hopeful and undaunted that with your wife's suggestions, I can persuade Miss Aimee to open to me. Am I too droll? No, don't answer lest I be disheartened. I will write again soon. Your servant,

Cedric

Dear Journal,

Mama insisted I walk with him. She underestimates my resolve not to marry. How can I marry someone with no genteel attributes? Any gentleman worth his cravat would make polite conversation with a lady, yet what did Viscount Hawthorne do? Walked in silence. His only question was as we parted ways. Do you enjoy riding? He asked. How droll! A gentleman should ask after a lady's bonnet, compliment her sense of fashion, or comment on the weather. I refuse to marry someone so dull.

Aimee

Peter,

I hope this letter finds you, Margaret, and the baby well. Your letters bring me comfort in this trying time. I believe Margaret is correct about Miss Aimee being as nervous about the arrangement as I am. This is the insight I need. My attempts at conversation have not gone well, leaving Miss Aimee displeased whether I initiate conversation or remain silent. I could only assume she was displeased with me, but with your wife's insight, I feel renewed hope. I will aim for a different tactic tomorrow. Your dearest friend,

Cedric

Dear Journal,

I could not get to you fast enough to share the morning's events. I went to breakfast to find him there again. This time, to my dismay, he presented me with a bouquet of wildflowers. What am I to make of this? I confess to you alone I wanted to be moved, but he presented them without a single smile, only that dashed angry brow. I hardly know what to think except this: I will not allow my parents to force me into marriage. I remain ever vigilant!

Aimee

Peter,

Having taken Margaret's advice once more, I've dispatched a message to Miss Aimee inviting her for a curricle ride. However anxious I am, I believe your wife is correct. More opportunities for conversation will be to my advantage. Thus far, my questions have displeased her, but I will not lose hope and instead, once more, try a new tactic. By our fathers' design, we will marry regardless. It is in our best interests to find commonality. Ever your servant,

Cedric

Dear Journal,

Lord Hawthorne is skilled with the reins. I'm not impressed enough to marry him. He is, after all, a stranger, and I refuse to be forced into marriage. He drove me to the village, bought me an ice, and then showed me a pleasing view of the valley. I found his manner almost gentlemanly. Not to be taken for rude, I engaged him in conversation about my interest in painting. I'm not swayed, but I confess only to you that his company was tolerable.

Aimee

Peter,

As Margaret promised, Miss Aimee enjoyed the set of paints I surprised her with at breakfast. You are a lucky man to have so clever of a wife. My intended remains aloof, but I believe she's warming to me. After the gift, she offered to show me one of her paintings. She spoke more to me this morning than she has collectively since my arrival. If I'm fortunate, she'll accept my invitation for a morning walk. I'm determined to win her before our fathers sign the contract. Ever your friend,

Cedric

Dear Journal,

You'll think me a traitor when I admit I walked with him this morning. Politeness dictated that I must. What else could I do after he surprised me with paints? Oh, the paints! They are the finest I've ever seen. I must remain strong and not let this kindness move me. I'm certain his gift doesn't come from the heart but from a forced hand. After all, he frowned when he presented the paints.

Aimee

Peter,

She enjoys dancing, picnics, and charades. You know I'm more interested in a good ride, but with the right company, dancing, picnics, and charades are favorable, as well. More to come. Your friend,

Cedric

Dear Journal,

He dances divinely! Conversation remains tedious, but who needs conversation when one has a superb dancing partner? Neighbors joined us for dinner, so Papa rolled the rug in the drawing room, and we made sport of the evening! Dancing and charades! Oh, did I mention the picnic this afternoon? He took me to the lake for a picnic. I meant to write after the picnic but had no time to waste. I've promised to ride with him on the morrow, but only on the condition he allows me to paint him. How diverting to paint a man who never smiles!

Aimee

Peter,

Time draws near. Father expects me to propose.
I'm convinced I've not wooed her despite my best
efforts. I've achieved a modicum of progress and
hard-won approval, but her gaze remains sidelong,
her conversation hesitant. Wish me all the best. Your
anxious friend,

Cedric

Dear Journal,

Do you suppose he's fond of me? I so enjoyed painting him. He makes the perfect model, forever still
and silent. I worry he finds my conversation tiresome.
Did I write about the ride? Oh dear, I believe I forgot
again to write. We rode for at least an hour, and he
challenged me to a race! Between the two of us, and I
know you shan't tell anyone, I admired his seat. He's
as good a horseman as he is a curricle driver. Do you
think, dear journal, I could coax a smile before tomorrow eve? I shall make it my mission!

Aimee

Peter,

I've received a missive from Father. By the end of today, I must propose. My heart is in my throat. Try as I might, I don't think she's taken with me. I worry she remains displeased with her parents' choice of bridegroom. Call me a fool, but I'm smitten with her. She's not at all the haughty young lady I took her for. She's just as Margaret said, nervous about an arranged marriage. She loves to laugh and loves to dance. Have you ever been painted, Peter? By the time this reaches you, I'll have an answer. For now, I remain your nail-biting friend,

Cedric

Dear Journal,

No time to write today, so I'll keep this brief. Long at last, I know how to make Cedric smile. Say yes to his proposal, and behold — the warmest smile I've ever beheld! Between the two of us, I knew all along Cedric and I would suit. Off to the lake with my betrothed!

Aimee

The Mad Monk

G eneva pulled her hand from the velvet bag, a smooth rock between her fingers.

"Let me see," said the gypsy seated across from her.

Laying the rock on the table, Geneva looked at the faces of her friends, all circled about the table for two.

"Odal," the gypsy rasped. "Rune of separation and inheritance, a noble rune."

The stone looked innocent enough. Etched into its face was what looked like a ribbon or perhaps an angular *o* with two legs.

"You must separate from your old self if you are to embrace the new. This is a time for retreat. By shedding the skin of the old, you'll inherit what's yours."

Around her, the party guests whispered, a few snorting or scoffing. Geneva studied the lined face of the gypsy, wondering how much the woman already knew of her life.

"Go!" shouted the gypsy, startling everyone. "This life serves you no more. Welcome the new, so you may be reunited with family, reunited with lost love."

A chill ran down her spine.

Her turn at an end, she rose from the chair to stand with two of her closest friends and watched as someone else accepted the seat to have their fortune told.

Belinda patted her hand. "What hogwash. Don't listen to a word that woman said. You've no need to retreat or leave or do anything except allow his lordship to take care of you."

That was the last thing she wanted, his lordship being her husband's cousin, now the bearer of the title, come to claim his estate, accompanied by his wife and children. The letter he had sent had been kind. Although they had never met, he had invited her to remain in residence, promising to see to her needs if she had no other relatives with whom she could reside.

To Belinda, she said, "I have no intention of being here when they arrive."

"It's never too late to change your mind."

Ariana leaned in to join the conversation. "If you would only see reason, Geneva. You need only remain at the estate long enough to remarry. You can't be serious about moving. Who's to take care of you? You need someone to look after you."

Belinda patted her hand again. "A woman can't live alone. See reason."

For the past few months, Geneva had heard the same argument from all her neighbors. They did not agree with her decision to purchase a home of her own, and one clear across the country where she would know no one. Who was to care for her? They insisted time and again, disbelieving when she said there would be a housekeeper and cook in residence. Not a full staff? Not a husband? Not a guardian? This was not safe for a woman and unseemly!

The gypsy was right. It was time to shed the old self and embrace the new. She was tired of the long faces and sympathy, even if her friends meant well. The year of mourning had ended, yet condolences they still offered. Tired of the pitiful gazes, she was ready to welcome the new, although she was anxious about what the gypsy said about reunions. Her only family, her only love lost, after all, had been her departed husband.

Two weeks later, Geneva arrived to her new home. She had purchased it sight unseen. Now seen, she could not believe her circumstances. Once an old monastery, all that remained was the priory and, behind that, a manor house situated prettily next to a picturesque river.

Her solicitor must be quite the negotiator, for the property had been a steal in price, so much so that she had believed the house to be a cottage, exaggerated in size to persuade her into purchasing it. Her mistake. The house was not a cottage but an impressively grand manor. No, it could not compete with the estate she left behind, but it was no less grand in comparison to the cottage she had in mind. The priory itself was quaint, but the medieval construct and stained glass windows brought a smile to her lips. There was history here, real history.

Standing at the front door of the house were her solicitor and a man she assumed to be the steward since he had agreed to greet her upon arrival. She waved to them both and began her hike up the gravel drive. The carriage she had taken from the village inn had offered to drive her to the door, but she insisted on being let out at the end of the driveway so she could take in the whole of the property and breathe in the air of her new life. The walk had not disappointed.

"Welcome, Lady Fenford!" greeted her solicitor.

A bevy of handshaking, pleasantries, and introductions were exchanged. The man to Mr. Milwick's left was, in fact, the steward. She was made to understand the housekeeper did not live on the property but rather had agreed to arrive late afternoon and stay every day until dusk. The cook, likewise, would arrive in the mornings and leave in the evenings. Neither gentleman was comfortable with her staying at the house alone, but they were both well-paid enough not to squabble with the widow of a nobleman.

As the trio turned to enter the house, something caught Geneva's attention. Just a shadow at the corner of her eyes. She glanced in the direction of the priory but saw nothing. Shrugging, she took one step forward, then halted.

A robed figure peeked around the church. She blinked. The figure was gone.

Mr. Milwick joined her. "Is anything wrong, your ladyship?"

"I saw someone. Just there." She pointed at the stone wall.

When neither man responded, she eyed them right in time to spy an exchange of glances.

The solicitor said, "Could have been the new groundskeeper. Strange fellow, but arrived with impeccable characters. Keeps to himself and shouldn't be any trouble. Takes to haunting the grounds, so to speak, as a groundskeeper does."

"Didn't look like a groundskeeper to me. I distinctly saw a monk's robe. Is the groundskeeper in a habit of wearing a monk's robe while on duty?"

The steward cleared his throat. As discreetly as he could, the solicitor shook his head, but the steward ignored him. "Could be the mad monk."

Mr. Milwick grumbled under his breath.

The steward said, "Seeing as how she already owns the property, she's a right to know." Turning to Geneva, he said, "A local ghost story is all, but you'll hear neighbors talk about it. No truth to it. Started with a couple of children who claimed to see the ghost of a monk walking the grounds. Rumor escalated, and before you could say *boo*, everyone in town claimed to have seen the mad monk. It's why your offer was the only one received. Nothing but rustling in the wind, I tell ya. I've never seen ghost or goblin. Only a few bats. To be expected."

Geneva squinted at the church. No signs of ghosts or shadows. With a nod to the gentlemen, she proceeded into her new home.

She loved the house. She loved everything about it. Everything except…

No, she must not think of Wesley. She had buried him over a year ago. It was time to move forward, time to embrace a new life and a new self. Everything about the old life was gone. The friends they shared, the picnics for two, the balls they hosted, everything. She could not look back.

They had been married ten years, eight of which were the happiest years of her life, two of which were spent in fear she would never see him again. He sacrificed all for Crown and Country.

Although evening darkness blackened the windows, she refused to close the curtains. There was no one around to see into her windows, to spy her curled on the chair by the bedroom casement, reading by candlelight. The morning light she knew would fill the room and wake her was something she looked forward to. This was her house, her property, her private utopia. She was surrounded by woodland, the river looping behind the house.

She turned the page of her book.

A faint sound called to her from outside the window. A moan? A whisper? She held her breath and listened. Silence. Cupping her hands to the glass, she tried to look out. Between the absence of moonlight and the glow of her candle, she could make nothing of the outside. But wait…

Inside the priory, a flicker behind the stained glass, a glance of reflected color.

Was someone inside the church?

With a quick snuff of the candle, her nostrils filling with the scent of smoke, she cupped her hands to the glass once more. Unmistakable, a candle flicker. A pane of stained glass lit then shadowed, another lit then shadowed, all along the length of the nave. Someone was walking from the entrance of the priory towards the back.

Geneva pulled her shawl more tightly around her shoulders. The mad monk? She would not be afraid. Alone though she may be, she was not faint of heart. How much harm could a ghost cause anyway? But… ghosts did not carry torches.

Oh, Wesley.

The next morning, she breakfasted in the kitchen with the cook, much to the consternation and fluster of poor Mrs. Bumbberton.

Geneva questioned her about the mad monk.

"No ghosts here," Mrs. Bumbberton reassured her. "Rumors, sure, but 'tis child's play. Kept the place from selling 'til you offered, but that's your fortune. No monks here, not since the dissolution. Could be the new groundskeeper. Strange fella. What you need, if ya don't mind me saying, is a husband. Won't see no bobbing candles with a man here."

Ignoring the woman's impertinence, Geneva said, "I've not toured the church yet. Is it unlocked?"

"Always. I said a few words there only yesterday before I returned home. Dust don't bother me. Rector Stevenson lived here a few years back. Held services there. Then the Tilstons moved in and let it collect all that dust. Not been used in years." A hint of melancholy whispered in the cook's words.

Services would not be held there again as long as Geneva owned it, but she would love to learn more about the history, especially of the monastery days, and if she could, she would restore it, even if only for personal use and that of her minimal staff.

Promptly after breaking her fast, she donned a cloak and walked the few paces from manor to church.

The wooden door squeaked on its hinges as she entered. One step inside, and the odor of stale air assaulted her. Unfortunately, no one had taken care of the old building. It had good bones from what she could see. Stones and windows were all intact, only pews littering the floor, some splintered with age.

A flutter caught her attention. She looked up at the soaring ceiling of the nave. Bats. Clinging to the ribbed vaulting. Most sleeping, a few darting from one roost to another.

The church seemed larger on the inside than it looked on the outside. The nave stretched from end to altar, behind which were three magnificent windows reaching to the ceiling. Along the nave to one side were round arches paralleling the cloisters, and to the other side were stained glass windows with grisaille panes. Further in, Geneva found the presbytery separated by an oak screen, a wood pulpit on a stone base, and a locked door.

A locked door? She lifted the iron handle and tugged. No movement. She gave the door a none-too-gentle push. Solid. She pulled and twisted at the ancient, round handle, wriggling it this way and that. No luck. Leaning down, she tried to peer through the keyhole. All she could see was an old wooden bureau.

When she returned to the house, she found the housekeeper in the kitchen with the cook. They both stood, curtsied, and fumbled through an awkward greeting, dismayed and embarrassed Geneva had come, yet again, into the kitchen.

Waving a hand at their nonsense, she asked, "Is there a key to the locked room inside the church? I wish to see inside."

"Key? There's no key to the church, my lady. It's always open," said Mrs. Bumbberton.

The housekeeper agreed.

"Well, there must be a key somewhere because one of the doors inside is locked," Geneva insisted.

"The groundskeeper may have it," said the housekeeper.

"Where might I find the groundskeeper, then?"

Both women apologized for not knowing, assuming he would be somewhere on the grounds doing what groundskeepers do, although they could not recall seeing him yet today.

Setting off to walk about the property, Geneva took in the scenery while scouring for the mysterious groundskeeper. The woodland went too far back for her to explore without better knowledge of the property lines, but she toured as much of the land as she could from one end of the driveway back to the river, across the sweeping lawn where the monastery's dining hall had once stood—a great loss, she thought, for the sake of lawn bowls—and into as much of the woodland as she dared. No signs of a groundskeeper.

Upon returning to the kitchen, where the two women were gossiping again, Geneva instructed them to tell the groundskeeper to seek her out. Both women encouraged her not to stay here alone but to hire more staff or consider marrying. With a steely gaze, she went about the rest of her day, the curiosity of the church never far from her mind.

Foolish.

Geneva, you're a fool, a gullible fool, and you're behaving foolishly.

Curled in her chair by the window, book ignored in her lap, she watched the church, her eyes having adjusted to the darkness some time ago. The only sounds were the occasional gust of wind whistling around the corner of the house and a soft thumping during the strongest of gusts that she suspected was caused by a branch hitting the side of the house. If she ever met the groundskeeper, she would have him trim the noisy branch.

There! Just there!

She sat up straighter, craning her neck.

A shadow at the nave door, a shadow in a monk's robe.

She waited. She watched. Nothing.

Wait. A flicker at one of the windows. Yes, a flicker as if of someone trying to light a candle. What was that? A sound. She strained to hear. A voice? If she would not have to admit she had gone mad, she would swear she heard chanting, however faint, however distant. A gust of wind and the thumping of the dratted branch silenced the sound. Blast.

Tossing the book onto the table, she retrieved her tinderbox and, with a bit of effort, lit her candle, donned a banyan and shoes, and headed downstairs and out the front door.

The wind bit through her dressing robe. She hunched over and used her free hand to guard the candle flame as it gutted violently. Before her, the priory stood silent and dark as the night. Not a whisper or a flicker from the stained glass.

She opened the door, the creek echoing through the nave. Stepping inside, she looked around but could only see as far as her candle's orb could reach. A gust of wind chose that moment to blow inside, circle about her, douse her flame, and then pull the door closed behind her. The door slammed with such force that the hibernating bats above fluttered and screeched. They were not the only ones. Geneva, too, screeched, about-faced, fumbled for the door, wrenched it free, and then scrambled back to the house with an empty candlestick.

Only when she made it back to her bedchamber and closed the door did she recall seeing a robed monk in her periphery just before the candle extinguished. Despite the cold, a bead of perspiration trickled down her back. *The mad monk!*

In the safety of daylight, she toured the church again. The dropped candle lay where it had fallen, just inside the doorway. For longer than she would ever admit to anyone, she sat in one of the pews and listened, watching the shadows at the corners of her eyes. No whispers. No chants. No robed monks. Did ghosts only come out at night, then? But no, she had seen something during her first day here, in broad daylight.

With the sun shining through the windows, she could wonder about the monk without fearing he would pop out and scare her, or at least knowing if he did, she could scream for help from the housekeeper and cook. The mad monk. A curious name for a ghost. What made him mad? Did he know he was a ghost and so intentionally haunted the priory, or did he think he was still going about his daily duties?

She chuckled to herself. If Wesley were here, he would accuse her of being a silly goose.

When she returned to the house, she headed for the kitchen, expecting to find the housekeeper and cook gossiping again. Instead, the kitchen was empty, although a pot of something that smelled delicious simmered over the fire. Peering around doorways, she determined the coast was clear. She slipped into the butler's pantry, where she knew the housekeeper kept her chatelaine with all the keys of the house.

Double blast. The hook was empty. The housekeeper must be wearing it. Geneva would have to retrieve it after the woman left for the day and return to the church then to try each key.

The wait was as long as the day, of course, but at least she was distracted during the afternoon by several neighbors paying call as a welcoming committee. All were kind. They arrived bearing a basket of gifts, ranging from embroidery thread to calling cards of those who could not come but hoped to meet her soon. The plan for her new life did not include much socializing; however, she would not live as a stranger to her neighbors. Remain cordial but distant. Allow them to think her kind but quiet, never solicitous of company. Maintaining a degree of anonymity was of the utmost importance to her new life.

Evening arrived at last. Hanging on the hook in the butler's pantry was the keychain with every key to the house, inside and out. As it was already dusk, she would have to wait until daybreak to try each key on the door in the priory. Another foolish decision. She should have instructed the housekeeper to accompany her to the church and try every key, but not only did she feel silly about the matter, she did not want to accuse the woman of lying about not having the keys to the church. What did she expect to find in the room, anyway? The mad monk, ghost extraordinaire?

Keys lying on her little table, Geneva situated herself comfortably in her window-side chair. She snuggled her feet against the arm of the chair, tucking the ends of her nightgown around her toes, and read her book. So engrossed, she lost track of time, reading well into the night. The candlelight waning shook her from the story world. Glancing at the candlestick, she was struck by an altogether different glow, one from outside. There could be no denying it. As clearly as it had been the first night, the flicker of a flame shone through the windows of the church, starting from the door and moving steadily the length of the nave. *To the locked room!* She knew it. She knew it without a shadow of a doubt. The mad monk? Ghosts did not need candles, did they? The groundskeeper, then? Children playing a game? A burglar?

Oh, Wesley.

She snatched her dressing robe, shoes, keychain, and candle, not about to waste time. If she were to confront this mystery, she needed to do it before the culprit had a chance to escape.

As she crossed the lawn, the night played tricks on her. Shadows danced. Trees moaned. A figure peeked around the church, then disappeared. A whisper spoke on the wind. Chanting thumped her heart wildly. Courageous, not willing to give in to fear or superstition or ghostly monks, she opened the door and stepped inside.

"Is anyone here?" she called out. "Show yourself!"

The bats rustled their wings, commanding quiet.

She closed the door and took five brave steps forward. Her eyes darted to the alcoves, watching for monks. The church stood silent as the grave. Making her way to the locked door, she shifted her gaze left and right, the keys clanking in one hand, the candlestick trembling in the other.

Only one stubbed toe later, she found the locked door. All the rationale, all the logic, all the courage could not steady her hand as she tried one key after the other. One failed twist after another.

But then, *click*.

She gave the iron ring a tug and twist. The door opened. With a deep breath to calm her nerves, she stepped into the room.

What she could see by the faint light of her candle shocked her as much as if she had been staring at the mad monk himself. Someone was living there. A cot with a downturned blanket was against one wall. Several sets of clothes were draped over the backs of chairs. A washbasin stood in the corner, and next to it, a table with a shaving set and washing supplies.

A glint flashed. The candlelight reflected back with a wink from something gold, something dangling.

Geneva took tentative steps towards the something. A locket? Yes, a locket on a chain. She licked dry lips and tried to swallow. Setting the candlestick on the table, she reached for the locket, fumbling with it, almost dropping it. With bated breath, she flipped open the latch.

Geneva gasped. Inside the locket was a miniature painting. Of her.

Strangling a cry, she dropped the locket onto the table and took a stumbling step back.

From behind, arms came around her, one clasping her around the waist, the other covering her mouth. Pressed against a stone chest, she struggled against the grip.

A voice rasped into her ear. "Please, don't scream."

She stilled.

"Relax," he said.

She obeyed, relaxing against him. His grip loosened, and then his hold released. She whipped around to face him. Before her stood a cloaked figure. Not a monk, not a ghost, but a man in a hooded cloak.

Geneva choked back a sob. "Are you frightful beneath the hood?"

"Do you wish to find out?" he asked.

She raised a hand, hesitated, then reached for the hood.

A fingertip away, he clasped her wrist. "Are you certain you wouldn't rather I disappear into the night? You could live easier not knowing."

Her cheeks felt wet. Was she crying? Of course, she was. He released her wrist. With him facing the candlelight, she would be able to see him clearly. Did she dare look? Touching the edge of the hood, she hesitated again, swallowed against her parched throat, and then tossed back the cloak to reveal his face.

She mouthed his name.

"Am I frightful beneath the hood?" he asked, echoing her original question.

She shook her head. "You're nearly unrecognizable, but you'll always be beautiful to me."

He groaned, then collapsed into her arms, burying his face against her neck. She ran her fingers through his hair, feeling where the burns had scarred into his hairline. There was so much to be said, but all she could do was laugh.

"Is this your idea of a new identity?" she asked. "Lurking about my priory? Haunting my new home?"

"I was instructed to keep a low profile. Did you ever dream your nobleman would become a groundskeeper?"

Sighing, she leaned back to study his face better. Once handsome, now scarred from torture at the hands of the King's enemies. What must he have suffered? *Oh, Wesley.*

A hand to his cheek, she said, "I hope whatever secrets you discovered as a spy for Crown and Country were worth it. You're forever mine now, though. They can't have you back. I'm only thankful it was torture, not death."

He chuckled softly. "But it did lead to my death, at least in name. For as long as I live, we'll remain in hiding. Not glamorous, but it's the safest choice. The life of a spy, namely one who escaped capture, is not for the faint of heart."

"What *is* your new name?"

"Mr. Winston Wilkerson. Like it?"

"No." She shook her head. "But I'll grow accustomed to it. Goodbye, Lady Fenford, and good evening, Mrs. Wilkerson. Yes, I'll grow accustomed to it, but only after we convince our new neighbors that I've fallen deeply in love with the groundskeeper. Then I can marry you all over again."

"Mmm. I like the sound of that. Are you certain, Geneva? Despite all our careful planning, I can steal away in the night, never to be seen again. You need only command it. If I stay, you'll have to look at this face every day. It's not the one you knew."

"No, it's not the one I knew, but I married *you*, not your face." To make her point, she stood on her tiptoes and kissed his cheek, where the scarring was the worst. "Now, where's that monk's robe you've been wearing? I want to put it over my dressing robe. I'm *freezing*!"

He stared at her, perplexed. "What monk's robe?"

"Don't be coy. You've been skulking about in a monk's robe, pretending to haunt the place so it wouldn't sell until I could purchase it."

"I only secured the job as groundskeeper after you purchased it, love."

"Stop teasing. I've *seen* you in a monk's robe. So have the villagers. They call you the mad monk. They all think it's a ghost, but I know it's you."

"A ghost?" Wesley, or rather Winston, laughed. "Don't be a silly goose. There's no such thing as ghosts."

As he said the words, movement behind him startled Geneva. She looked past him. Standing in the doorway, staring at them, was a monk. Geneva shrieked and pointed. Her husband turned to see, but the doorway was empty.

"Let me guess," he said, "your ghostly monk?"

She nodded, her gaze still trained on the door in case he reappeared.

"Well, I've not seen any ghosts, love, but a monk would certainly explain the nightly serenade of chanting."

Shy or Saucy

Connor Phelps, Lord Kilham, rode neck or nothing across the barren landscape; the only sounds the crunch of snow beneath his horse's hoofs and the bay of hounds. The pursuit led across the fields, over the hill, and into the forest. After a tree branch swiped his face, Connor loosened his hold on the reins, slowing his horse for safety. Warmth trickled down his cheek. With a brush of his glove to his numb flesh, he wiped away the blood.

"Baron!" The word echoed. "Baron! This way!"

Bringing his horse around, he searched the horizon. There. Some distance to the west. How had he lost sight of his prey? Heart pounding, he urged his horse into action, victory his only option. Motivation fueled his veins to the cadence of a lady's voice. To win her admiration, to secure her affection, meant everything.

Beneath him, the earth shook from the rumbling hoofs of the other riders. Ignoring their approach, Connor followed the sound of the hounds, the bays reverberating around him in all directions. Ahead, he could see his man's profile enlarging as he drew closer.

"My lord!" his man called, initiating the chase deeper into the forest.

Just as the baron pulled his horse alongside the other man, the horn sounded a long, wavering note, repeated three times.

"Blast," Connor said, drawing in the reins.

His companion laughed. "Did you truly think bringing her a foxtail would impress her? How little you know of ladies, my lord."

"One more snide remark, Laurel, and I'll demote you from best mate to neighboring acquaintance," he said with a smirk. "Come, let's wallow with our fellow hunters, then proceed to the fête. There's a contest to enjoy."

That the fox had gone to ground did not dampen spirits, not with the annual pie contest to warm their palate. The baron and Laurel joined the other riders before all proceeded to the fête, all except the Master of Foxhounds, who took the hounds back to the estate.

Laurel ribbed, "She's certain to notice you with caked blood on your cheekbone. Care to make use of my handkerchief?"

Accepting the proffered linen, Connor said, "I hoped to win favor, not sympathy." He dabbed at his cheek. "Is it unbecoming?"

"More to the point, should you not avoid her? Tongues will wag if you hover at her side."

With a shrug, he pocketed Laurel's handkerchief and guided his horse towards the village square. His gaze roamed the crowd, searching for the pie tent. Behind him, the huntsmen, still in their colors, began to dismount and tap their hats to the ostler. Connor followed suit, his eyes still trained on the tents.

Laurel leaned in. "By the well. The crowd is gathering, hungry for a taste."

Grinning, the baron left his horse with the groom and strode across the snow-covered green, hungry for a taste himself, only it was not the pies he craved. He spotted her behind a table, a figure hidden beneath a coat and apron. As with his chase of the fox, his heart pounded at the sight of this minx. Even from a distance, he could make out her smile. Would it be in too poor of taste for him to flirt? He knew it would, and yet how could he resist?

Just as she caught sight of him approaching, a man intercepted his progress, blocking the sightline. The villain, clad in a dark cloak, hood drawn, stepped up to the table, his back to Connor, his maleficent attention focused on the piemaker.

Quickening his pace, Connor shouldered into the crowd. Once villagers realized it was the baron, they stepped aside, a path widening to the table. Connor had no wish to taste the pie, not until he dealt with the man between him and his heart, a man he knew from posture alone. Ten strides away. Seven strides. Five strides. Three strides. His hand outstretched, he clamped his fingers around the man's shoulder and spun him around.

[proceed to the ending of your choice]

Ending A

The villain's eyes widened before crinkling at the edges.

Connor's brows snapped together. "Thought you could keep us waiting, did you? Hmm? What do you have to say for yourself?"

With a toothy smile, the gentleman lowered his hood before drawing Connor into a viselike hug. "Have I missed the wedding? No? Then stop complaining, brother! I was delayed by the snow but left the carriage behind to come on horseback, all so I could see you walk down the aisle with the best pie maker in town—oh wait, I shouldn't have let that slip, not when the contest winner has yet to be announced."

The crowd around them shared a laugh with the baron as he returned his brother's embrace. Only when the two released each other did Connor eye the young lady behind the table, her cheeks flushed from the cold. His bride.

Laurel joined them, clasping hands with the baron's sibling and pulling him into conversation so Connor could sneak around to the other side of the table.

"My lady," he said, smacking a cold kiss to her warm cheeks.

"Not yet," she said, giggling at his overtures. "Now, away with you! You've already caused a stir with that kiss."

"I can't kiss my bride on the day before our wedding?" He slipped a hand around her waist and dipped lower in a tease, his fingers inching towards her derriere.

"Connor!" she shrieked, dodging him. "Someone will see you. Go away so I can win the pie contest."

"Trying to impress me, Rosemary?" He waggled his eyebrows.

Batting her eyelashes, she whispered for his ears only, "Not with the win, only the flavor. After all, what's a wedding night without a slice of pie?"

Ending B

As soon as the man faced Connor, the baron knew his mistake. 'Twas not the villain he had supposed, rather Miss Rosemary's father. Blanching, he released the gentleman's shoulder.

"Oh, I say, Mr. Lockheed, I do apologize. I mistook you for someone else."

Rather than be offended, Mr. Lockheed lowered his hood, smiled, and shook Connor's hand. "No apology needed, my lord. With you to look after us all, we're assured safety." Lowering his voice, he said, "If you thought it the blacksmith's cousin, I thank you kindly for your quick actions. You know he has an eye for my daughter."

Connor looked past Mr. Lockheed to see Miss Rosemary watching their exchange with curiosity. Releasing her father's hand, he bowed to her. To his great pleasure, she blushed prettily.

"Lord Kilham," said the gentleman, "I know you have guests, so now is not the time, but would you permit me to invite you to dine with us as soon as you're able?"

It was the invitation Connor had been hoping for these long months, ever since first setting eyes on Miss Rosemary. Was it too much to hope she favored him, as well? The father's invitation was all the excuse he needed to begin his campaign to win her heart.

"A delight, sir," Connor said, unable to hide his smile. "I'm honored to be invited."

Laurel joined them, clasping hands with Mr. Lockheed and pulling him into conversation so Connor could steal a moment with Miss Rosemary.

Not one to miss an opportunity, the baron eyed the line of pies at the table. When he looked up, his gaze locked with hers.

With a shy smile, she asked, "Would you like to taste a slice of my pie, my lord?"

Anyone would agree it would have been impolite for him to decline, and so the baron made the only dignified response he could. "Miss Rosemary, it would make me the happiest of men to sample your pie."

Christmas Riddles

On the first day of Christmas, Viscount Hammond hosted a party, one to which all villagers of Lower Veleton were invited. The Reverend Jenkins served as majordomo, as he did every year. With a cheery speech and a clap of his hands, the Christmas Day festivities began.

Miss Dana Skellart stood near a window in Lord Hammond's ballroom, watching from one vantage point the snow flurries against the setting sun and from another vantage point her neighbors milling about the room, admiring the greenery adorning walls and doors, décor that had been hung the day prior by most of the same guests. From wreaths to kissing boughs, the decorations set the mood. Dana did not mill or admire but rather eyed the bowl in the center of the room, awaiting the ceremonial removal of the Holland linen.

Tapping her fingers at her waist, she waited. This was her most anticipated event of the year and had been for as long as she could remember.

Footmen circled with refreshments, providing guests time to exchange pleasantries, a task that took no more than twenty minutes but a lengthy twenty minutes for Dana, one that kept her fidgeting with mounting excitement. Whose name would she draw this year? She hoped for Mrs. Bear. Dana had in mind the perfect gifts for the music teacher, gifts that would serve well for Sunday service, to boot, as new sheets would give Mrs. Bear fresh music for her pupils and for the church choir.

If she did not draw Mrs. Bear's name, she would be happy with Mr. Embry. The inhabitants of Lower Veleton lived as a family, the only known villain being Mr. Embry, a grumpy widower who shook his cane at children and squinted his eyes rather than reciprocate with a good morning. He never played his role as villain well, though, as he had a soft heart for Mrs. Bear's cakes, Mrs. Bear being a widow herself. Dana imagined gifting him with those cakes along with a sly invitation to join her and Mrs. Bear for tea — not that she was a matchmaker, but what greater gift could there be than love?

She snapped to attention. The Reverend Jenkins stepped forward, raising his hands to draw everyone's eyes to him. Lord Hammond excused himself from a group to join the vicar. At last!

Another brief speech. The setting of the rules for the game villagers knew by heart. A flourish of the linen. The presentation of the bowl.

Giddy, Dana joined the circle of guests.

One at a time, they were waved to the table. Dana watched the faces of those who went first, spying expressions in hopes of a flicker to hint at whose name they pulled. With a touch of curiosity, she wondered if anyone's gaze would move her way. No one's did. No, that was not true. As her gaze swept across the room, her eyes met those of Mr. Gerald Wilson. She blushed and turned away. His name was the only one she hoped never to draw from the bowl. A gentleman, like her father, but with the misfortune to be both single and handsome in a village otherwise lacking single and handsome gentlemen. All the ladies of her acquaintance swooned over him. She refused to, even if his dark eyes and mischievous smile tickled her stomach.

Oh! The vicar waved her forward. Her turn!

She closed her eyes, dipped her hand into the bowl until she felt the edges of ripped paper, then plucked the winning slip. *Please don't say Mr. Wilson. Please don't say Mr. Wilson. Anyone but Mr. Wilson.* She opened her eyes to the smiling and expectant faces of her neighbors. Opening the paper, she read the scripted name of *Mrs. Beetle*. With a contended sigh, she returned to the back of the crowd to allow room for the next guest to have a turn.

Mrs. Beetle was one of the oldest inhabitants of Lower Veleton. A kind woman with failing eyesight, sloped shoulders, and a love for needlework, even if she could no longer see her embroidery. More than anything, Mrs. Beetle loved visitors. One of the best gifts would be Dana's time, offering the opportunity to share stories over thread and hoop. Well, that or a new roof, given the persistent drip drop from an unrepaired leak, but since it would take more than pin money to pay for a new roof, Mrs. Beetle would have to settle for companionship.

Dana looked up from her thoughts to catch the gaze of Mr. Gerald Wilson once more. *Good heavens!* Another blush. Another glance away. At least she had not drawn his name.

For the remainder of the party, Dana socialized with friends, neighbors, and family, never far from her mind the ten gifts for Mrs. Beetle, one for each day until Twelfth Night, when the villagers would meet again at Lord Hammond's manor for the grand reveal of who had drawn whose name. The fun part was not so much the reveal but the guessing, as each guest was challenged to guess who had gifted them.

The next morning, a surprise awaited Dana. Tucked to the side of her plate at the breakfast table was a folded letter.

> *On this second day of Christmas,*
> *The Yule Rider, hearty and hale,*
> *Presents the first witness.*
> *To the schoolhouse, you must go,*
> *But will you guess without assistance?*

A strange riddle, to be sure, but one that piqued her curiosity enough to speed her through breakfast. To the schoolhouse, she went posthaste.

Last year, the person to draw her name had been the milliner who had gifted her each day with a different color of ribbon — simple and sweet, as far as gifts went. The year before, she had been gifted by Lady Hammond with a series of hothouse flowers and perfumes. The year previous had been homemade cakes from Mrs. Bear. Never riddles.

Her approach to the schoolhouse did not go unnoticed. In fact, she was greeted with startling fanfare. The Reverend Jenkins had requested the presence of all children who attended his classes in the makeshift vestry-turned-schoolroom. Gathered around the vicar, the children cheered, whooped, and whistled Dana's arrival. They had been waiting for her, bundled in their winter warmth, a meager fire not quite warming the cold stone of the church.

One of the children, a pigtailed girl with a row of freckles marching across her nose, skipped to Dana and handed over a book. "This one is my favorite."

Turning the book over, Dana smiled. "How lovely. It is one of my favorites, as well."

A boy stumbled forward, his hair mussed and his breeches dirty, although how he found dirt beneath so many feet of snow, Dana could only guess. "This one is mine! Mr. Jenkins said I could take it home to read if I promised to return it."

As the children shared their enjoyment of the books, Dana turned a quizzical expression on Mr. Jenkins.

The vicar stepped forwards, his paw of a hand patting one of the children's heads. "You are kindness itself, Miss Skellart. I can't say who is more grateful, the children or old Mr. Mallard. He sent this morning the collection from his library, right happy to be rid of the lot, he said in his note. Donating to our humble school on your behalf, he said. This is your doing, and I'll not forget your kindness."

"*My* doing?" Dana touched a hand to her heart. "As wonderful as this is, I can't take the credit, Mr. Jenkins."

"However it came to be, Mr. Mallard donated in your name. Seems it's you we have to thank for the generosity."

She stayed for half an hour so the children could rifle through the books and show her each one they were eager to read and a few they were not so eager to read. As she trod through the snow on her return home, she could only surmise Mr. Mallard had drawn her name and sent the riddle. So, he was her gift-giver this year, was he? She liked that he had gifted on her behalf rather than gifting her directly, but… wait. He had not attended the party at the Hammond manor. How could he have drawn her name?

After a day spent with Mrs. Beetle, complete with the gifting of new thread, Dana returned home to sleep soundly. Almost soundly. At the fringes of her mind was the puzzle about Mr. Mallard.

The next morning, another letter was tucked into the side of her breakfast plate. Unfolding the letter with a quirk of her brow, she read,

> *On the third day,*
> *Prince Christmas*
> *Thatched the way.*
> *To the grove, you must go,*
> *But can you guess without delay?*

The grove was where Mrs. Beetle lived. With more haste than the day prior, Dana dressed for the cold and then set off to see what Prince Christmas was up to.

There was no opportunity to guess, however, as she arrived to find the roof of Mrs. Beetle's cottage teeming with young lads from Upper Veleton, the myriad sons of the Harper family, all in their teens, all idle as the day was long, but hard at work repairing more than the leak in the roof. The boys waved to her, smiling despite their rosy cheeks and cloud puffs of breath.

Mrs. Beetle greeted Dana at the door. "Oh, my dear, how can I ever thank you?" There was no mistaking the meaning of those watery eyes.

"You've not me to thank, Mrs. Beetle. It's the Harpers on the roof in a labor of love."

"Pish-posh. No humbleness from you, Miss Skellart. They arrived at sunrise with my Christmas surprise. A new roof on your behalf, they said. Not a penny they would accept. Said it was *their* gift to receive hard work and prove themselves in their parents' eyes, all on account of your inspiration."

"*My* inspiration?" Dazed, flattered, and confused, Dana followed Mrs. Beetle into the front parlor.

The gift she brought of freshly baked scones dimmed in comparison to a new roof, but that did not faze Mrs. Beetle as she noshed with bliss to have company, conversation, and compassion. Dana's concentration was anywhere but on her needlework, however. If her gift giver was not Mr. Mallard, then was it the Harper family? They had not attended the Hammond party, either.

She knew by now to expect a riddle. She was not mistaken. Next to her plate, just as anticipated, awaited the next happy lines.

On the fourth day,

Miss Skellart trekked to the barn.
Would this gift 'shoe' the way,
Or would she remain tangled in yarn?

Dana could hardly get foot into boot for the excitement to see what she would find in the barn. Cold and blustery though it may be, the barn was welcoming as her younger brother and father greeted her with hearty smiles and hugs.

Her Papa's first words took her as much by surprise as the past two days had. "To think of your papa and help the Tucker boy all at the same time… you make me proud, Dana."

It was then she caught sight of Mr. Will Tucker, the blacksmith's son. He was hard at work shoeing Papa's horse and gushing about this grand opportunity to show his own father he was ready to apprentice. To be given this chance meant the world, he said, and all on behalf of Miss Skellart.

Were the Tuckers her gift-givers, then?

Her day spent with Mrs. Beetle, the lady being gifted today with a handsewn shawl, was devoted more to Dana's puzzling over the riddles and gifts on her behalf than on any other thoughts. How shocked she then was to arrive home only to find Mr. Gerald Wilson leaving. He touched his hand to his hat as he passed. Dana blushed and looked away, her heart fluttering. He had called on her family while she was away? How peculiar. Perhaps he was her gift-giver. She giggled at that, for Mr. Wilson would neither notice her if she were the last eligible lady in Lower

Veleton nor go through so extraordinary measures to gift so many people on her behalf. No, it would be more likely Mr. Embry was her gift-giver. Now, *there* was a lark!

With these amusing thoughts, she spent the evening.

On the fifth day of Christmas,
You'll dine with friends.
A family affair not to miss.
To the Wilson abode, you'll go,
But can you guess who arranged this bliss?

Before she could march over to the Wilson home, an action that would have been nothing short of humiliating considering that single and handsome gentleman who resided within, her mother intercepted her with good tidings. It would seem Mr. Gerald Wilson had invited the Skellart family to dine with his own, an invitation curiously issued on Dana's behalf. How an invitation to dine with the Wilson family could be considered a Christmas gift, she could not immediately say, but that would soon become apparent.

The Skellarts were not the only ones invited. The Jenkins were, as well. Through an unexpected turn in the conversation, Jenkins invited Mrs. Marianne Skellart, Dana's mother, to sing with the choir at next Sunday's service, a long-held dream of Marianne's, but one she had shared with few others, least of all

with the Reverend Jenkins for fear he would think
her voice inferior, a silly notion from Dana's perspective, as her mother sang like an angel, although only
in private.

The one dark cloud over supper was Dana being
seated next to Mr. Gerald Wilson. She could scarcely
eat for blushing! His conversation was of fine quality, ever flowing with questions about her favorite
aspects of the season or voiced admiration for a
bonnet she might have worn one day at church — had
he really noticed? — yet as smooth was his dialogue,
she found herself short of breath to be his focus. In
a funny way, she wondered if today's gift had not
been her mother's invitation to sing but rather her
sharing conversation with Mr. Wilson. What a silly
thought, indeed!

On the sixth day of Christmas,
Your gift giver gave to you
Rainbow threading for a fleur-de-lis.
Can you guess who I am
Before knotting the green with a chef's kiss?

It took precisely one hour to learn the meaning of this riddle. Mrs. Turner, head of the sewing
club, arrived at Mrs. Beetle's door to thank Dana for
her kindness in donating so many different colors
of threads to the sewing circle. Both Dana and Mrs.
Beetle shared in the joy, for they were both members
of the club, as well, and would thus take advantage

of this gift given on Dana's behalf. Mrs. Turner shared that the milliner had received the wrong thread in her most recent order and did not know what to do with the excess, thus being instructed to send it to the sewing club to rid her storeroom of the unwanted threads while bringing delight to the members.

At this stage in the gift-giving, Dana forfeited guessing the identity of her gift giver. Twelfth Night could not arrive soon enough, so she might discover this generous and clever benefactor.

The seventh day brought a riddle, sending her to call on Mrs. Brumley and Mrs. Norris, sisters who shared a cottage while their soldier husbands toured with their companies. To Dana's amusement, they thanked her for thinking to invite Mrs. Nash to serve as cook and housekeeper, a task Mrs. Nash was ever grateful to receive since she had grown lonely and bored following her husband's passing, longing to feel purposeful and useful yet not knowing how. She was, now, where she felt most at home: in the kitchen preparing pies, pies, and more pies. All thanks to Dana, the trio chimed.

If only Dana could accept the accolades!

On the eighth day, she received a riddle inviting her to try the piano at the village inn. Sure enough, when she arrived, the private parlor of the inn was decorous with seasonal greenery, half the village present to sample the fare of the innkeeper's new cook, who happened to be his daughter. All in attendance thanked Dana for slipping the bug in the innkeeper's ear to give his daughter a try in the kitchen, inviting them to enjoy the fruits of the daughter's labor and gifting them so glorious of music as she could summon from the rickety piano. Everyone enjoyed the luncheon immensely, especially Dana, who had wanted to put fingers to those keys for years but lacked the courage to ask permission.

Then came the ninth day, and the tenth day, and finally the eleventh day, all with riddles, all with gifts of service arranged on her behalf. With today being the twelfth day, she did not expect to find a letter, yet she did.

> *On Twelfth Night,*
> *You'll receive the final gift.*
> *May you not take fright*
> *By my courtship laid bare*
> *Rather, see me as your white knight.*

A troubling riddle, one that had her skipping breakfast, fraught with indecision during her visit to Mrs. Beetle, and near dreading the Twelfth Night party at the Hammond manor. *Courtship* laid bare? This was not the average gift giver, then, nor was it Mr. Embry, Mr. Mallard, Mr. Wilson, the Tuckers, the Harpers, or anyone else who had been involved in the gifting on her behalf. No, this was someone who wished to *court* her.

The first person to come to mind was Mr. Marc Tomalin, her neighbor these many years, a young man who had attempted to flirt on several occasions. How unfortunate for him to draw her name, if true, for as kindhearted as he was, she was not the least interested. She saw in him only the friendship of a neighbor. In truth, he was almost like a brother to her. No, she could never consider him *romantically*. Oh dear. After all this work, after all these gifts on her behalf! What was she to do? What to say?

The party began auspiciously, with everyone sharing in the joy of their myriad of gifts and casting guesses as to their gift-givers. Most guessed correctly, although others remained in mystery. Dana searched the faces of her neighbors for hints, anyone who eyed her overlong, anyone who watched her unobserved. No clues were revealed.

The Reverend Jenkins stepped forwards at last, raising his hands to garner attention. "For those who have guessed your gift-givers, you've already had the chance to share thanks for the bounties bestowed. For those who have not guessed, now is the time to meet your gift giver. On my signal, benefactors who have not been discovered will reveal themselves. We'll allot twenty minutes for thanksgiving, then proceed to the dining room on Lord Hammond's signal. Ready? Set. Meet!"

Dana squeezed her hands at her waist, eyes darting about the room. Mr. Marc Tomalin smiled at her with a little wave. Her heart sank. But then he turned to shake hands with Mr. Turner. Oh. Oh! Relieved, she looked about her again. Mrs. Bear smiled on her way towards Dana before redirecting to Mrs. Norris.

"Pardon me," said a voice behind her. "I believe you're awaiting a white knight, although I can claim to be his squire if you're disappointed."

She turned around, heart in her throat, to see none other than Mr. Gerald Wilson standing before her. An unladylike gasp kissed her lips. *Mr. Wilson!* She knew not how to respond. For that matter, she knew not how to speak. All faculties fled. *Mr. Wilson?* Was the single and handsome gentleman who tied her stomach in knots but could never possibly notice her the generous gift-giver? Impossible!

His smile slipped at the corners. "Are you displeased? Was I too presumptuous?"

Dana gathered what courage she could muster. Shaking her head, she asked, "How could you think me disappointed? I'm merely in shock. You… you don't know I exist!" She covered her mouth, dismayed at having said that aloud.

Mr. Wilson cocked his head to one side. "Don't know you exist? I rather thought it the other way around. I've failed to find the strength to approach you. I'm… you see… I'm shy."

Before she could stop herself, she laughed. "You? *Shy?*" When a faint pink tinted his cheeks, she knew him to be truthful. "You must forgive me, Mr. Wilson. I always perceived you as confident, whereas I am anything but. I hardly know how to respond. I had hoped it would not be you. Wait, no, I said that incorrectly." She laughed again, this time a nervous titter. "I hoped it would be you, but I didn't. Oh, I speak in contradictions."

His smile returning, he said, "I believe I understand you, Miss Skellart. I have felt the same, each year hoping to pull your name or vice versa, yet fearing the result. Am I to assume, then, I may be the knight rather than the squire?"

Grinning now, Dana said, "Only if that means *you're* to be my gift."

He raised his brows at her boldness. "Yes. Or rather, no. You see…" He cleared his throat. "I had planned to riddle you towards the kissing bough for your gift. Is love not the greatest gift of the season?"

"Oh, Mr. Wilson. You've already gifted love. For every day of Christmas, to everyone in the village, and through them to me. Love in abundance." Touching her hand to his arm, she nodded to one of the kissing boughs. "One last gift, then, Yule Rider, one of pure joy."

A Note from the Author

Dear Reader,

Thank you for purchasing and reading this book. If you're interested in exploring some of the research that went into this book and others, do check out my research blog: https://www.paullettgolden.com/bookresearch.

Supporting indie writers who brave self-publishing is important and appreciated. I hope you'll continue reading my novels, as I have many more titles to come.

I humbly request you review this book on Amazon with an honest opinion. Reviewing elsewhere is additionally much appreciated.

One way to support writers you've enjoyed reading, indie or otherwise, is to share their work with friends, family, book clubs, etc. Lend books, share books, exchange books, recommend books, and gift books. If you especially enjoyed a writer's book, lend it to someone to read in case they might find a new favorite author in the book you've shared.

Connect with me online at www.paullettgolden.com, www.facebook.com/paullettgolden, www.twitter.com/paullettgolden, and www.instagram.com/paullettgolden, as well as Amazon's Author Central, Goodreads, BookBub, and LibraryThing.

All the best,
Paullett Golden

About the Author

Celebrated for her complex characters, realistic conflicts, and sensual portrayal of love, Paullett Golden writes historical romance for intellectuals. Her novels, set primarily in Georgian England, challenge the genre's norm by starring characters loved for their imperfections and idiosyncrasies. The writing aims for historical immersion into the social mores and nuances of Georgian England. Her plots explore the human psyche, mental and physical trauma, and personal convictions. Her stories show love overcoming adversity. Whatever our self-doubts, *love will out.*

Paullett Golden completed her post-graduate work at King's College London, studying Classic British Literature. Her Ph.D. is in Composition and Rhetoric, her M.A. in British Literature from the Enlightenment through the Victorian era, and her B.A. in English. Her specializations include creative writing and professional writing. She has served as a University Professor for nearly three decades and is a seasoned keynote speaker, commencement speaker, conference presenter, workshop facilitator, and writing retreat facilitator.

As an ovarian cancer survivor, she makes each day count, enjoying an active lifestyle of Spartan racing, powerlifting, hiking, antique car restoration, drag racing, butterfly gardening, competitive shooting, and gaming. Her greatest writing inspirations, and the reasons she chose to write in the clean historical romance genre, are Jane Austen, Charlotte Brontë, and Elizabeth Gaskell.

Connect online
paullettgolden.com
facebook.com/paullettgolden
twitter.com/paullettgolden
instagram.com/paullettgolden